W9-AVG-725

OCT - - 2022

WHERE THE
SKY
BEGINS

Center Point
Large Print

Also by Rhys Bowen and available from
Center Point Large Print:

In Farleigh Field
The Tuscan Child
The Victory Garden
Above the Bay of Angels
The Venice Sketchbook

**This Large Print Book carries the
Seal of Approval of N.A.V.H.**

WHERE THE SKY BEGINS

A NOVEL

RHYS BOWEN

CENTER POINT LARGE PRINT
THORNDIKE, MAINE

This Center Point Large Print edition
is published in the year 2022 by arrangement with
Amazon Publishing, www.apub.com.

Copyright © 2022 by Janet Quin-Harken,
writing as Rhys Bowen.

All rights reserved.

Originally published in the United States by
Amazon Publishing, 2022.

This is a work of fiction. Names, characters,
organizations, places, events, and incidents
are either products of the author's imagination
or are used fictitiously.

The text of this Large Print edition is unabridged.
In other aspects, this book may vary
from the original edition.
Printed in the United States of America
on permanent paper sourced using
environmentally responsible foresting methods.
Set in 16-point Times New Roman type.

ISBN: 978-1-63808-470-9

The Library of Congress has cataloged this record
under Library of Congress Control Number: 2022940560

I dedicate this book to my old and
dear friends Penny and Roger Fountain,
who always give me such a warm
welcome in their Lincolnshire home.
They have also helped me with my research,
taken me to RAF museums, shown me a
Lancaster bomber and generally
set the scene for this book.
You are both very special to me!

CHAPTER 1

London, November 1940

Josie Banks's favourite part of the day was when she walked to work down the Mile End Road at eight thirty every morning. That was when the street sprang to life around her: men returning from the night shift at the nearby docks—grimy, bleary eyed and stumbling with exhaustion; shopkeepers rolling up blinds on good days or sweeping up glass from a night of bombing on the bad. The smell of watery decay blew in from the Thames, mingling with the fumes of bus engines and the various scents coming from the opening shops. On the good days the greengrocer would be arranging turnips, swedes and cabbages in an attempt to make them look attractive, the fishmonger laying out what bits and pieces he had been able to scrounge from Billingsgate fish market that morning. The fishy smell overwhelmed the others as Josie approached. The fishmonger always had something to say to her.

"Fancy a nice bit of whale meat, Josie, love?"

"I ain't that desperate yet," she called back.

"Better than starving, some say."

"What's it taste like, anyway?" she asked,

frowning at the slab of pink flesh that lay on the marble slab.

"Don't ask me; you won't see me eating it," he replied, and she walked on, both of them chuckling. She had pegged him as a bit of a flirt, but she didn't mind. A few words exchanged in the high street were harmless enough, and the fact that the local shopkeepers now knew her made her feel alive—as if she belonged.

Her destination was an improbable sight amid the pubs and fish and chip shops, the working-class commerce of the busy East End street. Just past the Mile End tube station, she came to an unassuming shop window, draped with faded lace curtains. Josie paused outside the front door where a discreet sign read "The Copper Kettle Tearoom," took out a key and let herself in. Every morning, as Josie closed the door behind her, she looked around and gave a little sigh of contentment.

The tearoom had been started by Madame Olga back in the early days of the century after she had fled from Russia. She had attempted to create a tiny glimmer of civilization amid the bustle of the East End. Lace-edged tablecloths and pretty pink-and-white-flowered china, teacakes and sandwiches with the crusts cut off. These days the lace-edged cloths had been replaced with glass tabletops, the china tended to be chipped and mismatched, and there were no teacakes to be had, but Josie did manage scones when she could get the flour and the margarine. Otherwise it was toast and jam, baked beans on toast, Marmite on toast and occasionally Welsh rarebit if there was the miracle of a cheese ration.

However much it had come down in the world, the Copper Kettle still attracted housewives who wanted a cup of tea and a minute's escape from the chores and the children or to have their nerves calmed after a night of bombing. And to Josie it represented heaven.

Josie remembered clearly the first time she had discovered it—like a little mirage between the ironmonger's and the pawnshop. After five years of being a housewife, she was on her way to get a job. Stan had been called up into the army, and she had pointed out that every able-bodied person was supposed to help the war effort. Stan could hardly refuse. Josie set out with excitement mingled with a little apprehension. She hadn't worked for five years, and before that only in a garment factory. But it was a beautiful, clear January day, one of those rare winter days when a brisk wind coming up the Thames from the sea had cleared out the usual layer of choking smog that hung over the city. The sky above the warehouses and church steeples glowed like a blue arc. Josie found she had a spring in her step. Life seemed full of possibilities. She was heading for the civilian recruitment centre at Liverpool

Street Station when she happened to glance at a row of shops and saw the lace curtains in the window. And what's more, a sign pasted on the rather dirty glass: "Help Wanted." She peeked in through the window. It was a tea shop. The sort of tea shop she had seen in the West End and where she had very occasionally treated herself to a cup of tea.

Josie had opened the door gingerly. A bell tinkled above her head, and she stood taking in the improbable scene: little round glass-topped tables with proper china teacups and saucers on them. Small vases of tired artificial flowers on each table. A large older woman appeared from behind a curtain. She was rather an alarming sight—dressed all in black, her hair swept up and held with tortoiseshell combs. She was wearing too much make-up for her age—bright red lipstick and red circles of rouge on her cheeks, her eyebrows plucked to thin lines.

"We are not open yet," she said to Josie in a voice heavy with a foreign accent. "Come back at eleven."

"I came about the job," Josie said. " 'Help Wanted'? In the window?"

"You have experience?" the woman asked, eyeing Josie suspiciously. "This is an establishment with class. People who come here want to be treated properly. Where have you worked?"

"I haven't worked recently, and nowhere like

this," Josie said. "I've been a housewife, taking care of my husband. But now he's in the army and everyone is supposed to be getting a job."

The old woman shook her head so that the large earrings that hung from both ears rattled and jangled. "Sorry. No experience. Try somewhere else."

"Hey, just a minute," Josie said. "You could at least give me a chance. What do you need—a waitress or a cook?"

"Some of both, I suppose. My old legs are not as young as they were. I get tired easily."

"My husband ain't never complained about my cooking, especially my cakes and pies. And scones. Stan says I do a good scone, you know."

The woman sighed so that her many chins wobbled. "Not that there is much cooking these days. No flour, no sugar and certainly no butter or eggs. We have to make do. But you just condemned yourself with your words, my dear. You said 'ain't.' Too common. My customers seek refinement."

"In the Mile End Road?" Josie laughed. "Go on! I bet there ain't—isn't a refined person within five miles of here. And I can try. I'm a quick learner. And if you don't want them to see me, just shove me in the kitchen and I'll do your washing-up for you."

The woman was eyeing her with interest now. "Why do you want this job?" she asked. "Now there is a war on, there are jobs again. You could work for the government. Join the WAACs. Plenty of work."

Josie looked around the room. "I like nice things," she said. "I see you've got Royal Albert china. Nice pattern, that."

"How does a woman like you know about Royal Albert china?" she demanded.

"I may not be able to afford good stuff, but it doesn't mean I don't know about it. A cat can look at a king, they say, don't they?" She gave the woman a defiant stare, then continued, "I go up west and I look in Liberty's and Selfridges. And what I see here is that this place has got run down. You say you expect refined clientele— well, they wouldn't appreciate the dirty windows and the curtains what needs washing, would they?" When the woman didn't answer, she went on. "I could make this place look really nice again. I'm not afraid of hard work." The woman was still eyeing her, so she pressed on. "And anyway, you're a foreigner. Someone must have given you a start when you came here. Had you worked in a tearoom before this?"

The woman gave a sad sort of smile then. "Me, I had not worked at all before I came here. I fled from Russia at the turn of the century. Before that, I was married to a high-ranking government official in Moscow. We had a fine house and a dacha in the country. Lots of servants. I never lifted a finger. I went to balls and parties and lived a ridiculous life. But then the sentiment against Jews became strong. I am a Jew, you see. My husband was murdered before my eyes. I escaped through luck and came here with nothing. I sold my last good jewellery and bought this little shop."

"Why here? Why not the snooty part of London?"

"Because Jews are welcome around here. I think there is still prejudice in what you call the snooty part of London. And it was cheap enough for me." She gave a little chuckle. "And I thought the place needed some refinement, yes?"

"So?" Josie said. "Are you going to give me the job or not? Because if not, I'll be on my way. But if you do, you won't regret it. I'll make this place very nice for you."

The woman smoothed down the front of her dress as if she was wiping off her hands. "I'll give you a week's trial, and then we shall see. I am Madame Olga." She held out her hand.

"Josie Banks. Pleased to meet you," she said.

The week's trial at the Copper Kettle turned into a month, and it became quite clear that Josie was an asset. After years of looking after her six younger siblings, following their mother's death, the work didn't seem hard, and Josie loved chatting with customers, making sure all the china sparkled and trying to stretch the flour and margarine to bake the occasional cake or biscuit.

"You are a good little worker, I'll say that for you" was Madame Olga's grudging first compliment. "You have children at home?"

Josie shook her head, looking away, out of the newly cleaned window. "No. We haven't been blessed that way yet." She turned back to Madame Olga. "How about you? Did you have children?"

"I had a son. Sasha," the old woman said slowly, as if it was a pain to draw out each word. "The light of my life. Such a charming little boy. He made us all laugh. But he was very delicate. He caught a chill, out playing in the snow. It turned to pneumonia, and he died. It broke his father's heart. And mine, too. He was only four."

"I'm so sorry." Josie instinctively reached out and covered the old woman's hand with her own. Madame Olga recoiled at the unfamiliar contact, then her eyes met Josie's.

"I see you have much love to give," she said. "Your husband, he is a lucky man, I think."

"Go and tell him that." Josie gave a bitter laugh. "He ain't—isn't—too hot on compliments. Usually it's telling me what I've done wrong. And one of the things is not having any babies."

Madame Olga drew herself up, her eyes flashing. "You send him to me. I set him straight."

Josie had to laugh. "He's off in the army some-

14

where. And he wouldn't listen to no woman." She examined Madame Olga, sitting there erect and formidable. "They should use you against the Germans. Our secret weapon. I bet you'd know how to set that Hitler straight."

Madame Olga chuckled, too. "I'd certainly like to give him a piece of my mind. If only we women ran the world, there would be no war, don't you think?"

As the weeks went by, an unlikely friendship formed. During lulls, they sat together at one of the tables with cups of tea—Russian style, brewed in a samovar—and Madame Olga told Josie tales about her youth in Russia, about the grand balls and sleigh rides with handsome Cossacks. All of it sounded too good to be true. But Josie loved to hear the stories nevertheless. Couldn't get enough of them.

"Tell me again about that grand duke who was courting you."

Madame Olga smiled sadly. "It's all so long ago now. Like a beautiful dream for me, too." She patted Josie's cheek. "You are like a daughter to me. The daughter I never had."

Josie got the implication: Madame Olga had said she had no one in the world, except for her dear cat, Mishka. She was hinting that she was going to leave Josie the tea shop when she died.

CHAPTER 2

When she was a child, Josie was convinced that the stork must have left her on the wrong doorstep. The other members of her family were big-boned peasant stock with round faces and light hair. Josie was thin and dark with high cheekbones and interesting green eyes. Her mother once told her that her great-grandfather had run away with a gypsy and that she clearly had gypsy blood. She had meant this to be shaming, but Josie found it romantic. She was also blessed with an imagination—something none of her siblings possessed—as well as an appreciation for beautiful things, of which there were none in the cramped little house behind the gasworks. Her dad worked as a porter on the railway and sometimes would bring home magazines that passengers had discarded. Josie would pore over these magazines as if they were portals to a magic world—one she could transport herself to by wishing. She would cut out pictures of fashionable women and posh houses and try to imagine herself in those scenes of garden parties and horse race meetings at Ascot.

Josie's mother told her more than once that no good comes of daydreaming, and the sooner Josie faced the harsh reality of life, the better. She should know what she was talking about: nine children and a tenth on the way, plus a husband whose pay packet didn't stretch to enough food even when he didn't drink half of it. Josie's one ray of hope lay in her teachers at school. They were impressed with her quick brain, her desire to learn, her mathematical ability and her love of reading. They told her they would recommend her for teacher training when she left school at fourteen. This sounded wonderful to Josie, but the dream was crushed when her mother died in childbirth with her tenth child, leaving six children younger than Josie. Her older brothers were already out of the house, her older sister in service. So it fell to Josie to leave school and become the mother. This continued until her father married a widow who made it clear that Josie should be out and earning money— preferably living under someone else's roof. The chance for teacher training was now long gone. The neighbour's daughter, Alice, made good money at a garment factory and suggested Josie join her. "You have to work fast, but it's a lot of laughs," she said. So Josie found herself at a sewing machine in a room with fifty other women, all singing and laughing loudly as they worked. The clatter of machines and constant chatter of the girls took a lot of getting used to.

"Cheer up, love. Your face could curdle milk," her seatmate said. "You're never going to find yourself a husband if you don't make something of yourself."

There had been no opportunity in her life to meet a potential husband until Alice took her to a dance at the local workingmen's club. There Josie met Stanley Banks. He was tall and fashionably, almost flashily, dressed, with a Ronald Coleman moustache and a cheeky smile. To her amazement, he seemed interested in her. He was a good dancer, and after a slow waltz he steered her outside and kissed her. Josie was bowled over. Apparently he was the catch of the whole room, and he had chosen her. What's more, she realized she finally had an escape route. They were married three months later and moved to a small terraced house in nearby Bethnal Green. Stanley had a good job as a porter at a Smithfield meat market and made it clear that he didn't expect his wife to work.

"I'm the provider around here," he said. "You keep a nice clean house for me and look after the children when they come."

At first Josie thought it was bliss—the little house was easy to clean, giving her time to look in shop windows and occasionally money to treat herself to a ride up west to the shops in Oxford Street. She had time to visit the library, and to do the crossword in the newspaper, both of which Stan mocked as getting above herself. He only read the racing section and the funnies. But the children didn't come, and the cocky assertiveness that had seemed attractive in Stan now showed itself to be a cruel streak of bullying. The least little thing would set him off—an egg yolk that was too hard or too soft, unnoticed crumbs on the carpet, a crease in his shirt.

"What's bloody well wrong with you?" he demanded when his dinner wasn't on the table the moment he stepped in the door one evening. "What do you bloody well do with yourself all day, that's what I'd like to know. I didn't realize I married a barren cow. You better watch yourself, or I'll throw you out and get a proper woman— one who can give me lots of kids and get my meals on the table on time."

Josie wanted to suggest that he might be responsible for the lack of a baby, but she didn't fancy the back of his hand across her face. She thought of leaving him. She would have left if she'd had anywhere to go. But then fate stepped in, in the form of Herr Hitler. War was declared. At first nothing happened. Life went on pretty much as normal, although they were issued identity cards and ration books. Foodstuffs became scarce. Stan started to sneak home the occasional cut of meat. Josie was horrified.

"But that's stealing, Stan."

"You want to eat, don't you? Who's going to notice the odd bit of stewing steak gone missing, eh? Besides, all the blokes are doing it."

"It's still not right."

"Fine. You can cook it for me and watch me enjoy it, then."

Josie worried he'd get caught and prayed he'd get his call-up papers. Stan didn't seem at all concerned.

"I'll be all right," Stan said. "I'm in a protected occupation. The country has to have meat to survive, doesn't it?"

One by one all the other men on their street were drafted, and the sight of new soldiers in uniform marching past to Liverpool Street Station became a regular occurrence. Then came the threat of bombing, the evacuation of children out of London—lines of small girls and boys with labels around their necks, each carrying a tiny suitcase with a change of clothes. The mothers wept. Some children looked scared, but most seemed to view it as a great adventure.

Then, in January 1940, came the envelope Stan had not expected.

"Bloody 'ell," he muttered as he held it in his hands, staring down at it.

"What is it, Stan?" she asked.

"My call-up papers. I'm to report to the depot at Islington. I'll go and have a word with them blokes. They've made a mistake. This isn't right." The cocky grin returned. "Don't you worry. Clerical error. I'll soon set them straight."

He came back sobered and dejected. "They told

me the army doesn't make mistakes," he said, "and it's my duty to go where my country sends me."

"I'm sorry, Stan." Josie put a tentative hand on his arm. He shook it off.

"I don't know how we're going to afford the rent on this place with my army pay cheque," he said. "We'd better give it up while we can and have you move in with my sister."

Stan's sister, Shirley, and her husband, Fred, were a loud-mouthed pair of cockneys who were either laughing, drinking or fighting. They lived close to the docks in a grim little backstreet where the spare bedroom looked out on to a warehouse. There was no way that Josie was going to move in with them.

"It's all right, Stan," she said. "Don't you worry about it. I'll get a job." She saw he was going to object and added, "You've seen the government posters, haven't you? All able-bodied adults are supposed to report for work. And I'm able-bodied and willing. I could join the WAACs."

"I don't want you in no army," he said aggressively. "All them men around. You could go back to that dress factory where you used to work, I suppose. I expect they are making uniforms by now."

"Don't worry about me," she said. "I'll find something. You just go and take care of yourself."

Josie felt a twinge of worry mixed with guilt

21

when he left. Was it right to feel a sense of relief that he was going? He was her husband, after all. She must have loved him once.

"Bye, then. I'm off," he said, trying to sound jaunty, but clearly looking scared. "Come and give your old man a kiss."

"You'll be fine," she said after she had dutifully presented her mouth. "Tell them you know how to handle meat, and they'll put you in catering."

"Yeah. Good idea." He stood, looking down at her, clearly wanting to say something but not finding the words. "And you—you mind yourself, right? No looking at other blokes."

"Don't be silly," she said, attempting a lively laugh. "Go on, then. Off you go. Don't keep the army waiting."

As she watched him disappear down the street and then around the corner, the guilt bubbled to the surface. She had not been able to cling to him, weeping, like other wives on the street. She didn't like to admit, even to herself, that she was glad to see him go. All she could think was that she was free to do what she wanted for the first time in her life. And the first step became the tea shop and Madame Olga.

As winter turned into spring and then into summer, Josie received the odd note from Stan. The food was terrible. The army boots had given him blisters. She should hear how the other blokes snored. And then nothing for a while.

News began to trickle in about the expeditionary force in France, about the Maginot Line that was impenetrable. But then the German army swept around it through Belgium, catching the defences by surprise. And then, on June the fourth, the country learned about a little French port called Dunkirk—British soldiers trapped on the beaches being machine-gunned by German planes. Josie was sure Stan was one of them and felt fear in the pit of her stomach.

Then came word of the miracle. Thousands of tiny boats, some only sailing dinghies, crossing the Channel to rescue those soldiers, bringing back a handful and turning right around to risk enemy fire and bombs again. England wept and prayed and gave thanks. And on Saturday she came home from work to find Stan sitting in the kitchen, having made himself a cup of tea and toast and dripping.

"Where the bloody hell have you been all day?" he demanded. "I come home on a week-end's leave, and my wife isn't bloody well there to greet me."

"Oh, Stan. You're safe," she cried and flung herself into his arms.

"Of course I'm bloody safe, you silly cow," he said, pushing her away.

"But I thought—Dunkirk. All those soldiers trapped . . ."

"Nah, I wasn't over in France. Bloody lucky,

actually. We've been guarding the Essex coast in case of invasion. The closest we came was watching all them little boats coming up the Thames. Amazing."

"Thank God," she said. "You were close by, and I didn't even know it."

"It was bloody cold and boring if you want to know. Patrolling up and down beaches and watching for U-boats."

"Better than being on a beach in France, getting machine-gunned by Germans."

"Bloody right."

"And you're home now, and safe. That's the main thing."

"Only for the weekend. And what do I find? I come home, expecting a warm welcome, and my wife is gone all day. What am I to think, eh?"

"I'm sorry, Stan. I'd have stayed home if I'd known you were coming," she said. "I've been at work."

"On a Saturday?"

"Yes. We have to work shifts these days, you know." She felt a tiny pang of guilt about lying.

"You're not working at that factory, are you?" He wagged an accusing finger at her. "I went round there to find you."

"No. I'm working in a cafeteria. Helping feed everyone. What's more, it's nearby, so I can walk to work and not have to spend on the bus fare."

She had phrased it carefully. "Cafeteria" sounded suitably vague and harmless.

She saw the anger fade from his eyes. "Well, that's all right, then, I suppose. You're not waiting on no service blokes, I hope?"

"No. It's in the Mile End Road. What do you think? And besides, I'm mostly doing the cooking."

"So, you've finally learned to cook, have you?"

"What do you mean? You've always said I'm a good cook," she said. "And I've got a lot better, too. Madame—my supervisor has been teaching me. You wait. When you're home, I'll make you some great little rock cakes and scones."

"If I ever bloody well get home," he said. "They gave us weekend leave because we're supposed to be shipping out."

"Where are you going?"

He frowned. "They won't bloody well tell us, but the blokes have been muttering that it might be North Africa. The Krauts are bringing in troops to help Italy, so it seems."

"Oh dear. North Africa. That's a long way away." She gave him a sympathetic look. "So you didn't manage to get into catering, then?"

"Didn't have no choice. I enlisted. We walked down a line, picking up uniforms. They shoved a gun into our hands and said, 'You are part of His Majesty's infantry.' And that was that. Drilling. Parades. Learning how to handle a rifle, although

25

to tell you the truth, there aren't enough rifles to go around, and some of us have to do drills with sticks of wood. A lot of bloody good they are for defending our island from Hitler. 'You tanks stay back, do you hear, or I'll hit you with my stick of wood.' " He gave a bitter laugh. "The whole thing's a joke, Josie. Under-equipped and undertrained, and they're sending us out against the German fighting machine. What chance do we have? And you better be ready, because you mark my words, the invasion will come soon, and blokes like me won't be there to stop it because we'll be in bloody North Africa." He leaned forward, waving an aggressive finger. "So what will you do if a bloody Jerry shows up on your doorstep, and me not there to protect you, eh?"

"Make him a cup of tea and hope for the best, I suppose." She tried to chuckle, but then she touched his shoulder tentatively. "I'm really sorry, Stan. But at least if you are sent far away to Africa, you'll be safe for a while, won't you?"

"And what difference would that make?" he snapped at her. "Only delaying meeting those bloody Huns and being mown down."

"Maybe you'll be better trained before you meet them," she said. "And have real guns, too. I tell you what . . ." She put on a bright smile. "I don't have much food in the house because I mainly eat at the cafeteria, but I'll run down to the corner and pick us up some fish and chips, shall I? And a pint of brown ale for you at the off-licence, if they've still got any?"

He took her hands in his. "You're a good girl, Josie. I'm sorry if I'm a bit sharp with you sometimes. I guess you're as disappointed as I am that we ain't had no kids yet."

"You know I am," she said. "We'll keep on hoping, eh?"

"We'll give it another good try tonight, shall we?" And he gave her shoulder a squeeze.

On Sunday evening, he was gone. Josie couldn't help feeling a sense of relief. He was being shipped abroad. He wouldn't be home for a while. Her job at the tea shop was safe for now. As the summer progressed, she received a letter from him. Half of it was blacked out by the censor and the rest completely illegible. But she saw the signature *Love, Stan.* At least he was still safe. She wasn't sure if she felt happy or sad about that.

CHAPTER 3

The tea shop remained a charmed little haven, too good to be true, until the autumn of 1940, when the bombing started in earnest. Night after night, waves of bombers over London. The rumbling drone of hundreds of aircraft drowned out by air raid sirens. The sky criss-crossed with searchlights. The burst of anti-aircraft guns and then the first deep thump as a bomb landed. Then another. Then came the wail of fire engines and ambulances until finally the all-clear was sounded by the sirens and everyone crept out of cellars and shelters, giving a silent prayer that it wasn't them tonight.

When the air raid warning sounded, everyone was supposed to go down to a shelter. Some had dug corrugated iron shelters in their back gardens. Josie's house only had a small concrete yard, so the nearest shelter for her was the Shoreditch underground station around the corner. She went there for the first couple of air raid warnings, but it terrified her even more than the bombing. All those people crammed together on to the platforms. The smell of unwashed humanity, of cigarette smoke, of nappies that needed changing, some people eating, others drinking. Men who had drunk a bit too much.

"Come over here and join us, love," one called out, grabbing at her skirt as she walked past. "I'll protect you. Give you a nice big cuddle and keep you warm, eh?"

After that, she decided to risk staying put, making up a bed under the sturdy oak dining table. Then one morning she walked to work as usual, only to find the street blocked and a pile of smoking rubble beyond the cordons. She ran towards the barriers only to be stopped by an air raid warden on guard.

"Hold on, love. Where do you think you're going?" he asked kindly.

"The place where I work. It's just down there. Just past the station near the fish shop."

"Not any more it ain't," he said. "That row of shops was completely flattened." He paused, looking at her stricken face. "I'm sorry, love. There's nothing you can do."

Her first thought had been one of despair that she now no longer had her job, but then she realized—Madame Olga lived in a flat over her little tea shop.

"Was anyone killed?" She heard her voice tremble.

He winced as he nodded. He was an older man, his hair, poking out from under his tin hat, already grey. His face showed the strain of nights of bombing. "I'm afraid there were a few casualties, ducks. There wasn't much warning, so I understand. Some old lady who couldn't get down the stairs in time—trying to carry her cat, so it seems—and an old Jewish couple who were caught in the street. Luckily not too many people lived over the shops. Not the same as a residential neighbourhood." He saw her face. "Did you know any of them?"

Josie nodded, feeling tears welling in her eyes. "The old lady probably was my employer. She's been having difficulty with stairs, and she had a cat she adored. Did you see the bodies?"

"Not me, love. I'm on day shift this week. I reckon they were taken to the mortuary over at the hospital."

Josie was still staring past him to the smoking rubble.

"Could I take a look and see if anything can be saved? She'd want me to do that."

He shook his head. "I can't let you no further, love," he said gently. "They haven't checked for gas leaks yet. You don't want to get blown sky-high, do you? Besides"—he gave a little sigh—"there really isn't anything. And you'd likely find things you wouldn't want to see— blown-off bits of bodies."

He walked away, leaving Josie staring at the smoking ruins. She was still in shock, trying to digest that Madame Olga was gone, the tea shop was gone. It felt as if everything she cared about had been snatched from her in one instant. The

30

tea shop had been like home. She hadn't realized how fond she had become of the old lady. Madame Olga had become the grandmother she never knew, someone who had time to listen to and appreciate her. And now she was gone.

"If only . . . ," Josie muttered to herself, not sure what she was saying. If only she'd been there, she could have helped Madame Olga down the stairs? Out to safety? But then they would just have been killed on the street instead. It was what happened in a war. One minute you were safe, and the next you weren't. And there was no rhyme or reason who would be next.

She turned reluctantly and started to walk away, forcing her brain to think. She had to find out where they had taken Madame Olga. She didn't want her buried in an unmarked plot with all the other victims. One thing she could do for her was make sure she had a decent funeral. She went to the nearest hospital and found her way to the mortuary. The young attendant on duty looked harassed, as if he hadn't had a proper night's sleep in ages.

"An old lady brought in last night, you say? There were several. What did she look like?"

"She was heavyset, grey hair in a bun, and she wore too much make-up . . . but then it was night, wasn't it? She'd have washed her face before she went to bed. And she always wore lots of rings— but she'd have taken them off, wouldn't she?"

"There was a lady like that," he said. "It can't have happened too late at night. She was still in her day clothes and wearing several rings. And she had red lips, like she'd been wearing lipstick."

"Then it was her." Josie turned away, determined not to cry in front of this man.

"I'm sorry, love. Was it a relative? Your mum?"

"No," she replied, then, realizing there was no one else, said, "My auntie."

"Oh, then you'll want those rings, won't you? Unless you want her buried in them?"

"No, I'll take them," Josie said. "I want to pay for a proper burial for her, so she's not dumped with a lot of others in a mass grave."

She was directed to the hospital almoner, where she was asked to give the deceased's name and sign an affidavit that she was next of kin. Her innate truthfulness won out, and she told the whole story to the almoner, who shook her head. "I'm sorry, Mrs Banks, but I can't release a body to someone who has no authority." The almoner had the severe face of an upper-class member of officialdom, but her look softened, and she actually covered Josie's hand with her own. "I understand your desire to help. It's hard to lose a friend. But . . ." She let the rest of the sentence hang in the air.

"What about her rings?" Josie asked.

"You want them?"

Josie shook her head. "I don't know if any of them are worth anything, but maybe they could be used to pay for a burial, couldn't they?"

"I'll see what I can do," the almoner said. "If she was a building owner, she must have had a bank account and insurance. Leave it to me. I'll do my best."

"Thank you." Josie felt quite drained as she stood up. "And if I leave my address, can you let me know about a funeral? I'd like to be there. She was Jewish. I expect she'd want her rabbi."

"Write down her particulars, and I'll try," the woman said. "But I have to tell you we're getting a constant stream of bodies. The mortuary will be overrun soon, I'm afraid, and then I've no idea what happens."

The almoner stood up, having suddenly come to a decision. "But I will go and get you her rings, as a keepsake. Nobody's asking too many questions these days."

She brought back a small paper bag and handed it to Josie. Josie opened it briefly, looked in, and nodded. "Yes, I remember that one with the big stone. It's only paste, but she liked it."

The woman smiled. "But a nice memory, eh?"

Josie took the bus home in a daze. Each day she went to the Mile End Road to see if the barriers had been removed. On the third day there was a bulldozer at work, scooping up rubble into a dump truck. Josie watched in horrified fascination. Suddenly she gave a little cry and darted forward. There amid the rubble was a perfect pink-and-white teacup, untouched by the bombing. She snatched it up as the driver yelled out a warning to her. It felt like a small victory.

By the end of the week, Josie realized she needed to find another job. On Monday morning she would go down to the civilian recruitment centre and see what they needed. She wouldn't mind working in one of the government canteens that provided meals to workers at low cost. At least she'd be busy and meeting people—and doing her bit for the war effort.

In the middle of Sunday night, she was awoken by the wail of the air raid siren. She sat up cautiously, trying not to bang her head on the tabletop above her. How far off was the siren? She was already learning when she needed to take action fast and when it was all right to get dressed and then decide if she needed to shelter. In the distance came the rumble of approaching planes and the sound of the ack-ack. The rumble grew louder. So many of them this time. Josie wondered if she was doing the right thing, staying put under her table. But then the first wave of planes was overhead. No time to go to the shelter in the tube station now.

Suddenly there was a whooshing sound and a deafening explosion nearby. The windows were blown in, the blackout curtains luckily stopping most of the glass from flying into the room. Sooty air came around the shredded curtains. The smell of burning and brick dust. Instantly the sounds from outside were magnified—screams, shouts, the bell of a fire engine.

Some poor person on this street, she thought and wondered if she should come out from under the table to take a look. She was reaching out to find her slippers, mindful of the broken glass, when there came a second whoosh. Then, almost instantly, an ear-splitting blast. She was thrown back, the air sucked from her lungs as she tried to cry out. The world was falling around her. Bricks were raining down. Something hit her head, and she knew no more.

Josie opened her eyes to total darkness. It hurt to breathe. Something was across her face. *My hair,* she thought and tried to lift a hand to brush it away. But her arm wouldn't move. She tried the other arm. Then her legs. Something was pressing on her from all sides. She was trapped. Buried. She wiggled her toes and was relieved that they at least worked. So did her fingers. At least she wasn't paralyzed, but the implication of where she was began to dawn on her.

"A tomb," she said to herself. "I'm in a tomb." And she felt panic rising because she had been buried prematurely. But then she heard the sound of an all-clear siren and the closer clanging of an ambulance bell.

"Help!" she called, trying to make a parched mouth work and force air into her lungs. "Somebody help me." The latter phrase was stopped by a fit of coughing as she breathed in the dust and dirt that covered her. She tried to see where she was. She realized then that her house must have collapsed around her, and she was covered in debris. Odd slivers of red light came in through the gaps in the walls, creating a surreal glow through the layer of dust, but she couldn't make out the table under which she had been sleeping. Had she left her shelter before the bomb dropped? She couldn't remember. And then, as she looked up, a sudden gust of cold wind stirred up the dust, and it cleared for a moment, making her gasp. Above her she had a glimpse of the night sky, and she was looking at a star. She took it as an omen, a sign from heaven that everything was going to be all right.

"Help!" she called again. "I'm here."

As a searchlight strafed the sky above, she saw a jagged section of wall overhead, poised precariously as if about to collapse. She fought back the fear. Nearby an ambulance bell sounded again, and she heard the tone change as it moved away. Hope fought with despair. They'd find her. Of course they would find her. But how would anyone know she was here? Maybe all they saw was a pile of rubble like the one on the Mile End Road where Madame Olga had died. But they had found Madame Olga's body all right. When it got light, they'd come looking . . . if Josie could hold on that long. She had no idea if she was badly hurt or what might be broken or bleeding. She was beginning to be aware of pain.

The noises around her had subsided. The street had fallen eerily silent.

"Help. Somebody help me," she called into darkness.

Then, miraculously, a voice responded. "Hang on, Frank. Did you hear that? There's somebody alive over there." Footsteps crunched over rubble. A torch moved over that section of wall above her. Then it swung down and picked out her frightened face.

"Bloody 'ell, Frank. There's a woman buried over here." The man moved cautiously, and Josie heard the crunching of glass as the torch swung down to light the way ahead of him before returning to her face. He dropped to his knees beside her.

"It's all right, love. It's going to be all right. Don't you worry. We'll get you out."

The second rescuer came up behind him. "I don't like the look of that bit of wall, Joe. Looks like it could come down any minute. Can we find something to protect her if it falls?"

The torch moved off, and she heard one of them call out, "Give me a hand with this."

"Oh yeah. That might work."

She heard footsteps moving around, and then one of them came back with a kitchen chair, which he placed over her head.

"Just in case, eh, love? Best I can do right now," he said, giving her an encouraging smile. "But don't you worry. It won't be long now. Frank's gone off to get a shovel, and we'll have more help coming as soon as that ambulance comes back."

He started pulling away bits of debris until the second man returned.

"Looks like she's got something big on top of her," he called to his mate. They scraped away the layer of debris, and then the first man gave a whistle. "Boy, you must lead a charmed life, missus. This tabletop must have taken the worst of the blast. Look, it's split right down the middle—big, thick piece of oak like that."

So the tabletop had lost its legs but had still provided something of a shield. As the first streaks of red dawn highlighted the jagged brick wall, more help arrived. One by one her limbs were freed.

"Can you move your legs for me, love?"

She could.

"And your arms?"

She lifted them but then winced.

At that moment, an ambulance crew came with a stretcher. "Stabilize her neck. She might have broken her back," another voice said as she was covered in a blanket.

Panic returned to her. People who broke their backs never walked again, did they? As gently as they could, they lifted her on to the stretcher.

"Wait," she called out, as reality returned to her. "My handbag! It's got my identity card and ration book in it. It was on the kitchen table. And the teapot on the mantelpiece—it had the week's spending money . . ."

"I'm sorry, love." In the darkness, the voice came out of nowhere above her head. "All I can see is bricks and rubble. I've no idea where your kitchen was, and we have people to rescue. Identity cards can be replaced." Pain shot through her as she was carried over the rubble, out to the street and into an ambulance. The ambulance bell cut through her head, horribly loud as she was jerked around while the vehicle dodged to find a way through debris-covered streets. The journey seemed to take forever. Then at last she was carried down a tiled hallway that smelled strongly of disinfectant and into a waiting room.

"We'll leave you here, then, love," the ambulance man said. "We have to get back."

And she was left alone. The room was ice-cold. She had been covered in a blanket, but she still shivered now, with delayed shock. As she moved her head cautiously to look around, she saw that she was in a row of stretchers. Moans came from some of them; others were horribly still. A harried young nurse appeared, moving down the row, getting particulars from patients who were awake, reading ambulance preliminary reports. At the stretcher next to Josie's, she stopped, took a pulse and then called to another nurse, "This one can be removed and taken to the mortuary." And she covered the face with the man's sheet. Then she indicated another stretcher to be carried through a door to her right. It was all so efficient. So clinical. Josie found it strangely similar to her work in the factory. Take one collar from the pile, machine around the edge, move it to her left for the next girl. *A factory of broken humans,* she thought, almost finding this funny.

She couldn't stop shivering. "Nurse?" she called. "I know there's other people before me, but I'm so cold. Could I have a cup of tea or something?"

"I'm afraid we can't give you anything until we see whether you need to go into surgery," she said. "But it won't be long now. Two of the patients ahead of you have died, which is speeding things up a bit."

Finally, she was carried through into a brightly lit room.

"Had a bit of a rough night, I gather," the doctor

said. "Don't worry. We'll soon get you patched up. Let's take a look, shall we?"

He pulled back her blanket. That was when Josie discovered for the first time that she was naked. The blast had stripped off her nightgown. She gave a gasp of horror and tried to reach for the blanket again.

"Don't worry, missus, I've seen much worse," he said with a chuckle. "You've come through remarkably well, considering. Not many people can have a house fall on them without sustaining a crushed limb." As he talked, his fingers examined each part of her body. "Legs all right. Looks like you've broken your clavicle—your collarbone. We'll send you for an X-ray. Nasty bang on your head—probably a concussion, then. But apart from some cuts and scrapes, you've got off lightly."

"My back? It's not broken, then?"

"If you can move your legs and arms like you just did, I'd say your back is in fine shape. We'll have you transferred to a ward where one of the nurses can clean those cuts and put your arm in a sling to minimize pain in your collarbone."

"You're not going to set it in plaster?"

"We don't do that with collarbones. Almost impossible to set. You just have to keep it stabilized until the bone knits together again. But it should heal nicely."

"Thank you," she said.

He smiled. "It's a treat to see a lucky one. I've had enough bad news for one night. One woman blinded, one little kid is going to lose his leg. And I can't tell you how many didn't make it. Bloody Germans."

He gave a signal to a nearby nurse, and Josie was wheeled away to a long ward where she was washed, had her wounds cleaned and patched up, was dressed in a gown and then was given that cup of tea she had been hoping for.

It was only after she lay back in bed, feeling warm and comfortable, that reality dawned on her. She had nothing and nowhere to go.

CHAPTER 4

Josie spent the next night in hospital, but the following morning she was greeted by an efficient middle-aged woman in a severe, high-collared blue dress. Greying hair permed into neat waves—the type who usually ran the Girl Guides and sat on parish councils.

"Now, Mrs Banks, how are we feeling?" she asked after she had taken Josie's particulars.

"Not too bad," Josie said. "Bit of a headache still, and of course it hurts me to move my arm."

The woman nodded with what seemed to be sympathy. "Normally we'd keep you in for a week, but demand is so high we need this bed for the seriously wounded. I understand your house was bombed?"

Josie nodded.

"Were you in the house alone? No children?"

"No children," Josie said.

"And your husband?"

"Off fighting Jerry somewhere."

"Do you have family members you could go to for a while?"

"Nobody."

"You don't have parents alive?"

"My mother died. My dad married again, and there are three of my younger brothers plus two

43

stepbrothers now living in a little house with no inside bathroom. And even if they did have space, my stepmum was right shirty with me for marrying and no longer bringing home my pay packet. She told me not to bother to come back when I moved out."

The woman nodded again. "No other family or friends who could help out? I'm afraid the government hostels are full."

Stan's sister crossed her mind but was swiftly put aside. "Nobody," she said. "My older brothers are in the forces. My sister is a maid at a big house."

The woman examined Josie's chart. "It says here you experienced a bad concussion, so no job that involves heavy work or standing for a while. That leaves out moving into the armed forces yourself or signing on as a land girl. And I could get you into the hostel at the munitions factory in Woolwich, but you couldn't work at a factory bench at the moment, not with one arm out of commission." She looked up suddenly. "Might you have the money for a hotel for a while?"

"Oh yes," Josie said. "I've just been trying to choose between the Ritz and the Savoy."

The woman managed a little smile. "I take it that's a no."

"It was all I could do to pay the rent on my house," she said.

"You didn't work?"

"I did, until last week when a bomb fell on my tea shop and killed my employer. I was about to look for a new job when this happened."

"I'm sorry," the woman said. "It does seem like an awful lot to bear at once, doesn't it? The only thing I can say to make it easier is that you're not alone. I can't tell you how many people I talk to every day in similar circumstances. Many of them have lost family members in the bombing—children buried in rubble, you know. Everyone is grieving and in shock, and frankly we have no answers."

"What am I meant to do, then?" Josie's voice sounded suddenly harsh. "Sleep stark naked on the street? I've got no clothes, no possessions, no home. I've got nothing, missus." She fought back a tear. This woman would not see her cry.

"We can set you up with some clothing, at least," the woman said. "And basic toiletries. Toothbrush. Comb. Do you have any money in the bank?"

Josie shook her head. "Stan had his post office savings book, but that's buried with the rest of my stuff. Besides, I couldn't get at that money, could I? I've never had a bank account in my name. Stupid me—I put the extra money in a teapot on the mantelpiece . . ." She broke off, afraid she might disgrace herself by crying.

The woman looked down at her pad again, clearly wanting to end the interview. "I tell you what," she said. "I'll put you on the list for evacuation."

"Evacuation? Out of London, you mean?"

"Yes. Out into a rural area."

Josie toyed with the idea. It sounded as strange as suggesting she move to the Himalayas. The woman had no idea of the turmoil this was creating in Josie's head. She went on, with mounting enthusiasm. "Normally it's only mothers with children we send out of the city, but in your case, I think it would do you good to get out into the country. And when you feel better, why, then you can join the land girls, can't you? Fresh air and better food will work wonders."

She stood up. Josie's mind was still racing. So many pieces to a jigsaw puzzle of which she couldn't see the big picture. "Here, what about my identity card and ration card? They were in my handbag, and that's buried somewhere. I can't get food without them."

"We'll arrange for a reissue," the woman said, "but it will take a while. The Ministry of Health is overwhelmed at the moment. There's a convent at St Bridget's Church, where the nuns are taking in people in your circumstances, people who have nowhere to go. You can stay there until we can get you new cards and arrange for transportation out to the country somewhere."

Like many Londoners, Josie had an innate suspicion of the Roman Catholic Church and nuns in particular. She had heard all sorts of rumours about them—they prayed all night, they whipped themselves with barbed wire, they got walled up for breaking vows—but at this moment she couldn't come up with anything better.

"Righto. Thank you," she said. "I suppose it will have to do."

She could tell the woman had expected more gratitude, but she just couldn't find it. A nurse probationer came in to show her how to change the dressing on her wounds, how to tie her sling and put it over her head with one hand.

"It won't be easy going to the lav or anything," she said. "I'd keep my clothing really simple if I were you, until you can move your arm a bit more."

"Oh, that will be easy for me," Josie said, "seeing as how I don't have no clothing. Not a stitch to put on. Nothing. My nightdress was blown off in the bomb."

"Oh dear," the girl said. "But I expect they'll be coming round with a change of clothes for you before they release you later today."

"If they don't, I ain't going out of this ward wearing a gown that shows my bottom," Josie said, and the girl laughed.

"That's the ticket," she said. "Keep up your spirits, eh?"

"If you don't laugh, then you'd have to cry, wouldn't you?" Josie said.

They exchanged a smile.

"I'll go and see what I can do," the girl said, and true to her word she came back with a couple of pairs of flannel knickers, a couple of wool vests, a tweed skirt, a knitted jumper and a well-worn overcoat. She added a pair of lisle stockings plus a garter belt, and lace-up shoes, also well-worn.

"I hope these are about your size," she said.

Josie had the horrible feeling that they had belonged to someone who died in hospital and she was now wearing a dead woman's clothes. But she took them because she had no choice. The knickers and vests seemed to be new, or at least newly laundered, but the jumper still had a lingering smell of Ashes of Roses perfume—one that Josie particularly disliked. She had never been one for perfume, except for eau de cologne and lavender water. She remembered Stan had once bought her a bottle of real perfume that he claimed had fallen off the back of a lorry. It had been overwhelmingly heady and cloying, and she had never worn it. It was funny how the whiff of scent could trigger such strong memories.

When she was dressed, she was wheeled down to a waiting taxi and taken through streets that were so heavily bombed she had no idea where she was going. The convent was not far away, and Josie realized she must have passed it before, but it was so unobtrusive she would never have noticed. The aspect presented to the street was a plain brick wall with a small door in it. No window. The taxi driver assisted her to this door, rang the bell and waited. It was opened by a nun wearing a starched white wimple around a smooth and ageless face. The look was so alien that Josie almost changed her mind there and then, but the taxi driver said cheerfully, "Here you go, sister. Another new convert for you. Make sure you only feed her bread and water!"

It was the usual cockney humour, but to Josie it was almost the last straw.

"Now look," she began, but the nun held up a hand and smiled.

"My dear, don't listen to this awful man. We have been notified about you, and you are most welcome. Come on in, do."

Josie was led along a narrow passage and found herself in a courtyard with walls on all four sides. Someone had attempted a bit of a garden in the middle, but as it was November, only a couple of sorry cabbages were growing. Then they went into another hallway, this one warm and smelling slightly of boiled cabbage, until at last she was shown into a big room, now covered in army-style camp beds, many of which were occupied.

"This is normally our recreation room," the nun said. "We've converted it for the duration. Find yourself an empty bed and tuck your things under it. Anything else I can do for you?"

"A cup of tea might be nice," Josie said.

The nun smiled again. "The tea trolley will be round at four. And then supper at six. Lights out and silence at nine. We observe night-time silence here." She paused. "And you are welcome to join us for any of our services in the chapel."

"Thanks," Josie muttered, refraining from adding, "but no thanks."

She had been brought up completely without religion except for her early years, when she attended Sunday school at the local Methodist chapel because they had a once-a-year outing to the seaside for regular attendees. She had even won a prize, a book about a child who suffered abuse and then went to heaven. Josie had never found it too inspiring and hadn't been back since. It seemed that religion was all about a wrathful God and punishment for sins. Josie had decided long ago that if she were God, she'd do something about wars and people suffering.

She found a bed, equipped with two blankets and a pillow, under one of the high windows. She sank down on to it, feeling tired and a little dizzy now after standing and walking, and lay staring at the high, vaulted ceiling. In the distance, she thought she heard the sound of chanting.

"Like a ruddy mortuary, ain't it, love?"

Josie looked across at the next bed and saw a round-faced woman lying there, her face battered and bruised and her legs both in plasters.

50

"Still, it don't matter much," the woman went on. "I ain't going to be doing much dancing in the near future. How about you? Get bombed out, too?"

Josie nodded.

"And broke your arm?"

"No. Collarbone. And I have a concussion. I'm supposed to lie quiet for a few days."

"I suppose we're the lucky ones," the woman said. "I'm Ada, by the way."

"Josie. Pleased to meet you."

"At least we're still alive, aren't we?" Ada went on. "See that woman over there—the one in black who never moves? Lost all three of her kids in an incendiary bomb. House went up like a torch, and the kids were trapped upstairs. Husband's goodness knows where in the army. The poor soul just lies there. Never says a word. I wonder if she ever will be right again." She shook her head at Josie. "Makes you so mad, doesn't it? If those Germans knew what they were doing to ordinary people, don't you think they'd stop? Or are they all monsters?"

"I suppose they have to do what they are told, like all our boys," Josie replied. "But at least in the army, my Stan will be fighting other soldiers, not civilians."

"And British boys know better than to harm defenceless women and children," Ada said proudly. "I'm glad my daughter's grown up and gone. Emigrated to Australia before the war with her husband and the nippers. They wanted us to go with them, but my hubby didn't want to leave. Then, guess what? The blighter goes and dies on me. Heart attack right after war was declared. So now I'm stuck here with nobody, and no house now, of course. Not sure what I'm going to do next. I've got a brother, but his wife is a right cow."

"Same with me," Josie said. "My Stan has a sister, but I wouldn't last two minutes in that place. Always arguing and fighting, they are. And the swear words—the air turns blue there."

"So where do you think you'll be going, then?" Ada asked.

"They mentioned evacuating me. Sending me out to the country somewhere."

"That would be nice. All right for some," Ada said. "Plenty of good food out in the country, so they say. I wouldn't mind going myself, but I can't go anywhere while I need looking after like this. I can't even get up and go to the lav on my own." She paused, then gave a bright smile. "Listen. That sounds like the tea trolley now. They do their best here, that's for sure. Food's halfway eatable."

As well as cups of tea, there were jam sandwiches. As Josie came back to her bed with hers, she glanced down at the woman in black, just lying there.

"Here, love, have a cup of tea and a sandwich," she said, holding them out to her.

The woman barely moved her head enough to shake it.

"Come on, love," Josie said. "I know you've had the worst thing in the world happen to you, but you've got to go on fighting. Cos if you give up and you die, too, well, that's just showing that bugger Hitler that he's won, isn't it? We have to show him that we're British and he's not going to break us. Right?"

The woman opened her eyes and stared at Josie for a long minute, then she sat up enough to take the cup of tea. Afterward Josie found there was a small common room where they could sit on well-worn sofas, and a library they could use. Not all the books were of a religious nature, and she found plenty to interest her—a book on the history of the British Isles, one on the French Revolution and a couple of Dickens novels. Since she didn't feel like talking much, and as Ada was a great chatterer, Josie sat in a corner and read. She had to admit she found the books heavy going, full of a vocabulary she never had, but she persevered—until the headache returned again.

After a couple of days, she felt less dizzy when she stood up, and she approached the nun who came to check on them. "Sister, is there any reason I can't go out?"

"If it's to post a letter, one of the sisters can do it for you," the nun said.

"No. I see it's a fine day, and I thought I might just go and take a look at my house—at what used to be my house. I haven't seen it since . . ."

"Is that wise? It wouldn't distress you?"

"I'd just like to see for myself," Josie said.

"Well, I can't stop you. You're not a prisoner here," the nun said, "but I must remind you that you've had a severe concussion. You shouldn't do too much."

"I don't think I used to live far from here," Josie said. "I think I recognized the cinema on the corner. I wouldn't be long."

"I'm afraid I can't spare a sister to accompany you, but you can certainly take a little walk in the fresh air. Although"—she gave a rueful smile—"I think 'fresh air' is a loose description at this time of year. Make sure you bundle up warmly and put something over your nose and mouth, then."

"I would if I could," Josie said. "I don't have any clothes except the ones I'm wearing, and I get the feeling they came from a dead person. I was in my nightdress when the house was bombed, and the blast blew it right off me."

"Good heavens." The nun looked shocked. "Let me see what we can find in the donations bin, shall we?"

She went away, then returned with a red knitted scarf and an old black felt hat. "Better than

54

nothing. And when you return, you can come and check the donations for yourself. See if there's anything else there you can use—although don't take too much, please. There are many women like yourself here. Ones who have lost everything."

Josie had to be helped into putting her good arm into the overcoat, and the nun had to wrap the scarf around her. When she set out, she realized quickly that her gait was unsteady and told herself she was probably a bloody fool for doing this. But she walked on, discerning familiar street names and landmarks until she came to Bethnal Green Road, recognized the railway station, found James Street and then Cornwall Road. Or what used to be Cornwall Road. It was now rubble on either side. There were four houses standing at the far end, and a group of cheeky boys was having a fun game over the rubble. Josie moved cautiously until she came to number twenty-six, or what used to be number twenty-six. It was hard to tell. But then she saw her old brass bedstead sticking out of a pile of bricks. Stan had been so proud of that bedstead. He had bought it at a second-hand shop when they married. "Good quality, Josie," he had said. "Belonged to some toff."

She stared at it now with longing, knowing she couldn't take it with her. Soon a bulldozer would sweep it away with the rest. That made her wonder if anything might be saved. She presumed that someone would have had a good pick over all the bombed houses by now—just in case there was anything valuable. Her handbag would be gone, if it wasn't buried. And that teapot with the spare cash in it—well, that wouldn't have survived. Black despair came over her again.

She took one hesitant step after another, unable to balance herself properly with one arm out of commission. There was a smashed water jug from the upstairs washstand. Then there was one shoe. Her smart shoes for going out. Now if only she could find the other . . . but she couldn't.

"This is stupid," she said out loud, fighting back tears of frustration. "There's nothing here now."

But then she saw her old bedside table. It had had a marble top, which had saved it from utter destruction. She pulled open the drawer with difficulty, using only one hand, then smiled. Inside was her jewellery box—not a real jewellery box but an old cigarette tin, and the jewellery was nothing expensive, of course. Mostly costume except for a hollow bangle Stan had bought her when he had been lucky at the dog racing. But the box also contained fifteen gold sovereigns she had been putting by for a rainy day. And the little bag containing Madame Olga's rings.

"Oh." She gasped, her eyes welling up with

tears. "Oh." It was almost like a gift from heaven. Something of her own after all.

Josie shoved the box into her pocket. Further searching turned up nothing else of use. She walked away and returned to St Bridget's without looking back. As she entered the convent and walked down the narrow corridor to her room, she heard the sound of chanting coming from nearby. She pushed open the heavy oak door a few inches and peered around. The nuns' chapel was simple with hard pews and a crucifix at the altar. There was a statue of the Virgin Mary, another of St Joseph, but no fancy stained glass or side altars. The scent of incense hung in the air. The front pews were now filled with nuns, and their voices rose and fell with the chant.

Without quite knowing what she was doing, Josie let herself in and slipped into a back pew. The words were in Latin, but the effect was soothing. For the first time, she found herself uttering a little prayer: *I don't know if you can hear me or not. I'm not sure I even really believe in you. But if you are listening right now, it's Josie Banks, from London. I want to thank you for saving my life from the bomb. You must have something in mind for me, so I reckon I'm going to trust you and not worry about it too much.*

CHAPTER 5

Christmas came while she was at the convent. The nuns tried to make it cheerful, setting the resident women to make paper chains to decorate the rooms. Josie wrote to Stan, care of the battalion headquarters, telling him she had been bombed out and would let him know when she had a new address. Nothing came from him in return, but other women said it took months to get letters from their husbands overseas.

"And a fat lot of good they are, too," one woman said. "I had a letter that started *Dear Marjorie,* and everything after that was blacked out by the censor."

"It must have been too steamy for them," a young woman said, chuckling.

"My Reggie? Steamy? That would be the day. The raciest he ever got was to ask if I fancied a cup of cocoa before bed."

The women laughed, happy to have a moment when they could find something to laugh about.

On Christmas Day the nuns served a turkey— donated from another of their houses in the country—and everyone got one slice, as well as plenty of roast potatoes and parsnips and afterward, treacle pudding and custard. They sang Christmas carols around a piano. It was all very jolly, and Josie began to feel a small bubble of hope forming. Life in the country might not be bad. She recalled what she knew of the country. She had only been out of London a few times. In her childhood, there was the Sunday school outing once a year—a charabanc trip to Southend-on-Sea or Clacton, singing loudly all the way: "Pack up your troubles in your old kit bag and smile, smile, smile." She hadn't noticed the countryside much—the odd field of cows or vegetable patch, a couple of little villages with thatched houses. Very pretty, but she was intent on being the first one on the bus to see the sea. And then that delicious thrill of taking off her shoes and stockings and paddling in the cold waves.

Since then, her only countryside experience had been a few trips to Epping Forest when she and Stan were courting. It didn't really count as countryside as they could get there via the Underground, but it was pleasant and cool and leafy, and she remembered that Stan had tried to make love to her, under a big oak tree. She hadn't let him, though. "Not till I've got a ring on my finger," she had said. And the next week he had shown up with a little diamond. She smiled at the thought now. They had been happy once. It was the lack of children that had brought out the worst in Stan. That and a streak of jealousy. He was always worried she might look at another man.

"Poor Stan," she muttered. "Poor bugger out in God-knows-where for Christmas." Perhaps he was being shelled or bombed. Perhaps he was already dead. And she felt more charitably about him.

Since she had been brought to the convent, they had been spared any close calls with enemy bombs. There had been no ominous drone of enemy planes on Christmas Day, which was a miracle in itself. Then on Boxing Day the bombing resumed. The church beside the convent was hit, leaving a blackened hole where the nave had been. The blast blew out some of the convent windows, including those of the chapel. Josie wasn't the only woman who was upset by the bomb. It was a vivid reliving of their own prior experiences, and a couple of them got quite hysterical and had to be calmed with a cup of tea. Josie was not about to show her fear, even though her heart was thumping and she felt she might pass out at any second. She realized how fragile her nerves had become, and suddenly evacuation to the countryside seemed like a good idea. She sought out the nun in charge.

"Any idea when I might be getting my new identity papers and be able to move to the country?" she asked.

"Your papers were delivered a week ago, but the doctor thought you should stay here until you were over the concussion," the nun said. "If you're really feeling well enough to undertake a long journey, I can put your name forward in the queue."

"I think I'd like to go," Josie said. "Oh, don't get me wrong. I like it here. I think you're all bloody saints, but I can't take the bombing no more. Every time I hear those planes, I remember being buried. I just don't know if I'll ever feel safe again."

The nun nodded. "I do understand, Mrs Banks. You lived through a horrible experience, but the thing to remember is that you did live through it. God must have wanted you here for a reason."

Josie laughed then. "Go on. He just didn't want me in heaven, that's all."

The nun smiled softly. "I think He'd be happy to have you up there. Just not yet."

"But you'll tell them I'm ready to go out to the country, will you? I don't want to jump no queue or anything. I won't take someone else's turn. But if it's mine, then I'd like to take it."

"Of course." The nun patted Josie's good hand. "I'll pass the message along."

It wasn't until the first week in January 1941 that Josie was driven to King's Cross Station, carrying a canvas bag containing her pitifully few personal effects. Around her neck was a label, stating who she was and where she was headed. On the platform she joined a group of evacuees, mostly children but some mothers as well. The children stood together, huddled in a tight group as if there were safety in numbers, looking wide-eyed as a train pulled out with a great puff of steam. Josie guessed for most of them, it would be the first time on a train, the first time in a great station like this. Josie wondered how many of them were leaving their mothers behind and how many no longer had mothers.

An efficient-looking woman, one of the many the war seemed to have brought out of comfortable, middle-class drawing rooms to volunteer for the war effort, checked Josie's label and then consulted her clipboard. "You're bound for Peterborough, Mrs Banks. Go and stand with that group by the pillar."

Josie did what she was told and joined a group of mainly children.

"Hello," she said. "You coming for a nice adventure in the country with me?"

She got a few weak smiles in return. They boarded the train and set off. After a while the London sprawl turned into fields and trees— all stark and bare at this time of year. Their progress was painfully slow. When a goods train approached, their train had to pull into a siding and wait, goods having priority over people these days. As they moved further north, there were patches of snow in fields. This perked up the children in the carriage, who had never seen proper white snow before. Some of them had never seen a cow or a sheep, either, and they now peered out of the windows with interest.

"Cor, missus, them cows ain't half big, ain't they?" a little boy said to her. "Do you reckon they are dangerous?"

"Probably not, if they give us milk every morning," Josie said. "Someone has to milk them."

The boy looked at her as if he was just digesting what she said. "So the milk comes out of them cows, then?"

Josie nodded. "That's right. See them things hanging underneath? You pull on them, and milk comes out."

"Go on!" He looked at her and laughed. Josie didn't admit that she had never seen it herself either.

It was three hours later that the train pulled into Peterborough station. It had been a noisy journey, and the train had rocked and stopped and started, all of which brought on a headache for Josie. Another batch of efficient women with armbands and clipboards were waiting to direct the evacuees, moving like sheepdogs rounding up a herd of sheep. Josie was directed with a group to a waiting small green bus. She was one of the first to board and was ushered down to the back. Two children took the seat in front of her. The smaller one was crying with heart-wrenching sobs.

Josie leaned forward and put a hand on the child's shoulder. "It's all right, love. We're going to be taken where it's safe until you can go home again."

"But it's so far away," the girl managed between sobs. "How will my mummy ever find me?"

"We'll write and tell her, won't we? Those ladies will tell her, don't you worry. And soon you can go home again."

"But we don't have a home," the little girl whimpered. "They bombed our house, and my mummy is in the hospital."

Josie didn't quite know what to say to this. It echoed her own predicament, and she had no idea what might happen in her own future. The bus filled up, mainly with children, but there was one mother, with a baby and a toddler, who was given the front seat. The engine roared to life so that the whole bus shook, then it took off with a jerk, making her have to sit back in her seat. She found she was sitting next to an older girl, probably around twelve or thirteen, her hair in two thick plaits beneath a brown beret, her thin, pale and serious face not showing any emotion. She was looking down, focusing on her hands, avoiding eye contact.

"Doesn't look too bad, does it?" Josie said, glancing out of a window as suburbs melded into countryside. "No sign of bombs out here. What's the betting we'll get some decent food, eh?"

The girl glanced up and gave a polite smile.

"I'm Josie," Josie said. "I got bombed out. How about you?"

"I am Lottie," the girl said. There was something about her accent that was foreign.

"You're not English?"

The girl shook her head. "No, I am German." When she saw Josie's look of horror, she explained, "I am also Jewish. My parents sent me to England with the Kindertransport. Do you know of this?"

Josie shook her head.

"Before the war started, when things were getting bad for Jewish people, some parents sent their children to England to be safe."

"So you came here without your mum and dad?"

Lottie nodded, then looked down at her hands again. "They were not allowed to leave. Only children."

"That must have been very hard for you," Josie said. "How are they doing in Germany? Do you hear from them often?"

She saw a spasm of pain cross Lottie's face. "Since the war started, no letters come from Germany. I do not know if they are dead or alive. I hope for the best because my father is a professor at the university—an important scientist—but I do not know."

"So where have you been staying all this time? In London?"

Again a fleeting spasm on Lottie's face. "Jewish families took us in. I was sent to a house with two older women, sisters, in Golders Green. Do you know it? Many Jewish people live there."

"Oh. Well, that's a nice part of London. Was it a nice house?"

"Yes, a nice house, but the women, they were not nice. They did not want a child in the house, they wanted a servant. They made me do everything—carry the coal for the fires, scrub the steps. I heard one of them telling a friend that they had been able to save money and get rid of their cleaning woman now that they had me. I did not understand much English, and they scolded me when I got things wrong. I was very unhappy."

"Mean old cows," Josie said, making Lottie grin. "So what did you do?"

"When I could understand better English, I heard of a Jewish organization in London—a charity to help Jewish people. I did not go to school one day and went there instead. There I met a very kind lady, and she promised to help me. She came to see me at the house in Golders Green, and she told the two women they should be ashamed of themselves for treating a fellow Jew that way, and she took me with her. I stayed in her flat, then it got bombed. That is why you see me here."

"Was your kind lady all right? And you? Not hurt?"

"No. We went to the shelter. We were safe, but the house was no more."

"I got bombed, too," Josie said. "My house was flattened."

"And you were hurt?" The girl looked at her with concern.

"Not too bad. Not nearly as badly as some. I reckon some good country air will do us both good, don't you?"

"I hope so," Lottie said. "I hope the new family will not treat me like a servant as well."

"Don't you worry, my love," Josie said, wishing she had use of her right arm so that she could put it around the girl. "You've got me now. I'll make sure you're well taken care of."

And she saw Lottie blink back a tear as she glanced up again.

The bus had left the city of Peterborough behind and was now negotiating narrow country roads. On either side flat fields stretched away, covered in a dusting of new snow.

"It snows here," Lottie exclaimed, giving a hint of animation for the first time. "Just like at home in Germany."

"Where did you live?"

"In Munich. In the south, near the Alps. We

always went skiing in the winter. It was very nice. Papa is a good skier. He taught me, and he carved my first pair of skis from a plank of wood."

Josie heard the wistfulness in her voice. "Don't look like you'll be doing much skiing where we're going," she said. "Flat as a pancake here, isn't it?"

"Excuse me?" Lottie looked puzzled. "What kind of cake?"

"Sorry. English expression. 'Flat as a pancake' means—you know what a pancake is?" She mimed it.

"*Ja. Pfannkuchen*? You eat?"

"Yes. So as flat as that. Get it?"

The girl laughed. "Now I understand. I learn more English every day, but some idioms I still don't understand."

"I think you speak very well, considering you haven't been here very long."

"I did not learn much from the women. They called me things like lazy and stupid. But the school was good. I hope there will be a school for me to attend out here. I always expected to go to university one day."

"University! Blimey." Josie shook her head. Then she said, "You hold on to that dream, love. I had to leave school at fourteen. I've always regretted it. Always wanted to learn more."

"I love to read, do you?" Lottie asked. "They let me take books from the school library, but those women did not like me to read, so I had to read in bed, late at night."

"I like to read, too," Josie said. "Let's hope there's a library somewhere nearby, shall we?"

Lottie nodded, and they exchanged a smile.

CHAPTER 6

After about fifteen minutes, the bus approached a small town and came to a halt outside the railway station. Josie had no idea which town it was, as all names had been removed to deter an invading force. The mother and then children in the front rows were ushered off, carrying their bags. The bags looked as pitifully small as Josie's. How were they all going to survive with one change of clothes? She wondered. What would that mother do for nappies? At least Josie didn't play in the mud or wet the bed the way children would. The bus moved on again, leaving the little town behind. Flat countryside stretched out on either side, sometimes with water-filled ditches between the fields. Nothing was growing at this time of year. The only thing that broke the horizon was a distant church steeple. The bus passed through a village—just a small cluster of houses along the road and a church with a tall spire. Josie had noted there were no signposts, or they had been blacked out, but the board in front of the church read, "St Mary's Church, Deeping St Nicholas."

"Silly name for a place, isn't it?" Josie turned to Lottie, who managed a smile.

"I'm sorry, I feel not too well," Lottie said. "The bus sways and bumps, doesn't it?"

"I'm not feeling too chipper myself," Josie confessed. "It shouldn't be too much longer."

"Where do you think they will take us?"

"I've no idea, love. I don't even know what county we are in. Somewhere in East Anglia, it must be, because I've heard of flat, fenny country like this. See the water in those dykes? We must be quite close to the sea, I reckon."

"The sea?" Lottie's eyes lit up for a moment. "I have never seen the sea. I have been to lakes in Germany, but the sea is only in the north."

"I've only been a couple of times myself," Josie confessed.

They came to another village, and the bus slowed to a halt beside a war memorial from the Great War. The woman who had been riding at the front called out two names, and two small boys got out. There was a farmer waiting nearby. The woman and the farmer had a conversation, then he nodded. The boys were introduced to him. He lifted them up on to the back of a horse-drawn cart, and they moved off as the bus started up again. This was repeated until there were just four of them in the back of the bus. Josie was definitely feeling sick, although maybe it was from hunger, as it had been hours since breakfast, when the bus came to another cluster of houses.

"If we don't get them placed here, we're out of luck," the woman said to the driver, glancing back at Josie and the children that remained.

"We haven't tried here before because of the proximity, you know, but we'll have to see what we can do." She looked back down the bus. "All right, everyone. This is where you get off."

"What's it called, miss?" a girl who had been sitting in front of Josie asked.

"I believe it's Sutton St Giles, if we are in the right place. Let's see, shall we?"

They climbed down, one by one. The big-boned girl of about ten or eleven went first, then extended her hand to help a tiny mite of about four down. The little one was like a pretty china doll with lots of light, curly hair tied up in a red bow and wide blue eyes that now looked around her in terror. Josie let Lottie go next, and she came last. The four of them stood, gasping in the frigid wind that swept across the bare fields. The woman in charge looked around.

"I don't see . . . ," she began. A woman had just come out of the village shop, a basket over her arm, a scarf held up to her face.

"Excuse me," said Efficient Lady. "This is Sutton St Giles?"

The woman looked at her suspiciously. "We're not supposed to say, in case it's the enemy."

"Of course we're not the enemy, you silly woman," Efficient Lady snapped. "This is the group of evacuees from London that you were notified about. There were supposed to be volunteers here to take them in."

"They were expecting you hours ago," the woman said. She had a country accent, with its pronounced *r*'s, and spoke slowly and deliberately compared to the staccato speech of the cockney Josie was used to. "Mrs Badger got cold waiting, and her husband sent her home on account of her weak chest."

"Mrs Badger." Efficient Lady consulted her clipboard again. "Yes. She is down as a possible volunteer host. Can you tell me where her house is?"

"See there, across the vegetable patch, with the smoke coming out of the chimney."

"Oh yes," Efficient Lady said. "Can we get up to the house by bus?"

The woman laughed. "I don't reckon so. It be only a muddy track, you see. Alf Badger takes his horse and cart up it, but no motor vehicles."

"I don't suppose they are on the telephone?"

This produced signs of mirth from the woman. "None of us have the telephone around here, except for her at the big house and the police station in Holbeach."

The clipboard lady sighed. "Right. It looks as if we have to walk. Are you ready, children?" She glanced down at the little girl's shoes. They were dainty ankle straps in red patent.

"I'm afraid those shoes are most unsuitable, Dorothy. Do you not have gumboots with you?"

The little girl shook her head, about to cry again.

73

"I can carry her maybe," said the big-boned girl. She had a round, eager face and ash-blonde hair that poked out from under a knitted hat. In many ways she reminded Josie of her siblings, and she remembered that her family had supposedly come from Norfolk in this part of the country.

"Are you her sister?" the woman asked, sounding surprised.

"No, miss. I just took care of her on the platform because she was in a right state about being left alone. She didn't want to leave her mum."

"Well, you're a kind girl. What's your name again?"

"Sheila, miss."

"Are we all going to that house?" Josie asked.

"I'm not really sure. I believe it's just the two younger girls, but you'd all better come along." She turned to Lottie. "Maybe you can carry the little one's bag, dear, and I'll carry Sheila's, and Sheila can give her a piggyback."

They set off. The track had been muddy but had frozen hard, making the going treacherous. At times there were icy puddles, and they slithered and stumbled. On either side were garden beds with cabbages and other winter vegetables growing. Beyond them were what looked like fruit trees. The cottage itself was whitewashed with a red roof and looked appealing, but Josie was already worrying. What if they got all this way and then were not welcomed? She knew so little about the evacuation process. Did people have to take in strangers, or was it purely voluntary? It seemed as if this village hadn't been tapped before for some reason. They were all panting so that their breath hung in the frigid air like steam by the time they reached the front door. Efficient Lady was gasping harder than any of them and had to wait a while to catch her breath before she rapped on the door. At once came the sound of barking, and little Dorothy cried out, wrapping her arms tightly around Sheila's neck.

"Quiet, you stupid beast," boomed a deep voice, making little Dorothy give a whimper of fright, then the door was opened. A large, hairy sheepdog rushed out and started sniffing at them.

"Mr Badger?" the efficient lady said, still having to talk between gasps while she evaded the excited dog. "You were on my list to take in evacuees."

"That's right." He pronounced it *roight*. "You'd better come in out of the cold, hadn't you?" He opened the door, and they stepped into a delightfully warm kitchen. It smelled of freshly baked bread. There was a big coke-burning stove on one wall and a scrubbed pine table in the middle of the room. A string of onions hung in the window.

"Wipe your feet on the mat. Nan don't like muddy footprints on her clean kitchen floor."

Sheila put down the small girl, who promptly hid behind her skirt.

"You sit yourselves down," he said. "You look fair tuckered out, walking all that way in the cold."

He noticed that the small girl was clinging to her companion in terror as the dog approached. "You don't need to worry about old Gyp," he said. "He's never hurt a fly in his life. He might want to give you a big wet kiss, but that's about all."

Josie went to sit on the bench in the window and held out her hand to the little girl. She came over hesitantly, and Josie hoisted her on to the seat beside her. The big dog approached, tail wagging, and Josie petted him, even though she had no experience of dogs herself and was a little bit afraid. But she wasn't going to show this to Dorothy.

"I am Mrs Sanderson," the efficient lady said. "I'm the volunteer coordinator, and these are Mrs Banks, Charlotte, Sheila and Dorothy."

The big man held out a meaty hand to her and shook heartily. "Badger's the name. Alf Badger." He released her hand, then went to the kitchen door. "Nan, get yourself in here right now, my dear. We've got company. The little ones have arrived."

As they waited, he went across to the stove and poured boiling water into a teapot, then put a pink-and-green-striped knitted cosy over it. Josie had time to observe him: he had a mop of white hair above a round, red face with brows that stuck out like spiky prawns and white stubble around his chin. Josie put him at sixty or more. But his eyes were remarkably bright, and when he chuckled, his whole face came to life, as if he were appreciating a good joke. She made an instant assessment that the children would be fine here. She wouldn't mind it herself.

There was the sound of hurrying footsteps in the hall, and Alf's wife appeared. She was a female replica of Alf, a round apple of a woman with the same kind of good-natured, weathered face.

"Well, now. Finally you've come," she said. "They told us twelve o'clock, and now it's gone two. We thought you'd got lost or you weren't coming after all."

"And the wife was right disappointed, weren't you, my love?" Alf asked.

"I was at that." She beamed as she looked at them. "And who is this precious little mite?"

"Her name's Dorothy," Sheila said for her.

Nan squatted down so that she was at the same level as the child. "Dorothy. Such a pretty name. And what a pretty ribbon you've got in your hair. Did your mummy do that for you?"

"My mummy is in the hospital," Dorothy said. "A bomb fell on us."

"Goodness me. But thank the good Lord you're safe here now."

Dorothy stared at her and then nodded. While Nan was speaking, Alf was pouring large mugs of tea, adding a generous amount of milk and sugar and then handing the mugs around.

"Here, get that down you. You'll all feel better," he said.

Efficient Lady, now identified as Mrs Sanderson, had been standing by the door. She shuffled her feet impatiently. "I should be going, then," she said. "I can leave them all in your capable hands, can I?"

The smile clouded on Nan's face. "Hold on a moment there, missus. We only said we'd take in two children, you know. We don't have space for more than that. Certainly not for this lady."

"Ah. Of course." Mrs Sanderson glanced at her clipboard. "Well, you two had better come with me, then."

"Will there be anywhere else for us here, then?" Josie asked. She had the alarming thought that she'd be sent back to London, unwanted.

The woman looked up from her clipboard. "There is another house that has yet to take in any evacuees and seems to have plenty of room. A Miss Harcourt."

"Miss Harcourt?" Alf demanded sharply. "You're surely not intending to send anybody to her?"

"She's on my list. Apparently she has six bed-rooms and only herself in the house."

"That's right enough, I suppose, but she's a mean old cow, pardon my language." He glanced at his wife, then gave Josie a regretful look. "Are you all related?"

"No, none of us is," Josie said.

"Well, I'm sorry, ma'am, but we just don't have the accommodation for a lady like you. You'll be all right with Miss Harcourt, I've no doubt. But I don't think she much goes for children. I wouldn't want to wish her on no child."

Josie was watching Lottie's face. She saw the alarm in the girl's eyes. She was clearly imagining another situation like the one in London.

"Is there no way you could keep young Lottie here?" she asked. "She's had a raw deal, and I think she needs to be somewhere with a little warmth and kindness, if you get my meaning."

Alf looked at Nan. "We could squeeze the other young lady in here, couldn't we, Nan? Maybe put a camp bed in the attic? I could clear some space up there, if she don't mind sleeping with the apples and taters?"

"We could do that, I reckon," Nan agreed. "She's only a skinny one, isn't she? Won't take up too much room or eat too much."

"The children have brought their ration books," Mrs Sanderson said. "That should help out."

"Ration books? I don't reckon we'll be needing

much of that," Alf said. "We eat what we can grow and raise here. The local miller gives us flour in exchange for eggs. All we need really is sugar and tea."

The mention of tea made Josie drink her cup hastily before she had to move again. The sweet warmth spread through her cold limbs. She took a deep breath and got to her feet. "Well, I'd better be going, then. This lady needs to get back with her bus before it gets dark. Thank you for the tea. I hope I'm close enough to visit you girls. And you be helpful to Mrs Badger, then, eh?"

They all nodded solemnly.

"You come and visit us whenever you like," Nan Badger said. "It's not that far, and you can cut across the field. Come and have a decent meal. We'd enjoy the company, wouldn't we, Alf?"

"We would right enough," he said. "And don't you take no nonsense from that old cow. Thinks she's superior to everyone."

Josie picked up the bag she had set down by the door and wound the scarf around her neck as they went back out into the cold. It was starting to snow, big fat flakes falling from a leaden sky.

"Oh dear. I hope we can make it back to Peterborough before things get too bad," Mrs Sanderson said. Josie looked at her now with understanding. She, too, was living a life for which she didn't sign on. In normal circumstances, she'd be hosting tea parties and playing bridge and arranging church flowers. Everyone was doing their bit, and Josie realized she'd be expected to do the same as soon as her collarbone healed.

They made it back to the bus and climbed on board.

"Now we just have to find a place for this lady," the woman said to the driver. "If you can turn around by the church, then it's on the right as we are going out of the village." He did as he was told. Josie noticed a small row of shops and a pub called the Green Man, and then they came to a halt at a low brick wall beside the road. Beyond the wall were formal gardens, the flower beds lying desolate and empty at this time of year, half hidden in patches of snow. The house was a well-proportioned Georgian, made of the red brick that seemed customary in this part of the country. It had a central door with windows on either side and reminded Josie of a child's doll house—the sort she had always craved but never owned. She followed Mrs Sanderson from the bus and then up the garden path.

"You should be quite comfortable here, at least for now," Mrs Sanderson said. "And if things don't work out, we can think again as soon as your arm heals and you are able to take up some form of employment."

She was about to say something more when

there came an ominous rumble that grew louder until it was deafening. Josie looked around in alarm, her mind immediately going to enemy planes. But at that moment a large plane rose into the air, just beyond a line of yew trees. It was followed by another, then another.

Mrs Sanderson gave an apologetic smile. "That's why we haven't placed evacuees here before," she said. "RAF Sutton Deeping. It's an aerodrome of Bomber Command."

CHAPTER 7

They waited until the bombers had risen and then disappeared out over the horizon.

"I don't suppose it will be more than once or twice a day," Mrs Sanderson said, again with an apologetic smile.

"I don't mind, just as long as they're ours," Josie said, but even as she said it, she was wondering if being next to a bomber airfield would put her in danger of being bombed. Still, she expected their defences were good.

Mrs Sanderson went up to the front door and rapped on a knocker in the shape of a lion's head. It was presumably brass but had been allowed to tarnish over the years. After what seemed like a long while, the door was opened by an older woman wearing a flowered overall. Her appearance was slightly unkempt, with hair wisps escaping from an untidy roll. "Yes?" she said sharply, her eyes darting from one woman to the other. "If you're asking for donations, we already gave."

"We are not asking for donations," Mrs Sanderson said. "We are here to see the mistress of the house, a Miss Harcourt, is it not?"

"That's right." She eyed them with suspicion. "I'll see if the mistress is receiving visitors."

"This is not a social call, but a governmental one," Mrs Sanderson said firmly.

The woman shot her a look of distrust, then grudgingly stood aside for them to enter. They stepped into a foyer. There was an ornate hall stand with several hats and coats on it. On the other side was a large mirror with a marble-topped table beneath it and a vase of silk flowers on the table. A flight of stairs went up to a landing above. Josie barely had time to take this in before the woman opened a door to the right of the hall. There was a muted conversation, then she returned. "The mistress will see you," she said.

Josie followed Mrs Sanderson into a big sitting room. At the far end was a large brick fireplace, but the fire glowing in it did little to warm the room as there was still frost on one of the windows. Josie had never been in a room of that size before, at least not in a private house. The oil paintings in gilt frames on the walls and vases and knick-knacks on little tables reminded her of a visit she once made to a museum.

"Yes, how can I help you?" said an upper-class voice from the far end of the room.

It took Josie a moment to realize that the voice came from a high-backed Queen Anne chair next to the fire. An elderly woman was sitting in it, her feet on a stool and a rug over her knees. She had what Josie would call a snooty sort of face—the sort that looked as if there were a perpetually nasty smell under her nose, which was beakish. Her face could have been chiselled from white marble, expressionless and with few wrinkles for a woman of her age. Her hair, streaked with grey, was cut in a mannish crop. She had a woollen shawl around her shoulders.

"I'm Mrs Sanderson," Efficient Lady said, not showing the trepidation Josie was feeling. "My task is to place evacuees from London, and we see from our records that you have not assisted us to date."

"I contribute to the war effort in other ways," Miss Harcourt said. "I have knitted socks and wound bandages for the wounded. I have donated jam as well as some of my precious railings for scrap metal. But I have no wish to have my privacy invaded and my house ransacked by a lot of unruly brats. Children and I do not get along."

"In this case, we're not expecting you to host children," Mrs Sanderson said. "It's just this one lady. Mrs Banks. Her house was bombed. She was actually buried alive, and she needs a place to recuperate."

"I am also not a sanatorium," Miss Harcourt said. "I am down to just the one servant and thus not equipped to provide nursing for a wounded person."

"I don't need looking after much," Josie said. "I can take care of meself. Just need someone to wash me clothes and tie me shoes at the moment."

Miss Harcourt looked at Josie as if she had been physically struck. "I think you'd better try and find somewhere more suitable."

"And what could be more suitable than a large house occupied by one woman and one servant?" Mrs Sanderson asked. "My job is to place Mrs Banks today, and that is what I intend to do. And I'm afraid you have no choice in the matter, Miss Harcourt. The government directive is that those with extra space have to take in evacuees when asked to do so. If you refuse, things could be made rather difficult for you. A hefty fine and maybe confiscation of your ration book."

Miss Harcourt looked affronted. "It's black-mail. That's what it is."

"It wouldn't be for too long," Mrs Sanderson said, realizing she had won an important point. "As soon as Mrs Banks is well again, she will want to do her part for the war effort and join the Women's Land Army or get another civilian job."

"Well, if it's only temporary and you indicated that I have no choice, I suppose I had better acquiesce, hadn't I?" She gave an audible and exaggerated sigh, then picked up a small brass bell from the table beside her. It was in the shape of a crinolined lady, and she rang it forcefully.

"Kathleen!" she called.

The untidy servant reappeared. "Yes? You were wanting something, madam?"

Josie had now identified the accent and the faded reddish hair as Irish.

"Kathleen, this woman will be staying with us for a short while," Miss Harcourt said.

The Irishwoman shot Josie a look of complete distrust. "Staying here? With us? You'll not be wanting that, surely?"

"It seems I have no choice," Miss Harcourt said, examining Josie as if she were a specimen. "Would you please see that a bed is made up for her in a suitable room?"

"One of the proper bedrooms or one of the servants' rooms on the top floor?"

"The lady has been quite badly injured," Mrs Sanderson said. "I don't think it would be right to expect her to climb up too many stairs. Or to have a room too without heat."

Josie tried not to give her a grateful grin.

"Very well, but not one of the good guest rooms at the front," Miss Harcourt said.

"If I were you, I'd count the silver," Kathleen muttered as she turned to leave.

"That is quite uncalled for and inappropriate," Mrs Sanderson said. "You are merely doing your national duty, as you should have done earlier when there were homes needed for so many evacuee children. And I'm sure Mrs Banks will be a delightful guest in every aspect. Now, if you will excuse me, we need to get the bus back to Peterborough, and it seems to be snowing."

Josie followed Mrs Sanderson out to the front hall. Now she no longer seemed like Efficient Lady but a warm and understanding person, trying to do her job. "I'm most grateful," Josie said. "And if it doesn't work out here, who do I contact?"

"It is your choice to stay here for as long as you want, unless there are really extenuating circumstances, such as the hostess dying or going into hospital." She glanced back into the sitting room. The two figures inside appeared to be frozen and motionless, staring after them. "Or if the house is bombed," she added as the roar of another plane came overhead. She gave Josie an encouraging smile. "Chin up. At least you've got the Badgers and the girls to visit nearby. And we will be checking on you from time to time." She gave a brisk little nod, then ventured out into the swirling snow.

Josie returned to the doorway of the sitting room. "If someone can show me where to put my things," she said. "And then maybe which rooms in the house I am welcome in. I wouldn't want any thoughts that I might be nicking the silver."

"Of course not," Miss Harcourt said quickly. "I am not sure of your past circumstances, but you may feel more at home in the servants' hall and the kitchen. I am down to one servant these days, and I'm sure Kathleen would welcome the company."

"As you like," Josie said, trying to decide whether time spent in the company of the mistress of the house would be preferable to that with the grouchy servant.

Kathleen sighed. "Come along, then," she said. "I suppose we'd better find you some bedding and a place to sleep." She shuffled ahead. Josie picked up her bag and followed, but when she reached the staircase, she paused, staring up and realizing she could not hold the banister and her bag at the same time.

"Do you think you could give me a hand here?" she called to Kathleen, who had already started up the broad staircase. "I don't think I can manage my bag."

Kathleen gave a sigh and grudgingly took it from her. "It's not my job to look after an invalid," she said.

"I don't need no looking after. It's just I'm still a bit wobbly, and I might need to hold the banister," Josie said as she followed Kathleen up the stairs. Portraits of haughty-looking ancestors frowned down from the wall. At the top was a landing, and Kathleen hesitated, as if deciding where Josie could do the least harm.

Then she gave an exaggerated sigh and turned to the left.

"I suppose it will have to be down here, then," she said. "Away from the mistress so she don't ever encounter you on her way to the bathroom.

You've a washbasin and lav on this side, and you can arrange with the mistress when you're allowed to have a bath. She has hers once a week, and we heat up the boiler for her. You could have what hot water is left, I suppose."

"That would be fine," Josie said.

Kathleen stopped in the middle of the dark hallway and opened a door. Frigid air came out to meet them.

"This room hasn't been used in twenty years or more," Kathleen said, as if enjoying imparting this news. "In fact, I can't remember when it was used last. When guests came, they got the good rooms, you see. And there have not been any guests in quite a while now." She paused, and Josie gave a nod to show she was paying attention. Kathleen walked ahead into the room. Josie followed.

"I give it a once-over occasionally, but I don't know if we'll find mice in the mattress or not." She put Josie's bag down on the floor with a thump and gave the mattress lying on the single, iron-framed bed an experimental prod. Then she walked around, removing dust sheets from hidden pieces of furniture. These she gathered into her arms.

"Wait here," Kathleen said. "I'll go and find bedclothes." She then left.

Josie looked around her. The room was small but not bad. It contained a single bed, a tall mahogany chest of drawers, matching wardrobe and a low, upholstered chair by the window. There was also a small fireplace, unlaid. A fine layer of dust lay on the top of the chest of drawers, but otherwise the room looked clean enough. The floor was knotted wood with a braided rug beside the bed. Hardly what anyone would call cosy, but at least it was a space of her own. She'd have to see about coal for her fire, since she had brought her coal allowance. She went over to the window to look out. The room was so cold that there were frost patterns on the inside of the glass. Beyond them, snow-flakes were now swirling over an impossibly flat countryside. The horizon was broken by a line of bare trees. The view beyond was blurred by the snow. She wondered where the airfield was and felt sorry for those pilots who had to fly in such weather. Surely it was dangerous enough waiting to encounter enemy fighters without having to negotiate a snowstorm.

Kathleen re-entered. "Oh, there you are," she said, spotting Josie by the window.

"Yes, I checked it out. Nothing worth stealing," Josie said with heavy sarcasm. Kathleen had the grace to blush.

"I brought sheets and blankets and the eider-down off the bed in the next room," she said. "Can you make your own bed?"

"I'd appreciate some help," Josie said. "As you

can see, I can only use one arm at the moment."

"How do you manage, then?" Kathleen asked.

"Not very easily. It takes me ages to get dressed and undressed. The nuns where I was staying usually came to help."

"You were with the nuns?" Kathleen's expression softened. "You're a Catholic, then?"

"No, I'm not. I was sent to this convent when I came out of hospital. They needed the hospital beds for people more badly wounded, you see, so the nuns took me in. Very nice they were, too."

"Any Irish nuns amongst them?"

"Yes, there were," Josie said, not quite sure whether this was true or not but hoping to find a way to win over this hostile woman. "Lovely girls. All very kind."

Kathleen nodded with satisfaction, as if she were personally responsible for creating the kind Irish nuns. She pulled the bed out from the wall and went around it, and together they put on the sheets and blankets.

"We've a hot water bottle down in the kitchen," she said. "You can come down when you've put away your things."

"That won't take long." Josie laughed.

Kathleen eyed the bag. "That's all you brought? I thought the rest of your stuff was downstairs."

"That's all I own," Josie said. "I was bombed at night, wearing my nightie. Even that was blown off me, so I had nothing. Not even a stitch of clothing. What I'm wearing now came from people who had died at the hospital."

For the first time, she saw compassion in the other woman's eyes.

"Oh, that's too bad," Kathleen said. "You can have a look through the things the mistress is donating to the clothing drive. She's quite a bit bigger than you are, but there should be some jumpers that might fit you. Otherwise, you could unravel them and knit them up again for yourself."

"When I can hold needles," Josie said, and Kathleen returned the grin.

"Oh, you're right. I keep forgetting."

Now that she had broken through that initial layer of hostility, Josie decided to press ahead. "So you now have to take care of this big house by yourself, do you?"

"I do," Kathleen said. "There were two maids, a cook and a gardener before the war. Now they've all gone and enlisted into the army or God knows what, leaving me all alone here. And let me tell you, it's a lot of work. Luckily, she only uses a few rooms, and we keep the others closed off under dust sheets. But I do all the cooking, too."

"I'm happy to give you a hand," Josie said. "I'm not sure how useful I can be right now, but when my collarbone has healed, I can take over some of the cooking. I used to work in a nice tea shop, you know. I love to bake."

"That's good news," Kathleen said. "I wouldn't say no to some help. She's very picky about her food, the mistress is. Well, picky about everything, actually." She brushed off her hands. "Well, that's that, then. I'd best be getting downstairs. She'll be wanting her tea soon. Come on down when you're settled. The kitchen's down the hall at the back."

"I will. Thank you," Josie said. "I'll try not to be a nuisance."

"I'm sure you won't, Lord love you," Kathleen said. "In fact, you'll be a bit of company for me in the long evenings. She keeps herself to herself, you know. Listens to the wireless or reads but never was one for a chat. She's one of the old school. She's the mistress, and I'm the servant, and there's a line between us that can never be crossed."

"Have you been with her long?"

"I have. I came here as a young housemaid when the old master was in charge. Her father, you know. Oh, he was a proper tartar. Everything had to be just so, and heaven help you if you made one tiny mistake. He sacked a parlour maid once for knocking over the gravy jug. And I'm afraid she's inherited his nature, too."

"Was she an only child?"

"She was. Her mother died giving birth to her. Maybe that's why the father was so bitter and harsh. He blamed the child for his wife's death."

"And he never married again?"

"He never did."

"And she never married?"

"I think I heard she had a sweetheart once, but nothing came of it. She went away to a fancy finishing school, and then she worked for a while in London as some great lady's companion. But then she came back here during the last war and stayed with her father until he died. In any case, she was already here when I came in 1918, at the end of the war. That was before Ireland was divided, you know. Plenty of troubles in those days with bombings and executions and the like. I wanted a bit of peace and quiet for myself."

"Do you miss your own country? Do you ever go back?"

A sad look came over Kathleen's face. "I didn't have the money to go back in the early days when my family was still alive—not that the old master would have given me the time off. Only one half day a week it was in those days. They did let me travel to my mother's funeral, God rest her beautiful soul. Now I don't go back any more. I've a brother and two sisters, but they have their own families and their own troubles. And quite a few nieces and nephews. So do you not have a family, missus?"

"The name's Josie," she said. "And I do still have a father and brothers and sisters, but they certainly don't have room for me, even if my stepmother would make me welcome, which she doesn't."

"But you're married, aren't you?"

"I am. My husband's off with the army somewhere. No idea where. I got one letter from him and couldn't read a word. Most of it was blacked out by the censor, and the rest was impossible to read."

"And children? You don't have children?"

"No children," Josie said. "We have not been blessed that way. But thinking about it now, I'm glad, for any child would surely have perished when the house was blown up."

"Ah, 'tis surely a wicked, sorrowful world," Kathleen said. "But you'll be safe enough here. They've got plenty of guns around that aerodrome. Oh, you should hear the noise if any enemy planes try to come too close."

"It's a new aerodrome, built just for the war, is it?"

"It is. Oh, you should have seen how the mistress tried to stop it from being built here. Tried to take it all the way to Parliament. But nobody cared that she had a house close by and that the planes were interrupting her sleep. Well, they wouldn't, would they? The defence of the country has to come first." She stopped. "And here am I chatting away when there's work to be done. If you come down to the kitchen, there will be a cup of tea."

"I don't suppose there might be something to eat?" Josie said. "I've not had a thing since breakfast, and I'm starting to feel quite woozy."

"You poor woman. You come down, and I'll make you a ham sandwich to keep you going."

"You have ham?" Josie could not disguise her astonishment.

Kathleen gave a knowing little smile. "We got a piece for Christmas. It came from Mr Sparks, a local farmer. Apparently this was a pig that died and thus couldn't be part of the government distribution programme."

"What did it die of?" Josie asked suspiciously.

"Nothing catching, that's for sure. Probably banged its head." Kathleen laughed.

"On what?"

"On the farmer's poleaxe! The local people all chipped in to buy the pig and divvy it up, and the mistress decided to throw caution to the winds and join in. Unusual for her. She usually keeps herself to herself. But she does love a slice of ham." She paused, then nodded. "I'll be off, then, and let you get settled."

Josie heard her footsteps receding down the hallway. She hung up her overcoat and scarf, put her few items in the top drawer, then went to find the lavatory and washbasin. They were next door, which was convenient. On returning to her room, she was painfully aware of how cold it was. Not a place to linger when there was a promised cup of tea in the kitchen. She realized then that her feet were cold and wet, the inherited shoes not having the best of soles, and changed into the spare pair of stockings she had been given. There wasn't much to be done about the shoes. She hoped that Miss Harcourt might have a pair of rubber boots to spare, or even a pair of house shoes. She combed her hair, then set off in search of the kitchen.

CHAPTER 8

Josie went cautiously down the stairs and turned towards the back of the house. There were several doors along the dark little hallway, and she was afraid to open the wrong one. Luckily she heard the clatter of pots and pans and opened the door into a big, warm kitchen. There was a sturdy solid fuel-burning stove on one wall and a Welsh dresser on the one opposite, with rows of cups, saucers and plates arranged neatly. A window looked out on to a back garden with bare garden beds and, beyond them, fruit trees and a pond. All in all, a pleasant room. Josie had little chance to observe it, however, because her eyes were focused on a ham sitting on the kitchen table. Ham had been a rare treat even before the war. The grocer used to have a whole leg of ham sitting on his counter, and he'd carve off wafer-thin slices. This was only a small portion of a leg, and Josie felt guilty about eating something that was a treat for the mistress.

"Look, I shouldn't take any of the ham," she said. "Not if it was your Christmas treat."

"It won't keep much longer, will it?" Kathleen brought the teapot over to the kitchen table and took down two cups from the dresser. "Besides, one slice won't hurt nobody." Then she cut a slice of ham, which she placed between two thick hunks of bread.

"You like mustard with it?" she asked.

"That would be lovely, thank you." Josie started eating while Kathleen poured the tea. She felt warmth coming back to frigid limbs.

"It's good to be warm again," she said. "That room is ruddy cold. Any chance of having a bit of coal for the fire in there? I do have my ration book with me."

"You'd have to ask the mistress," Kathleen said. "We haven't had much luck with the coal. We're too far out from Spalding, you see. The coalman won't come out here for a small order, since he can sell everything he's got closer to town. We've been trying to make do with wood, but again we don't do too well. If a gale brings down a tree, there are plenty of men with saws out to get it for themselves. It's not easy being women alone at a time like this." She gave an apologetic little smile. "So I'm thinking you'll not be wanting to spend too much time up in that room."

"Where do you sleep?" Josie asked. "Up on the servants' floor?"

"I do not," Kathleen said firmly. "I used to when there were other servants, but these days I've taken over the old butler's room next to the kitchen. It's tiny, but it gets the warmth from this stove, you see. Nice and cosy. And not as noisy as up on that top floor. Are you a sound sleeper, then?"

"I was, before the war," Josie said. "Back in London, there weren't many nights when there wasn't an air raid."

"And you'll be hearing the planes here, right enough. They always seem to be returning at night." She pulled up a chair opposite Josie. "Still, it's not for long, is it? You'll be off somewhere as soon as you've recovered."

Josie nodded between mouthfuls, trying to think where that might be. Would she be strong enough to work as a land girl? But Stan had made it clear he didn't want her joining any of the armed forces, where she might come in contact with men. And she didn't fancy going back to the city, even if she could find work and somewhere to stay.

"So what's it like in London now?" Kathleen asked. "Pretty grim, is it?"

Josie nodded again, still getting every ounce of satisfaction from the ham in her mouth. "It's bad," she said eventually. "Bombing every night recently. Whole parts of the city burning. And it's becoming hard to get food. We have the coupons in the ration books, but there's nothing on the shelves. I suppose it's easier out here in the country?"

"In a way," Kathleen said. "It would be if we grew our own food. We have the grounds, the space to do it. But Ted, our gardener, he went and joined up, and I don't have the time to work in the garden as well as run this house."

"Of course you don't," Josie said. She looked around the kitchen, taking in the various crockery on the dresser. "You have pretty cups and saucers," she said. "The café where I used to work had nice china. I used to love handling it."

"These are only the everyday set," Kathleen said. "She's got some lovely china in the dining room—Royal Doulton, Royal Worcester, Rockingham. The very best, you know. Only she never uses it these days. Her old father used to entertain, but she's not the type. Between you and me, I think she's a bit shy."

Josie nodded, cradling her cup in her hands before finishing her tea.

"Your mistress has lots of lovely things," Josie said. "I've never seen pictures on the walls like that, except in a museum."

Kathleen leaned closer. "She used to have a lot more," she whispered. "The old man inherited from his father, and the family had made a tidy packet out in India in the early days. They had land, too—where the airfield is now, you know. And a home farm. But that had to be sold when her father died, because of the death duties. It doesn't seem right, does it, for the government to take so much when someone dies.

"Anyway, she was still left quite comfortably

off until the Depression came and her stocks lost their value. It gets harder by the minute. In fact, I know she's sold off her mother's jewellery and a couple of good paintings. She doesn't think I know, but I know most things that go on around here." She gave Josie a triumphant little smile that made Josie feel a bit uneasy.

Josie finished her tea and wondered what to do next. A return to her room did not seem inviting, and yet Kathleen would want to get on with preparing Miss Harcourt's dinner, and Josie didn't want to feel in the way.

"I'd offer to peel some spuds for you if I could hold the peeler," she said. "If there's something I can do, I'd be happy to do it."

Kathleen paused, as if sizing up Josie's ability with one arm. "Well, you could get the tea tray laid to take in her tea at four o'clock. Tray's in that slot. Tray cloths are in the second drawer of the dresser. You can see the cups and the spoons are in the top drawer."

Josie obeyed, running a loving hand over the embroidered tray cloth as she placed it on the tray and then adding a cup, saucer and tea plate. Kathleen boiled more water and filled a small Chinese teapot.

"She likes China tea in the afternoons," she said. "Lapsang souchong, served with lemon if you please. Tastes like dishwater to me."

She opened a cake tin. "I don't know what there

is left to eat. I made mince pies over Christmas with the last of the mincemeat we had put away before the war, but they are long gone. No biscuits to be had at the shop. No sugar either. So it will have to be a watercress sandwich. She won't be too pleased about that."

She loaded the tray and then turned to Josie.

"You can bring the sandwich plate if you don't mind. Save me going back again."

Josie picked it up and followed, feeling strangely reluctant to face those critical eyes again. Kathleen put the tray on the hall table to open the sitting room door.

"I've brought your tea, madam," she said.

Miss Harcourt barely acknowledged her as Kathleen pulled up a small table and placed the tea tray on top. Then she poured the tea and added a slice of lemon and two lumps of sugar. Josie looked for a spot to place the sandwiches, then squeezed them on to the table.

"What is this?" Miss Harcourt looked up sharply.

"Watercress sandwiches," Josie said.

"And where are the cakes?"

"No cake, I'm afraid, madam," Kathleen answered for her. "We've finished what I made for Christmas, and there was no sugar to be had last time I was at the shop."

"What is the world coming to?" Miss Harcourt said. "And now I suppose we've another mouth to feed."

"You'll be getting my ration book, too," Josie said. "That should be a help."

Miss Harcourt's cool gaze studied her as if she were surprised that a worm had suddenly spoken. She went to say something, then gave a sharp nod. "Yes. I suppose another ration book will be useful. And we'll have to decide what your duties will be. Obviously no heavy work until that sling comes off. Is anything actually broken? I don't see a plaster."

"It's my collarbone," Josie said. "You can't set a collarbone. You just have to keep it from moving until it rejoins."

"Ah," Miss Harcourt said. "Not too long, one hopes. In the meantime, I suppose light dusting—"

Josie interrupted. "Let's get one thing straight. I'm not your servant. I'm a guest. Billeted on you as your part of the war effort. And I'm no more thrilled about it than you are. I'm happy to help out while I'm here, but I don't have no duties."

Again Miss Harcourt opened her mouth to say something, then closed it again.

"That will be all," she said and calmly picked up her teacup.

Kathleen was clearly amused and impressed by Josie's speech. "You told her, didn't you?" she said when they were back in the kitchen. "You put her in her place."

"Well, the way she was looking at me, it got up

my nose," Josie said. "It's not my fault that Hitler chose to drop a bomb on my house. I didn't ask to come here. And I mean what I said. I'm happy to give you a hand when you need one."

For dinner that night, Miss Harcourt had a fillet of smoked haddock with potatoes, followed by a baked apple. Kathleen shared the leftovers of a vegetable pie with Josie.

"One thing we can get around here is swedes and parsnips and the like. They grow them in the fields, and some are always falling off the carts when they go to market. So at least we don't starve."

Josie attacked the food on her plate. It was a mound of indeterminate mashed veg under a pastry crust so hard she worried about breaking a tooth. The pie wouldn't have been too flavourful to start with, and reheated it was downright nasty. Josie got the impression that Kathleen was not the best of cooks. *As soon as I can move this hand,* she thought.

That night Josie lay curled in the narrow bed, hugging the hot water bottle to her, trying to come to terms with what her life had become. All alone in an unfamiliar place with one woman who wanted to get rid of her as soon as possible and another woman she found it harder to make out. Kathleen seemed to switch between hot and cold, at one point saying she was glad to have

106

someone to talk to and share the workload and the next looking at Josie with suspicion and distrust. She was clearly a person to whom life had dealt a raw deal, Josie could see that. And she understood it. She hadn't been dealt the best of deals herself.

The hot water bottle made her bed bearably warm, and at last she fell asleep, but Josie awoke the next morning to find her window completely covered in patterns of frost. When she cleared some of it away, she looked out on a sparkling world. A red sun hung over the eastern horizon. Snow-covered fields seemed to go on forever, divided by dykes and canals that glowed pink in the rising sun. After the narrowness and confinement of a big city all her life, this landscape took Josie's breath away. She had never imagined such an enormous sky. As she watched, she heard the muffled roar of a plane and saw two aircraft coming in to land. Two bombers, heavy, unwieldy. She noticed that one of them was pitching and shuddering like a wounded insect, and then she saw the reason—part of one wing had been destroyed. She watched the unscathed plane lower its wheels and dip behind the line of the trees, then the damaged plane dipped, too. Suddenly there was an explosion. A fireball rose over the trees, and she realized that the plane had crashed trying to land. She turned away, feeling sick. The enchanted, sparkling landscape now had a new dimension—it was a place of danger. And the sick feeling gripped her stomach. She had thought she'd be safe out in the country, but it seemed that nowhere was safe any longer.

CHAPTER 9

When Josie had washed and dressed, she came downstairs to find the house still sleeping. An icy chill hung in the hallways, with cold drafts wafting up the stairs. But the kitchen offered reassuring warmth. No sign of Kathleen or a morning cup of tea. She hesitated to make one herself, not trusting her one good hand to be able to fill a kettle or pour boiling water. Instead she started to look around the house. It would be good to know the lie of the land and which rooms she might be welcome in. Behind the sitting room, facing the back garden, she found the dining room—clearly in use as the large mahogany table was set for one. Josie paused to admire the china in the impressive mahogany china cabinet along one wall. Blue Wedgwood tea sets, coffee sets with tiny gold-rimmed cups. Soup tureens, gravy boats and presumably the big dinner plates down below in the cupboard. Josie sighed at the delicate workmanship. On the sideboard were remnants of a bygone era—silver stands to be filled with hot water to hold breakfast dishes. Before the war, they might have contained bacon and kidneys, kedgeree, scrambled eggs. Now there was nothing to put in them, and they stood there, abandoned and tarnished.

Josie tiptoed out of the dining room and opened the other doors, one by one. On the other side of the foyer, opposite the sitting room, was another reception room, this one with what had to be a grand piano under a dust sheet. And then behind it a library. Josie took a hesitant step inside, marvelling at the shelves of leather-bound volumes that ran around the whole room. They rose right up to the ceiling, and on one wall was a ladder to reach the highest shelves. Early sunlight shone in through dusty windows. Dust motes danced in a sunbeam, and the room smelled of old books. It felt like stepping into an enchanted world. That one person could own so many books was inconceivable to Josie. She remembered treasuring that one Sunday school prize and hadn't owned a book since. She had checked out some from the local library but hadn't really known where to start or what she might want to read. She moved closer and ran her finger gently over the book spines. Dickens. Shakespeare. *The Forsyte Saga. The History of the World.* And she pictured herself coming into this room, selecting a book and then parking herself in that chair by the fire in the sitting room while a servant brought her a cup of tea and a slice of cake. That would be heaven, she decided.

She was reluctant to leave, but it was comforting to know that such rooms existed. She turned to go and gasped as she saw Miss Harcourt standing in the doorway, staring at her.

"And what were you doing in this room, may I ask?" Her voice was ice-cold.

"I just came in to look," Josie said, her voice a little shaky.

"And I've caught you red-handed," she said, now blocking the doorway to prevent Josie's escape. "You thought you'd do a little spying around before anyone was awake. To decide what might be worth something or I wouldn't miss?"

Josie was no longer scared. Her cheeks flushed, and she took a step forward. "For your information, just because someone hasn't had a chance for your sort of life doesn't mean they are a criminal. I've never taken a thing that wasn't mine in my whole life—even when we didn't have enough food to put on the table." She paused to take a breath. Miss Harcourt was standing like a statue and said nothing, so Josie went on. "If you want to know the truth, I love looking at beautiful things. I've never owned any, but that doesn't stop me from getting a thrill just from looking. And books are something I've never had. I had to leave school when my mum died and take care of six little kids. So no more education."

"Do you know how to read?" Miss Harcourt asked.

"Of course I do. My teachers thought a lot of

me. I was always top of my class. They wanted to recommend me for teacher training before I had to leave school too soon. I've gone to libraries since, but there's so many books, I don't know where to start. And I like doing crosswords, too, but sometimes there's just too many words I don't know."

Miss Harcourt was suddenly looking at her as if she might be a fellow human being after all. "I know the feeling," she said. "Some books are indeed too unnecessarily wordy." She came into the room, standing beside Josie at the bookshelves. "Very well. You are welcome to borrow a book from this library if you wish and read it in the sitting room. I would not want you to risk getting grease on it in the kitchen."

"Thank you very much," Josie said. "I'll take good care of it, I promise. I may look like a scarecrow now, but that's just because all my things were destroyed in the bomb. These aren't my clothes."

"How very upsetting for you." Miss Harcourt cleared her throat, as if expressing a sentiment was uncomfortable for her. "I'm sure we can find you some things to wear in this house, although I'm a good deal larger than you, and I confess I haven't bought any new clothes for at least ten years. Still, you might be able to alter some items if you are good with your needle."

"I am when I've got two good hands," Josie said, and Miss Harcourt actually smiled.

"Would you like to choose a book now while I'm here to advise you?" she asked.

Josie turned back to the shelves. "They all look too good to take out," she said. "I don't like to touch them."

"So what have you read that you have enjoyed?"

"I tried Dickens," Josie confessed. "He was a bit heavy going for me."

"I quite agree. You might want to start with a good crime novel. They are always fun." She went across the room and removed a slim book with a dust jacket. "Dorothy Sayers. One of my favourites. It's called *The Nine Tailors*, and it's about this part of the country. Easy reading."

"Thank you, miss." Josie took the book carefully and stood, staring down at it. "I never tried a detective novel. I thought they might be too gory, you know."

"This one isn't. And when you've finished it, there are plenty more on that side of the room." She gave Josie a knowing look. "I had to hide these from my father when he was still alive. He did not approve of books that were not great literature. He called these 'feminine fluff,' although I've no idea how murders could be classed as fluffy." As she talked, she walked down the line of books, checking titles, then stopped and smiled. "And you might even enjoy some of my old children's books. I find them very comforting in times like these. *Little Women*. What great fun that was."

Josie's eyes lit up. "I read that one. I took it out of the library. How I envied the sort of life those girls led."

"Me too," Miss Harcourt agreed. Suddenly she shivered. "But it's too cold to stay in here for long. Let's see if Kathleen has managed to rouse herself enough to make breakfast, shall we?"

And she ushered Josie from the room, paused in the hallway and rang the brass bell on the table. "Kathleen!" she called.

Kathleen appeared from the kitchen. "Oh, good morning, madam. I didn't know you were up. And the lady, too."

"We've been talking about books in my library. And now I'm ready for breakfast. I don't suppose there are any eggs?"

"Only the powdered egg like usual," Kathleen said, eyeing Josie suspiciously now.

"Then it had better be the same old toast and marmalade," Miss Harcourt said. "If we still have any marmalade left."

Josie now found herself in an awkward position. She sensed Miss Harcourt might suggest that she join her for breakfast, but she didn't want the housekeeper to think she had been currying favour with her employer. "I'll come and help you get things ready in the kitchen, Kathleen," she said, "as soon as I've taken this book up to my room."

"Nice for some to have time for reading," Kathleen muttered and stalked off to the kitchen.

"Don't mind her," Miss Harcourt said. "She's temperamental. All the Irish are. Hot-tempered. Emotional. She'll soon get over it."

Josie hurried upstairs to deposit the book, then came into the kitchen, a little breathless.

"Sorry about that," she said. "Now, what would you like me to do?"

"Not much you can do with only one arm, is there?" Kathleen said in a sullen voice.

"I could at least put the toast under the grill for you. And butter it if you like."

"She likes her toast in the toast rack and butters it herself," Kathleen said, still sullen. "At least, she marges it herself these days."

"Kathleen, you don't have to be angry with me," Josie said. "I was just having a look around this morning, seeing where all the various rooms are, and I found the library. I was just looking at her books when she caught me. She was pretty angry to start with until she found out that I like to read. Then we had a nice little chat. That's all."

"I've never been one for reading myself," Kathleen said. "I never had much schooling."

"Neither did I," Josie said. "But that shouldn't

115

stop us from wanting to learn and better ourselves, should it?"

"I don't see the point in trying to better ourselves when we'll always be stuck where we are. You can read as much as you like, but when you open your mouth, they'll know that you're a cockney and they'll put you in your place, just the same way that they know I'm Irish and good for no more than a servant to the English."

As she spoke, she sawed off slices of bread. "It's an unfair world however you look at it," she said. "Look at you. You had a house of your own and clothes and things, and then Hitler drops a bomb, and now you've nothing. That's not fair."

"But other people died, and perhaps it's not fair that I lived," Josie said. "I reckon we all have to do our part to defeat that Hitler as quickly as possible."

Kathleen gave her an incredulous look. "You don't really believe England can win, do you?"

"Of course I do."

Kathleen gave a sad little smile, as if Josie was an idiot. "Germany is a big fighting machine. They can invade whenever they want to, and the sooner the better if you want my opinion. Then we can stop having these infernal bombers roaring overhead every night, and life can get back to normal."

"As German slaves?" Josie demanded. "No thank you."

"We Irish have been English slaves for four hundred years. You get used to it," Kathleen replied.

Josie took the slices of bread and put them on the grill pan. "Were you awake when that plane crashed this morning?"

"No? When was that?"

"The sun was just rising. Two planes came in, and one of them was badly damaged. Half a wing blown away. He tried to land but . . ." To her horror, she felt a big sob in her throat. "Those poor boys, probably burned alive," she said.

"That's war for you," Kathleen said. "Makes no sense."

CHAPTER 10

After breakfast had been cleared away, Josie would have liked to start on the book, but she didn't fancy being with Miss Harcourt in the sitting room while Kathleen was doing all the work in the kitchen.

"What can I do to help?" she asked. "I could dust for you."

"If you really want to help, you could pop to the village shop for me," Kathleen said. "We're out of several things, and I should really do the laundry since it's a fine day."

"I don't mind doing that at all," Josie replied, "but you wouldn't happen to have an extra pair of boots I could borrow, would you? These shoes I've been given let in water something shocking. My feet were frozen yesterday."

"The gardener might have left a pair of Wellingtons in the shed," Kathleen said. "I'll go and look for you in a minute."

"I can go," Josie said.

"It's all right. I'm the one in charge of the keys," Kathleen said defensively. "You've already seen the mistress don't want you snooping around where you shouldn't be."

"Fair enough." Josie shrugged, not wanting to show she was hurt that the woman still didn't trust her. "Although I don't think there's much for me to steal in the garden shed."

"Spades and rakes and a wheelbarrow," Kathleen said, "but I wasn't hinting that you'd steal something. I just don't want you to go making yourself too familiar here, seeing as you're not here for long."

Josie waited until Kathleen returned with a big pair of battered rubber boots. "These are all that's left," she said. "I suppose I could lend you mine, just this once . . ."

"That's all right," Josie said. "I can make do with these. You said I could look through your mistress's donations to the clothing drive yesterday. Is there any chance there might be a pair of shoes there that don't let in water?"

"You can look and see if you like," Kathleen said. "The bag's in the laundry room."

She led Josie through the scullery and into a small room with a stone floor, big sink and old-fashioned gas-heated copper.

"Take the bag through where it's warmer in the kitchen if you like," she said, now seeming to be perfectly friendly again. Josie didn't quite know what to make of her, but she dragged the heavy bag through and up a step into the kitchen. She felt awkward going through clothing with another woman's eyes on her. A thoroughly humiliating experience, so she rummaged quickly and found a pair of old-fashioned button-strap shoes with low heels. Quite elegant but useless for going into the village through snow.

"I'll go through the rest of these later when I have time, up in my room," she said, "but I better get your shopping done first, hadn't I?"

Kathleen watched her putting on the big boots, then gave a sigh. "I suppose you could borrow mine," she said. "You'll fall and break your neck in those."

She returned with a newer pair, though almost as large. Josie was a small size five, and her feet still slithered around in the boots, but she didn't want to appear ungrateful. As soon as she could get herself into any kind of town, she'd buy herself a pair of thick wool socks with some of her secret money. This made her pause and wonder where any more money might ever come from. If she got a government job, she'd be paid, wouldn't she? And maybe receive free housing? It all seemed rather bleak when she thought about it. Still, she reminded herself as she managed to get her coat on and wrapped the scarf around her head, at least she was safe for now. Housed and fed in a nice place. She couldn't complain.

She set off with a basket over her good arm and a list in her pocket. She realized quickly that the item of clothing she still didn't own was a pair of gloves. It was bitterly cold, with an icy wind racing in from the North Sea across marshes and flat fields. A wind that took her breath away and stung her cheeks as if she had been slapped. She plodded carefully along the edge of the road, never having walked in fresh snow before, her feet sliding around in the too-large boots. In London snow was rare, and when it fell overnight, it was soon walked on, crushed, soiled and swept away. This was pristine snow, and hers were the first feet to touch it. She liked the satisfying crunch as each foot made an impression.

It would not have been a taxing walk to the village under normal circumstances, but Josie was out of breath by the time she approached the first houses. The pub stood guardian to the village on the left side, its "Green Man" sign swinging and creaking in the wind. Josie stared at the picture on the sign. The green man was an alarming figure—a glaring face with leaves sprouting from it. It watched her critically as she approached, so she turned her attention to the rest of the cluster of buildings. After the pub on the left were a couple of shops. Then a row of cottages with thatched roofs. On the other side a blacksmith, three more cottages and then the church—St Giles, she supposed, if the village was indeed called Sutton St Giles. It was an imposing building for such a small hamlet, with a big arched window at the front and an incredibly tall spire. Josie saw the wisdom in this. A traveller could spot the next village from miles away by its church spire in this flat land. She imagined in peacetime the bells of each church would have rung out on Sundays, and their sound would have echoed across the fields. Now there were no more Sunday bells. They were only to be rung in the event of an invasion.

Josie stood for a long moment outside the village shop, catching her breath before she ventured inside. As she went to enter, the door opened, and a woman came out, wrapped like a mummy with a big crocheted shawl over her head.

"Morning," she said, giving Josie a slightly hostile stare.

"Good morning," Josie replied.

The woman went to walk away, then turned back, lowering the scarf around her face. "You're the one that came from London, aren't you?" the woman asked. "The one what's been put with the old girl at the big house."

"That's right," Josie said.

The woman's expression instantly became less guarded. She gave Josie a pitying smile. "I hope you survive that, my dear. I reckon if you can take her on, you'd be good against any invading German. A right tartar she is."

"It won't be for long," Josie said, "and she's been quite nice to me so far."

"Has she now? Well, perhaps she's getting ready to meet her maker, and she's repenting for the rude way she's treated everybody around here."

"She's been as bad as that, has she?"

"Never a friendly word have I got from her in all these years. It's like we're the simple country folk and therefore beneath her. She'd pass you on the street as if you didn't exist. Her old father was the same. He once thrashed young Jimmy Burton for sneaking on to his land and helping himself to a few cherries." She moved a bit closer. "And that Kathleen, she's not the easiest either, is she? Also keeps to herself. Funny lot they are. But we have the local WI at the church every Thursday if you've a mind to join us."

"WI?" Josie asked.

The woman looked at her as if she had just landed from Mars. "Women's Institute. Don't they have that where you come from?"

"I'm afraid not. I lived in the middle of London."

"Well, come and join us sometime. We have a sewing and knitting circle these days, making things for the soldiers. Get you out of the house and some friendly company, that would."

Josie gave an apologetic smile. "I'd love to come, but I'm not much good for sewing at the moment. I've only one good arm until my collar-bone heals."

"Oh no. You were injured in a bombing, were you?"

"That's right. Whole ru . . ." She was going to say "ruddy," but she sensed that country people would not appreciate even the mildest of swear words. "Whole blooming house fell down on me," she said. "They had to dig me out. Luckily the tabletop was over my chest so I could still breathe, otherwise I'd have been a goner."

"Mercy me," the woman said. "Well, you take care of yourself, and I'll see if my Tom can spare a little cream for you to build you up again. We keep cows, you know. Rose Finch is the name."

"Josie Banks. I'm pleased to meet you."

"We're up the lane, just past the last house in this row," Rose said. "On the other side from the Badgers—I know you've already met them."

Josie left her there, thinking that news travelled fast around a community of this size. She pushed open the shop door. A bell above her head rang, and she stepped down into an interior that smelled faintly of spices as well as other welcoming scents. On one wall were tall glass jars of boiled sweets, next to matches, candles, smaller jars of tobacco. In the glass-fronted counter were various useful items—tin openers, bootlaces, shoe polish, fish hooks, needles and thread. In front was a rack for newspapers and magazines— no longer glossy and colourful. At the back of the shop was the post office counter, and along the other wall were racks of vegetables as well

124

as big bins, containing heaven-knows-what. The shelves lining the wall should have displayed tins and packets of foodstuffs, although they were rather bare.

"And what can I do for you, then, ma'am?" the stout woman behind the counter asked, coming forward to greet Josie. "You'd no doubt be the lady who arrived yesterday to stay with Miss Harcourt?"

"That's right," Josie replied. "I'm Mrs Banks. And Kathleen sent me to do the shopping for her."

"She would," the woman replied. She seemed about to say more, then stopped herself and asked, "So what would you be needing, then?"

Josie took out her list. "A box of matches, please. And a pound of flour."

"You have the ration for it, do you? Cos I've already given her flour this month."

"Yes, I've brought you my book," Josie said. "The extra ration should help."

"You're in luck. I can give you a pound today." The woman went over to one of the bins and started shovelling flour into a paper cone, twisting it shut at the top. She placed it on the counter.

"And any eggs?"

"I can give you two."

"What about tins of meat? Corned beef?"

"Sorry, love. All gone. The only tins we've

got are baked beans and pilchards. You can have them if you like. They're off ration."

"I'll take a tin of baked beans, then," Josie said. "And I was to ask whether the sugar had come in yet."

"It has. Came in yesterday. I can give you four ounces on your ration book, dear."

"And any cheese on my book?" Josie asked hopefully.

"I don't have no cheddar, but I've got some of the cottage cheese the local farmer lets us have. It's not bad, and it's good nourishment." She lowered her voice, although they were alone in the shop. "And it's off ration, if you know what I mean."

"Thanks. I'll try some, then. And vegetables. Kathleen said to see what you've got."

"Not much at this time of year." The woman came around the counter to the vegetable rack. "I can give you a cabbage and a few carrots. I can only let you have one onion. Oh, and here's the last of these potatoes."

Josie took them, noticing that the carrots looked rather old and tired. So did the potatoes.

"Sorry, but we don't get much call for veg around here," the shopkeeper said. "Most folks grow their own or have family that has a farm." She shook her head. "I don't know why she don't grow her own stuff," she added. "Great big garden like that. The ministry said we are all

126

supposed to grow our own food to help the war effort, but she don't make no attempt, does she?"

"I suppose it's only the mistress and Kathleen in the house," Josie said. "Kathleen is overworked, and you couldn't expect Miss Harcourt to dig her own garden at her advanced age."

"I don't see why not," the shopkeeper said. "Colonel Alford over at the Grange must be nearly ninety, and he's dug up his lawn to put in vegetables. And Miss Harcourt is not that old. What is she? Sixty? Maybe sixty-five. We've plenty of folk of her age around here who walk three miles into church on Sunday. Spoiled, that's what she is. Always was too hoity-toity." As she talked, she jotted down prices on a piece of paper, then put the items into Josie's basket. "At the very least, she could let local folk come in and grow things in her beds, but she wouldn't hear of that either."

Josie paid and was putting the various items into the basket when the woman noticed she was only using one hand. "Oh, you've damaged your arm. Let me help you," she said. "Alf Badger said you'd been wounded. You'll heal soon enough out here with good fresh air and food." And she gave Josie an encouraging smile.

Josie thanked her and was about to walk out when a thought struck her. "There isn't a cobbler in the village, is there? I only have one pair of shoes, and they let in water."

"No cobbler closer than Holbeach, I'm afraid," she said. "But you could try Dan over at the blacksmith. He's real handy with fixing most things, and he can probably keep you going for now."

"Is there a bus into Holbeach?" Josie asked.

"Not any more. There's one into Spalding. Used to be three times a day. Now it's only twice, eight thirty and then five thirty, and not at all on Sundays. No petrol, see."

"Thank you again," Josie said and went next door into the baker's, where she bought a small whole wheat loaf. She looked around hopefully for currant buns, but there were only some oatcakes and a few white bread rolls.

"I'll take a couple of the rolls, please," she said.

The baker shook his head. "I've promised those to the vicar's wife, I'm afraid. She has her parish council meeting tonight, and she likes to do things proper."

Josie came out, looking for a butcher's shop, but then noticed that a van was parked, with its back doors open. She read on the side *Henry Broadfoot, Butcher and Purveyor of Fine Meats.* A man in a striped apron was standing beside the van. She went up to him. He also seemed to know who she was. He told her bluntly that Miss Harcourt had already used up her coupons until the middle of the month.

"So you don't have any meat I can buy today?

I have my ration book here," she said. "Between you and me, I can't face another of Kathleen's vegetable pies."

"I can give you a nice bit of liver," he said, giving her a sort of sideways grin that she couldn't interpret.

"That would be lovely." Josie returned the smile. "Liver and onions. One of my favourites."

"There you are, then." He put two slices on to the paper and wrapped them. "And some sausages?"

"Oh yes. Very nice. Thank you."

"You're not as fussy as some people," he said, giving her a knowing wink. "I reckon we'll get along just fine, missus."

"It's Josie," she said. "Josie Banks."

"And I'm Henry Broadfoot. Which I am, too. I wear a size twelve and a half." And he laughed loudly at his own joke. Josie was tempted to say that the boots she was wearing would probably fit him better than her.

"Are you here every day?" she asked.

"Every morning between ten and twelve, except weekends."

She set out for home, feeling better about things. She already had allies in the village. She had liver and sausages, so they wouldn't starve for a couple of days.

CHAPTER 11

The basket was now heavy on her left arm, and she staggered to keep her balance in the big boots. She was just passing the Green Man when she stepped on to an icy patch. Her feet shot out from under her, and she landed heavily. Potatoes rolled out into the snow. For a moment she sat there, winded and terrified that she might have done more damage to her broken bone. Her basket was still over her arm, and she wasn't sure how to get up. Tears of frustration came into her eyes. It was one thing after another. Just when she thought she could handle what life threw at her, it chucked something else from the side. She had started to pick up the objects that had been thrown out of the basket, praying that the two eggs might have survived, when she heard the sound of a motor car approaching. It came to a halt beside her, and a man got out. She noticed he was in an RAF uniform.

"Hey, are you all right?" he called.

"Oh yes. I enjoy sitting in the snow. It's my favourite pastime," she said. She looked up at him. For a moment, he had taken her seriously and was eyeing her as if she might be not quite all there. "Just joking," she said. "I slipped on some ice, and I can't get up because I can only use one arm."

"Hold on there." He came over to her. "Let me help. Here. Give me the basket. We'll rescue the things that have fallen out once you're up on your feet again. Can you hold on to my arm with your good hand? I'll put my other arm around you. Let's see if that works."

He bent to put his arm around her, and as he started to lift her weight, his own feet slid out from under him, and he fell on his rear beside her.

"I see what you mean about the icy patch," he said. They looked at each other and started laughing. He was still chuckling as he scrambled to his feet. "I'm glad none of my men saw that little indignity. Let's try again, shall we?" Cautiously this time, he put his arm around her and lifted her up. Josie was conscious of his arm around her waist and the rough feel of his uniform jacket against her cheek.

"No major harm done, I hope?" He bent to retrieve the potatoes that had rolled away.

She was about to say she might have a bruised bottom, but that didn't seem polite to say to a strange man. "I seem to be all right," she said. "How about you?"

"I'm tough," he said. "I used to play ice hockey. You spend half your life falling down on the ice. Now, let me give you a lift. Are you going far?"

"Not far at all. Just to that big house down there."

"It's no weather for walking," he said. "Come on. Hop in. I'll drive you." He took the basket and placed it on the back seat, then opened the front door for her, helping her climb in. They drove off. Now she had time to look at him properly. He wasn't unattractive, probably in his thirties, with a rugged, outdoorsy look with a strong jawline and creases around his eyes. He was wearing a blue RAF uniform, and she saw his wings over his pocket. A pilot, then.

"Nice motor car," she said, wanting to break the silence.

"It's a bit of an old banger, but it does the job and gets us around. Four of us clubbed together, and we take turns driving it."

She had been trying to place his accent but couldn't. Those deep, rumbling consonants certainly weren't British.

"Are you American?" she asked.

"Canadian. When my country was in no hurry to get into the war, I came over to join the RAF."

"That's very noble of you."

"I just wanted to do my part for the motherland," he said, "and, I confess, I was itching to fly."

"You weren't a pilot before the war?"

"No. I'd taken flying lessons in a small plane, but nothing like these brutes we fly now."

"Do you fly the bombers at the airbase here?"

"That's right."

"I saw one crash this morning," she said, realizing as she said it that it might be a tactless thing to say. "It was horrible. Was anyone killed?"

"The pilot was. The gunner was already dead. We managed to get the co-pilot out, but he's badly burned. I don't know if he'll make it. Let's hope so. He's a good man." He sighed. "Such a pity. How they managed to fly the crate back from Germany with only half a wing, I'll never know. But the undercarriage had been blown away. All this way home only to die at the end."

"How can you do that?" she blurted out. "How can you keep flying over Germany, knowing that you might never come back?"

"I suppose the answer is that somebody has to do it. Everyone's in some sort of danger these days," he said quietly. "At least I'm doing something to stop the madness, and I make my own danger, rather than sitting at home and waiting for a bomb to fall on me."

"That's what happened to me," she said. "A bomb fell on my house. I've been evacuated out here from London because I had nowhere to go."

"And you were hurt?" He glanced at her with sympathy. She noticed he had kind eyes.

"Yeah. Not too badly, thank God."

The car came to a halt outside the gate. "This is the place?"

"That's right."

"Not bad digs to have."

"Depends what you mean by bad," she said, grinning at him. "The woman who owns this place wouldn't get a medal for friendliness. Neither would her housekeeper. But I'm not complaining. It's a place for me to heal so I can go off and find work somewhere."

"So you're not here for long?" Did he sound disappointed?

"Only until my collarbone heals, I think. That's what they told the old woman—that she'd soon be rid of me."

He got out, came around and opened the door for her. "I'll carry your basket," he said. "We don't want a repeat of earlier, do we?"

"Thank you," she said. "You've been very kind."

"Careful!" He grabbed her arm again as one foot threatened to slide off the path.

"It's these blooming boots," she said, laughing with embarrassment. "They are ten sizes too big, and they seem to have a life of their own."

"You don't have any your own size?"

She shrugged. "I lost everything in the bombing. The only pair of shoes they gave me let water in. The woman at the village shop knows someone who can probably put a new sole on. In the meantime, it's the former gardener's boots, left behind in the shed, or the housekeeper's if she decides to lend them to me." He was now walking beside her. "I'll have to take the bus into the nearest town—Spalding, is that what they said?—one day and see if I can find a pair to fit me there. I reckon that's what I'm going to need out here in the country." As she said it, she was wondering again how quickly she'd get through those fifteen golden sovereigns and where she was likely to get any more money.

"Maybe I could drive you in one day," he said. "Although I can't tell you when that will be. We're on standby most days. I'm on the night flight today, so I am supposed to be sleeping now, but who can sleep in the middle of the day?"

He was very tall, she noted. Over six feet. He opened the front gate for her and let her walk slightly ahead of him up the path.

"My name is Mike Johnson," he said. "And yours?"

"Josie Banks. Mrs Josie Banks," she said, turning back to him and wondering why she had added the Mrs.

"And your husband's away fighting somewhere?"

"Somewhere. He thought it would be North Africa. I've only had one letter, and that was all censored out. So it could be Timbuktu as far as I know. Have you left a wife back home in Canada?"

"No," he said. "No wife." He put the basket

down on the doorstep. "Well, nice to meet you, Mrs Banks." He held out a hand, then realized her right arm was in a sling.

"And you, Officer Johnson. Or are you something more important? I'm not too well up on RAF ranks."

He smiled. "Actually, I'm a squadron leader."

"Oh, sorry. I didn't mean to put my foot in it. That's pretty high up, isn't it?"

"Don't apologize. I don't know how I managed the promotions. One of the advantages of joining up right at the beginning. But you can call me Mike if you like. We are less formal in Canada."

"Then you can call me Josie," she said. "Thank you for your help, Mike. If you hadn't come along, I think I'd still be sitting there, frozen to the ground like a ruddy snowman."

"My pleasure, ma'am." His hand went to his cap in a formal salute. He stood there, as if he was going to say something else, then gave her a nod. "Take care, now," he said.

"No, you take care," she said. "Don't fly tonight," she wanted to shout as he walked away.

Realizing that she was wearing boots that were both snowy and muddy, she didn't enter through the front door but went around to the back entrance into the scullery. Kathleen was there, lifting sheets out of the copper and into a mangle.

She was red-faced and grunting as she turned the handle.

"Oh, you're back," she said. "You took your time."

"It wasn't easy to walk in these boots, I'm afraid," Josie said. "I kept slipping and sliding, and I fell down once."

"Well, you're back now," Kathleen said. "How did you get on at the shops? Was the butcher's van there?"

"It was. They didn't have any meat for us, though."

"Spiteful pig, he is," Kathleen said. "Just because we don't always pay the bills on time and the mistress wouldn't pay his price for a chicken at Christmas."

"But I did manage to get us some liver and sausages," Josie said.

"Liver? She won't eat that. She never touches offal," Kathleen said, "except kidneys for breakfast. They are all right, supposedly."

"Well, I reckon you and me can have a nice liver and onion casserole," Josie said. "And what about sausages?"

"She won't eat them either," Kathleen said. "You don't know what's in them, and awful fussy she is about what she eats."

"So what do you feed her when there's no meat to be had?"

"The fish van comes around twice a week,

and she likes a fillet of plaice or even cod with a parsley sauce. And right now she has to make do with the last of the Christmas ham with boiled potatoes." She removed the sheet from the mangle and dropped it into a waiting laundry basket. "Did you manage to get any eggs? She does like a boiled egg."

"Only two," Josie said. "You should consider keeping chickens."

"And who'd feed them and look after them, I'd like to know?" Kathleen demanded, again the hostility coming into her voice.

"I wouldn't mind."

"But you're not going to be here long, are you? As soon as that arm is working again, you'll be off."

"Yes, I suppose so," Josie said. "I'll put these things away in the kitchen, then, shall I? And I don't mind making the liver and onion casserole to save you time. I think I can manage that much with one hand."

"I'd appreciate that. I can't say I've ever cooked liver myself, with her not eating it."

"We'll have it for our supper today, then, shall we?"

Kathleen nodded. "If you like. Now let me get these sheets out before we lose the sun."

"I can't be much help with hanging them on the line, but I can pass you the pegs," Josie said. She picked up the peg basket and followed Kathleen out to the back garden. The clothes line stood off to one side, in the former kitchen garden. Josie studied the bed, now full of dead or dying weeds. If she stayed here, she could get some vegetables growing again. There were fruit trees, too. And it shouldn't be too hard to make a chicken coop . . . Then she shook her head. But she wouldn't be staying here. They couldn't wait to get rid of her.

That afternoon she approached Miss Harcourt hesitantly. "I wonder if I might have a sheet of writing paper and an envelope to write to my husband and let him know where I am," she said.

"Very well." It was always impossible to tell from Miss Harcourt's face what she was thinking, whether something annoyed her or not. She walked over to an inlaid desk in the corner of the sitting room and took out a writing pad.

"Will one sheet be enough?" she asked.

"I think so," Josie said. "They'll censor most of what I say anyway, but I want him to know why I haven't written sooner. I didn't want to upset him with the news of the bombing and the house being destroyed."

"Of course not." Miss Harcourt handed the sheet of paper and an envelope to Josie. "And you'll need a stamp."

"I can walk down to the post office, thank you," Josie said. "I'm quite enjoying being out in the fresh air. Do you get out and walk much?"

"Not since I had pneumonia two years ago," she said. "When my father was alive, we went for walks together, usually on the dykes near the sea. But I don't enjoy walking alone. Father always said it wasn't seemly for a woman to walk unescorted."

"You should come out with me one day. Even if it's only to the village shop."

Miss Harcourt shook her head firmly. "I try to stay well clear of the village. I am not the most popular person there. And frankly, I have no wish to interact with those people."

"Don't you think you are punishing yourself by shutting yourself away?" Josie asked.

Miss Harcourt's face flushed. "Such impudence. You forget your place. You go too far. Now take the writing paper and go. I shall contact the authorities about finding you somewhere else to stay. The sooner the better."

Josie took the paper and fled up to her room. It was almost too cold to hold the pen up there, but she needed to be alone. She addressed the envelope to Stan's brigade headquarters again, not knowing if the letter would ever reach him, wherever he was.

Dear Stan, she wrote. *Such a lot has happened since I wrote to you last. I did let you know the house had been bombed, but I couldn't give you an address to write back then. The good news is that I'm still alive, luckily.*

She described the bombing, the hospital, the convent and then this house. *Now I'm out in the country. It's a lovely big house, and I would be very happy here if the owner wasn't such . . .* She had been about to write *an old cow* but changed it to *a difficult person. A proper snob. So I don't think I'll be here long. I can't go anywhere until my collarbone heals, but then I'll try and get a job somewhere out in the country. I like it out here. It feels different when you're not crammed together with so many other people. And the air is so clean, too. I wouldn't mind working on a farm if I'm up to it when I recover. So you might come home and find your wife milking cows!*

Take care of yourself. Love, Josie.

She hesitated over the last words. Did she feel love for him? She couldn't really say. But he was out there somewhere in danger, and she supposed that she wished him well.

CHAPTER 12

Josie was upstairs going through the bag of discarded clothing when Kathleen called her. She hadn't had much success. The clothes were too large and hopelessly old-fashioned. She rescued a couple of tea dresses and a tweed jacket, also an old velvet cape that could be turned into other things, then added a large, mannish cardigan and a navy jumper that could be unravelled and knitted up again when she had the use of two hands. The rest she was putting back into the bag when she heard her name. She hurried out and saw Kathleen standing at the bottom of the stairs.

"There's a package for you. Left on the door-step," she said.

"For me? Who can possibly know I'm here?" She came down to take it. Kathleen was standing, eyeing it expectantly, clearly wanting Josie to open it in her presence.

"A lady I met in the village said her husband would send me some cream to help build me up," she said. "That must be it. But I didn't expect it so quickly." She tore off the brown paper, then said, "Oh."

Inside was a pair of galoshes and a note. *This was the best I could do until I have time to go into a town,* it said. *At least these will keep your feet dry for now. Mike.*

Kathleen was peering over her shoulder with unabashed curiosity. "Who's Mike?" she asked.

"He's an RAF chap. He helped me up when I slipped," she said, "and he drove me home. I told him the boots were too big and my shoes let in water. It was really nice of him." She could feel her cheeks burning.

"You want to watch those airmen, they are all out for one thing," Kathleen said. "And you a married woman, too."

"He's a squadron leader, Kathleen," Josie said. "An older man, not some boy. And he knows I'm married. He's just being kind."

"Oh yes?" Kathleen smirked. "I don't think the mistress will approve of gentlemen callers here. Really strict about that sort of thing, she is."

"I can assure you there will be no gentlemen callers," Josie said and made a hasty exit, carrying the galoshes up to her room. She remained up there in the cold for a while, watching her breath hang in the frigid air. Was it all right to accept a present from Mike? Was he only after one thing, like Kathleen said? She'd had so little experience with men. She married the first one who showed an interest in her, and then because she was looking for any excuse to escape from a less-than-perfect home life. Since then, there had been no opportunity. It was usually women or married couples who frequented the tea shop. Banter with the fishmonger was about as far as her interactions with the opposite sex went.

"But he seemed so nice," she muttered to herself. And she realized what a kind thing it had been to use part of a day when he should have been sleeping to find galoshes that were the right size for her.

She came down in time to make the liver casserole, layering the meat between slices of onion and carrot, and then making a thick Bisto gravy. She had to ask Kathleen to slice the onion and carrots, using only half the onion to make it last. Then she baked it in the oven with three potatoes, since Kathleen had mentioned that potatoes were one of the few things Miss Harcourt would eat. At six o'clock, she took the casserole out of the oven. Stan always liked his dinner at six o'clock on the dot, so she was used to eating at that time.

"We can eat ours first," Kathleen said. "The mistress doesn't eat her dinner until seven thirty or eight. She always says it's common to eat any earlier, but then it's all right for some, isn't it? She never gets up until almost nine. Never had to carry coal upstairs to get the bedroom fires going before it's light. She's had it too easy all her life, and now she lives in a world that doesn't exist anymore." She glanced up fiercely at Josie.

"Nobody these days cares if you have a relative with a title, do they? Or if your family was out in India?"

"I don't suppose they do," Josie admitted. "The Germans don't care where their bombs land, do they?"

Kathleen nodded. "We had her sort out in Ireland," she said. "The English landowners, acting as if it was their country. They drove the Irish people off their land, you know, so they could graze their sheep and cattle. And last century, when the potato famine hit, they let us all starve. In fact, the more of us that starved, the better. More land for them, you see."

"So why did you come here if you dislike the English so much?" Josie asked.

"No jobs to be had in Ireland. Simple as that. I came over before the country was divided. It was all English in those days—part of Great Britain. And the only jobs were in Belfast at the linen mills. I had no wish to move to a big city, so domestic service was the only other choice."

She paused, staring out of the window, past Josie. "It's not been a bad sort of life," she said. "At least it wasn't too bad when there were other servants. Someone to chat with in the evenings, and the work was divided between us. Now it's just me, and I'm not as young as I was. The work seems too much, and the local people still treat me like a foreigner."

"So why don't you go home?"

Kathleen now looked down at her hands. "Nobody left, is there? My parents both died. I've brothers I haven't seen in years, my nieces and nephews, but they've their own families and their own troubles. And there's still no work." She lifted the lid off the casserole. "My, but that smells good. I don't think I've ever had liver. It wasn't that we didn't eat offal when I was growing up but that we didn't get any sort of meat that often. Tripe we had, I remember. I hated it. So what animal is it from?"

"Lamb," Josie said. "Calves' liver is more expensive, and pigs' liver is too strong. But lamb is just right." She spooned a helping on to Kathleen's plate and added the baked potato. She was just serving the second helping when Miss Harcourt came into the kitchen. Kathleen stood up hurriedly.

"Was there something you needed, madam?" she asked. "We're just about to have our supper, and we'll serve your meal at seven thirty, the way you like it."

"I just wondered what smelled so appetizing?" Miss Harcourt said.

"It's a casserole I made," Josie said. "Do you want to try some with us?"

"And was I not to be offered any of this, even though I pay the bills?"

"I went shopping for Kathleen today," Josie

said, "and the only meat they had was liver. And Kathleen said you wouldn't eat it."

Miss Harcourt stared at the rich brown gravy. "I have never eaten offal," she said.

"Would you like to try it now?" Josie asked. "There should be enough for three."

She could see Miss Harcourt wrestling with wanting to dismiss any offal as inedible and wanting to see what that smell tasted like. The latter desire won.

"Very well," she said. "I might try just a little. Since proper meat seems to have vanished from the face of the earth."

She pulled out a chair and sat at the kitchen table. Kathleen shot Josie a nervous look. Josie put a small helping in front of Miss Harcourt. The lady prodded at it with her fork, cut a small mouthful, then brought her fork to her mouth. Josie and Kathleen both watched in fascination. Josie saw the look of surprise on Miss Harcourt's face.

"It's rather good," she said. "Reminds me of the kidneys and bacon we used to have for break-fast in the old days."

"There's a baked potato to go with it if you'd like to eat now, with us," Josie said.

"Well, since I've already started on it, I'd better finish it here," Miss Harcourt replied.

The three of them sat in silence and ate, Kathleen still staring at her employer in wonder.

When she had finished, Miss Harcourt stood up.

"Thank you," she said. "I can see you have cooking skills. Let's hope you can work more magic with the pitiful odds and ends of food we are allocated these days."

"I'm happy to try," Josie said, noticing Kathleen glaring at her.

Josie didn't understand Kathleen. She complained about too much work, was glad of Josie's help, yet seemed put out when Miss Harcourt suggested Josie take over some of the cooking.

"I don't see how you think you're going to do the cooking with only one arm," Kathleen said, when her employer had left the room. "Because as soon as your shoulder is better again, you'll be moving on, won't you?"

"Let's just say I'm happy to help if you need me," Josie replied. "And I do have to build up some strength before I go off to work somewhere. I got a nasty bang on the head, you know. A bad concussion, they called it, and told me I was not fit for heavy work."

"Hmm" was all that Kathleen replied.

Josie watched Kathleen as she bustled around the kitchen, picking up the dirty plates. Clearly, she felt threatened by Josie. Was she worrying that her own position would be in jeopardy if Josie stayed? Perhaps she felt that Miss Harcourt might turf her out in favour of a better cook?

Josie watched her with new-found sympathy. She was afraid of losing her job because she'd have nowhere to go.

The next day Josie hesitated to volunteer to cook the sausages, but Kathleen sent out the challenge. "So what do you reckon you can do with a few sausages, then?"

"My husband always liked my toad-in-the-hole," Josie said. "I think we can make that with powdered egg and not waste a real one."

"And how do you make that?" Kathleen demanded.

"You've never eaten toad-in-the-hole?" Josie was incredulous.

"I told you. Sausages are not an item suitable for the upper classes. That's the message given in this house. And at home we had black pudding, but I hardly remember sausages."

"It's quite tasty," Josie said and made the batter.

"Go on. I dare you to serve some of this to Miss Harcourt and see what she says," Kathleen said, grinning with anticipation.

"All right. I will." Josie went through to the sitting room, where Miss Harcourt was listening to the wireless.

"Sorry to interrupt you, missus," she said, "but I am about to serve our supper, and I wondered if you wanted to try some."

"What is it?" Miss Harcourt turned down the voice on the radio.

"It's toad-in-the-hole, missus."

"We are reduced to eating amphibians now, are we? No thank you."

"It's not a real toad. That's just its name. It's sausages in a Yorkshire pudding."

"That sounds equally bad."

"Suit yourself," Josie said. "We'll go ahead with our supper, then, and bring you your ham later." She headed for the door.

"Perhaps I could just try it," Miss Harcourt called after her.

"I'll bring you some in the dining room if you like."

"You are most kind," Miss Harcourt replied.

Josie allowed herself a little smile as she went back to the kitchen.

The meal was at least a partial success. Miss Harcourt described it as "interesting" and "not bad at all." Josie suspected she didn't want to admit she had been wrong about sausages, but she also realized that sausages were not what they used to be. Now there was very little meat to a lot of rusk filler, but she still enjoyed her dish anyway. So did Kathleen, who chomped it down greedily. Josie could see Kathleen was warming to the idea of Josie taking over some of the cooking.

When she was getting undressed that night, an

exercise that usually took a considerable time and was painful, she noticed that she didn't wince as her arm came out of the sleeve of her jumper. She moved it tentatively. It was stiff and sore, but it only produced minor discomfort. Her collarbone was healing. This created conflicting emotions: she'd welcome the use of two arms again, but as soon as Miss Harcourt and Kathleen saw she was healed, they would want her gone—unless her cooking had given her an excuse to stay. Josie wasn't sure herself whether she wanted to be placed somewhere else. Her situation wasn't the most comfortable, to be sure, but at least she had a warm kitchen to sit in when Kathleen went off to her own quarters after supper and an endless supply of books to read. She even dared to break Miss Harcourt's rule and read in the kitchen, making sure the book was not put down on any surface except her own knees. And she had to admit that she rather wanted to see Mike again. It was stupid, she knew, but it was heady, too. *He was just being kind,* she told herself firmly. But kindness had been in short supply in her life until now.

CHAPTER 13

Josie was anxious to see the girls at Alf Badger's cottage, but she didn't want to intrude while they were getting settled in. She gave them a week and had made up her mind to go the next day, if the weather allowed, when Lottie appeared at the front door.

"You've got a visitor," Kathleen said, giving Josie an accusatory look.

Josie heart leapt, thinking it would be Mike Johnson. But instead the schoolgirl stood there, looking apprehensive.

"Hello, Lottie, love," Josie said. "You look frozen to the marrow. Come on in and have a cup of tea."

She led Lottie through to the kitchen. Lottie looked around her, worried now. "Oh, should I have come to the back door? I'm sorry. I didn't realize."

"It's all right. No harm done. Take your coat off and sit down," Josie said. She turned to Kathleen. "This is Lottie. She's billeted with the Badgers in the village."

"I am pleased to meet you," Lottie said.

Kathleen's expression changed. "You're foreign?"

"I'm German," Lottie said. "I am also Jewish."

"Her parents put her on a train and sent her away before the war started," Josie explained. "She was with people in London who didn't treat her well. I hope the Badgers are better?"

"Oh yes." Lottie smiled. "They are very kind. Mrs Badger says she must feed me up because I am too thin. They have good food, too. Eggs from their chickens, and they keep a pig and grow vegetables. Mrs Badger is a very good cook."

"I'm glad," Josie said. "And what's it like in the attic? Freezing cold?"

"It's not bad," Lottie said. "They have made me a space over the kitchen, so the warmth comes up. The other girls offered to let me share their room. Dorothy wants to share a bed with Sheila anyway. She's afraid to sleep on her own. So there would be a spare bed, but I feel that I need a private space, especially when I have to do my homework."

"So they've got you into a school, then?"

Again Lottie smiled. "Yes. The lady who brought us here came and arranged for us to attend schools. The other two go to the primary school in the next village, but I am attending the grammar school in Spalding. It's quite a long way on the bus, but it seems like a good school."

"So you're going to be happy there?"

Lottie shrugged. "I hope so. It is always the same. The girls hear my accent, and when they find out I am German, they are suspicious of me. But I hope to make friends and to show my teachers what I can do."

"Good for you."

Lottie looked up shyly. "I came to ask you a favour, Mrs Banks. I met a man . . ."

"What?" Josie's voice was sharp. "You're too young for that sort of thing."

"No, nothing like that," Lottie said hastily. "He is a very nice man. A man of good repute. He is a doctor—an eye doctor at the hospital in Peterborough. My first day at school, I did not know where the bus stop was, so I missed the bus coming home. I didn't know what to do. It is a long way, as I told you, but I had to walk. I started off. He saw me walking and stopped to give me a lift. He is also German, and he has invited me to tea on Saturday." She hesitated. "I wondered if you would come with me, Mrs Banks. I do not think it would be right for me to go to a man's house alone."

"Who is this man?" Kathleen asked. "He lives around here?"

"His name is Dr Goldsmith," Lottie said.

"Oh, him." Kathleen nodded. "Yes, we know him. He bought that big house on the other side of the village. Out on the marsh."

"How do we get there?" Josie asked. "Is it too far to walk?"

"Dr Goldsmith says he will send his motor car for me on Saturday at three o'clock. So if you can meet me at Mrs Badger's house before then . . ."

"Of course I can," Josie said. "Although I shall feel like a gooseberry."

"What? Why should you feel like a fruit?"

Josie laughed. "That's another silly English expression. If we feel like the odd person out, we say we feel like a gooseberry. You will want to speak your language to a fellow countryman, so I won't be able to join in."

"Oh no. That would be rude," Lottie said. "We shall speak English."

As soon as they had gone, Kathleen stared at Josie, frowning. "What's this place doing, crawling with Germans, then?" she said.

"They are Jewish, Lottie. They escaped from Germany, where they were being persecuted."

"That's what they all say," Kathleen muttered. "Still, it's up to you who you mix with. You won't be here long."

"You still want me to go?" Josie said. "Even if I help with the cooking for you? And the other chores?"

She could see Kathleen struggling with not wanting her in the house but wanting the help Josie could provide. "We'll have to see what the mistress says," she said at last.

On Saturday Josie tried to make herself look respectable with her mismatched items of clothing. She had a choice between a dark-green wool skirt and a red-and-blue faded tartan. Nothing really went with the red and blue, so it had to be the dark-green skirt, to which she added a beige jumper and then Miss Harcourt's long, mannish cardigan over it. Not in any way fashionable but at least respectable. She added her necklace of imitation pearls, which softened the appearance a little. She looked at her face and wished for make-up. She had been supplied with necessities—comb, toothbrush, face flannel, but no rouge or powder or lipstick. No clips to hold back her hair. She resolved to buy some of these things when she went into the nearest town with Mike Johnson—if he remembered his offer to drive her into town, that is. She paused, thinking about this. If he had safely returned from his bombing mission.

She had started counting the planes going out in the evening, wondering which one was his, and then the numbers returning. But after two flights had returned with missing aircraft, she stopped doing it. No sense in getting upset about something she couldn't control.

She slipped her new galoshes over her own shoes, put on her coat and scarf and had just opened the front door when Miss Harcourt appeared in the foyer.

"Where are you off to, then?" The way she phrased any question always made it sound like an inquisition.

"I'm taking the young girl who was evacuated with me to have tea with a local doctor," she said.

"Really? Dr Hammond? He doesn't seem like the type to ask people to tea."

"No, this man is originally German. German Jewish, that is. Now he's a doctor at a hospital."

"Oh, that one." Miss Harcourt's expression was cold. "Yes, we heard about him when he moved in right before the war. We found the timing suspicious. I don't know why he'd want to ask you to tea."

"It's the little girl he's invited, because she's also a German Jew."

"Gracious. The community is being invaded with them, then." Miss Harcourt sniffed. "Isn't it rather suspicious that so many Germans happen to take up residence beside a major RAF station? Those Germans will stop at nothing, you know. They parachute in spies disguised as nuns. I'd be very careful if I were you."

"Don't worry, I won't divulge any of the state secrets that Mr Churchill shared with me yesterday," Josie said.

Miss Harcourt sighed. "I knew it was a bad idea to open my home to a stranger from London. First it's cavorting with airmen and then bringing Germans into my house. Still, that shoulder of yours should be healing quite soon, should it not? And then you'll be off."

With that encouraging message, Josie went to

meet Lottie. The snow had started to melt, and it was now wet and muddy underfoot, but the galoshes did their work, and her feet remained dry. From Miss Harcourt's attitude, it seemed that any plan to stay on and help with the cooking was not going to be acceptable, however useful Josie might be.

Lottie was standing by the street at the end of the Badgers' path. She waved as Josie approached. Josie noticed her face had lost that pallid, pinched look already, and her smile was hopeful.

"Hello, love," Josie said. "Been waiting long?"

"A little while," Lottie said. "I didn't want to miss Dr Goldsmith."

As she finished speaking, a sleek maroon Aston Martin motor car approached, reversed in the gravel area in front of the pub, then came to a halt in front of them. The driver got out—a tall, slim man with receding fair hair and heavy rimmed spectacles. His face had a worried expression, but when he smiled, he suddenly looked much younger.

"Ah, here you are. I hope you do not wait too long in the cold."

"No, we just got here," Lottie said. "And Doctor, this is Mrs Banks. I asked her to come with me."

"Quite right," he said. He extended his hand to Josie. "I am Dr Goldsmith. How do you do." He gave a little nodding bow.

"I'd shake hands if I could," Josie said and opened her coat to reveal the sling.

"Ah, you have an injury," he said. "Here, let me assist you into my car."

He helped her in and then opened the back door for Lottie. They set off, out of the village and across a marshy area, dotted with water-filled dykes.

"So, Mrs Banks," the man began tentatively, "you are a resident of this village? I don't believe I have seen you before."

"Oh no, I arrived with Lottie," Josie said. "Evacuated from London like her. My house was destroyed by a bomb, you see."

"I am very sorry for this," he said. "So much needless suffering."

Josie nodded, unsure how to respond to that. Half a mile out of the village, they came to a house beside the road. It was another Georgian house, square, built of brick, but it stood in splendid, lonely isolation.

"Here we are," the doctor said. He pulled into the driveway, then opened the doors for his guests, leading them into a front hall, where he took their coats, then into a warm sitting room with a blazing fire. It was about the same size as Miss Harcourt's sitting room but had a more comfortable, lived-in feel to it. Two large leather armchairs were on either side of the fire. A sofa faced the hearth, and on the low table in front of it was a tray containing teacups, sugar and milk, plus a cake stand with small cakes and biscuits on it.

"Do sit down," he said. "I will make the tea."

They sat on the sofa. Josie noticed Lottie looking longingly at the cakes on the stand.

Dr Goldsmith reappeared with a teapot under a cosy and poured the tea. "Please," he said. "Help yourself to a cake."

"Do you have a cook?" Josie asked him. "Or did you bake these yourself?"

"Ach, no." He laughed. "I am no baker. I can manage to boil an egg. I only have a cleaning woman who comes in twice a week. Otherwise, I am alone here. These cakes are gifts from a patient. I operated on her cataracts, and she owns a bakery. Good timing, yes?"

His English was clipped upper class with just a trace of accent. He offered the cakes, and they both took one.

"So how long have you been in England, then?" Josie asked. "Your English is very good."

He smiled. "I came over here after the last war. In 1919. I was a prisoner of war, and I decided never to return to Germany."

"You were in the army, then?"

"I was in my last year of medical school in Tübingen when they came for us. The army, you know. All final-year students were required to serve as army doctors on the front. I cannot describe what that was like. I still have bad dreams about it. Men dying in mud and filth, torn apart on barbed wire. It was the same for both sides. A living hell. Such a stupid, meaningless war directed by old men who knew only about cavalry charges. But in England, as a prisoner, I was treated with respect. I made up my mind that I wanted to stay in a place that did not glorify war. When I was released, I finished my medical training at St Thomas's Hospital and have practiced as a doctor ever since."

"But why come out here, to the middle of nowhere?" Josie looked out of the window at the endless flat expanse.

He sighed. "I was working as an eye surgeon in Birmingham. I liked my job. I was content. Suddenly everyone was suspicious. My neighbours did not wish to talk to me. There was talk of my being taken to an internment camp as an enemy alien, even though I told them I was a Jew. So I decided to lie low. Besides, I like the feel of this countryside. It is remote but beautiful. I have been writing poetry since the Great War. I have published two volumes, and now I think I may wish to write a novel. This is the perfect place, no?" He looked at Lottie and smiled. "Do not be shy. Is the cake good?"

Lottie nodded, her mouth full of crumbs. "Very good," she said.

"You must miss your home," Dr Goldsmith said. "And the food?"

Lottie smiled then. "I miss my mother's cooking. The Knödel. The Spätzle and Leberkäse."

"Ah, Spätzle!" He gave a little sigh. "Ich hatte fast vergessen."

And they lapsed into German before he corrected himself. "I am sorry. It is rude to speak in a language someone else does not understand. I am afraid it was the memory of food that took us both back home."

"Do you have family you left behind?" Josie asked.

"I did have," he said. "I am afraid they have been rounded up with other Jews. My father kept a jewellery shop. It was smashed and everything taken. That was the last I heard, two years ago now."

"But you didn't marry?" Josie asked, feeling awkward as soon as she said the words. "I'm sorry. I shouldn't be questioning you like this."

He shrugged. "I had a sweetheart when I was a student in Germany," he said. "After the war I found she had married someone else. Someone who had stayed home because his father had connections. And here . . . at first I was too occupied finishing my training and establishing my career. Then I wanted to find a nice Jewish girl, to please my parents. But nice Jewish girls are hard to find in England. And then . . . then it all seemed a bit late. And I am used to my own company." He put down his teacup. "But you are married? Your husband is in the army? The air force?"

"The army," Josie said. "And abroad somewhere. He's not allowed to say where. They censor the letters."

"How sad. How you must miss him."

Josie decided not to answer this truthfully. "It's the same for everyone," she said. "We all have to do our part, don't we?"

"You are a brave woman," he said, and turned to Lottie, asking her about her family.

"You can speak German if you like," Josie said. "I won't mind. I might even sneak a second cake while you are not looking."

They laughed. It felt good to be amongst pleasant people in a warm room, laughing easily. And she realized that Dr Goldsmith treated her as an equal, unlike the upper-class English who might be polite to her but always with a hint of condescension.

CHAPTER 14

As they were driven back, Josie realized she had been alone for too long. She had cherished Madame Olga's company and had become friendly with the customers. She hadn't really had close friends on her street. When she first married, there had been an older woman neighbour who had shared her cooking skills and provided a motherly influence, but she had died, and the other neighbours all had children, and that set Josie apart. She was not one of them.

Dr Goldsmith let them out of the car at the bottom of the path leading to the Badgers' cottage.

"Thank you for coming with me," Lottie said.

"Thank you for inviting me," Josie replied with a smile. "It's not often I get invited to tea in a posh house."

"Dr Goldsmith is posh, is he?"

"Dear Lottie," Josie said, "you'll soon understand that England is all about your class. If you talk like me and grew up in the slums of London, you can never mix with people who live in big houses and send their kids to private schools. Oh, they might be polite if they have to, but they'd never invite me to tea. That's just the way it is here."

Lottie nodded seriously. "Yes, I suppose it is

the same in Germany. The same for Jews, anyway. There are many people who would not have my parents in their house, even though my father is a distinguished man—a professor. How silly, is it not?"

"Very silly," Josie said. She looked around. The early twilight of winter was now melting into darkness, and because of the blackout no lights shone out. Josie felt a shiver of apprehension. She had never experienced a place where she was not amongst people and noise. "Come on. I'll walk you to your front door."

"That is not necessary," Lottie replied. "It is not far."

"All the same, I don't like you walking alone in the dark." Josie put an arm around the girl's shoulder. Lottie looked up at her.

"But you must now walk home alone. How will you find your way?"

"Look, there's a moon rising," Josie said. "That should give me enough light."

They walked together up the rutted path, stumbling a little here and there. When they were close to the front door, it opened. Light streamed out for a second, and Mr Badger came out.

"Well, here you are," he said, giving the girl a beaming smile. "The wife was getting worried that it was dark and you weren't back. So I thought I'd come to look for you. Come on in. Did you have a good time?"

"Yes, thank you, Mr Badger," Lottie said. "Goodbye, Mrs Banks. Thank you again."

"Oh, Mrs Banks. I didn't see you at first," Mr Badger said. "Won't you come in for a cup of tea?"

"Thank you, but I should get home before it's completely dark," Josie said, "or I won't find my way."

"I'll lend you a torch. You can return it when you come past next time. I can't let you go without the wife seeing you. She's been wanting to know how you're getting along in that big house. Come on in."

Josie could hardly refuse. She stepped into the warm kitchen and was greeted with the smell of herbs and onions cooking.

"Look who I've found," Alf Badger called, and his wife looked up from the stove.

"Why, it's the lady from London," she said. "We've been thinking about you. Worrying about you, actually. I said to Alf, 'I wish you could build on one more room in a hurry, then we could have her here.'" She gave a sad little smile. "I didn't like the thought of you stuck there with that woman. How are you holding up?"

"It's not too bad," Josie said. "Not exactly warm, if you know what I mean. But I can be useful, even if Miss Harcourt does think I'm an extra servant."

"She would." Nan Badger nodded to her husband. "Proper toffee-nosed, she's always been. From the very beginning. Never wanted to mix with the likes of us or say a friendly good morning. I don't know what she's got to be so proud about anyway. Only cos she inherited a house from her dad. Never done a day's work for it."

"Now Nan, stop talking for a moment and give the lady a cup of tea and some of your ginger-bread," Alf said.

"Oh no, really, I shouldn't disturb you when you're cooking your supper," Josie said. "I did have a lovely tea at the doctor's house."

"He's a strange one, too, isn't he?" Nan said, pouring tea as she talked. "Choosing to live out there in the middle of nowhere. Not married. All alone. They say he's nice enough to talk to, but he doesn't mix with anyone."

"That's probably because he's a Jew," Lottie said, making them turn to look at her. "It is not easy for us when people think we are German. They don't understand that Jews in Germany are the enemy, to be destroyed. I see the other girls' faces at school. He must feel the same way."

"You tell me if any of those girls bothers you, Lottie, my dear," Alf said. "I'll go up to that school and have a word with them."

A look of alarm crossed Lottie's face. "Oh no, please. Then they would dislike me even more."

"Where are the other girls?" Josie asked.

"Playing some sort of game in their room," Nan said. "They're awfully good at amusing themselves. The little one spends half her time playing with my button box. She makes button families and button schools and even button hospitals. Amazing little imagination she has. And Sheila is wonderful with her, just like a little mother. I reckon this has been good for them both. Taken their minds off what they've just left." She went to the door. "Sheila, Dorothy? Where are you? Come and say hello."

"Oh no. Leave them if they are having fun."

But the two girls appeared in the doorway. "Is it time for supper?" Sheila asked.

"Not yet, but the lady from London is here and wanted to see how you're doing."

They smiled shyly at Josie. "So what were you playing?" Josie asked.

"Dorothy is the princess in her castle, and I'm a wicked witch," Sheila said.

"And she turned my mother and father to stone," Dorothy said. "But a prince is coming to save me, and he knows a spell so he won't be turned to stone."

Josie chuckled. "Sounds like you've settled in well, then."

They both nodded. "Auntie Nan is a really good cook," Sheila said. "She made gingerbread."

"I've just put a piece here for Mrs Banks," Nan said. "Now you let her eat, and you can get back to your castle until it's time to set the table. Right, Dorothy?"

"All right." The little girl grabbed Sheila's hand. "Come on, wicked witch," she said.

As they went, Mrs Badger turned to Josie. "I've given them both chores around the house and asked them to feed the chickens. It makes them feel that they belong here."

Josie finished her gingerbread and tea, then stood up. "I really should be getting back, but I'd love to come and visit again."

"Any time you like, my dear. There will always be a welcome in this house," Nan said.

Alf put on an overcoat and took a torch from the window ledge. "I'll walk Mrs Banks to the main road, seeing as it's tricky on our path, Nan. And I'll lend her our spare torch to get home safely."

"Good idea," Nan said. "Well, bye bye for now, my dear. You take care of yourself."

Josie followed Alf Badger into the frosty night air. The moon had now risen, and she could make out the shapes of bushes and trees. Alf's torch had the required black paper covering the glass so that it didn't give off too much light. She stayed close to him down the path, then plucked up enough courage to ask, "Mr Badger—"

"Oh, please call me Alf. We're not big on formality around here."

"Alf, then. I wanted to ask what vegetables could be planted in the winter. As soon as my arm is better, I thought I might try and get something growing in Miss Harcourt's garden. The beds are all there, and it seems silly to pay for potatoes and carrots."

"It does indeed. I've always thought that. When you come back with the torch, I'll have some seeds for you and onion sets and seed potatoes, too."

"Thank you very much," Josie said.

"And when the weather's warmer, I'll fix up a henhouse for you, and you might look into getting some chicks. Having your own eggs is the way to go these days. We'd never survive without our produce and our chickens and the pig."

"You are very kind," she said.

"Happy to help. You show that old woman what she's been missing all these years."

They had reached the road. Alf handed her the torch. She shone it up the path for him as he stomped away, then she set off for home. The village lay in blackened silence, only the rising moon glinting on the windows of cottages giving a hint that people lived nearby. Josie walked on, savouring the satisfaction of good food and good company. And plans for the future—a garden that grew vegetables, and maybe chickens. Then reality washed over her as she remembered that

Miss Harcourt was anxious to get rid of her as quickly as possible.

She'd be going somewhere else and starting over again.

CHAPTER 15

Sunday came—no different for them from the rest of the week with the church bells silenced. Kathleen lamented not being able to go to her church because the buses were no longer running.

"Why don't you go to the church in the village?" Josie asked her.

She looked as if Josie had suggested she dance naked in the snow or attend a satanic rite. "Because the church in the village is heathen," she said. "Not the true faith."

"It's all Christian, isn't it?" Josie asked. "Don't you all pray to the same God?"

She shook her head vehemently. "It might be what they call Christianity, but I doubt that the one true Catholic God hears their prayers."

Josie thought this was a strange way of thinking, but she could see there was no reaching Kathleen when it came to her religion. She wondered if Miss Harcourt would go to church, and if Josie would be expected to accompany her. She went cautiously into the dining room, where Miss Harcourt was finishing her breakfast of porridge and toast. There had been no more eggs for a few days.

"I wondered if you go to church?" she asked.

"I do not," Miss Harcourt replied. "God and I

fell out years ago. He let me down. I see no need to worship him." She gave Josie a long stare. "But of course, you are free to go if you like. The service is at ten o'clock in the village, I believe."

"I haven't been much of a churchgoer myself," Josie said, "but recently it seems we need all the help we can get from God."

"A touching innocence." Miss Harcourt almost smiled. "But by all means, hold on to your belief and your hope. I lost all mine years ago."

Josie left the room and made a decision. She would go to church. She remembered the feeling of peace in the nuns' chapel, and she needed that feeling right now. Besides, it would be a chance to meet more of the villagers. She put on her coat and scarf and pulled her galoshes over her shoes, and off she went. It was a cold, overcast day, the sky already heavy with rain or snow, and Josie had to lean into the wind as she walked. She was quite out of breath by the time she reached the church and found she was one of the last to go in. She slid into a back pew just as the choirboys were processing into the choir stalls. Nobody seemed to notice her as the first hymn began. "Oh God, Our Help in Ages Past." It seemed most appropriate. The elderly vicar gave a sermon about being a light in darkest times, that the love of God could break through the darkest clouds. He was a persuasive speaker, and Josie did feel better by the time they prayed the final prayers for those serving on land, at sea and in the air. Then the last hymn was sung: "Fight the Good Fight."

As they began to file out, some people stared at her, then walked past, saying nothing, instead turning to friends and neighbours to chat in the entrance. She was trying to slip out unobtrusively when Rose Finch saw her.

"Hello," she called. "Mrs Banks, isn't it? How are you feeling now? A bit better than the last time we met?"

"Yes. I'm definitely on the mend," Josie said.

Rose Finch nodded. "I can see that. You looked proper poorly then. I told my Tom, 'I don't think she's long for this world.' But now you've perked up a bit already. So you might join us at the WI this week, then?"

"Yes, I might," Josie said. "Thank you."

"And how are you doing with . . . them?"

"I'm managing," Josie said.

"Not exactly the warmest house in the world, I should think." Rose gave her a wink.

"Not exactly," Josie replied. "But I'm grateful to have a roof over my head at the moment. I don't know what I'd have done if she hadn't taken me in."

"Well, of course she should have taken you in, old witch," Rose said. "The farmer over towards Holbeach took in a couple of boys. We took in

174

one for a time, but then he went back home. And Alf Badger with only one spare room—they've taken in the three little girls. But her, with all those rooms—never offered to help. Still, I shouldn't speak ill of her. I expect she's got her own troubles." She shrugged. "If you come on Thursday, I'll see if we can find a pot of cream for you. And maybe a couple of eggs, too."

"That would be lovely, thank you." Josie felt tears stinging her eyes. It seemed so long since anyone was warm and friendly or cared what happened to her, and now it felt as if she was amongst friends.

When they came out, the promised rain had started. Rose tied her scarf over her head. "I wouldn't be surprised if this didn't turn to snow later," she said. "I do hate the snow. Having to go out and feed the livestock is no joke, especially now that Tom and I are getting on in years. We were expecting our Reggie to take over the farm. That was always the idea."

"And he's been called up?" Josie asked.

Rose shook her head. "He was killed at Dunkirk. Drowned trying to get to one of the boats, they say. He was such a lovely boy."

Josie wrapped the scarf around her head, wishing she had thought to take one of the umbrellas she had seen in the stand in the front hall, as the rain was already starting to come down hard. She bade farewell to Rose and set off for home. Luckily, the rain came off the sea and was at her back, blowing her along. As she approached Miss Harcourt's house, she noticed a man in an RAF uniform sitting on the wall beside the gate. For a second her heart jolted, hoping it was Mike. But it was a younger man, and he was wearing an ordinary airman's cap, not the peaked hat of a pilot. She saw then that a bicycle was propped beside him.

"Hello," she said. "Are you taking a rest?"

"No," he replied. "The wretched bike has a flat tire. I've got to wheel it all the way back to the base. I borrowed it from my mate, and he's going to kill me, but it wasn't my fault. I went on to the gravel when a lorry came past, and bang—that was the tire gone." His accent had undertones of an upper-class upbringing that he was now trying to disguise.

"How far is the entrance to the base?" Josie asked.

"About half a mile from here, I suppose," he said. "It didn't seem far when I was riding. Now it does."

"It wasn't the best of days to go for a ride, was it?" Josie gave an understanding smile.

"I wasn't on a bike ride," he said. "I went to church. I know there's a chapel on the base, but it's non-denominational and cold, and I missed the sort of church I'm used to. I sang in the choir when I was a kid. My dad's a vicar."

"So you wanted to feel like you were home for a while?" Josie asked.

He nodded. "Yes."

"How old are you?" she asked.

"Nineteen. I was planning to go to university, but I thought I ought to do my bit. It didn't seem right to be studying Classics when other chaps were getting killed."

Josie glanced at the house behind her. "Look, would you like to come in for a cup of tea?" she asked. "Warm you up before you face that walk home?"

"I'd love that," he said. "Is this your house?"

"I'm staying here at the moment," Josie said. "I got evacuated out of London. I don't suppose they'd mind if I brought you round to the kitchen. It's nice and warm in there because of the stove."

"Lovely. Thank you."

"What's your name?"

"Charlie," he said. "Charlie Wentworth."

"I'm Mrs Banks, Charlie," she said. "Wheel the bike around the side. It will get a bit of shelter there." He followed her as she went around the house and opened the back door. Kathleen was working in the kitchen.

"Oh, you're back," she said, not looking up. "You've come back nice and holy now, I suppose?"

"It was a nice service," Josie said, "and I've rescued a young man. His bike has a flat tire, and he's soaked and cold. I thought we could give him a cup of tea."

Kathleen eyed him up and down. "Oh yes?" she said.

"You get on with what you're doing, and I'll make it," Josie said. "And if we drip on the kitchen floor, I'll mop it up for you.

"Take a seat, Charlie," she said. She went to fill the kettle and put it on the stovetop, then put tea in the teapot. "So do you have to fly those ruddy great planes?"

"Oh, gosh no," he said. "I'm ground crew. I just have to service them. Clean them out. Refuel, get them ready to go off again." He paused. "I wanted to be a pilot, actually. That was why I joined the RAF and not the army. But I failed the maths exam. Maths was never my strong point at school."

"At least you are safer on the ground," she said.

"I suppose that's true."

The kettle whistled, and Josie poured the boiling water over the tea. Charlie looked around with a smile. "This is almost like our kitchen at home. We'd all eat in the kitchen when the weather was cold. Vicarages can be rather draughty, you know."

"I'm sure they can." She turned to Kathleen. "Charlie's dad is a vicar. He came to church this morning."

"Well, I suppose it's better than going to the pub," Kathleen said, "but not much."

"Kathleen's Irish," Josie said. "Catholics think we're all doomed to damnation."

"Well, you are," Kathleen said. "Not one of you recognizes the pope or the true church."

"Surely, we are all God's children, aren't we?" Charlie said. "Even Jews and Buddhists. I'm sure He loves us all."

"If He loves the Jews, He has a funny way of showing it," Kathleen said angrily.

"I don't think we'll ever understand," Charlie said. "I was planning to go into the church myself, but after this war, I'm not sure any more." He drank his tea with satisfaction, his hands cradling the cup. "We have the same china at home," he said. "They'll be getting ready to sit down for Sunday lunch soon. My mother and father, and my three sisters."

"Where is home, then?" Josie asked.

"In Devon. Quite different from this. Rolling hills and little villages in the valleys. Fast-running streams with stone bridges over them. And Dartmoor. Parts of it are quite high. My mother wrote that they'd had snow, too." He drained his cup. "I shouldn't disturb you any longer, but I can't thank you enough. Just being in a normal place for a little while has made all the difference. Sometimes being with all the other chaps, sleeping in long huts, waiting for the planes to come back, counting them in—well, it seems like another world altogether."

"I'm sure it does," Josie said. "Well, if Kathleen doesn't mind, why don't you stop in for a cup of tea again on your day off?"

"Really? Could I bring a friend?" he asked. "There's a couple of chaps who are really far from home. I'd like them to see a proper English kitchen."

"It's not up to me," Kathleen said. "It's up to the mistress."

"They'd only be in the kitchen, Kathleen. We wouldn't disturb Miss Harcourt," Josie said. "I'll ask her myself, if you like."

"You do that." Kathleen glared at her.

"I'll walk you back to your bike," Josie said and opened the back door.

"It was nice to meet you, ma'am," he said to Kathleen, putting on his cap again.

She didn't reply.

"She's a bit on the grumpy side," Josie said as she shut the door behind them. "I don't know why. She resents me, even though I've volunteered to help with the housework and brought another ration book."

"Some people are just born grumpy, I suppose," Charlie said. Their eyes met, and they laughed.

"Tell me, Charlie," she asked, trying to sound casual. "Do you know Squadron Leader Johnson?"

"I know who he is," Charlie said. "The senior pilots don't exactly hobnob with lowly chaps like me. I see him when he climbs into his planes. That's all."

"He is—still okay, then? Still alive?"

"Oh yes. Very much alive."

" 'Very much alive,' " she muttered, cherishing the words as Charlie wheeled the bike away.

CHAPTER 16

As Josie returned to the kitchen, she realized that she probably should tell Miss Harcourt about her visitor before Kathleen had a chance to embellish the tale. She tapped cautiously on the sitting room door. Miss Harcourt was in her usual armchair, a book of photographs open on her knee. She looked up.

"You've returned from church, I see."

"Yes," Josie said. She made a point of not saying, "Yes, madam," like Kathleen. She didn't want Miss Harcourt to get it into her head that she was a servant. "It was a nice service. Quite comforting."

"That's good." Miss Harcourt looked down at her lap and firmly closed the book.

"You've been reliving old memories?" she asked.

"A stupid waste of time, I suppose," Miss Harcourt said.

"Not at all. I think we need to try to cling to the good times because we can't really look ahead, can we? Nothing much to hope for at the moment, and we need to keep going."

"Yes," Miss Harcourt said. "We need to keep going. So what great delicacy is Kathleen preparing for our luncheon today? Roast beef with Yorkshire pudding and all the trimmings?"

"How about steamed cod with a white sauce?" Josie had to smile. "I don't know who gets the beef these days, but that butcher never seems to have any."

"I suppose it goes to feed the troops. And of course, there are no imports from Argentina any longer. No lamb from Australia and New Zealand. We have to rely on what we can grow ourselves, and it's not enough." She realized Josie was still standing there. "You wanted something?"

"Yes, I thought I should tell you. I brought a young airman into the kitchen for a cup of tea. I hope that was all right? He was standing in the rain, soaked through, and his bike had a puncture, so I felt sorry for him."

"I admire your compassion, but don't make a habit of it," Miss Harcourt said. "I am averse to sharing our meagre rations with outsiders."

"It was only one cup of tea." Josie fought to stay calm. "And you do have my tea ration now."

"Another thing you should consider is your reputation," Miss Harcourt said. "If you are seen inviting airmen in through the back door, people will talk. People gossip. They can be terribly harmful. You are a married woman, after all."

Josie had to laugh at this. "He was nineteen. He looked like a little boy. And he was homesick. You should have seen how he looked around the kitchen and said it was just like his mum's."

"All the same," Miss Harcourt said, "I don't want you inviting strangers into my house. He could have been scoping the place out to rob us."

"I don't think that's likely," Josie said. "You would have liked him. He talked posh like you, and his dad's a vicar. Next time he calls, I'll bring him to meet you."

"I certainly have no interest in meeting strange airmen," Miss Harcourt said. "And I just told you that I do not want strangers in my house."

"Don't you have any feelings for those poor boys who are far from home? Those ones who have to fly to Germany every night and never know if they are coming back?"

"I gave up compassion years ago," Miss Harcourt said. "I learned that life is not fair and that life is cruel and that human life is cheap. My advice is to stay away, not get involved, and then you won't have to grieve. Now I suggest you go and help Kathleen with the luncheon and let me get back to my memories."

Josie came out of the room and stood in the dark hallway, thinking. Miss Harcourt must have suffered a loss at some stage. Had she lost a sweetheart in the Great War? But no, she would be too old for that, surely. Whenever it had happened, she now chose to shut herself off from life. And that just wasn't healthy, Josie decided. She went back to Kathleen in the kitchen.

"You've been with Miss Harcourt for years," she said. "You said she had a sweetheart?"

"She was already middle-aged when I arrived," Kathleen said. "Certainly no sweetheart since I've been here. And she doesn't talk much about herself. Occasionally she'll mention something her father did. She was born in India, you know, and she does talk about that from time to time. Very grand lives they led there. They came back when she was about twelve. Since then, she and her father lived in this house, apart from when she went off to finishing school and then was in London for a short while. That's all I know."

"Well, something must have made her rude and bitter," Josie said. "It's not natural to want to shut yourself off, is it?"

Kathleen shrugged. "That's how the upper classes behave, isn't it? They keep their children shut away in a nursery, then they send the boys off to boarding school. You're right. It's not natural. None of it is. Just be glad that you're working class and you've got a husband, and when he comes back after the war, you'll return to your old life and a normal home."

"Yes," Josie said. "My old life. That's what I'll do." And she felt the weight of those words pressing down on her.

That night Josie was getting ready for bed when she heard the drone of aircraft approaching. Bombers on a training run? she wondered.

Returning from a daytime raid? Then, in the distance, a dull thump. Then another. And she heard the pitch of the engines. Enemy bombers. She fought back the panic as she scrambled back into her day clothes, put on her shoes and grabbed her ration book before she ran downstairs.

"Kathleen!" she called as she went through the kitchen. "Kathleen! German bombers."

She opened a door to find herself in a narrow hallway with several doors. She hammered on each of them until one door at the end of the hall shot open, and Kathleen appeared in a flannel nightgown with curlers in her hair.

"What on earth is going on?" she asked. "What do you think you're doing, coming into my private quarters?"

"Listen," Josie said. "German bombers. Where do you go during a raid?"

"We hardly ever have raids here," Kathleen said.

"Should we go to the garden shed, do you think?" Josie asked.

"No! Of course not," Kathleen snapped. "Pull yourself together. They won't bomb a house like this. They've come for the airfield, that's what they want."

Josie opened the back door. Thumps and explosions echoed through the night air. She thought she saw bright flashes, but then the planes passed over, and the sound of their engines receded, and the night became still.

"They'll be going to the Midlands," Kathleen said. "That's what normally happens. Leicester or Nottingham. Where the factories are. We're pretty safe here."

Josie took a last look in the direction of the airfield. Had any buildings been struck there? Was everyone all right? When she crawled into bed, freezing now, and hugged the hot water bottle to her, she found herself thinking about Mike.

"Please let him be safe," she prayed. Then she felt guilty for thinking about him and reminded herself that it was absurd. He was a squadron leader. An important man. An upper-class man probably, as all the pilots seemed to be public school boys. He'd see her as beneath him. Although perhaps in Canada there wasn't the distinct barrier between classes that could never be crossed. He had been kind, that was all, Josie told herself again. And she was a married woman. Someday in the future Stan would return home, and she'd move back to London and her old life. She shouldn't be dreaming about something she could never have.

The next morning there was excitement in the village about the bombing raid. Two of Farmer Moulton's cows had been killed in a field beside the airstrip, but the bombs had apparently not done much damage to the RAF base itself.

"See, what did I tell you?" the butcher, Mr

Broadfoot, proclaimed. "Useless lot, those Germans. Can't even hit an RAF base in the middle of blooming fields."

And the women who were queueing up at his van laughed, hoping this was true. Before Josie set out for home, she had to deliver the torch back to the Badgers. She felt guilty that in the rain yesterday she had forgotten to do so. Alf Badger didn't seem at all put out.

"Don't you worry one bit, my dear. It's our spare, and we don't go out much after dark these days. And I'm equally guilty. I told you I'd have seeds ready for you, and it was raining so hard yesterday that I didn't go near the garden or the shed. So I'll tackle that today for you, I promise."

"There's no rush, Mr Badger," Josie said. "I don't think I'm up to digging a bed yet. I don't think that arm will be good for much for a while."

"I could come over and dig it for you," he said. "If that woman wouldn't make a fuss about it, that is."

"Oh no, I wouldn't want that, Mr Badger. You've got a big plot of your own to take care of, and as you say, she'd be bound to make a fuss. Don't worry. I'll tackle it soon."

"Right you are, my dear. That will give me time to find you some onion sets and seed potatoes to get you going."

She left him and walked home. Life in the country clearly agreed with people. He must be at least seventy, and yet here he was taking care of an acre of land, sprightly as a young man.

Miss Harcourt deigned to eat the liver she had just bought, and Kathleen even suggested that Josie might be getting close to taking over more of the cooking.

"So you want me to stay, then?" Josie asked.

She could see conflicting emotions battling. In the end, Kathleen shrugged. "It might not be a bad idea," she said. "Two people will mean halving the work, won't it?"

"If I stay, I was thinking of getting that vegetable garden going again," Josie said. "It would be nice to have our own veg, wouldn't it? Not to rely on what they've got at the shop."

"And paying their prices," Kathleen agreed. "Sixpence for one onion? I've never heard the like."

The next day dawned bright and cold. Josie bundled up and went out to inspect the garden beds. There were dying weeds, but she thought she recognized plants that might be vegetables gone wild. She'd have to bring Alf Badger to identify them—if Miss Harcourt would allow that much. Personally, she couldn't see why anyone would object to having a gardener again when Miss Harcourt had been used to one before the war. Josie nodded to herself. That's how she'd put it. A free gardener.

She was standing there, wondering where to

start, when she saw someone coming around the side of the building. It was Mike Johnson. Immediately she was conscious that she looked a fright, standing in the mud, her scarf wrapped around her head and wearing Kathleen's too-big boots.

"Hi," he called. "I finally got a day off. Are you busy?"

"I was taking a look at the garden," Josie said. "I thought I might get these veggie beds going again, but I'm no gardener, and I don't know where to start. Mr Badger from the village is going to show me what to do and give me seeds to plant."

"So you're adapting to country life, then?"

"I don't know about that. It's more like survival," Josie said, walking towards him gingerly across the earth. "I don't like being dependent on what the village shop has to offer."

"I wondered if you'd like to take a run into town today," he said. "I've managed to snag the motor car."

"I'd love to," she said. "I've been making a list of things I can't do without, and I'll have to see which ones I can afford. I'll just go and get changed."

"Great," he said. "I'll wait for you out at the car."

"So your gentleman caller is back, I see," Kathleen said as Josie took off the boots in the scullery and then came up to the kitchen in stockinged feet.

"He's not my gentleman caller. He's a kind man who has taken pity on me. He has to go into the nearest town, and he invited me to come along, that's all. Is there anything we need that we can't get at the shop?"

"Too many things," Kathleen said. "Unfortunately, they all cost money. I'll write you a list, and you can ask the mistress if she has the cash to spare."

Josie rushed up to brush her hair and put on Miss Harcourt's cast-off good shoes and the one respectable jumper. She had made her own list of things she needed. It ranged from new soles for her shoes, her own pair of Wellingtons, another pair of stockings, a torch and maybe a lipstick. She debated whether to spend more of her precious sovereigns on clothes, if they were even to be found these days. Or at the very least on wool to knit a new jumper. The trouble with someone else's jumper was that the smell of that person never really went away with washing. That Ashes of Roses still lingered enough to annoy her.

Then she went to find Miss Harcourt, who was standing in her library, lost in contemplation as she ran her hands over a shelf of books. Josie rapped loudly on the door and coughed as she entered.

"What do you want?" Miss Harcourt demanded.

"I have a chance to go into a town, and Kathleen gave me a list of things you needed for the house. So if you'd like me to get them, I'll need the money for them." She stood there, her gaze defiant.

"Let me see the list," Miss Harcourt said. Josie handed it over. Miss Harcourt studied it. "Yes, I suppose we have to have laundry soap flakes and more candles in case the electricity goes off again." She mulled over the items, one by one. "Very well," she said. "Stay here. I will get you the money." Josie stood still in the cold library, worrying that Mike was sitting outside and would be waiting for her. Miss Harcourt returned. "There is a man in a motor car outside. Is he the one who is driving you into town?"

"That's right," Josie said.

"The one you brought in to tea the other day?"

"No. This one's a squadron leader. He helped me carry home the shopping last week."

"My," Miss Harcourt said, raising an eyebrow expressively. "You've been here two weeks, and already you have made friends with half the RAF. I suppose that's how things are in London."

"You mean a kind man being friendly?" Josie demanded. "I would hope that people try to help each other everywhere during a war."

"Men usually want something in return," Miss Harcourt said. "At least that is my experience."

"I'm sorry you have such a poor view of men. Squadron Leader Johnson treated me with nothing but respect the other day."

"Being driven by squadron leaders? My, we are moving up in the world, aren't we?"

"He's Canadian."

"Huh!" She made a disparaging grunt. "They are almost as bad as Americans from what I've heard."

Josie's patience was wearing thin. "He's taking me shopping, not to the casbah," she said. "Now do you want me to get those things for you or not?"

"I suppose so." Miss Harcourt gave her a ten-shilling note and four half-crowns. As Josie was leaving the library, Miss Harcourt called to her, "Have you finished that book I lent you yet? I haven't seen you doing any reading. I told you that you were welcome to read in the sitting room."

"I didn't feel right in there," Josie said.

"I hope you haven't been reading it in the kitchen where it could become soiled," Miss Harcourt said. "I am meticulous about the way I keep my books."

"I made sure I put a clean cloth on the table before I read in the kitchen," Josie said. "And yes, I've finished *The Nine Tailors*."

"What did you think?"

"I wouldn't have wanted to die that way," Josie

said. "And why are the detectives always upper-class people?"

Miss Harcourt looked surprised. "I suppose it's because they have time on their hands. The working classes are working, are they not?"

"That's right," Josie said. "I've never thought of it that way."

"So have you chosen another book yet? I have plenty more by Sayers, although you might find Agatha Christie is easier going."

"Maybe you can suggest one for me when I get back. I don't want to keep the squadron leader waiting any longer."

CHAPTER 17

Mike was standing by the car and opened the door for her, making her feel ridiculously like a princess. "I'm so sorry to keep you waiting. The lady whose house this is had a list of things she wants me to buy."

"No problem. I'm not in a rush."

She gave him a little smile as he got in beside her.

"Sorry, it's still cold in here. The heater isn't working properly," he said. "There's a rug in the back seat. Let me get it for you."

He reached between them, then covered her knees with the rug. It came to Josie that it was the first time in her life that a man had shown concern for her. Stan would never have noticed.

"It's very nice of you to give up your time like this," she said as they drove off.

"Don't you see, it's a treat for me, too," he said. "Living in the barracks, on standby most of the time, knowing we might have to drop what we're doing and jump into a plane at any moment—it gets to you after a while. What we guys all want is a touch of normality. Life as it used to be." He looked across at her. "Tell me about your life, before you came here. You lived in London? Did you grow up there?"

And Josie found herself telling him about the house behind the gasworks and looking after her younger siblings, and then the garment factory and meeting Stan, and then the tea shop. He didn't interrupt, and when she was finished, he said, "You know, the first time you smiled was when you mentioned that café. It obviously meant a lot to you."

"It did," she said. "It was a place that was special—elegant, you know. Refined. The people who came there, they wanted a moment in their days that was peaceful and an escape from their usual boring lives. We worked hard to give them that. Nice cups and saucers. Flowers on the tables. Little cakes when there was still flour. And Madame Olga—she was a Russian toff, even though she was Jewish. She told me all these stories of life in Russia. It all sounded so magical, you know. And what else I liked was she didn't treat me as if I was beneath her. She treated me like a friend, almost like a daughter."

"Why would anyone treat you as if you were beneath them?" he asked.

"That's the way it is in England. Haven't you noticed?"

He gave a brittle laugh. "Yes, I suppose I have. I've certainly seen how cruel and judgemental people can be. The other officers here—public school boys, most of them—I sometimes feel they are all in an elite club I can never belong to. They speak a secret language, you know. Good old Toddy and Foggy and God knows what other awful nicknames. And parties with debs. Of course, they are mostly younger than I am. They deserve their moments of fun, poor blokes. Those years when we all were reckless and silly. They know too well that their lives may end tomorrow."

"Were you ever reckless and silly?" Josie asked.

"Not really." He smiled. "Never had a chance to be. I grew up in rural Nova Scotia. No big city lights to attract me. Certainly no parties with debutantes. My father was a doctor. He wanted me to follow him, but between you and me, I didn't like the thought of cutting people open. All that blood." He glanced at her and grinned. "So I went to university in Halifax and studied pharmacy. Then I became a pharmacist—a chemist—at the university hospital."

"So what made you leave Canada and come over here to join up? I think that was a really noble thing to do."

"Not really noble. Just a desire to do something constructive, I suppose. And to face some danger. My life until then had been rather dull and predictable."

"And you never met the right girl and married?" She blurted out the words before she decided they were prying.

197

"Oh, I did. I was married, but my wife died."

"I'm so sorry."

"So am I," he said. "But we all have to keep going, don't we? You must miss your husband terribly."

"Not too much," Josie said. "I can't believe I'm saying this, but it was a relief when he went. He's not the easiest man. When everything's going well, he can be fun and quite charming. But the least little thing that goes wrong, he just explodes. It's like walking on eggshells all the time."

Mike looked at her with concern. "I'm sorry," he said. "No one should have to live like that." He paused. "So will you go back to him, when he comes home?"

Josie stared out of the windscreen as frosty fields moved past them. "I suppose I will," she said. "I married him, didn't I? And if he's been off fighting somewhere, it wouldn't be right to leave him on his own."

"Maybe you'll both have changed—in a good way," Mike said. "You'll know what life is like in the big world and that you can survive well on your own. And he might have come to appreciate the comforts of home and a loving woman."

"Let's see, shall we," Josie said. "So what's it like in your part of Canada?" she asked, moving away from the uncomfortable subject.

"Cold," he said. "Our winters are bitter. Lots of

snow. But it's a beautiful place. Hilly countryside with pine forests and little fishing villages and such good seafood. You should see the scallops the fishing fleet at Digby brings in."

"I've never heard of a scallop," she said.

"Never?"

Josie shook her head. "We get winkles and cockles and whelks, and Stan used to like jellied eels. That's about it. They're all quite tasty in their way. You don't see them any more since the war started. I suppose it's too dangerous to be digging up things on beaches. You might find yourself digging up a mine."

"True enough." He exchanged a grin with her. Suddenly they both caught the sound of approaching aircraft. Mike immediately pulled over to the side of the road, where a large oak tree was growing. The planes came closer, dropping lower and lower, as if coming in to land. Josie pressed her lips together, determined not to let him see that she was afraid. The noise became deafening. The planes passed over, and she let out a sigh of relief as she saw they were Spitfires. Mike frowned as he watched them go.

"Missing-man formation," he said quietly. "Those boys are our fighter escort. We lost two planes last night and now another one. That's too bad."

"Do planes get shot down all the time?" Her voice was unsteady. "Every time you go out?"

"Not every time, if we're lucky," he said, "but it's quite a usual occurrence. It just depends if we have fighters to accompany us, and they can keep the enemy busy. Sometimes it's just us, and we have to rely on our rear gunners. Not all that successful, really. Our planes aren't as fast as enemy fighters."

"Let's talk about something else," Josie said.

"All right. What do you need to buy when we get to Spalding?"

"I made a list," Josie said. "Things I really ought to have, and I've brought that pair of shoes to see if they can be repaired while we're there."

"The galoshes worked for you, did they?"

"They did. Thank you so much. It was so kind of you. And they fit perfectly."

"My wife was about your size," he said. "I made a lucky guess. But let's see if we can find you a pair of boots today."

Josie chewed on her lip. "I'm not sure how much I can spend," she said. "I don't have any money coming in, and I don't know when I can start working again. So it's just the basics."

"Boots are basic around here, I would have thought," he said.

They drove into a little high street, and Mike parked the car outside a hardware shop.

"Let's find your cobbler first," he said.

They walked together, Josie looking with interest in the shop windows. There was a

Woolworths, where Josie thought she could find most of the things on her list, but Mike asked and was directed to a shoe shop through an alleyway, where the cobbler agreed to put on new soles by lunchtime.

Then they returned to Woolworths. She bought a pair of thick stockings and a bar of Pears soap that was now on ration, and she couldn't resist a Coty lipstick. She managed to find most of the items on Kathleen's list. When she went to pay, the salesgirl stared at her sovereign. "What's this?" she demanded.

"It's a sovereign. Same as a pound. Ain't you never seen one?" Josie demanded.

"It's not like real money," the girl said.

"Of course it is. Ask your supervisor."

"Here, let me pay." Mike stepped forward, but Josie waved him aside.

"No, there's nothing wrong with this. Ask your supervisor, please."

An older woman came, took the coin from Josie, disappeared into a back room then came back with change for a pound. "It's not often we see one these days," she said. Josie gave her a grateful smile. After that they found a wool shop, and Mike helped Josie select a pretty shade of blue-green wool. She hoped Kathleen would have needles. And lastly, they searched for the boots. This proved the greatest challenge. There had been a run on boots, given the bad weather, she was told, and no more coming from suppliers. No rubber to be had these days. They finally tracked down a pair in an ironmonger's, of all places, when she was buying candles and paraffin for the house.

Josie hesitated when she saw the price, but this time Mike insisted on paying. "Absolutely my treat," he said. "We don't want you falling on the ice again, do we? I might not be there to help you up."

"Or to fall beside me," she reminded him, and they exchanged an amused glance. His eyes held hers for a long moment before she gave an embarrassed giggle and turned away. She could feel her cheeks burning, but that one glance had stirred up feelings inside her that she didn't know she had.

CHAPTER 18

They came out to see heavy clouds gathering on the eastern horizon.

"Going to rain soon," Mike said. "Perhaps we should buy you a raincoat, too."

"That's not necessary," Josie said. "I can borrow an umbrella when I have to go out. And anyway, I can't have you buying me things. I hardly know you."

"I suppose you British would say we haven't been properly introduced or something?"

"Not my kind of people. Where I come from it's 'whatcha mate,' and anyone who buys you a pint is a friend. We don't stand on ceremony when we're packed in like sardines."

"I figure that during a war there isn't much time for standing on ceremony," he said. "You have to make the most of the moment. Besides, I feel comfortable with you. I have from the moment you laughed when I fell down beside you."

"Yes," she said. "I've told you things I don't tell other people. I'm not usually one for talking about my life, you know. I haven't had many close friends apart from Madame Olga."

"Everyone should have a friend they can turn to," Mike said. "I know how it feels when there is nobody." He looked around. "It's too early to pick up your shoes yet," he said. "Come on, let's find somewhere for a hot cup of something." He took her arm, and it felt so natural that she didn't resist. Further along the high street they came to a café. It was called the Spinning Wheel. Mike opened the door for her, and they stepped into a pretty room with white tablecloths and flower prints on the walls.

"Oh." Josie stood, taking deep breaths.

"What's the matter? Not the right sort of place?" Mike asked.

"It's lovely. It's just like that tea shop I told you about. The same sort of feel to it. As if you've stepped through that door and escaped from the real world."

"Then let's sit down and see what they have to offer," Mike said.

A cheerful woman, her sleeves rolled up, came out of the kitchen, drying her hands on her apron. "Morning, ma'am. Morning, sir," she said. "What can I get for you?"

"You don't happen to have coffee, do you?" Mike asked.

"As a matter of fact, I do. Coffee's not rationed, you see, and there's not much call for it. But I hope you don't like it with too much milk, because the milk ration's been cut."

"No, I take mine black." He turned to Josie. "Do you like your coffee white?"

"White, I think," Josie stammered. She wasn't

going to let that woman know that she had never drunk coffee before.

"And any little cakes?" Mike asked.

"Afraid not, love." She gave a regretful smile. "I can't get the ingredients. But what I do happen to have is a malt loaf with currants. It's very nice toasted."

"All right," Mike said. He waited until she had gone, then leaned forward and whispered to Josie, "What the heck is a malt loaf? Will I like it?"

"It's good. Sort of brown bread with fruit in it. You've never had it before?"

"Never heard of it."

"Then I've got a confession to make to you," she said, still leaning close to him. "I've never drunk coffee before in my life."

"Never?"

Josie gave an embarrassed shrug. "People don't, where I come from."

"I can see I'm going to have to teach you about a lot of things you've been missing," Mike said. Josie wondered if that sentence had a double meaning. He was looking at her with that relaxed smile that she found so attractive. "First scallops, and now it's coffee. Goodness me. I couldn't live without my coffee."

The café owner appeared with a tray containing two slices of malt loaf, cups of black coffee and a small jug of milk.

"Try it black first," Mike said, "so you know what real coffee tastes like."

Josie took a sip, wrinkled her nose and shook her head. "It tastes bitter."

"Then add some milk and sugar," he said.

She tried again. "Oh, that's not so bad," she agreed. "A funny taste. I suppose you get used to it."

"Not too bad? It is the nectar of the gods, woman," he said, laughing as he said it. "I can see I'm going to have to convert you."

The door opened, sending in a blast of cold, damp air, and two women entered, taking a table in the window. They glanced across at Josie and Mike and, seeing Mike's uniform, gave an encouraging nod.

"So this is like your tea shop, is it?" he asked.

"Very much. Ours wasn't quite as fancy as this. But it had the same feel. It's funny," she added, remembering, "but I met one of your blokes the other day. It was pouring rain, and I invited him in for a cup of tea."

"You're fraternizing with airmen now, are you?" he asked, raising an eyebrow.

"Oh, come on, Mike," she said. "He was still a kid, and he looked lost. You should have seen him in our kitchen. The way he looked around it with wonder, as if he were remembering how real life used to be before the war."

"Was he air crew?"

"No, he said he didn't pass the pilot's exam so he works on servicing the planes."

"Then he might be quite young. A lot of them are eighteen, first time away from home, poor little buggers. It's not a job I'd want, cleaning out those planes that often come back with blood or vomit spattered over them." He checked himself. "I'm sorry for using bad language. You get used to that way of speaking amongst the men all the time."

Josie laughed. "You should hear what my Stan says. He's got a terrible mouth on him. But I can't believe you're sorry for the ground crew when you're the one being shot at."

"I suppose most of us who train to be pilots like the danger," he said. "At least it makes us feel alive."

Josie looked up, frowning. "You didn't feel alive before the war?"

"No," he said. "Not for a while."

After his wife died, she thought and rapidly changed the subject. They finished their malt loaf, and Mike drained his coffee cup. Josie left some of hers—the taste would take some getting used to. They left the tea shop and picked up the shoes, which now looked as good as new.

"You've done a beautiful job," she said to the cobbler.

"Ah well," he said, nodding with satisfaction, "nobody's going to be buying new shoes for a long while, are they? So it's up to me to keep them going."

It was with regret that she climbed into the car beside Mike. It felt like a beautiful fantasy that was about to melt away. "I've had a lovely time," she said. "Thank you for taking me."

"No, thank you," he said. "It's the first time I've spent time alone with a woman in years. I thought I might have forgotten how to talk to one."

"You must have loved your wife very much," she blurted out.

There was pain in his expression. "I did," he said.

They drove the rest of the way home in silence. It was raining in earnest now.

"This will probably turn to snow tonight," Mike said. "Not the night I'd want to be flying."

"You're not going up tonight, are you?"

He nodded. "I'm on the roster. They only abort if conditions are really terrible."

"So you were supposed to be sleeping today." She gave him an accusing look.

"I told you, I don't sleep very well in the daytime. It's too darned noisy, for one thing. Guys shouting in the corridor outside my room, trucks driving past. And of course we can't take a sleeping pill because we have to be one hundred percent alert when we fly."

"Where will you be going tonight?"

He chuckled. "What are you, a spy? Sorry, can't help you with that. We won't get our briefing until this afternoon. It's been German supply routes across France lately. Blowing up railway lines. At least that's less dangerous than flying over Hamburg or Bremen. I just feel sorry for the French. Sometimes a storage depot is next to a lovely old church. That's the part I hate about a war. I don't mind bombing the enemy, although I feel for those guys who didn't want to be in uniform, but I hate it when we get the command to bomb a city. Retaliation bombings, you know. Every night there's a raid on London, the next night we're over a German city doing the same. It's all so senseless." He was staring straight ahead as sleet now peppered the windscreen. "I wish now I had opted for flying fighters. Man-to-man battle in the air. That's more honourable, isn't it? But they said they needed bomber crew, and here I am."

"Well, someone's got to do it," Josie said. "If we didn't hit back and slow them down, they'd be in England by now."

"I still don't know if we can stop the invasion," he said. "It seems as if Jerry has endless supplies, and us—we're tying engines together with rubber bands and string."

"That's what Stan said," Josie agreed. "Some of the men had to train with sticks of wood because there weren't enough rifles."

"The Germans have been preparing for years. We should have intervened sooner."

The village was approaching, and Mike turned the car so that Josie was beside the front gate. "Got your shopping?" he asked.

She nodded. "Thank you again," she said, then she reached out a hand and placed it over his. "Take care of yourself tonight, won't you?"

"I'll give it a darned good try, Josie." He gave an easy laugh. Josie tried not to look back as she hurried up the front path.

After Josie had deposited the items on the kitchen table, she found Miss Harcourt in the sitting room and gave her the change. Miss Harcourt nodded. "You managed to find the items for Kathleen, then?"

"Except I could only get half the amount of paraffin she wanted. It's rationed," Josie said.

"Everything is." Miss Harcourt sighed. "Life has become so tiresome. Sometimes I wonder if it's worth continuing."

"We have to keep going, or Hitler will think he's won," Josie said.

"Quite right." She stood up. "So, do you want me to find you a book now?"

"That would be nice of you," Josie said. She went ahead of Miss Harcourt into the library. "Brrr. It's freezing in here today. You wouldn't want to stay long, would you?"

"No, you wouldn't," Miss Harcourt agreed. "In my father's day, we had big, blazing fires in all the rooms, and the house was lovely and warm. But then in those days, we always had plenty of wood from fallen trees on the estate. I had to sell that land to pay his death duties." She shook her head, as if ashamed of displaying a sign of weakness. "So, another mystery novel?"

"Do you have any books on Canada?" Josie asked.

"Canada? This is because of the man in the motor car?"

"It is, actually. I can't quite picture it. It's all snowy in winter, he says."

Miss Harcourt stared at her for a moment, then said, "Let me think. Ah, I do have some that fit the bill."

She examined the shelves and then pulled down a book. "Here you are. *The Whiteoaks of Jalna.* It's about a house in Ontario, on a lake. Quite light reading but enjoyable."

"Thank you." Josie took it. "I'll take good care of it. I don't read in the kitchen until all the food is put away and the table's been scrubbed."

Miss Harcourt nodded. "And your shoulder? Is it finally healing?"

"Yes, it is," Josie said. "I can start to move that arm again." She looked up at Miss Harcourt. "So I suppose you'll want me out of here soon, then. Only . . ." She broke off, summoning courage.

"Only I have a proposition to make to you. If you let me stay on here, I'll get your garden going again. Alf Badger is going to give me seeds and show me how to work a vegetable garden. And chickens, too. When the weather gets warmer, we could start chicks. Have our own eggs. And I'll take over the cooking, too. Kathleen's not the world's best cook, is she?"

"She is not!" Miss Harcourt actually smiled. "But should you not apply for war work as soon as you are well enough?"

Josie hesitated. "The doctor did say I was not to undertake any strenuous work because of my injuries," she said. "And besides, I'd be contributing to the victory gardens, wouldn't I?"

Miss Harcourt's cold eyes examined her. "Well, what you say makes sense, only I couldn't afford to pay you, you know. My own finances have taken a turn for the worse because of the Depression."

"I don't need paying as long as I get room and board," she said. "And who knows, if we get extra produce, extra eggs, maybe we can make a few bob selling them."

"A few bob!" Miss Harcourt looked amused at the terminology. "That would certainly come in handy."

That night Josie went to bed feeling satisfied for the first time in ages. She was not going to be turned out. And what's more, she had a purpose in life. She pictured the garden full of growing things, a henhouse with eggs every day. She pushed aside the reality that she had never grown anything in her life and had no idea how to start. She only knew she was determined to make it work. And if her decision to stay had anything to do with a certain pilot being nearby—she was just considering this when the rumble of planes taking off made things rattle. She jumped out of bed and went to the window. The moon was now half full, and she could see their shapes as they rose, one after the other. Five of them. And Mike was in one.

"Bring him home safely," she prayed.

CHAPTER 19

On Thursday, Kathleen remarked that they could do with more potatoes if Josie felt like walking down to the shops. Josie was always looking for an excuse to get out of the house and a chance to try out her new Wellington boots. When she saw two women walking together up to the church, she remembered the WI meeting with the women's sewing circle. The household chores had been done for the day, and Kathleen wouldn't need the potatoes for that night, so Josie decided to join the gathering. She bought the three remaining potatoes from the shop, added another tin of baked beans, and then went across the street and into the church hall. Inside there was already a buzz of chatter as the women sat around a long table. There was fabric spread out on the table, and others had knitting in front of them. Rose looked up and waved to her.

"Come on in, love. Sit down. Join us." She turned to the group. "This is Mrs Banks, who has been billeted on you-know-who. I thought she might like some friendly company for a change."

"Oh, of course. Come and sit down," several of the women said at once. The smiles were welcoming.

Nan Badger waved from across the table. Another older woman with her hair in a bun and a round, red-cheeked face was patting a seat beside her. "Come and sit here, my dear," she said. Josie smiled and slid gratefully into the chair.

"I'm afraid I won't be much use at sewing yet," Josie said, indicating her arm in a sling.

One of the women laughed. "We're not going to put you to work. We do the occasional bit of sewing or knitting, but it's really an excuse to get together away from the men—or in your case the women."

They all laughed then.

"I'm Mrs Adams," the woman beside Josie said. "Annie Adams. That's easy enough to remember, isn't it? First in the alphabet. How are you getting along so far?"

"It's a roof over my head that I didn't have before," Josie said.

"I'll bet you're not finding the occupants too friendly, are you?" Annie asked.

"Not the warmest," Josie said. "I think Miss Harcourt has been on her own for too long. She's rather set in her ways."

"She's too stubborn, that's what she is," Annie said. "I can't tell you the times we've invited her to village functions, and to the WI, too. But she's always turned us down, looking as if she has a bad smell under her nose." Annie looked across the table. "There's no place for snooty behaviour like that in a war, is there? We all have to pull together."

Conversation soon turned to news about the war and various sons and husbands who were off fighting. It didn't seem that any of the news was good. Annie reported that she hadn't heard anything from Jack for a while. It seemed he was on an Atlantic convoy.

"And where's your husband, Mrs Banks?" a woman across the table asked her.

"Off fighting somewhere," Josie said. "When he left, he thought he was being sent to North Africa . . ."

"That's where they're all being sent these days, isn't it?" another woman chimed in.

"But I only had one letter before my house was bombed, and I couldn't read most of it. It was all blacked out by the censor. Now he won't know where to find me until he gets the letter I sent him."

"I don't know why they think they have to fight Jerry in Africa," someone said. "What's wrong with defending our own island, I want to know. What good would it be if they beat Jerry in blooming Africa and come home to find he's on their doorstep?"

There were nods of agreement.

Nan Badger got up and returned with a cup of tea and a biscuit for herself and Josie.

"So how are the girls settling in, then?" Josie asked.

Nan smiled. "They are doing well, apart from Lottie getting some nasty comments at school. One of them from a teacher, too. Alf said he'd go to that school and have a word with them, but Lottie didn't want to make a scene. I can understand that. She's such a quiet, studious little thing. Goes up with her homework and hardly says a word. On the other hand, the little one, Dorothy—well, she doesn't stop talking. Such a change from when she first came here. She was worried about her mum in hospital, you know. And so afraid of everything, including our dog. But Sheila's been a big help. A lovely girl, and after what she's been through, too."

"What was that? Bombing, you mean?"

Nan moved closer. "Her mum sent her to be evacuated because she's got a new boyfriend and didn't want Sheila around. She told me that. She said her mum started not liking her when she wasn't a pretty little girl anymore."

"That's terrible."

"It is. So I'm glad I can give her a warm home here for a while. And the little one, too. We haven't had any news about the mum for a week now. I hope she's doing all right. The dad's off in the army somewhere like your man."

Josie dipped her rich tea biscuit into the insipid

217

mug of tea. Clearly they were trying to make tea rations stretch for as long as possible.

"My Alf was planning to come to see you tomorrow," Nan said. "You'll be home, will you?"

Josie got the feeling that the whole village knew she had been out in a car with an airman earlier that week. But Nan's voice did not sound judgemental.

"Yes, I'll be there," she said. "I'm looking forward to it. All those good garden beds just sitting there. I can't wait to get my hands on them."

Nan nodded. "It will be hard work," she said, "but good to be in the fresh air and even better when you can eat your own veggies. Alf's got all sorts of seeds for you and some good compost."

Josie gave an embarrassed grin. "He'll have to be patient with me, I'm afraid. I've never had a garden all my life. I was born and raised in the middle of London."

Nan shook her head, commiserating. "I don't think I could stand living in a city, not seeing open fields around me."

"To tell the truth, I was a bit scared when I first came here—all this openness. I felt—well—exposed. But now I'm getting used to it."

"You won't want to go back to the city when your husband comes home," Annie Adams said. She was intending it as a joke, but to Josie it felt like a punch in the stomach. Because she realized that she didn't want to go back to the city with Stan.

Alf Badger came over the next afternoon. Josie took him out to show him the garden. He showed her which bed she should start on first. He looked at the remnants of foliage, now blackened by the frost. "I reckon this might have been some curly kale, growing on its own," he said, "but I'd dig it all out, if I was you. Start afresh. Do you have garden tools handy?"

"There must be tools in the shed," Josie said, "but I think it's locked. I'll have to ask Kathleen."

Kathleen was not in the kitchen but having an after-meal snooze. Josie went into the little hallway and tapped on her door. Kathleen appeared, red-faced and dishevelled. "Jesus, Mary and Joseph," she said. "What do you mean by disturbing me all the time? Didn't I tell you not to come to my private part of the house?"

"I'm sorry, but how else would I be able to ask you for the key to the shed?" Josie said. "Alf Badger is here, and he's going to show me how to dig the vegetable beds, so I'll need garden tools."

Kathleen sighed. "No peace for the wicked, I suppose. Well, I'd better come and get the tools for you, hadn't I?"

"I can get them myself. Just give me the key."

Kathleen shook her head. "No, I promised the mistress that this key never leaves my hands," she said. She stomped through to the kitchen and put on her garden boots before going down to the shed. Josie followed. Kathleen opened the door and went inside.

"You see," she called back. "It's a mess in here. You'd never find a thing. But here's a spade and a fork. They should keep you going for now, and I'll try to straighten things out a bit so you can find what you need."

"You don't have to do that now," Josie said. "I can help later."

"No, it's up to me to oversee anything to do with this house," Kathleen said. "You're just a temporary guest here, aren't you? I'm the one who's accountable."

Josie carried the big spade and fork back to Alf, wondering why Kathleen was so possessive about everything. From what she had seen, the shed didn't look too disorganized. She could see plant pots on a wooden bench, bags of what might be fertilizer and plenty of cobwebs in the window. She wondered if Kathleen still had it in her head that Josie might want to steal something, but frankly she couldn't see anything worth stealing.

Alf started digging, breaking up clods of earth with the fork and then turning the dirt over with the spade. "Good soil you've got here, my love," he said. "And when we've added some compost,

I reckon this garden will do you proud when you get it going again."

"Let's not go for too much to start with," Josie said, as she watched him working his way down the bed, turning the soil over with apparent ease for a man of his age. "I still probably won't be able to use this arm properly for a while yet."

"Very well, my love," Alf said. "We'll just get some potatoes and onions in today, then, shall we? And you can start your seeds indoors, on a bit of flannel, then move them to pots in the shed and finally into the garden bed."

"Start them on flannel?" A memory flashed into Josie's head. She had grown something once! Someone had once given her some mustard and cress seed, and they had sprouted on a wet cloth. The childhood memory made her smile. She recalled the satisfaction when the family had eaten what she had grown.

"Piece of damp flannel. Put another piece on top to start with, and that should get them going," he said. Then he produced some sprouting potatoes from a bag, dug a trench and positioned them before covering everything with soil mixed with compost. Then he planted the onions. "They should do you all right," he said. "And once you get the hang of it, you can have this whole place producing food."

"Can I make you a cup of tea in the kitchen?" Josie said. "I made some scones."

"Thank you kindly, but I promised Nan I'd be back to help her get in the washing. Her old back isn't as good as it once was. Neither is mine, for that matter."

Josie felt a flash of guilt that she had given him extra work with his bad back. "Give her my best regards, won't you? And the girls."

He smiled. "I will and all. I reckon those little girls have given her a new lease on life. Our own daughter died when she was small, from complications of the measles. But these little girls—well, I reckon it's going to break her heart when they have to go back to London."

CHAPTER 20

Josie was walking with Alf around the house when they heard a shout. "I say. Hello there! We've come to pay you a visit." And the young airman, Charlie, was opening the front gate. Two more airmen stood outside the gate, looking uneasy.

"Looks like you've got company," Alf said.

"Oh yes." Josie waved to Charlie. "That's the airman I took in for a cup of tea on Sunday. He looked a bit homesick."

"I reckon they all are," Alf agreed. "I'll leave you to get on with it, then. Ta ta."

"Thanks, Alf. You're a real pal," Josie said. "You don't know how much I appreciate this."

The airman stood aside for Alf to walk up the path. "Is it a bad time?" he asked.

"Not at all," Josie said. "We just finished putting spuds in the garden, and I'm about to make a cup of tea anyway. Come around the back."

"I've brought some friends," Charlie said. "I hope that's all right. Only I told them about your kitchen and how nice it was, and they wanted to come along."

"Of course," Josie said, pushing aside Miss Harcourt's comments about entertaining strangers.

"And you're in luck. We got some flour, and I made scones."

"Wonderful." He looked as if she had given him a present. He turned and beckoned the other men. "It's all right, chaps. Come on in."

They came forward eagerly now. "Let me make the introductions. This is my good friend Dickie Dennison, and this is JJ. Don't ask me to give you the rest of his name because none of us can pronounce it. He's Polish, you see. Polish air force and managed to get out in time. He's a bona fide pilot. Flew his plane out over Germany. But he deigns to speak to us plebs, who just do the dirty work."

"How do you do, madam?" JJ said in stilted English.

"Nice to meet you, boys. Come inside, but make sure you wipe your feet. The housekeeper looks for things to criticize."

They followed her in through the back door, wiping their feet meticulously on the doormat.

"See," Charlie said. "What did I tell you, Dickie? Just like our kitchen at home, isn't it?" He looked up at Josie. "Dickie and I were at school together. We joined up together, too. Both wanted to be pilots, but he's colour-blind, and I failed the maths exam. So we're humble ground crew."

"You're doing your bit," Josie said. "Those planes wouldn't fly if you didn't take care of them, would they?"

"I suppose you're right if you put it that way," Charlie said.

"Well, take a load off your feet," Josie said. "The kettle should boil soon." She bustled about the kitchen, then put a scone in front of each of them. "Go easy on the marge and the jam," she said. "Luckily the old cook bottled a lot of it before the war, but we have to make it last."

"Jolly good show," Dickie said. "Scones. What a treat. Our cook at home used to make them."

"I do not know scones," JJ said. He watched the others cut theirs in half, then spread them with margarine and jam.

"Of course, they should have clotted cream," Charlie said. "That's how they are served where I come from."

"A local farmer has promised me some cream," Josie said. "Next time you come, maybe we can try it that way."

"Of course, it won't be proper Devonshire cream," Charlie said with a grin to Dickie.

"Devonshire cream?" Dickie snorted. "Only second best, of course. Now I come from Cornwall, where there is the real clotted cream."

Josie sensed the friendly rivalry. Frankly, she had no idea what clotted cream was.

JJ was busy devouring his scone. "This I like very much," he said. "I think English baking is good. Just not in our mess."

"Is the food bad?"

"Pretty bad." Dickie nodded in agreement. "Isn't it everywhere these days? Lots of stews with vegetables but no meat, and stodgy meat puddings with only scraps of meat. Or dreadful dried-out cod. And you sit amongst all those men, who are trying to shovel down as much as possible as quickly as possible."

"And you dream about sitting around the dinner table at home, don't you?" Charlie said quietly. "No rush. Plenty of time to talk over the day and laugh about insignificant things."

The other two airmen nodded and fell silent.

"And you're so far from your home, JJ," Josie said. "How long since you left?"

"Just over a year now," JJ said. "I do not receive letters from my parents. I do not know if they are still alive. Things are bad in Warsaw, I know. I just wish I could have got them out, too, but it was impossible."

"Cheer up, JJ," Dickie said, giving the slim blond man a slap on the back. "You've got us now."

"Thanks a lot," JJ replied, giving a mock frown. "You are good company, but you cannot cook like my mother. I'd give anything for her piroshki and plum dumplings." He corrected himself and turned hastily to Josie. "But this tastes very good, ma'am," he said.

"It really does," Dickie said. "As good as our cook makes at home. Well done, Mrs Banks."

They looked up as a door opened and Kathleen came in. "What's this?" She looked from one to the other, glaring at the young men. "Is my kitchen going to be full of interlopers every time I take ten minutes to myself?"

"This is the same young man who visited the other day, Kathleen. Don't you remember?" Josie said. "And two of his friends." She nodded to the airmen. "This one is a Polish pilot, far from home."

"I thought I heard a foreign voice," Kathleen said. "Polish, eh? How do we know he's not German?"

"Mainly because he flies bombing missions over Germany every night," Charlie said, with a cheeky grin.

"You might have asked me before you brought them in," Kathleen said.

"But you told me not to disturb you when you were taking a rest," Josie said sweetly. "And I'm sharing the scones I made with my flour ration. Why don't you help yourself to one?"

"I'm not hungry, thank you," Kathleen replied stiffly. "And what have you done with the mistress's garden tools?"

"I would have put them back in the shed, but you locked it again," Josie replied. "We could get an extra key cut for me if you're afraid of things getting stolen."

She could see that she had stumped Kathleen

there. Before she could reply, Dickie asked her, "You're Irish, are you?"

"I am. What about it?" She gave him a defiant stare.

"We've got a chap in our squad who is Irish, too. Northern Irish, of course. Or else he'd be on the other side." He grinned. "We'll bring him over next time we come. I bet he'd love to talk to a person from home. O'Brien is his name. Patrick, of course. Aren't all the men in Ireland called Patrick?"

"They are not," Kathleen said huffily. "We have our share of Michaels and Brendans and Brians and Georges, just like everybody else. But it's true that families do honour the blessed saint quite a lot. The Catholic families, that is. Not the heathen Protestants."

"Ah, you see, we have much in common," JJ said. "I, too, am a Catholic and stationed amongst many heathens. We do not even have a Mass every Sunday, only when a local priest can visit us. They do not think it important—there are very few Catholics amongst us."

"I can't go to Mass at all at the moment," Kathleen said. "The nearest church is in Holbeach, and there's no Sunday bus service now. It's inhuman, that's what it is. The English heathen Protestants don't care one bit that people like me can't practice their faith on Sundays."

"You could get a bicycle and cycle into

Holbeach," Charlie said cheerfully. "It's only about five miles, isn't it?"

"And five miles on a bicycle in the snow does not seem like much to you? But then you're not an old woman of fifty, are you?" She crossed the kitchen and started banging around pans on the stove, her back to them.

Charlie got to his feet. "I think we should probably be going," he said. The other men rose, too.

"Thank you so much, Mrs Banks," Dickie said. "It was a rare treat. If we spill the beans to the rest of the chaps that there is somewhere nearby where they can get a homemade scone and a cup of tea, I reckon they will be lining up at your gate."

Again Miss Harcourt's haughty face flashed into Josie's mind. "I don't think the lady who owns this house would be thrilled about that," she said. "She was quite shirty that I'd given Charlie here a cup of tea."

"We won't tell them," Charlie said. "It will remain our secret."

"So where do you blokes go if you get a few hours off?" Josie asked.

Dickie shook his head. "It's almost impossible to get into the nearest town unless you've a motor car, which none of us has. We've tried walking to the pub in this village, but the landlord made it clear he doesn't like sharing his beer allocation with us. So it's the bar in the mess hall, really. And usually we're on duty in the evenings because flights go out at night. So not much time for recreation apart from ping-pong or darts during the day."

They thanked Josie again and bid a polite farewell to Kathleen, who didn't reply. Josie closed the door behind them. A strange, unsettling thought was crystallizing in her head. She tiptoed across the front hall and found the door to the unused sitting room half open. She peered inside. Miss Harcourt was standing at the piano, its dust sheet turned back, running her hand over the polished black wood. She looked up and started with a guilty expression when she sensed Josie standing in the doorway.

"What do you want?" she demanded.

"I'm sorry. I didn't mean to startle you," Josie said. "Do you play the piano?"

"I used to," Miss Harcourt said, "but we don't have the coal to heat this room as well as the other sitting room, and one cannot play with cold fingers."

"Maybe in the summer you can be playing again," Josie said.

Miss Harcourt stared at her again, as if Josie were a creature from a new and different species whose behaviour was foreign to her. "What was it you wanted?" she asked. "Or were you just snooping on me?"

"Oh no, Miss Harcourt. I came to find you," Josie said. "I wonder if we could have a little chat."

"Very well," Miss Harcourt said. "Come into the other room, by the fire."

Josie let her lead the way and get herself settled in her favourite chair before Josie perched on the edge of the chair opposite.

"Well?" Miss Harcourt said, her voice sharp and suspicious.

"I understand that you're hard up these days," Josie said. "Short of cash."

"Isn't everybody?" Miss Harcourt snapped. "Apart from those dreadful men who deal in the black market. They are certainly profiting."

"I have a suggestion," Josie said. "That young airman came to visit again this afternoon. He brought two friends with him, and they were saying how they are stuck there, on the aerodrome, because it's too far to the nearest village. I gave them each a scone I had baked, and they really appreciated it. So I started thinking . . . You have all these rooms you don't use. You have all this lovely china you don't use. Why don't we turn that room with the piano into a little café? We'll serve them tea and a cake maybe, and it will feel like home for a while. And they'd pay us, and that would let us get more coal and the supplies you need."

There was a silence.

"Absolutely not!" Miss Harcourt finally spat out the words. "How dare you come here—foisted on me whether I wanted it or not—and tell me how to run my own house? As if I'd want common airmen in my drawing room, damaging my furniture, breaking my china. I thought I made it very clear that I do not wish to mix with outsiders, and certainly not riff-raff in uniform."

"You wouldn't have to mix with them if you didn't want to," Josie said. "I'm prepared to do all the work—to make the room look nice and clean, set up the tables, bake the food."

"Are you extremely stupid or just obstinate?" Miss Harcourt shouted. "I said no, and that is that. Do not mention this again." She was waving her arms at Josie. "And now that your shoulder seems to have healed enough to be baking food for strange men, I suggest that you find yourself more suitable accommodation, and the sooner the better."

Josie stood up. "What exactly are you gaining by shutting yourself away?" she demanded, her own voice rising now. "You're clearly not happy. You've got no friends. Nobody to cheer you up when you're feeling depressed. You've got all these lovely things—things I'd give my eye teeth for—and you keep them locked up, gathering dust, because you're not willing to share them."

"That's enough. Please go now," Miss Harcourt said.

"If you'd only give it a try, you might find that having young people in your home would make you feel alive again, rather than withering away like a cold old statue with no heart."

"I said go!" Miss Harcourt also rose to her feet. "I want you out of here by tomorrow morning. I shall be getting in touch with that woman who brought you here immediately. I will not tolerate this impudence a moment longer. You come here, out of the gutters of London, with the gall to tell me how to run my life. Well, for your information, I am perfectly content with my lot in life. I do not need anybody. Now, get out of my sight before I—"

Suddenly she clutched at her chest, gave a gasp and collapsed on to the chair.

CHAPTER 21

"Kathleen!" Josie yelled. "Kathleen, come here quick! The mistress has been taken ill."

Kathleen came running. "Holy Mother of God," she exclaimed. "What happened?"

"She was shouting at me, and suddenly she clutched her chest and collapsed."

"It's her heart. The doctor warned her." Kathleen crossed the room and knelt beside Miss Harcourt.

"We should get her up to bed," Josie suggested. Her own heart was thumping so wildly that she almost put her hand to her own chest.

"No, don't move her!" Kathleen shouted. "Telephone for the doctor."

"Shouldn't we call for an ambulance?"

"No. She hates hospitals. She wouldn't go."

"I'll stay with her, you telephone," Josie said.

Kathleen shook her head. "I've never used that contraption in my life, and I'm not about to start now. I wouldn't know how."

"Where is it?" Josie asked, not taking her eyes from Miss Harcourt, whose head was lolling back, deathly pale. She didn't recall seeing a telephone in the house.

"In her study."

"Study? Where's that?"

"Passage next to the library, at the back of the house," Kathleen shouted. "Hurry! Go now."

"What's the doctor's name?"

"Packer. Dr Packer!" Kathleen screamed the words. "Now for the love of God . . ."

Miss Harcourt stirred. "What's all this commotion?" she asked feebly. "What's going on?"

"You fainted. Josie's calling for the doctor," Kathleen said, still kneeling beside her and patting her hand. "Don't worry. I'll stay with you."

Josie didn't wait another second. She ran down the hall and found the small corridor behind the library. It ran along the back of the house and ended in a door. Josie opened it and saw the desk, the shelves and the telephone. She had hardly ever used one in her own life, but she'd seen one in the pictures when someone had to call the police. She picked up the receiver and pressed the little pad.

"Operator," said the voice. "What number, please?"

"I need a doctor right away." Josie could hardly get the words out. "Dr Packer, I think. I don't know the number."

"What is the address?"

"I don't know the street address. It's in a village. Sutton St Giles, I believe, and I need him to come to the big house just on the outskirts. A lady just had a heart attack. Miss Harcourt's her name. Please hurry."

"And who are you?"

"I'm just staying here, temporary like. I'm Mrs Banks."

"Don't worry, Mrs Banks. I'll find Dr Packer for you. And if he's out, I'll send for the ambulance."

Josie hung up, her hand trembling. She was about to leave when she saw a photograph on the desk, in a black frame. It was of a young, good-looking man, staring out at the world with hopeful eyes. So Miss Harcourt had had a sweetheart years ago! She returned to the sitting room. Miss Harcourt was still sitting, eyes closed, Kathleen holding her hand.

"He'll be coming soon," Josie said. "Shall I get her a glass of water?" She hurried through to the kitchen, wanting to keep busy and not think. She brought back the glass and placed it at Miss Harcourt's lips. Miss Harcourt took a sip, choked, coughed and murmured, "What are you trying to do? Leave me alone."

"The doctor is on his way," Josie said, praying that this was true. It seemed an eternity while they waited. All Josie could think was that she was responsible for this. She had caused Miss Harcourt to lose her temper and thus put a strain on the lady's heart. *I should have minded my own business,* she thought. *Not wanted to help. Just got better and moved on, like they expected.* What if she died? What would happen to the house? What would Kathleen do?

And she was surprised at the pang of regret she felt that she would have to move on and find another place to stay.

"Here's the doctor now." Kathleen jumped up and rushed to the front door. An aged Daimler motor car had drawn up outside, and an older man with a balding head and heavy rimmed glasses got out. Kathleen brought him into the room. "I said we shouldn't move her. It must be her heart."

"Is she conscious?" the doctor asked, turning to Josie.

"She spoke a few times," Josie said. "But she's sort of only half there."

"So what happened?" He opened his black bag as he spoke, bringing out a stethoscope.

"I was talking to her," Josie said. "She got upset and started yelling at me. Then suddenly she put her hand to her heart and just collapsed."

"Silly woman," he said, opening buttons on Miss Harcourt's front to access her heart. "I've warned her about her heart condition and that she shouldn't get excited."

"What are you doing?" Miss Harcourt rallied enough to slap his hand.

"It's Dr Packer. I'm listening to your heart." Miss Harcourt faded into silence again as the doctor took her pulse. He withdrew the stethoscope. "I suspect a minor heart attack, I'm afraid. She should probably be in hospital, but knowing how she feels about those, she'd probably recover just as quickly at home. Is there a man-servant in the house?"

"No, just us two," Kathleen said.

"Then maybe you two ladies can help me move her up to her bedroom. Easy now. I expect she'll be rather heavy."

"I resent that," said the ghost of a whisper.

They staggered up the stairs with her, Josie trying not to put too much weight on her broken collarbone. Down the long hallway and into the bedroom at the front of the house. It was a big room with blue velvet curtains at the windows and a matching blue silk eiderdown on the bed. The wardrobe, chest of drawers and dressing table were cherry wood, and the wallpaper was swags of blue flowers, tied with pink ribbons. There was a small wicker chair in one window, adorned with silk cushions. A pretty room, very much a girl's room, and Josie wondered if it had originally been designed for Miss Harcourt as a young girl. They deposited her on the bed.

"Can you get her undressed for me?" the doctor asked.

Kathleen retrieved a nightgown from under the pillow, and between them, they removed her dress and petticoat. Josie was not surprised to see that she still wore stays but felt intensely embarrassed to be seeing Miss Harcourt in this state.

"Perhaps I should go," she said. "She wouldn't want me here to see her like this."

The doctor nodded. "This lady can loosen her stays, then, and put her into a nightgown. I'll have some medicine made up. Do you have a means of going into Holbeach to fetch it?"

"No, we don't," Kathleen said. "She got rid of the motor car before the war. And there's only a bus into Spalding now, and then only twice a day."

"Then I'll have to see if someone can deliver it for me," Dr Packer said. "But in the meantime, I want her lying flat on her back. No pillows, understand. And nothing to eat or drink for the time being except sips of water. She is not to get up. You are to insist on that." He unwound his stethoscope and listened to her heart again, shaking his head as if he didn't like what he heard. "I'm afraid there has been permanent damage done to the heart this time," he said. "The lady will need the most solicitous of care. Only invalid food when she is able to take nourishment. Junket, jelly, broth. And she should not be moved. I'll leave you my card so that you have my telephone number at hand. And I'll arrange for the medicine to arrive as soon as possible."

He stuffed the stethoscope back into his bag and gave them a curt nod. "I can see myself out," he said. "One of you should stay with her, probably through the first night."

Kathleen gave Josie a despairing look. "This is

terrible," she said. "The poor, dear woman. Do you think she's going to die?"

Josie put her finger to her lips. "She may be awake enough to hear us," she whispered. She took Kathleen's arm and drew her outside the door. "Listen," she said. "We were in the midst of an argument when she collapsed. She told me to leave immediately. Now I don't know what to do. If she wakes up and finds me here, might that not bring on another heart attack?"

"But then, I don't want to be left in the house alone with her," Kathleen said. "And I can't be on my feet for twenty-four hours."

"Of course you can't," Josie said. "How about you stay and look after her, and I'll take care of the kitchen. That way she won't have to see me when she comes to."

"That's a good idea," Kathleen said. "We've some of that stew left for our dinner tonight."

"I'll go into the village first thing tomorrow morning and see if I can get some good, nourishing food for her," Josie said. "And I'll go and make us a fresh cup of tea. I reckon we both need one for shock, don't you?"

Kathleen managed a weak smile.

After she had taken up the cup of tea, Josie tried to keep herself busy. She swept the kitchen floor, cleaned the sink and put away the items on the draining board. Anything rather than let the guilt overwhelm her. She knew she'd had the best intentions. She had wanted to help, she told herself. But a small voice whispered that she had wanted to help herself. She had wanted to recreate her dream of the tea shop, with the lovely china and the smiling customers, making her feel she was in a place where she was appreciated, where she belonged.

She was just checking the larder to see if there was anything she could use to make invalid food for Miss Harcourt when there was a rap on the front door. She went to it to find Dr Goldsmith standing there.

"Good evening, Mrs Banks," he said. "I have brought medicine from Dr Packer."

"That's very good of you," she said.

"I happened to be in the chemist's having a prescription made up when he came in. Since I had to pass this way, I volunteered."

"Thank you." Josie took the mixture. "Would you like to come in?" she asked. "I could make you a cup of tea?"

"It would be churlish to refuse, would it not?" He smiled. "Actually, I am grateful. I have had a long day in the operating theatre. Many hours of standing."

"I can't take you into the sitting room, I'm afraid," Josie said "It's not my house. But the kitchen is warm." She led him through and sat him at the table, then put a plate and the tin containing the scones in front of him.

"My, what a treat," he said, taking one. "You baked these?"

"I did. We just happened to have enough flour for a change."

"I do not use my entire allowance," he said. "I eat my main meal at the hospital, and as I told you, I am no cook. If I brought you some flour and lard, maybe you could make one or two extra of these next time you bake?"

"I'll be happy to," Josie said, "if I'm here long enough."

"You are leaving?"

Josie turned away, trying to hide the conflicting emotions going through her. "I'm afraid so. Miss Harcourt was very angry with me before she fell ill, and she ordered me to leave. I would have gone already, but Kathleen can't look after the mistress and the house by herself, so I'm staying to help out."

"Why is Miss Harcourt so anxious to get rid of you?" he asked gently.

"I'm afraid I said some things that must have touched a nerve," Josie said. "I suggested that we might use her lovely china and her unused room to open a little tea shop. Somewhere where the RAF men could come and get the feel of home." She gave an apologetic sigh. "Miss Harcourt flew into a rage when I told her the truth—that she was shutting herself away and punishing herself."

"People do not like to hear the truth," he

agreed. "So she had a coronary event, so I hear."

"Yes, a heart attack. She's lying upstairs now, and Kathleen's with her. We're afraid she might die."

"I cannot go up and see her because she is not my patient," he said, "but I will give you my telephone number in case you need a doctor in a hurry during the night."

"That is very kind of you," Josie said. "Do you think it's likely, then, that she'll die tonight?"

"I cannot tell you. Some people have major heart attacks and survive, others have what seem like minor ones that are precursors to the final event."

"I see." Josie shuddered.

"You should not blame yourself," he said gently.

"Yes, I should." She swallowed back a sob. "I had no right to tell her how to live her life. The tea shop just seemed such a good idea, but I should have considered her feelings first."

Dr Goldsmith reached across and covered her hand with his own. "Do not distress yourself, my dear lady. You are a kind person. Your intentions were good. Not everything we do turns out satisfactorily. During the last war, I had to assist in many operations that resulted in the death of the patient. I was only in my last year of medical school, with no real experience, but I had to make many rapid decisions. I could never tell whether the patient would have died anyway or whether my decision to do surgery was not the best idea."

She noticed that his hand still covered hers. She withdrew it awkwardly.

"So when should she be given the medicine?" she asked, focusing on the bottle.

"One teaspoonful as soon as she is awake. The instructions are on the bottle."

"Thank you. As soon as you've gone, I'll go up and see to her," she said.

He stood up. "Would you like me to stay the night?" he asked. "In case a second heart attack follows?"

"It's very kind of you . . ." She hesitated, but then remembered his hand on hers. Had he meant anything by it, or was it just a friendly gesture? "But you need your own sleep if you are at the hospital all day. You said you'd give me your telephone number, and you are close by if we need you."

"Very good." He gave a little Germanic bow. "In that case, I will take my leave of you, Mrs Banks. I wish you all the best."

Josie followed him to the front door, where he turned back. "If you are required to leave this house, you could have a place with me. I could use a housekeeper, one who can cook, so it would suit us both."

Now she was really confused, not sure what he really wanted. Was it someone to cook for him or something more? She chose the former. He was an educated man and obviously saw her as a domestic servant.

"That's a very kind offer, Doctor," she said, "but I'm afraid my husband would not think kindly of my moving into a house with a single man."

He gave an embarrassed little smile. "Yes, I might feel the same way as your husband," he agreed. "I bid you adieu, Mrs Banks."

And he was gone.

CHAPTER 22

Kathleen stayed with Miss Harcourt through-out the night. Josie found her asleep in the chair by the window when she brought up tea in the morning. She hadn't slept much herself, waiting to be summoned if necessary. Miss Harcourt lay asleep, looking quite peaceful. For a moment, Josie wondered if she had died, but then she saw the rise and fall of the woman's chest beneath the bed sheet.

As soon as the shops were open, Josie walked into the village, where she managed to secure some beef bones from the butcher and two eggs from the shop, as well as spinach, an onion and a packet of Robertson's jelly. The woman in the shop went as far as wishing Miss Har-court all the best for a speedy recovery. The news had obviously spread quickly—when Josie was in the middle of making the beef tea, Rose Finch and Annie Adams arrived at the back door.

"We heard what happened," Rose said. "I've brought you round some cream and a couple of eggs. She'll need building up, and maybe you can make her a rice pudding or a custard."

"That's very kind of you," Josie said. "Will you come in?"

Rose looked around hesitantly. "Oh, I don't think . . . ," she said. "Where is Kathleen?"

"She's sitting up with Miss Harcourt. I'm taking over the cooking for her."

"Well, in that case, I don't mind stopping for a few minutes," Annie said. She came up the steps. "I don't think I've been in this room for years," she said. "Nothing changes much, does it? Just like it's always looked."

Josie offered them a scone and a cup of tea.

"Someone's a good baker." Rose nodded with approval. "Nice, light touch."

"I used to work in a tea shop," Josie said. "I made scones all the time there."

Rose took a sip of tea. "So her bad temper finally got the better of her, did it?" she asked. "My Tom always said that she'd come to a bad end. When you have all those hurtful thoughts, it has to come out some way or another, doesn't it?"

"I suppose it does," Josie agreed.

Rose stood up and gestured to Annie. "Well, we won't keep you. I see you've got a broth going on the stove. You're making beef tea for her, are you?"

"I am," Josie agreed.

"That will do her good. I'll stop by again to see how you're all doing." Rose let herself out of the back door, with Annie following. "Come to the sewing circle on Thursday. Do you good to get away for a bit."

Josie didn't have the heart to tell her she might be gone by Thursday.

Dr Packer stopped by in the afternoon and declared the patient was making good progress. "She told me to go away and leave her alone," he said, chuckling. "I think she may be back to her old self soon."

Josie suggested that she'd take over from Kathleen that night so that Kathleen could get some proper sleep. She sat in the chair with a rug over her and dozed from time to time. She awoke to find it still dark outside. The bedside lamp was on, its pink shade bathing the room in soft light and shadow. Josie tiptoed over to look at Miss Harcourt. She was standing beside the bed when the woman opened her eyes. Josie stepped back hastily, terrified that the sight of her might upset Miss Harcourt again.

"Is there anything I can get you?" Josie whispered. "I could warm a little beef tea or some Benger's Food?"

"Just a sip of water, thank you," Miss Harcourt replied.

Josie helped her to sit up and lifted the glass to her lips. Miss Harcourt took a drink, then nodded for Josie to put the glass down. Josie laid her back and replaced the covers.

"Miss Harcourt," she said, "I want to tell you I'm very sorry for what happened. It was my fault. I was quite wrong to tell you what you

248

should be doing with your own house. I will leave as soon as Kathleen can handle things on her own."

She started to tiptoe away.

"Mrs Banks," Miss Harcourt called after her. Josie turned back, eyeing the old woman cautiously.

"I've had some time to think while I've been lying here. You weren't wrong in what you said. What is the point of having nice things if I don't use them? Or share them? When I die, this house will go to a charity for widows of the Indian army. It will all be auctioned off and probably go for pennies." She took a deep breath and then gave a sigh. "A complete waste, you would say." Another long pause. Josie said nothing. "So, I would be willing to give this idea of yours a try. Nothing too extreme, you understand. I don't want the world coming in here. But a couple of young men—well, that might be acceptable. And not my best china. Not my Royal Worcester or Wedgwood, you understand."

Josie said, "We could use your kitchen china. It's nice enough. But I should serve you your meals on the Royal Worcester. At least let you enjoy your own things."

"That is hardly necessary when I eat alone."

"No reason not to enjoy eating alone, is there?" Josie said. "We've all got to do something to cheer ourselves up these days. Everything I had is buried in a ruin, all bulldozed away by now, I suppose. But I'm not about to give up."

"You have a formidable spirit, Mrs Banks. I compliment you. But then, you are still young. You can still have hope." Another long pause. "So you have my permission to give this scheme of yours a try," she added. "But I wonder how you would accomplish it. Where would the necessary groceries come from? The extra flour and fat and tea and sugar?"

"I'm hoping the airmen can share their rations with us or maybe find us some extra ingredients at the base," she said. "When the garden gets going, I may be able to trade veggies for flour or fat."

"You plan to take care of a garden as well as this tea shop of yours?"

"I've never been afraid of hard work," Josie said. "When I was fourteen, my mum died, and I had to look after six younger brothers and sisters. There was a new baby, nappies to wash every day. Anything since then has seemed easy."

Miss Harcourt stared at her, long and hard. It felt as if she was looking into Josie's soul. Embarrassed now, Josie said, "I'll go down and warm you up some beef tea. Help you get back to sleep."

The next morning Josie got straight to work. She removed the dust sheets from the drawing room, polished the furniture and arranged it in groups—two armchairs around one small table, another table in front of a sofa. She decided to borrow a third table from Miss Harcourt's sitting room, where it had only held a Victorian glass dome of dried flowers. Now she could seat eight people, which seemed to be the maximum she should attempt at the moment.

She was in the middle of dragging furniture when Kathleen interrupted her. "What in heaven's name do you think you're doing?" she demanded.

"I'm setting up this room as a little café," she said.

"Jesus, Mary and Joseph! Have you taken leave of your senses, woman?" Kathleen's face had turned bright red. "What do you think the mistress will say when she finds out? Or are you convinced that she won't survive, and then you'll take over this house?"

"Calm down, Kathleen," Josie said. "The mistress has given her permission. We're going to have a little tearoom in here and see how it goes."

"Well, you're not touching my tea ration, for a start," Kathleen said.

"That's fine. We'll manage somehow," Josie said.

"So does that mean you won't be leaving now, I suppose?"

Josie looked at her angry face. "But I thought you wanted me to stay on and do the cooking and shopping for you?"

"Those things, maybe, and just for a while, too. But not have this house full of strangers, making more work."

"I promise you won't have more work," Josie said. "I'm going to handle this room and everything else. All right? You can still have your long naps after your lunch without being disturbed."

"I do not have long naps. Just a little lie-down, as any normal person would," Kathleen said. "I value my privacy." She tossed her head and stalked out of the room. Josie would have liked to ask her to help finish moving the table but decided to let her go. She was a strange person, Josie decided. At one moment friendly and even grateful, and the next wanting Josie out of the house. Was she fearful that Miss Harcourt might like Josie better? she wondered.

When she had the room arranged to her satisfaction, she thought about how she was going to manage to provide tea and scones or cakes. If Kathleen wasn't willing to share her tea ration, there would hardly be enough. And they were already running short on flour after her scones. She remembered that Dr Goldsmith had said he'd be willing to part with some of his rations in return for her baking him scones, but she hesitated to ask him. She still remembered that hand over hers and the uneasiness she felt. Foreigners were known to touch people more, she thought. Didn't Frenchmen kiss each other? And Italians embrace? But not Germans. They always seemed to be stiff and correct. But anyway, she'd wait until he came to visit again before she'd ask him. And in the meantime, she had to rustle up supplies from somewhere. She walked down to the village shop to see if she could persuade the shopkeeper to find a little extra flour or lard or tea.

"You've used up your ration for this month, love," the shopkeeper said.

Josie sighed. "I'll just have to wait a while, then, until the next coupons come due. We're going to open a little tea shop for the airmen," she said.

"Open a tea shop? Where would this be?"

"Miss Harcourt's house. One of her unused rooms."

"Never!" The woman burst out laughing. "That old woman? Letting people into her house?"

"She's agreed to give it a try," Josie said.

The woman shook her head. "Then you must have a magic touch, my dear. Nobody's been allowed inside that house for donkey's years. A tea shop, you say?"

"Nothing fancy. Just a place where they can get away from the base and enjoy a cup of tea and a biscuit." She paused. "Do you have any ideas where I might find extra flour? I don't suppose there is still a miller around here? I've seen a couple of windmills. They don't operate, do they?"

"I believe one is still working, over Long Sutton way," the shopkeeper said. "But not in the winter, of course. You need grain to grind, don't you?"

Josie gave an embarrassed grin. "Of course. Silly me. I've no idea how anything works in the country."

"So you're settling in nicely, then?" the woman asked. "I thought this was only a temporary arrangement for you."

"I'm staying put, at least for the time being. I'm getting the garden going again and now this tea shop. I imagine I'll be quite busy."

"That woman was lucky when you arrived on her doorstep," the shopkeeper said. "Tell you what I'll do. I know a couple of people around here who don't drink much tea and might be persuaded to part with a bit of their ration."

"That's very kind of you," Josie said.

"Well, we all have to do what we can for our boys in uniform, don't we?" The woman gave a wistful smile. "My own son's in the navy—part of the Arctic convoys. I don't hear from him for months, and I worry all the time."

"I haven't heard from my husband for quite a

while either," Josie said. "I've no idea where he is."

"We're all in the same boat, aren't we?" said the woman, and Josie nodded, privately battling with the thought that she hadn't missed Stan much recently. As she came out of the shop, she found herself thinking about Mike. He was another person who drank coffee rather than tea. And coffee wasn't rationed. Perhaps he could be persuaded to give her his tea ration. That would be an excuse to see him again. She wondered if she dared write to him. No, that would be too forward. If he wanted to see her again, he'd show up when he had a day free. The thought created a bubble of happiness inside her.

She saw nothing of Mike or the young airmen for the next week and decided not to push things ahead while Miss Harcourt recovered. The doctor was pleased with her progress. She was allowed to sit up in bed and have soup and egg custard. Then she was allowed to come downstairs and sit by the fire for a short while. The fire was another matter of concern for Josie's plans. She would need coal for the fireplace in the drawing room, and they only had a small supply. She mentioned this when she went to the WI sewing circle on Thursday afternoon. The ladies were intrigued to hear about her tea shop. None of them could believe that Miss Harcourt had agreed to such a thing, and they looked at Josie as if she were some kind of magician.

"I might know where you could get your hands on some extra flour or fat," one of the women said. Josie thought she was Mrs Hodgkins.

"Not your Johnny, Lil," another of them said hastily. "Mrs Banks doesn't want to find herself fined for dealing on the black market."

"He's not black market," Lil said. "He just happens to know people. He's a friendly sort."

"People who find things that fall off the backs of lorries," Annie Adams muttered, and the group chuckled.

"I don't think you'd say no to a bottle of Scotch or a pair of stockings, Annie," Lil said. "But no matter."

"I'm hoping the airmen themselves might be willing to share some of their rations," Josie said, sensing the tension. "Does the RAF keep their ration books?"

"Probably does," they agreed.

Josie was beginning to feel discouraged and thought that she might not mind getting the occasional packet of black-market tea from Johnny.

"I wouldn't mind coming myself for a cup of tea," Annie said as they cleared up, ready to go home. "I didn't get a proper chance to look around last time. And I could bake a few extra biscuits."

"And if you like, I'll bring you up a few biscuits or cakes when I next bake," Nan Badger said.

The vicar's wife waved her hands excitedly. "I've just had a thought. About your lack of coal. We had a tree blow down in last month's storm. If we could get someone to come and cut that up, we'd have plenty of firewood. I haven't managed to find any volunteers to do the job, but if you say you've got airmen coming to the house, maybe they'd be prepared to put in some muscle."

"That's a good idea," Josie said. "I'll have a little talk with them."

"Oh, isn't this exciting?" An elderly lady with wispy white hair nudged her friend. "Something new in the village."

Josie walked home feeling energized and hopeful again. The village women had embraced her vision and were trying to help.

CHAPTER 23

Josie had sat down to write to Charlie Wentworth, asking him to come and see her when he next had free time, when she looked out of the window and saw him bicycling towards the house with another man. She ran outside to greet him.

"Sorry to interrupt you," she said, "but there's something I'd like to discuss with you if you have a moment."

"We were coming to see you anyway," Charlie said. "I know it's early in the day, but we've only got the morning free. Night shifts for the rest of this week. But I've brought another chap with me—Patrick O'Brien. When I told him about your Irish lady, he wanted to meet her. Is she available?"

Josie took in the freckles, the sandy hair, the unmistakably Irish face. He gave her an embarrassed grin. "Sorry to disturb you, ma'am," he said. "If it's a bad time . . ."

"Not at all. She's here. Leave your bikes and come round the back," Josie said. She led them around the house to the back door.

"Kathleen," she called, "you've got a visitor."

"A visitor? Who in God's name would that be?" Kathleen wiped her hands on her apron as she came across the kitchen. She saw the two airmen in their uniforms, and a look of surprise crossed her face. She took an involuntary step backward.

"And what would airmen be wanting with the likes of me?" she demanded.

"This young man is Patrick O'Brien from Ireland," Josie said, gesturing towards him.

"He thought it would be nice to meet a country-woman of his, since he's stuck amongst the heathen English," Charlie added. "And I believe he's from your part of Ireland, too."

"Very nice to meet you, missus." Patrick came forward and held out his hand to her. She hesitated, then took it.

"I've no time for idle chat now," she said. "I'm in the midst of my morning chores."

"You don't have time to give him a cup of tea?" Josie demanded. "Come on, Kathleen, he's far from home and wants to talk to a friendly soul for a few minutes." She went across to the stove. "You sit down, and I'll get them a cup of tea."

"I really won't keep you if you're busy," Patrick said, also looking uncomfortable now, "but I just thought—what part of Ireland are you from?"

"I'm from Derry myself," Kathleen said. "Do you know it?"

"Do I know it?" He laughed. "I know it well enough. I was born and bred there. You no doubt know the Rossdowney Road?"

"I do indeed," she said. "I'm from not too far away myself."

"Then you might even have met my mother," he said, still chuckling.

"And what would her name be?"

"Rosie O'Brien now, but before she was married, she was Rosie Murphy."

"Isn't half the city called Murphy and the other half O'Brien?" Kathleen replied, not taking her eyes off the boy's face. "And I left at a young age. I came to work in England when I was just a girl, so all my family and friends were left behind long ago."

"Is that right?" he said. "Left all your family behind? That must have been a wrench for you."

Josie put cups of tea in front of them.

"While these two are talking, I wanted to have a word with you, Charlie," Josie said. "Can you step outside with me for a moment?"

"Of course." He opened the back door for her. As briefly as possible, she told him of her scheme.

"I think that's a brilliant idea, Mrs Banks," he said. "I imagine plenty of chaps would come for a homemade cake or scone—and a chance to sit in a normal living room."

"So you don't think they'd mind paying?" Josie asked. "I'll have to try and get my hands on extra rations, which won't be easy." Her mind went to Johnny Hodgkins, who might happen to know people who could get things . . .

"They won't mind paying," Charlie said. "We

get our weekly packet and have nothing to spend it on. The officers have to pay mess dues, but we lowly types get fed in the mess hall for nothing." He paused, thinking. "Let me see what I can do. I do know a few chaps who work in catering." And a wicked smile crossed his face.

"Nothing that would get you into trouble," Josie said hastily.

"Of course not," Charlie agreed and gave her a wink.

"And there's one more thing . . ." She went on to explain about the tree that had fallen in the vicarage garden. "If we could get someone to cut it up, we could have our share of the wood and that would warm the room until the weather improves."

"I'll see what I can do," he said. "Round up a few chaps who have a day off at the same time, if the vicar can provide the saws and axes."

They came back in to see Kathleen standing on the far side of the table. Patrick got to his feet as they entered. "I think we'd better go, Charlie, old man," he said. "This lady's got work to do. It was nice meeting you, Miss Kathleen. You won't mind if I pop in from time to time, will you?"

"I don't know what for," she said. "I told you I've got no connections with my old home any more."

"But you've got the accent and the sweet smile," he said.

"And you've still got the blarney," she replied. He went out laughing.

"I thought you'd be pleased to meet someone from home," Josie said, "but you couldn't wait for him to be gone."

"What would I have in common with a twenty-year-old boy?" Kathleen asked. "And what would he have in common with an old woman like me?"

"You're not old. Don't act as if life has passed you by," Josie said. "You may be due for some excitement yet."

"And maybe I won't welcome it," Kathleen snapped in reply. "Maybe all I want is a quiet life and to be left in peace. Ever since you came here, the place has been in turmoil. People coming and going, the mistress nearly on her deathbed. I can't wait for you to leave, if you want my opinion."

"You're a strange one, Kathleen," Josie said and walked out of the kitchen.

Charlie was as good as his word. He turned up with a group of fellow airmen to attack the vicar's tree. At the end of the day, there was a pile of logs stacked beside the shed at Miss Harcourt's. And as he was departing, he drew Josie aside. "My mate in catering says he can get his hands on extra tea for you. He's not sure about flour. That comes in big sacks. But maybe a stick or two of lard."

"Not if it's stealing, Charlie," Josie said.

"Oh, come on. They take our ration books, and all the good stuff goes to the officers," he said. "No one will miss a little here and there." He gave her a bright smile. "How soon do you think you can have your tearoom up and running?"

"Well, now that we've got wood, thanks to you, it can start as soon as I've enough supplies," Josie said.

When he had gone, she dared to write to Dr Goldsmith: *Dear Doctor, you mentioned that you don't use all your rations because you take your meals at the hospital. I wonder if you could spare some of your flour and tea rations? I'd like to do more baking and can keep you supplied. Sincerely, Josie Banks.*

Dr Goldsmith paid her a visit the next day. "I can give you these," he said and handed her a two-pound bag of flour and a stick of margarine. "The flour's been sitting in my pantry for ages, so I have the coupons to get more when you need it."

Josie took him into the drawing room and showed him the plans for the tea shop.

"What a splendid idea," he said. "Now if I want to sample your excellent baking, I shall not have to do it in the isolation of my own home, but in the friendly atmosphere of this place, perhaps with good conversation, *ja*?"

Josie watched him going, wondering if she was doing the right thing by encouraging him.

Later that week, a package arrived on her doorstep. It was a bag of tea, presumably from the RAF, by way of Charlie and his friends. It seemed at last she was ready to begin her undertaking.

CHAPTER 24

The first snowdrops were appearing on the grass verges when the tea shop was ready for its grand opening. Even Miss Harcourt seemed a little excited, although her expression was always hard to read. Her doctor had been pleased with her progress, and she was allowed to come downstairs for a larger part of the day now. She was assisted into the newly transformed drawing room and looked around with a nod of approval. "As long as you don't let them put their cups on my piano," she said as she seated herself in an armchair by the fire.

"I'll make sure. Maybe sometime you'll play for us," Josie suggested.

"Hmmpf." Miss Harcourt made a dismissive grunt. "It's been years since I've played in front of anybody. I haven't practiced in God knows how long."

"I'd like to hear you one day," Josie said.

"Knowing you, you'll take it up yourself and be performing at the Albert Hall before we know it," Miss Harcourt said.

Josie gave an embarrassed laugh. "I don't claim any skills, ma'am. Just plenty of energy and wanting to make things better."

"A proper little Florence Nightingale." Miss

Harcourt turned away and went over to the window. "I wonder if God is punishing me by sending me a saint."

"I'm certainly not a saint," Josie said. "And to tell you the truth I'm a bit surprised at myself. I never did anything like this before. First I was too busy at home, taking care of my siblings, then I was working ten hours a day in a factory, and after I married Stan, he wanted me home, not doing anything outside the house."

"And you let him boss you around?" She sounded a bit stunned.

Josie realized she was now surprised that this was true. "He had the job and the money, you see. I had nothing. He didn't want me working. And he was always jealous. He wouldn't have minded me visiting other women, but the neighbours on our street all had children and I didn't. That made me the outsider, and it was something Stan couldn't forgive."

"You wanted children, did you?"

"Of course. Doesn't every woman?" She realized as she said it that it was a tactless thing to say to an old spinster. But that photograph in her study—maybe Miss Harcourt had wanted to marry and have a family with that man, and for some reason it hadn't worked out. He was too old to have been killed in the Great War, but there were other reasons for a man to die. Or he had found someone he liked better. That happened, too.

At two thirty, the first guests arrived. Charlie with Dickie, his Polish friend and Irish Patrick.

"Sit where you like," Josie said. "This is Miss Harcourt, who owns this house, so please be very respectful of her property. And don't touch the piano." She indicated the older woman, who had remained sitting on the armchair by the fire.

"Oh, really?" Dickie said with a cheeky grin. "I was going to give us all a tune."

"I don't mind if you play it," Miss Harcourt said, giving him a warning stare. "Just don't put your cups on it."

"These men are from good families," Josie said. "They are used to drawing rooms like this."

"Not me," Patrick said. "I grew up in a tiny cottage with five brothers. Three of us shared a bed. Never enough to eat. That's how it is in Ireland."

"You're from Ireland?" Miss Harcourt asked. "What is an Irishman doing fighting for England? I thought you hated us."

"I'm from Northern Ireland, which the English still claim as their own," he said. "And the men there were called up at the same time as the English boys. I thought the air force sounded a bit better than being cannon fodder."

Josie left them and went through to the kitchen to make the tea. She brought out a Rockingham china teapot with matching cups and saucers.

Then she went back for a plate of scones and jam. "And you'll never guess," she said. "We have cream to go with them today. A neighbour called Mrs Finch persuaded her husband to let us have some from his dairy cows."

"I say, this really is civilized," Dickie said as he reached for the cream and started to spread it on his scone. "Of course, we got ribbed by the other chaps for going out to tea, rather than the pub, but there is only that one pub in the village, and the locals are downright hostile." He grinned. "Besides, it's a long way to stagger back after a few beers."

"So you don't think more men will want to come here?" Josie wondered whether her efforts were all for nothing.

"I think it's just bravado," Charlie said. "Wouldn't want to admit that they fancied a cup of tea rather than a beer."

But it still left Josie wondering if these were to be her only customers.

The concern proved to be true when nobody came the next day or the day after that. Josie was disappointed but also embarrassed. She had pushed her idea, against Miss Harcourt's will to begin with, and now she looked like a fool with scones too stale to eat and wasted resources. She used the stale scones to make a bread pudding and worried about making more and having to waste them. So she compromised and only made a small batch, in the hope that there would be customers. Then, on the third day, there was a knock at the door and two more-mature men, both pilots, stood there.

"I say, is this the place that's supposed to be some kind of café?" one of them asked. He wore the trademark waxed moustache of the RAF and had the supercilious smile of someone who thought a lot of himself.

"That's right," Josie said. "Won't you come in?"

She led them through to the drawing room and seated them at a table.

"How quaint," one commented to the other. "Almost like a set from an old-fashioned drawing room comedy. Any minute now the maid in the very short skirt will walk in with a feather duster . . ."

Josie was conscious that he was eyeing her.

"Are you the waitress?" he said.

"That's right," Josie said.

"I must say you don't look the part. You ought to smarten yourself up a bit, dear. Black dress—nicely above the knees—little white apron and one of those lacy caps?"

"There's a war on," Josie said, her face blank. "No black dresses or frilly aprons to be had, I'm sorry to say. I expect all the black material is now in blackout curtains."

"Just a little joke, what?" The man chuckled.

"Now be a dear and get us a pot of tea, and make it snappy, will you? We don't have all day."

"Oh, and cakes," the other added. "What sort of cakes do you have?"

"It's scones today," Josie said.

"No cakes? What kind of café is this, then? You're not going to do well if you can't offer cakes."

"It's not exactly a proper café. It's just something we set up so that your men can have a place to come and escape, that feels like home," Josie said. "And at this moment, we're giving up our own rations to do this."

"I say. Steady on," the man said. "We weren't to know. We just heard there was some kind of café, and we fancied a cup of tea that wasn't out of a NAAFI urn."

"I'll go and get your tea, sir." Josie walked out of the room, letting out a grunt of anger when she was well clear. She heard one of the men say to the other, "Go easy, Rogers. After all, we are in the middle of nowhere here. We can't expect a London level of service."

It hadn't occurred to her before that they might have to deal with rude customers. Then she realized that this was a classic case of upper-class attitude towards the lower classes. To them she was servant class, someone to be ordered around.

She brought the tea tray and set out the cups.

"I say. This is Rockingham china," one of the men commented in surprise.

"That's right. The mistress of this house is kind enough to supply her own china to you boys," Josie said.

"So you're the maid here, are you?" he asked.

"No, I'm not the maid. Do you want to try the scones?"

"I suppose so, if there's nothing else."

Josie brought them, putting the jam pot and the last of the cream beside them. The pilots started to eat.

"I say, these aren't half bad," one said. "My compliments to the cook."

Josie nodded and said nothing. They were about to leave when another pilot came in. The two men rose to their feet and saluted. Then Josie saw that the newcomer was Mike.

"Watson, Rogers." Mike nodded to them. "I wouldn't have put you two down as tea drinkers."

Josie was delighted to see they looked uncomfortable.

"Nor you, sir," one of them said.

"No, I'm usually a coffee man myself," Mike said, "but when I heard one of the mechanics say that he had been for a cup of tea in a little café— well, I had to see for myself."

"No cakes, I have to warn you, but the scones weren't half bad," Watson said. "But I've just been telling the little waitress here that she needs to make herself look the part. You know—nice, short black dress . . ."

"With frilly panties under it when she bends down," Rogers added, and they both chuckled.

"I think you'll find that this lady is not the waitress here but rather the proprietress, and she doesn't appreciate comments like that," Mike said.

"Oh gosh. Just a bit of fun, old chap," Rogers said, his face turning red now. "No harm meant, miss."

"It's missus," Josie said. "If you gentlemen are finished, it's ten pence each."

One of them put a two-shilling piece on the table. "Keep the change," he said, and they made a hasty exit, under Mike's critical gaze.

"I'm sorry about them," he said as the two men walked down the front path. "I'm afraid you find that type too often in the RAF. Lots of bravado, you know. It goes with the territory of having to fly into the unknown every damned night."

"No harm done," Josie said, "but I didn't expect to see you here. Did you really come for tea?"

"No. In fact, it was a surprise to see two of my officers sitting at a tea table. I had no idea you'd started a little business."

"Remember what I told you about the boy I invited in for a cup of tea on a rainy day and how he looked around the kitchen as if he couldn't believe he was somewhere like home again? I thought there might be more of them who'd like a few minutes of normal life. So I persuaded the lady who owns this house to let me give it a try. I don't know how it's going to go—rations will be a problem, and it's hard to know how much to bake because I don't want to waste anything—" She broke off, realizing she was rattling on, maybe a little nervous in his presence. "So you don't want a cup of tea?"

He smiled, pulled out a chair and sat down. "I suppose I may learn to like tea eventually, but not the way they serve it in the mess. Strong enough to rot your insides. I expect yours will be better."

"I'll get you some." She rushed into the kitchen, poured him a cup of tea and brought out a scone. He ate and drank, nodding with satisfaction. "I always knew you'd be a good baker," he said.

"I don't know how you knew that." She gave him a defiant stare, making him chuckle. "Another scone?"

He shook his head. "Actually I have to drive into Holbeach, and I wanted to see if you wanted to come with me."

Josie was torn. Of course she wanted to go with Mike, but could she risk closing the tea shop early? "It's after four," she said. "I don't suppose anyone else will come today."

"I wouldn't think so. It's all hands on deck tonight."

"A big raid?" she asked.

He smiled. "I'm not allowed to divulge . . ."

"You're not going up tonight, are you?"

"Absolutely. Like I said, all hands on deck. But I don't have to check in until twenty-one hundred hours." He grinned. "That's nine o'clock to you."

"Shouldn't you be resting if you're flying all night?" she demanded.

"I'd rather see you than try to sleep. You want to come, then?"

"I'd better just clear away these dirty dishes first," she said.

"I'll help." He picked up his cup and plate and followed her through to the kitchen. Kathleen was peeling potatoes and looked up as they came in.

"One of my customers is being helpful," Josie said. "But I can't wash them up if you're at the sink. Just leave them, and I'll wash up when I get back. I'm just popping out for a little while."

She didn't wait for Kathleen's reply. She took her coat from the hall cupboard and walked with Mike to his motor car. As they drove away, Mike commented, "That woman does not look happy."

Josie sighed. "She's always got a grievance. In fact, she's her own worst enemy. She wants me gone, but she likes the fact that I've taken over a lot of her work. And she's jealous when I get along well with her employer."

"So the woman in the kitchen is the hired help?"

"Yes, she's the only servant left these days. There used to be several."

"And the woman who owns the house—didn't you say she was a bit of a curmudgeon and didn't want you there?"

"She's not the easiest," Josie said, "but she's come around a bit. She seems softer since she had a health scare. She had a heart attack, you know. But she's recovering nicely."

"Oh, what medication did they give her?" he asked, and she remembered that he was a pharmacist by profession.

"I've no idea. Some pills and a bottle of tonic. That's all I can tell you."

"They seem to have worked, if she's up and around again," he said. "I expect medicine has advanced since I last practiced. They are inventing new drugs all the time."

"You don't miss it?"

"Oh, I do," he said. "I hope to take it up again one day. But you—it sounds like you're planning to stay here now?"

"At the moment. I've got plenty to do. I'm going to get the vegetable garden growing, some chickens, maybe . . . and the tea shop. By the way—if you are a coffee man, could I have your tea ration?"

"I see. You only like me for my tea ration."

"No, I . . . I . . . ," she stammered, blushing, caught off guard. She sensed this was moving to a level of flirtation that she wasn't sure about.

Mike laughed at her red face. "I'll see what I can do."

The bare fields were showing the first signs of spring. Hints of green were pushing up from the earth, and when they passed a meadow, there were newborn lambs. Josie cried out in pleasure. "Look at them! They are so tiny. And they bounce around as if they are on springs. Aren't they adorable?"

Mike chuckled. "You act as if you've never seen a lamb before."

"I haven't," Josie admitted. "Until this, I'd only left the city a few times in my life."

"Do you miss it? Do you want to go back?"

"I honestly don't," she said. "All those people, packed in together. No fresh air. Lots of smoky fog. And now this. It's amazing, isn't it?"

"I grew up in the country," he said, "so I feel at home here. I don't think I'd ever want to live in a city."

"You'll go back to Canada after the war?" she asked.

"If I make it that long," he said, "I don't know what I'll do."

"Oh, look." Josie pointed out the window at the long runway stretching out from the road, and at the huts and hangars with planes standing outside them. "Another RAF station so close to yours?"

"There are plenty of them up and down this

coast," Mike said. He paused. "I think I can trust you with a secret. The locals know, of course, because they helped build it, but that one isn't real."

"What do you mean?"

He grinned. "They've built fake airfields with fake planes so that the Germans don't bomb the real ones," he said. "See those planes? They are made of plywood. Clever, huh?"

They drove into the small market town of Holbeach. It had a high street of shops and square red-brick houses, an impressive church called All Saints and several pubs. They parked the motor car outside one of these called the Horse and Groom, and Mike went into the tobacconist's, where he bought a tin of pipe tobacco and some spills. Josie hadn't pictured him smoking a pipe before.

"I didn't know you smoked a pipe," she said as they came out of the shop.

"I've just taken it up," he admitted, looking a little embarrassed. "Some of the other chaps are pipe smokers, so I thought I'd give it a try. It seems to be the done thing. I'm still not sure whether I enjoy it or not."

"I think you'll look very distinguished," she said, then wished she hadn't.

He smiled. "It's supposed to be relaxing, but the darned thing goes out so often that I'm constantly relighting it. I expect I'll get the hang of it."

They came out into red twilight. "Is there anything you want to do here?" he asked. "Anything you need to buy?"

Josie shook her head. "I don't need anything, apart from a short black dress, apparently."

"Damned cheek of that guy. At least I made him feel uncomfortable. Being a squadron leader does have its benefits." He put an arm around her shoulder, steering her back to the car. The gesture felt so natural that she didn't even react to it. "Come on, let's go for a walk before it gets dark. Stretch our legs."

They drove out of the town again, and Mike brought the car to a halt beside one of the small waterways. A raised dyke ran beside it, with farmland stretching away on either side. They left the car and walked along the top of the dyke. The setting sun was turning the water pink.

"Did you know," he said, "that everything you see here used to be under the sea? Holbeach was near the coast and used to get flooded. Then they drained the land hundreds of years ago, and now the sea is nine miles away. But all this is below sea level, and it's only dykes like this that stop the sea from coming back."

"Goodness," she said. "You know so many interesting things."

"I make a point of learning about places," he said. "See over there—that's a sluice gate. If the sea breaks a dyke or it looks like it's going to flood badly, a man's job is to open that gate and flood the fields instead. His title is lord of the dykes." He saw her face.

"You're pulling my leg," she said.

"Seriously. I'm not making this up. A local chap at a pub told me about the whole thing. And the rivers are called drains, and when they drain out to the sea at low tide, they flow so fast that anyone who fell in would be swept away and drowned. Fascinating country, this."

"I read a book," Josie said tentatively, "called *The Nine Tailors*. It's about this place. Quite interesting but horrible ending. And I didn't like that chap Wimsey. He thought too much of himself."

Mike laughed again. He looked down at her. The wind was blowing her hair from her face and making her cheeks sting. "You never cease to surprise me," he said. "I didn't know you liked to read."

"Oh yes. I love it. I haven't had much chance until now, but Miss Harcourt has a lovely library and lets me borrow books."

"So what are you reading now?"

She didn't like to say she was reading a book about a family in Canada. "I've been too busy with the tea shop," she said. "I expect I'll start another one soon."

She stopped suddenly, staring into the sky. "Oh, look. Up there." A flight of ducks moved across the last glow of sunlight. The sight of their black silhouettes against the startling redness of the sky was almost magical. Josie didn't think she'd ever seen anything so beautiful.

"Oh," she said again, stepped back and almost lost her footing down the embankment.

"Hey, careful." Mike grabbed her and pulled her back. "I don't want to lose you into the drain."

Josie realized he was holding her firmly, and she was horribly conscious of his closeness.

She gave a nervous giggle. "I seem to make a habit of needing to be rescued," she said. "It's lucky you're around."

"Someone has to keep an eye on you," he said and released her shoulders. She sensed that he was feeling uneasy, too. They walked back together in silence. On the way home she remembered that he'd be flying out tonight. A big raid. Planes would not return.

"You must come back and have tea again soon," she said, reverting to politeness as they pulled up outside the house. "If I get any currants, I'll bake rock cakes."

"I suppose I have to learn to like tea sometime," he said. "And whatever rock cakes are. Thank you for this afternoon. It's good to take the mind off things."

Josie wanted to say more. She felt a rush of emotion. She wanted to hug him, tell him to take care, but she said, "I'll see you soon, I hope."

"I hope so, too." He came around to open the car door for her, then waved as he went back to the driver's side. She watched him drive away. As she came to the front door, she saw a brown paper bag beside it and a note: *I came to have tea at your café, but it was closed. Are you still planning to run it? I brought some flour and sugar for you. Sincerely, Jakob Goldsmith.*

Then, of course, she felt guilty that she had shut up the shop to go with Mike but relieved that she hadn't had to be alone with the doctor.

That night she heard the low rumbling of planes taking off, one after the other. She went to her window but could see nothing in the pitch-darkness. Mike would be on one of those planes. How many would be coming home this time?

CHAPTER 25

She lay awake for a long time, her hearing fine-tuned for the sound of returning planes, but finally she drifted off to sleep and awoke to find the world bathed in early morning mist. She felt apprehension as she stared out of the window. Had the planes been able to land in that thick whiteness that now hid the earth? She told herself that she couldn't worry every night. This was the reality, and there was nothing she could do about it. And it wouldn't be wise to become too fond of Mike.

After breakfast she went into the village to see what meat the butcher might be able to let her have. As she approached the butcher's van, she saw several of the local women, standing and talking in a tight little huddle outside the shop. Josie recognized Rose Finch and Lil Hodgkins, as well as Mrs Adams and the older Mrs Wilks. She didn't know the pretty young woman who stood with them. Josie went to walk past, but one of them looked up and noticed her. "Hello, Mrs Banks. So how's your café going, then?"

"I can't say it's a roaring success at the moment," Josie said. "We'll have to see if it takes off or not. I don't think it's easy for the airmen to get away."

"Well, I wouldn't mind coming myself some

time," Rose Finch said. "Did they like the cream?"

"Oh yes. It was a big hit," Josie said. "I had a couple of snooty pilots in, and they couldn't believe I was serving them cream."

"Oh, some of them pilots think they're the cat's whiskers," Annie Adams commented. "Harry at the pub says they come in there acting as if they own the place."

"But they do liven things up around here, don't they?" the young woman said. "It was as dull as ditchwater before the RAF came."

"You want to watch yourself, my girl," Mrs Wilks warned. "They only want one thing. I've had to warn my daughter about them."

"It's not a case of 'you know what sailors are,'" Annie Adams said. "It's that airmen are twice as bad."

And they laughed, uneasily.

As the group was breaking up, Nan Badger came up the street towards them.

"What's all this, then?" she called. "Nobody has housework to do today?"

"We're just getting the news, that's all," Lil Hodgkins said. "Keep your hair on."

"Sorry," Nan said. "I'm a bit upset, that's all. We've just had a telegram that little Dorothy's mother has died. She was in hospital for a long time, and she was almost ready to come home when she caught scarlet fever and went just like that."

"Poor little thing," Josie said. "What will happen to Dorothy now?"

Nan shrugged. "I can't say. She has a father who is serving overseas, but other than that—I know she said her grandma died, but I don't get the impression there are other relatives. Of course, she can stay here for now, but after the war—who can say?"

"It's a good thing she's got you," Josie said. "And Sheila, too. At least she's got some love and comfort."

Nan nodded. "I don't know how I'm going to tell her. She's been doing so nicely, too. Really come out of her shell. Not afraid of the dog or the chickens. And now this. It doesn't seem fair, does it?"

"There's a lot that's not fair right now," Mrs Wilks commented. "We just heard my nephew Ron has gone down with his ship. Lost at sea. Merchant navy on the transatlantic run. And him only nineteen."

"You don't want to get the post these days, do you?" Rose said. "Afraid every letter will bring more bad news."

"Bring Dorothy up to the house after school one day," Josie said. "I'll serve her a proper tea. It will be a little treat for her."

"I'll do that," Nan agreed. "And I'll bring some of my gingerbread, too, if you like."

They didn't come that afternoon. Josie wondered if Nan had broken the news to little Dorothy. As it happened, it would not have been the right day to host a grieving child. Two women in air force uniform arrived, and shortly after them, four airmen turned up. Dickie Dennison, the Polish JJ, plus two others Josie hadn't seen before.

"Were you following us?" one of the WAAF women demanded.

"Of course not. We found out about this place first," Dickie said.

"We came here to get away from RAF men," the other WAAF said. "We need to feel civilized for once."

"We won't even look in your direction," Dickie said. "We're only here for the tea and cake."

At that moment Rose Finch and Annie Adams came in, looking around with interest, as if they had just stepped into another world.

"What was this room before?" Rose asked.

"Just another sitting room. Nobody used it," Josie said. "Sit where you like, and I'll bring tea."

The meal began in silence, each group pretending to avoid the other. But then Dickie went over to the piano, tried a tentative melody, then broke into show tunes. One by one the others joined in, singing along. First they sang "If You Were the Only Girl in the World" and then "The White Cliffs of Dover."

"When will you be back again?" Rose Finch asked. "I know some of the other girls would enjoy a good singalong."

"I'm afraid we can never tell," Dickie said. "Sometimes we go a couple of weeks with no time off. They don't tell us in advance when they plan to bomb Hitler."

Josie was bringing a second pot of tea from the kitchen when she saw Miss Harcourt, standing in the front hall, out of sight, observing the scene.

"Why don't you go and join them?" she asked.

Miss Harcourt shook her head. "I only wanted to make sure he was taking good care of my piano," she said and went across to her sitting room instead.

The two women had just left and the men were settling their bill when Dr Goldsmith arrived. "Oh, I see you are quite busy," he said. "I was sorry to miss you yesterday."

"I'm sorry, too," Josie said. "I thought there wouldn't be any customers when it got late, so I had some errands to run. Thank you for the supplies. I've already made some rock cakes. You can take some home with you."

"I'd like to enjoy one right now, if you don't mind," he said and pulled out a chair at an empty table.

Josie could sense the airmen watching him warily. He nodded in their direction. "Good after-noon."

"You sound like a German," one of them said.

"I was born in that country," Dr Goldsmith said, "but I have lived in England most of my adult life. I studied medicine at St Thomas's Hospital, and I am now an eye surgeon." He paused, then added, "I am also a Jew, hence I have no love for Herr Hitler, if that is what you were thinking."

That produced embarrassed mutterings and assurances that he was certainly a good chap. But the tension remained in the air as the airmen left.

"You see how it is," he said to Josie as she came to clear away the china. "Everywhere I go, there is suspicion about me. It is not an easy life."

"I'm sorry," she said.

"But kind people like you make it easier." He looked up at her. "And the rock cake is delicious."

"I'll put some in a bag for you to take home," she said. "I really appreciate the extra flour and sugar."

She was escorting him to the front door when Miss Harcourt appeared from her sitting room.

"The visitors have all left?" she asked.

"The last one is leaving now," Josie replied. "This is Dr Goldsmith. I don't know if you've met before."

"Ah yes. You were the kind man who brought my medicines when I had my heart trouble," she said. "Thank you."

"I was glad to be able to help," he replied. "I trust you are on the road to recovery now?"

"I am much better, thank you. Still a little breathless when I go upstairs."

"That is to be expected. You must make sure you do not exert yourself too much and put too much strain on the heart. I am glad you have this lady to take care of you."

"Yes, she has been most solicitous," Miss Harcourt said.

There was a noise behind them, and Josie turned to see Kathleen standing there, a look of anger on her face.

"Are you going to wash up those tea things now so I can get at my own sink to peel the potatoes?" she demanded, then stalked away.

"That woman gets worse every day," Miss Harcourt said. "I don't know why she has cause to be so grumpy. She has a job, she is well fed, and now she has her workload halved. You'd think she'd be grateful."

"I'm afraid she resents me," Josie said. "I'm an intruder on her domain, even if she does like the help she gets." She turned back to Dr Goldsmith, who was standing by the door, looking embarrassed. "I'm sorry, Doctor. Let me walk out with you to your car."

CHAPTER 26

Halfway through March, spring burst upon the countryside with bright green shoots sprouting from bare fields, new leaves on trees and primroses crowding the hedgerows. The dawn chorus of birds awoke Josie every morning with an overwhelming volume of song. Alf Badger brought the girls to help make a chicken coop. Little Dorothy skipped around, telling Josie about their chickens and which one was her favourite. "And Daisy is the brown one with the funny beak, but she's really gentle, and she lets me lift her off her eggs."

She seemed to be little affected by her mother's death, and Josie wondered how she would adjust if she had to go home to her father after the war. When the henhouse was ready, Mike drove Josie to the nearest farm supply shop and they picked out six young hens. He seemed to enjoy it as much as she did. Their relationship remained friendly but reserved, as if both were making sure it stayed that way. Josie didn't see too much of him because her days were now fully occupied. The first vegetables were sprouting well. The chickens needed to be fed, and the tea shop was busy most days. Kathleen not only refused to help, she retreated to her own domain whenever possible. Josie took this in her stride and said nothing. She liked to be kept busy and to feel that she was doing something useful. She enjoyed the feeling of belonging to the community, of being welcomed when she met other women or when she visited the Badgers. It felt as if she had found her true home for the first time.

Easter was approaching. The area around the church was a mass of daffodils. Josie encountered the vicar's wife as she was picking some to decorate the church.

"We usually have our flower festivals at Easter time in this part of the world," the vicar's wife said with a sigh. "Before the war we were the big flower-growing region. Lots of tulips and spring bulbs, just like Holland. But of course the fields have all been put to growing wheat and sugar beets now. Such a shame. The church used to look so pretty. Now it will just be a few vases of daffs."

"It all looks lovely to me," Josie said. "You only really appreciate the country when you've grown up in a city."

"Yes, I suppose you do." The vicar's wife smiled. "So you've taken to life here?"

"I really have. I can't think of going back now. All that dirt and noise and people crammed in together, everyone in a hurry. Out here I work hard, but there always seems to be time to notice and enjoy things."

"Then maybe you'll be able to persuade your husband to make a new life with you out here after the war," the vicar's wife said.

Josie walked away, saddened by the realization that Stan would never move to the country. He was the typical cockney Londoner, proud of who he was and where he was. He enjoyed his job at the meat market, his mates and the local pub. She couldn't picture him amongst these fields. And now she found she couldn't picture herself back in the city. She pushed the images from her mind as she walked home, stopping along the way to pick some primroses to put in vases in the tea shop.

On Maundy Thursday, Mike drove her into Spalding to see if there was anything to make Easter more festive. No chocolate eggs, for sure, as sweets were rationed and almost impossible to find. She found some cardboard eggs, clearly having sat in a box since before the war, as they appeared to be German in design. They were the sort that have a little hole at one end, and when you peep inside, you can see paper cut-outs of chicks and lambs. She bought some and decided she would try to make some kind of sweets that didn't require too much sugar to be added to the interior.

"Don't you need a new Easter bonnet?" Mike asked as they walked past a ladies' dress shop.

She laughed. "Don't be silly."

"Don't women buy new clothes for Easter over here?"

"Nobody buys any new clothes these days," she replied. "Haven't you heard of 'make do and mend'?" She paused, thinking. "Besides, I never had anything new for Easter. I suppose we never went to church, so we didn't make any fuss over it. I might borrow one of Miss Harcourt's hats if she'll let me."

"I'll buy you a new hat," he said.

"Don't be silly," she repeated. "The last thing in the world I need is a new hat."

"Then a new coat."

Josie was tempted. The coat she had been given was well worn. But caution won out. "I can't let you buy me things, Mike. It wouldn't be right."

"I've money to spend and nobody to spend it on," he said. "And I'd like to make you happy."

"You do make me happy," she confessed. "Just being with you, I feel—well, alive."

He gave her a long, intense look. "Me too," he said.

As they drove out of the town, she noticed the placards outside the cinema. "Oh, look," she said. "*Gone with the Wind* is coming to this picture house soon. I always wanted to see that, but it was reserved seats only when I was back in London."

"I'll take you if you like," he said.

Again Josie felt she should refuse but found

herself saying, "All right. Thank you. That would be lovely."

Back at the house, Josie looked through recipe books for any kind of sweets she could make for Easter. When the toffee recipe started with two cups of sugar and two cups of butter, she knew that was not possible. Turkish delight had four cups of sugar. It became clear that no sweets were going to be made. Then she remembered hot cross buns. She had never tried making bread or buns with yeast because these were things you bought at the baker's shop before the war. She took down Mrs Beeton's cookery book from the shelf and read the recipe. Not too hard, it seemed. And not needing too much sugar or fat. She tried it, and the buns came out of the oven looking just as she had pictured them. Josie beamed with satisfaction. But she still needed something to put in the cardboard eggs. The best she could do was some simple biscuits that she cut out in the shape of rabbits. In the pantry she came across a jar of hundreds and thousands and used a thin sugar glaze to sprinkle them on the biscuits, making them look quite festive. She put two in each of the eggs and took them round to the girls at the Badgers' house. She was sure Nan would have made her own buns, even better than Josie's, so she didn't include them.

On Easter morning, she was delighted to find that one of the new hens had laid. She boiled the egg for Miss Harcourt, then put one of the cardboard eggs on her breakfast plate as well as a hot cross bun.

"What's this?" Miss Harcourt stared before she picked up the cardboard egg, then gave a little chuckle. "Why, I haven't seen one of these since I was a girl. Where did you find it?"

"In a shop in Spalding," Josie said. "I looked for chocolate, but of course there isn't any. And the real egg is from one of our hens."

"How splendid! Well done. And a hot cross bun, too. We haven't done anything special for Easter for years. It quite reminds me . . ." Her voice cracked. She broke off and put a hand to her mouth, looking away as if embarrassed at displaying emotion. Then she gave Josie a genuine smile. "You really are an asset to this house. I'm sorry that I was so unwelcoming in the beginning."

"It's all right. I understand," Josie said. "I'd be a bit leery about taking in a stranger, too. But I do have a favour to ask you. Do you think I might borrow one of your hats for church today? I don't have a hat any more, and I'd feel wrong without one today."

"My dear," Miss Harcourt said, "help yourself. It's been a long time since I've needed hats. I expect you'll find them all horribly old-fashioned, but they are in the hatbox in my wardrobe."

"Would you like to come to church with me?" Josie asked. "Seeing as it's Easter?"

Miss Harcourt hesitated, then shook her head. "No, I don't think so, thank you. I don't think I'd enjoy the stares. And God and I have nothing to say to each other."

Josie nodded and left Miss Harcourt to her breakfast.

She went upstairs into Miss Harcourt's bedroom, then opened the great carved oak wardrobe. On the top shelf there was a hatbox. She brought it down carefully as it was heavy and made of leather and opened it on Miss Harcourt's bed. Some of the hats were indeed old-fashioned, but there was a simple beige straw boater with a navy ribbon around it. No sense in a fancy hat when she would be wearing her everyday hand-me-down coat and shoes.

"Here, what do you think you're doing—snooping in the mistress's bedroom?" Kathleen stood in the doorway with a triumphant grin on her face, as if she was delighting in catching Josie in the wrong.

"I'm choosing a hat for church today," Josie said. "Miss Harcourt told me to go up and help myself. Do you think it suits me?"

"It's too good for the likes of you," Kathleen said and stalked out.

"Don't worry. I'm only borrowing it," Josie called after her. She could see how it looked like Kathleen's employer was showering things on Josie but ignoring her. Josie hurried down, attempting to make amends. "Here, Kathleen," she said. "Happy Easter." And she put the cardboard egg in front of her. "Happy Easter, Kathleen," she repeated.

Kathleen eyed the egg. "For me?"

Josie nodded.

"And what would I be wanting with a cardboard egg?" she asked.

"If you don't want it, I'll have the biscuits myself," Josie said. "And the egg, too. I think it's pretty."

Kathleen held it up and peered inside. "That's clever," she said. "But what's the use of an egg when I can't even attend the sacrament at my own church on the holy day?"

"I'm truly sorry for you," Josie said. "I wish there was something I could do. If I had a bike, I'd lend it to you."

"And how would I be cycling ten miles, I'd like to know?" Kathleen demanded, but then she shook her head. "You're a kind woman. I'll give that to you. And I do appreciate the thought. And the biscuits."

That was about as gracious as Kathleen was ever going to be, Josie realized.

For their Easter lunch, Josie would have liked a leg of lamb, but the best the butcher could do was half a pound of stewing steak for a meat pie. But it was tasty enough with cauliflower in a white sauce and roast potatoes. Miss Harcourt suggested that they both join her to share the meal in the dining room. That in itself was an Easter miracle.

It was the first week in May that *Gone with the Wind* came to the Regal Cinema. Josie persuaded Kathleen to hold the fort at the tea shop that afternoon so that she could go to the matinee. She didn't mention that she was going with Mike, just that she had a lift into town. Kathleen gave her a knowing, judging sort of look, but Josie offered no more explanation.

"You can keep the profits from today for yourself," Josie said and noticed Kathleen perk up at this thought.

She went upstairs and tried to make herself look presentable. It was warm enough for one of Miss Harcourt's tea dresses. Was that going a little too far, a little too fancy? She stared at herself in the wardrobe mirror. The impression was one of elegance. You'd never have known that this was Josie Banks from the East End. The green of the silk matched her eyes, but then they'd be in a dark cinema, so did it really matter? Then she realized she wanted to look nice for him. How many years had it been since she had wanted a man's approval? She tried to remember if Stan ever told her she looked nice—not since their courting days, in any case. He had been quick to point out things he didn't like: "Why are you wearing your hair like that now? It doesn't suit you." Or conversely, "Why aren't you wearing your hair in waves like the fashionable women?" She sighed and pushed aside a pang of guilt that she was going out with another man.

Not going out, she told herself. *Just going to a cinema with a friend.* The important thing was seeing *Gone with the Wind.*

Mike was waiting outside in the motor car. He came out and opened the passenger door for her. "You look nice and summery," he said. "It's a fine day. Almost a pity to be sitting inside."

"I'm not going for a hike dressed like this," Josie said. "I've been waiting to wear this dress all year."

"Where did it come from?"

"One of Miss Harcourt's she had discarded to the poor box."

"Rather too good for the poor, surely?" he asked, laughing.

"The poor deserve nice clothes, too, you know."

"I dare say, but you can't see them going to tea parties, can you?"

"You'd be surprised," Josie said. "In London I ran a little tea shop in the middle of the Mile End Road. The heart of the East End—the poorest part of the city. But every day we'd have people come in that you'd describe as poor. Old ladies who had known better times or housewives who just wanted to sit in peace and quiet for a few minutes before going home to a house full of kids." She turned to look at him. "I grew up poor, Mike, but I always dreamed of better things."

"I'm sorry." He looked embarrassed. "I didn't mean to offend you."

"I know," she said, "but you should know about me that I'm not from a refined background like you. I'm working class, uneducated."

"But you haven't let it stop you," he said. "That's what I like about you. You've got spunk. I saw that right away, when you were sitting on that freezing road."

She chuckled then, and the tension between them was broken. They queued up at the Regal. Mike paid for the one-and-sixpenny seats at the back—proper plush chairs. Since it was a matinee, the cinema was only half full. Josie watched impatiently while the cartoons and the newsreel played. The latter showed the latest scenes of bomb damage in British cities as well as small victories at sea and news from North Africa. "General Montgomery assembles a mighty force to take on Rommel," said the announcer. Josie wondered if Stan was one of those men driving in armoured cars through the desert. She didn't think he'd approve of his wife sitting in a cinema with a strange man.

But then the feature film started. From the soaring opening music, Josie was transfixed. Pictures had been a luxury that didn't happen often in her life—and there were the glorious costumes of the old South, Vivien Leigh looking glamourous, Clark Gable looking dashing. The romantic tension between them was palpable. It seemed almost part of the film when Mike slid his hand into hers. Their fingers intertwined. She glanced at him, and he met her gaze. She could see his eyes sparkling in the flickering light coming from the screen, but she didn't pull her hand away. In fact, she savoured the warmth of his touch, making the film into a shared experience.

Then came the burning of Atlanta. Josie bit her lip, distressed by what she was seeing. It was too close to what she had witnessed in London.

"Why does everything have to be about war?" she whispered.

Mike slipped his arm around her shoulders and pulled her close. She rested her head on his shoulder. When she looked up at him, she knew he was going to kiss her, but she didn't turn away. The kiss was soft and gentle and not at all demanding, and she didn't want it to stop. She remained snuggled against him until the closing credits. They were still holding hands as they walked back to his motor car.

It was a shock to find the world outside bathed

in bright spring sunlight as they drove back to Sutton St Giles.

"You don't have to fly a mission tonight, do you?" she asked as reality returned.

"I'm afraid I do."

"But you gave up your rest time to see a stupid picture with me. You should have said." She sounded upset, angry with herself.

"Best thing that's happened to me in years," he replied. "I wouldn't have missed it for anything. Now when I fly, I'll remember how it felt having you beside me." He smiled at her, and she felt her cheeks flush.

They pulled up at Miss Harcourt's gate. "Thank you again. It was wonderful," Josie said. "Sad but wonderful. I'm glad I saw it with you. It made it even more special."

She opened the car door and was getting out when she saw a soldier approaching the house, walking as if tired, carrying a kit bag on his shoulder. She went to intercept him.

"Have you come for the tea shop?" she called. "I'm afraid you're a bit late. We usually close at five."

Then she stopped with her mouth open. The soldier was Stan.

CHAPTER 27

"Stan?" She could hardly get out the word. "Is it really you?" She came closer. "It really is you. I can't believe it."

"Of course it's bloody well me," he said. "Stop looking as if you were seeing a ghost and come and give your old man a kiss." He put down his bag and opened his arms.

She took tentative steps towards him. He wrapped his arms around her, hugging her fiercely to him, and planted a kiss that crushed her mouth. There were bristles where he hadn't shaved in a while. Josie fought back the desire to pull away. He released her, staring down at her critically.

"You don't seem pleased to see me."

"I'm just shocked, that's all. I thought you were in Africa," she said.

"There was a change of assignment at the last minute," he said. "I've spent the best part of a year in Ireland of all places. Northern Ireland, of course. Making sure them lot in Southern Ireland don't get too pally with the Germans. Watching for German U-boats. Standing on cold headlands all night. But now my lot are due to ship out, for Africa, we think, because they've given us tropical kit. We have four days' leave, and I've taken up almost two days trying to bloody well find you."

"Aren't the trains running, then?"

"What do you mean? I'm not a bloody magician. I didn't have the address, did I? The last I heard was when you were in that convent. I went there, and then to Shirley and Fred, and of course they hadn't seen hide nor hair of you. So then I was sent to the evacuation centre, and nobody seemed to know where you were."

"But I wrote to you as soon as I got here and gave you the address," she said.

He gave a derisive snort. "Well, the letter never got to me." He looked around. "What the devil are you doing in this godforsaken place, anyway?"

"I wrote to you," she repeated. "I told you the house got bombed. They had to evacuate me because I had nowhere else to go."

"You should have gone to Shirley and Fred. I told you I wanted you there when I was called up. Why didn't you go to them?"

"I needed to get out of the city after I was bombed," she said. "Somewhere I could recuperate."

He looked around again. "Well, I'd rather have you where someone can keep an eye on you. Go and get your things. I'll take you to their place with me right now. Get you set up."

"What?" She took a step back.

"I'm taking you home to London with me. I want you safely with my sister before I ship out. You've no business being in a place like this."

"Don't be silly, Stan." She gave a nervous little laugh. "I can't just up and leave. I've got a life here. I'm needed here."

"Doing what?"

"I look after an old lady and run a tearoom in her house," Josie said. "She'd be lost without me. Besides, I like it here. I'm growing veggies, and we keep chickens. It's good. Fresh air and nice people. It makes me happy."

He was staring at her, frowning. "What's come over you? You look different. You sound different, too. You're talking more posh than you used to."

"Am I? Well, I suppose I talk to the lady who owns the house, and she's about as posh as you can get."

He reached out and put a hand on her shoulder. "Come on, Josie. You can't really like it out here. And what about after the war when I'm home again? You'll be back in London then, living your old life, so there's no point in getting used to things you won't be able to have. Now, be a good girl and do as I tell you. Is this where you're staying? This posh house?"

"Yes. I help with the cooking and things."

"So you're a bloody servant, then? What's so good about that?"

"I'm not a servant. I help out because I want to. And I've started the little tea shop, and it's doing well. We're making a bit of money, and people like it. It cheers them up."

"You can go back to the cafeteria where you worked in London if you like cheering people up."

"The place where I worked was bombed. The owner was killed. And I'm not going back to London."

His hand now gripped her shoulder, his fingers digging into her. "You'll bloody well do what I tell you to. Now go inside and pack."

"I said I'm not going, Stan."

She heard footsteps crunching on the gravel and a voice behind her. "Is everything all right, Josie?" She hadn't realized that Mike had not driven away. He came towards them.

"Who's this, then?" Stan demanded.

"He's one of the officers who comes to the tea shop," Josie said quickly. "He gave me a lift home from Spalding today."

"Oh, so that's how it is, is it?" Stan demanded. "The moment my back's turned."

"Don't be silly. A lot of the RAF pilots come to the tea shop. They are all proper gentlemen."

Stan released Josie and took a step towards Mike. "You'd bloody well better keep your hands off my wife, or I'll knock your block off."

"Is it not customary in the army to salute a superior officer when you're in uniform, soldier?" Mike said in a calm voice.

Stan grudgingly managed a salute.

"And I'd like to see you try and knock my block off. I've fought many a bigger and better man than you."

Stan was clearly unnerved by Mike's composure and confidence.

"You're a bloody Yank? What's a Yank doing here?"

"I'm Canadian," Mike said. "A member of the British Commonwealth. An ally, remember? Now an RAF squadron leader. And you should be proud of the work your wife is doing. She's created a place where a lot of young airmen feel they are getting a taste of home. She's well respected around here."

Josie could see the uncertainty on Stan's face, then the bluster returned. "I don't care a rat's arse what she's been doing here. Her place is with the family in London. And that's where she's going right this minute."

"I told you, Stan. I'm not leaving," she said. "I don't know how much of my letter you could read, but I was buried alive in that house when the bomb struck, covered in bricks and rubble, and it was only a miracle that someone heard me before I suffocated. I broke my collarbone and got a bad concussion, and I've only just recovered. I'm not going to face any more bombs. My nerves wouldn't take it."

They stood there, unmoving, three statues, none of them knowing how to make the next move. Then Josie said, "Where are you shipping out from?"

"Southampton," Stan said. "On Monday."

"Listen, Stan," she said. "I'll come back to London with you right now and stay at your sister's until you ship out. That's only right and fair that you should spend your last days of leave with me. But then I'm coming straight back here again, and nothing you can do or say will make me change my mind." She glanced at Mike and saw appreciation in his nod. Then she turned to Stan. "Do you want me to introduce you to the lady who owns the house? Have a cup of tea while I go and pack a bag?"

"I could do with a cup of tea," he admitted. "I've been travelling since this morning, trying to get to this godforsaken place."

"How did you get here?"

"I had to hitch-hike from Spalding."

"Well, if we hurry up a bit, we can catch the bus at five thirty," she said. "Come on, then. Let's take you inside and get you that cup of tea."

She gave Mike a little smile. "I'll see you, then."

"Josie, are you sure this is all right?" he asked gently. "You do know what you are doing?"

"I'll be fine, thank you," she said. "And thank

you for the ride home. You'd better get going now, or you'll be late reporting for duty."

He looked at her, long and hard, then he nodded. "I'll see you when you get back, then."

And he turned and went back to his car.

"Well, come on, then, if we want to catch that bus," she said to Stan. He was frowning, watching Mike walk back to his car. She led him around the house and entered at the back door.

"There you are, finally back," Kathleen said, coming into the kitchen. She stopped when she saw Stan. "Who's this, for God's sake? If it's not the RAF you're bringing into the house, it's the army now."

"Kathleen, this is my husband, Stan Banks. He has leave before he ships out. I'm going down to London with him to see him off."

"So you're finally going, eh?" There was triumph in her eyes.

"Just for a couple of days. Don't get your hopes up." She went over to the stove and put the kettle on. "I'm going up to pack some things. Make him a cup of tea, will you? And there's a rock cake in the tin."

She didn't wait any longer. She ran up the stairs and flung some items into a carrier bag. Was she crazy to be doing this? What if Shirley and Fred wouldn't let her return when Stan shipped out? Then she thought, *They can't keep me a prisoner. I can leave when I want to.*

She looked at herself in the mirror and realized she was wearing the tea dress. She wondered what Stan had thought about that. Hastily she changed into a skirt, blouse and cardigan and put on her one pair of ordinary shoes. She even wiped off the traces of rouge and lipstick she had put on. Then she came down again.

"Almost ready?" she asked. "I better go and tell Miss Harcourt that I'm leaving. You should come and meet her, Stan—so she doesn't think I'm running off with a strange man." She gave a little nervous laugh.

She took his hand and half dragged him into the sitting room. Miss Harcourt was reading, engrossed in her book. Josie tapped on the door, and the older woman looked up.

"Miss Harcourt, this is my husband, Stan. I'm going down to London with him for a couple of days before he ships out," she said. "Kathleen will take care of the tearoom and collect the eggs."

"How do you do, Private Banks?" Miss Harcourt said in her cold, cultured voice. "I hope you are proud of the work your wife is doing here. She is an asset to our community. Don't worry about us, my dear. You go and enjoy your time together. It may be the last for a while."

"She's a right toffee-nosed old biddy, ain't she?" Stan said as they boarded the bus. "How can you stand it here, knowing she's looking down her nose at you all the time?"

"She's not so bad when you get to know her," Josie said. "She's been quite kind to me. She's given me some clothes and lets me read books from her library."

"Blimey, I'd go mad stuck out here in the middle of nowhere, but then I suppose you've found some things to amuse yourself with, like the RAF blokes—like that one who drove you home? I saw him looking at you."

"He's just a kind man, Stan. Just a friend."

"Well, I suppose he is a squadron leader, after all," Stan said. "Not going to be interested in a little cockney nobody like you." He paused, clearly to see if that remark had hurt, then he went on. "But there are the privates, aren't there? The ordinary airmen?"

"Who are mostly about eighteen years old," she said. "And homesick and scared. And the most I give them is a cup of tea. Besides, since I'm running the café every afternoon and getting dinner in the house at six o'clock every night, there's not much chance for high jinks. What's more, the bombers go out at night, so they all have to report back to base by five."

"Well, I suppose that's all right, then," he said, "but you better not let another bloke touch you, or you'll be for it."

"And how do I know that you haven't been

flirting with an Irish lass for the past year?" she asked. "Or meeting up with an Irish tart?"

"Well, men are different, aren't they?" he said. "Men have needs."

She decided to drop that subject. They rode on in silence and caught a train out of Spalding at six thirty, connecting to the London express at eight, arriving at King's Cross at ten.

CHAPTER 28

The area around Stan's sister's house was almost unrecognizable as they picked their way over rubble, moving cautiously by the blacked-out glow of the torch. In the eerie darkness Josie could make out jagged walls rearing up where houses used to be. The warehouse on the docks beyond was now a blackened shell. The row that contained Shirley and Fred's house was still untouched. Stan hammered on the front door, and Shirley answered it.

"Well, here you are at last," she said. "I thought you'd got lost." Her gaze went to Josie. "So you found her, then? She hadn't run off with a sergeant?"

"No, but she was living out in the middle of bloody nowhere. You should have seen it, Shirley. Nothing but bloody flat fields in all directions and this one house where she was living just sitting there. Nothing around it. No shops, no pubs. Nothing."

As he talked, he pushed Josie ahead of him into the narrow hallway. The place smelled of beer and stale cigarette smoke.

"So what was you doing out there?" Shirley asked. "We heard you got bombed out, and we thought you'd come here."

"I had to get out of the city," Josie said. "My nerves, you know. I was buried in the rubble, and I got a bad knock on the head." She heard herself speaking, conscious that she was deliberately reverting back to their cockney speech, which now felt coarse and foreign to her.

"But you're going to stay here now?" Shirley said. "Fred's doing long hours at the docks, lots of night shifts, and I'd welcome the company."

"Where is Fred?" Stan asked.

Shirley laughed. "Where the bloody hell do you think he is? Down the ruddy pub, ain't he? Then he'll go straight to his night shift." She shook her head, still smiling. "He's making good money with all the overtime, so plenty to spend. I won't fault him. He gives me my share—except there's nothing to spend it on if you don't have coupons, and not even then." She looked at Josie. "Well, come on. Don't just stand there. Take a load off your plates of meat, girl. So what you been doing out in bloody nowhere? Land girl, are you? Rolling in the hay with the local farm boys?" She laughed loudly at this.

"I wasn't allowed to do heavy work on account of my concussion," Josie said, "but I've been helping the older lady whose house I'm staying at, and I've started a little tea shop, like the one I worked at here. The local airmen come in the afternoon for a cuppa and a cake."

"Cuppa and a cake? Is that what they call it now?" She was still chuckling.

"No, really," Josie said.

"Blimey. Not a pint? Bunch of sissies, are they?"

"I expect they have the pints, too," Josie said. "But they are young, Shirley, and they want somewhere that reminds them of home."

"So who will take it over now?"

"Oh, I'm not staying," Josie said. "I'm going back as soon as I see Stan on to the train."

Shirley and Stan exchanged a look. "Didn't you say you were bringing her back to be with us?"

"She's not budging, apparently," Stan said.

"Tell her what to do then. You're the bloody boss. Stupid cow." Shirley's tone had become sharp, and Josie saw that she also must have been drinking.

"Look, if that's the way you're going to talk, I'll turn right around and catch the next train back," Josie said. "I came down with Stan because it's the right thing to do. But he's not going to control my life when he can't take care of me. What's more, I haven't had a penny from him since he joined up. You owe me a lot of housekeeping money, Stanley Banks."

"You think I'm getting a fortune in the army, do you? Shilling a day, that's what I get." He gave her a long, hard stare. "What's more, you ain't getting nothing out of me unless you stay down here in London where the family can keep an eye on you. You go back to that godforsaken place, and you support yourself."

"Fine. Then I will," she said.

She stalked out of the room and went up the stairs. As she went, she heard Shirley say, "Let her go where she wants, Stan. We don't need her here if she's going to be like that, stupid, surly cow, and she can't get up to much stuck looking after an old lady in the country, can she?"

Stan followed Josie upstairs. She was getting undressed and turned deliberately to ignore him.

"Where did you get that ruddy awful skirt?" he asked.

Josie spun and glared at him. "Where do you think? I was given it at the hospital because I was stark naked when they dug me out of the rubble. My nightdress had been blown clean off me in the blast. So I expect it belonged to someone who had died. That's where all my clothes come from at the moment because I've got no money and nothing."

"Look, I'm sorry," he said. He ran his fingers awkwardly through his hair. "You've been through a rough time, and I was upset because it took me so long to find you. In the morning we'll go down to the post office, and I'll take out some money for you, all right?"

"Thanks, Stan," she said.

She noticed his expression change. "Come

here," he said and started to unbutton her blouse. "You certainly ain't put on weight," he said. "You're skinny as a bloody rake."

"We don't exactly get a lot of food," she said. "It's getting better now we've got chickens and can have our own eggs, and the veggies are growing nicely, too."

He looked at her as if he didn't quite recognize her. "You sound quite different. You're proud of what you're doing, aren't you?"

"Yes, I am. It's the first time in my life that I've achieved anything—that I feel I belong somewhere."

He reached around and unfastened her brassiere. "Nice little boobs," he commented. "God, I've missed this." And he shoved her down on to the bed, grunting with impatience as he pulled down her panties.

"Stan, no—she'll hear," Josie said.

"So let her hear. What does she think a man's going to do if he hasn't seen his wife in a year? Hold her hand?" Then he roughly pushed her legs apart and made love so forcefully that she had to stop herself from crying out. She got the feeling it wasn't just his need that was being fulfilled. It was his way of showing her he was still the master in spite of what she had accomplished in her new life.

Stan fell asleep, his arm draped over her on the narrow, cold bed, but Josie lay awake, listening to the noises of the city—the toot of tugboats on the nearby Thames, the grinding and shrieks of machinery on the docks, the laughter of men coming out of the pub. She was just drifting off when there came the familiar wail of the air raid siren.

Stan shot awake. "Bloody 'ell," he said. "That's all we need."

There was pounding on their door. "Come on, you two. Down the shelter, quick," came Shirley's voice.

Stan was hurriedly pulling on his trousers and jacket. Josie's hands were shaking so much it was hard to put on her clothes.

"Come on. Hurry up," Stan urged. From above came the distant thrum of approaching planes. Josie struggled into her shoes and coat, then took Stan's hand and followed him down the stairs. Shirley was standing by the back door.

"Down the shelter, quick," she said.

In the darkness Josie could make out the humped shape of the Anderson shelter, dug into the narrow back garden. She reached it, started to climb down the steps cut in the side, then froze. Shirley was shining a blackout torch to light the way, and Josie could see the roof of the shelter, a foot or so above her head. The tiny area was damp and smelled of rotting vegetation. Something scurried in the torchlight. Josie gave a little cry and scrambled back up again.

"I can't go down there, Stan. I simply can't. It's like a grave."

"We don't have time to get to the tube station now," he shouted, his own fear sounding in his voice. "Go on. Get down there." He tried to push her.

"I can't. I can't," she wailed, fighting her way up past him. "You go, then. I'll stay out here. I'd rather be blown to bits than be buried again."

The first wave of planes was now overhead. From the darkness came the dull thump of bombs. Searchlights strafed the sky, picking up the Maltese cross silhouettes of German bombers. Anti-aircraft guns boomed out, and tracers lit trails across the sky. One plane burst into flame and spiralled to the ground. Stan stood, hesitating, halfway into the shelter, his hand still grasping Josie's.

"Do come down, love. I don't want to lose you," he said softly now. He eased her as far as the steps and put his arms around her. "Blimey, you're shaking like a leaf," he said.

"I know. I can't take the bombs no more," she said. "I just can't bear it." And she started to sob silently. Stan held her close as the planes passed over.

"They don't think this street's worth bombing," Shirley said cheerfully, "since most of it's already gone. That's one blessing, right?"

The all-clear sounded, and she climbed out of

the shelter to join them. Stan was still holding Josie tightly in his arms. "I'm sorry, love," he said quietly. "I didn't realize how bad it was for you. Now I do. I'm scared, too. I'm scared to be going to Africa and fighting in a bloody desert. I'm scared of dying out there."

They stood together, hugging long after the all-clear siren had died away.

In the morning they went out and had breakfast in a transport café—a big slab of fried bread with a small sliver of bacon on top. Then they went to the post office, and Stan drew out twenty pounds. "Can I add my wife's name to the account?" he asked. "Can she have her own book?"

It seemed this was quite easily accomplished.

"Now don't you go spending it all at once," he said, teasing her.

"As if I would," she replied. "Have you ever known when I wasn't careful with money?"

"Come on," he said. "Let's go up west and see if we can buy you some proper clothes, so you can ditch that old skirt."

They caught the tube to Oxford Street and marvelled at the prices in John Lewis's and D H Evans.

"We're not spending that much, Stan," Josie said, "even if I have got the coupons."

So they pressed on until they came to C&A, where the shoppers were definitely more their type of people. Here they found a cotton summer dress, a white cardigan and a pair of sandals, all at budget prices. Josie came out, beaming. "It will feel so nice having something new again, Stan."

That evening they all went to the pub, where they had sausage rolls and beer. It wouldn't have been Josie's choice for her last night with Stan, but she could see he needed to be around people and noise and not have time to think. The next morning, she accompanied him to Waterloo Station and joined the crowd of soldiers and wives boarding the boat train to Southampton.

"Take care of yourself, Stan," she said.

"You too, old girl."

"And don't you go looking at any of them belly dancers in Egypt," she said.

"Don't you go looking at any of them farm boys out where you are. Nor them RAF blokes, you hear?"

They stood there, gazing at each other. There was a whistle further down the platform. Doors slammed. "Well, I'll be off, then." Stan hoisted his kit bag, leaned down to give her a last kiss, then boarded the train. Josie waved as it steamed out of the station, not knowing which of the waving hands and handkerchiefs were Stan's.

Then she took the Northern line to King's Cross and the train back to Lincolnshire.

As the train steamed out of the dismal London suburbs, each with evidence of recent bombings close to the track, and passed the first bright fields of springtime green, Josie found she was letting out a big sigh of relief and was shocked at herself. She had just said goodbye to her husband. He was going off to war, and she might well never see him again. She should be feeling heartbroken. Now her feelings were definitely mixed. She had seen a softer, kinder side to Stan during their last day together, as if he wanted her to be left with good memories of him. And she realized something that she had never thought of before: a lot of his bluster had to do with fear. His bullying happened when he felt he wasn't in control. And after the air raid he had admitted his own fear when he acknowledged hers. He had allowed himself to show weakness. That was, at least, a step in the right direction—something they could build upon when he came home again.

But for now, the future looked hopeful. She was going back to her tea shop. To the village where people smiled when they saw her. Where three little girls loved to come and check on the chickens. And where Mike was. She considered this with consternation. She was a married woman who had just sent her husband off to war. Was it so wrong to enjoy an afternoon out with Mike? He made her feel special and worthy in a way that Stan never had. From the very beginning, Stan had given her the impression that she was damned lucky he had chosen her. Mike made her feel that he welcomed her company. "Just a friend," she muttered to herself. But that kiss in the cinema had changed everything.

CHAPTER 29

"Oh, you're back at last, are you then?" Kathleen greeted her. "I thought you might have decided to stay down there."

"No thank you," Josie said. "You can't imagine how awful it is in London right now. Half the city lying in ruins. More bombing at night. I couldn't wait to come back. Anything happen while I've been gone?"

"Not much," Kathleen said. "None of your airmen came to the café yesterday. It seems they lost quite a few planes the other night. Seven out of fifteen didn't come back."

Josie's heart did an uncomfortable jerk. It seemed as if Kathleen was almost enjoying imparting this news.

"Did you hear who was killed?" Josie could hardly make her mouth move to ask the question.

Kathleen shook her head. "I'm not in on the local gossip, am I? I only heard this because those WAAF women stopped by. They said everyone at the station was pretty shaken up. It's their biggest loss so far."

Josie carried her bag upstairs and hung up the new cotton dress. She was finding it hard to breathe. How could she find out if Mike was safe? She knew that Miss Harcourt had a telephone because she had used it when she had to call a doctor. She washed the soot from the journey off her face and went down to the sitting room. Miss Harcourt wasn't there.

"Where's the mistress?" she asked Kathleen. "She's not been taken ill again, has she?"

Kathleen shrugged. "She was right as rain when I took her breakfast in." She glanced around, then exclaimed. "Oh, there she is. Outside. Looking at the chickens. Wonders will never cease."

Josie went out through the back door and saw Miss Harcourt standing next to the chicken run. She looked up as she heard Josie approaching.

"Oh, you've come home," she said. "I never did like chickens. They seem to have evil eyes, don't they? But I do appreciate the eggs. It makes such a difference when one starts the day with a fresh boiled egg. It makes one think that perhaps life is getting back to normal when it's not." She looked around the garden. "You are bringing it back to life," she said. "Maybe soon we'll have flowers as well as vegetables. I wouldn't mind helping out, if you show me what to do."

Josie nodded. "Righto. I can't say I know that much myself, but I'm happy to pass along what Alf Badger is teaching me."

Miss Harcourt examined her critically. "Is something wrong, my dear? You look distraught. It must have been hard to say goodbye to your husband and watch him go off to war."

"Yes," Josie said. She hesitated, plucking up courage. "I wonder, could I possibly ask for a favour and use your telephone? It's only a local call."

"Yes. Of course. You know where the instrument is."

Josie tried not to run as she returned to the house. She heard the operator's voice and asked to be connected to RAF Sutton Deeping.

"Bomber Command, Sutton Deeping," came a crisp female voice.

"Hello, I wonder could I speak to Squadron Leader Johnson?" she asked.

"Just one minute." There was a long pause. Then the voice said, "I'm afraid the squadron leader is not available at the moment."

"He's—he's still alive, isn't he?"

"What? Oh yes. He's in a briefing meeting. Can I take a message?"

"No message. Thank you."

Josie hung up, put her hands to her face and burst into tears.

Knowing he was safe, she threw herself into her work with renewed energy all week long. She went to visit Alf and Nan to ask advice about what to plant next.

"It looks like we might have the first new potatoes, Alf," she said. "And plenty of carrots and cabbages."

"You want to get the runner beans and the broad beans and the peas going now, then, my love," he said to her. "And lettuces, radishes. Oh, and the marrows. Let's see if I have any seeds I can give you."

Josie sat at the kitchen table while Nan poured her a cup of tea. "How are the girls doing, then?" she asked.

"Good as gold, all three of them," Alf said. "Dorothy talks nonstop. She seems to have accepted her mother's death without a murmur, and she's certainly taken to Nan. Sheila is turning into a lovely little helper. Ever so willing, she is. And Lottie—well, you hardly get a word out of her. She's always got her nose in a book, but I think she misses her home, too. Well, you would, wouldn't you?"

"Especially when you hear things on the news about what they are doing to Jewish people in Germany," Josie said as Alf ducked out of the room. "The poor little thing must worry constantly about what has happened to her parents. She hasn't heard from them in two years now. It may just be because there is no post delivery from Germany, but then it might be worse than that."

"They are monsters," Nan agreed. "Can you imagine arresting people and carting them off just because they are not your religion? I mean, look at our Lottie. She's as sweet as the other two. No different because she's Jewish, is she?"

"Of course not," Josie said. "My old boss was Jewish, too, and she was driven from her country because they were trying to get rid of Jews. I don't understand it myself."

She broke off as Alf came back in. "Here you are, my love," he said. "I've got some beans and peas for you to plant here. You're going to need poles for them. Let me know when they start sprouting, and I'll bring some bamboo over and help you tie them up."

"You're very kind, Alf. Are you sure you can spare the time? I can see all the work you're putting into your own garden."

"Don't you worry about it," he said. "I need to keep busy. You ask the wife. She don't want me getting in the way around the house. She wants me outside in all weathers—ain't that true, Nan?"

"It is, right enough," Nan agreed. "He's not the sort of man who can sit there puffing away at his pipe and reading the newspaper. Always has been a goer, my Alf. He'll be a goer until the day he drops dead."

Josie went home, turned over the soil and planted the beans and peas and the marrow and lettuce seeds the way Alf had told her. The sense of satisfaction from picking something she had grown was enormous. The one concern was how to keep the tearoom going on limited supplies. Dr Goldsmith had not been back since the uncomfortable day when his identity had been questioned. So he hadn't brought any ration stamps for her. Josie admitted to herself, reluctantly, that she might have to contact Lil Hodgkins's wayward husband, Johnny, who could get things on the black market. She was intending to do this at the WI meeting the next Thursday, but at the beginning of the week a strange man showed up at the tea shop. It was early afternoon, and as yet there were no customers.

"Have you come for tea?" she asked him. It was hard to identify who he might be. He wore a suit—rather threadbare—and a trilby hat. Not a farmworker, then—not the sort of clothes that the local men wore.

"Are you the owner of this place?" he asked.

"No, that would be Miss Harcourt. I'm Mrs Banks. I just take care of the tea shop here."

He looked around the room. "So you are running a business from this house?"

"Just providing tea and a snack for the local people," she said.

"But you have no permit from the local authority?"

"Are you from the local authority?"

"I am," he said. He handed her a card: *Robert Harris. Lincolnshire County Council, Wartime Trade Regulations.* "And running a business without a permit amounts to underhand trading, black market, during a time of war." He gave a

328

sigh. "I'm afraid I'm going to have to fine you and close you down."

"Here, hang on a minute," Josie said. "First of all, I only started this because I brought a young airman in out of the rain and gave him a cup of tea. And he said it reminded him of home. And he brought his friends. And I realized they all needed to be reminded of home. They fly bombers out of the airfield here. Every night they go out not knowing if they'll come back, and you want to stop me making them feel as if their mum is looking after them for an hour? Shame on you."

"I have a job to do," he said, shifting uneasily and not meeting her gaze. "There are local business laws to stop people from profiteering."

"Profiteering?" Josie laughed. "We don't make a profit, ducks. I charge them just enough money to buy more supplies."

"And where do you get these supplies from?"

"Until now they've been coming out of our own rations, plus local people who don't drink tea have been giving me coupons, but it's a struggle, especially on days when we get a good crowd. You see . . ."

She broke off as she heard the front door open, then footsteps across the foyer. Three airmen came into the room. Charlie was one of them, plus Polish JJ and Irish Patrick.

"Hello, Josie. How are you?" Charlie said.

"Sorry we haven't been in for a while. Things have been pretty grim lately. You heard, did you? Two flights in a row with horrendous casualties. We lost forty-two men. It shook us all up, I must tell you. And then a scramble to get replacement planes flown in and prepared for action. They sent us the new Wellingtons. Should be good. Better than the old Blenheims. The trouble with those is they are slower than the Messerschmitts. Can't outrun or outmanoeuvre them. The Wellingtons should be a big improvement, don't you think, boys?"

"They should," JJ agreed. "This week has not been fun, I can tell you. We approach target and suddenly Luftwaffe appear out of nowhere. All around us. So much flak. We were lucky to make it home. You should see the plane—full of holes, like Swiss cheese!"

Josie had forgotten he was a pilot while the others were ground crew.

"You were flying one of those planes?"

"I am just co-pilot, of course. My squadron leader was piloting. He was brilliant. He got us out of there."

"Which squadron leader was that?" She fought to keep her voice even.

"Johnson," he said. "Do you know him? Foreign like me. Canadian, actually, but a good bloke."

Josie felt a ridiculous swell of pride but at the

same time the realization that he could so easily have been killed.

"We suddenly decided we needed to get away for a few minutes, before this evening's briefing," JJ said. "We're on lockdown as soon as that starts."

"So how about a cup of tea, Josie?" Patrick said. "And any chance of a cake today?"

She glanced at the inspector, who was standing there, watching. "I'm not sure," she said. "This man is telling me he's come to shut us down, because we're running an illegal business."

"What?" Charlie glared at Mr Harris. "You can't do that. This is the only place for miles, apart from our canteen, and their tea would kill an elephant. We do need somewhere, you know, and the local pub isn't exactly welcoming. Besides, our flights are all at night, so we're stuck on base all evening. And who wants a beer at three o'clock?"

"And us pilots, we can't drink before we fly," JJ said.

"She's operating without a permit," Mr Harris said, not looking too happy now. He was a small man, and the RAF chaps were brawny.

"Then give her a bloody permit," Charlie said. He turned to Josie. "I apologize for the language, ma'am, but the situation called for it."

Josie found this rather funny, given Stan's colourful language, but nodded graciously.

Mr Harris now shifted from foot to foot. "I suppose I could request that a permit be issued retroactively. There will be the need for a kitchen inspection, of course. Health and Safety will want to do that."

"You couldn't find a nicer, cleaner kitchen," Charlie said. "Just like our kitchen at home." He took a step closer to Mr Harris.

Mr Harris looked as if he wanted to retreat but wasn't sure how. "I tell you what," he said. "I'll do my best. I'll put in a good word for you. But you have to understand that this is wartime. We have to be stricter than we would be in normal times, on account of black marketing."

"Oh, come on, man," Charlie said. "Do you want us to win this war or not? We should all be on the same side, or are you a secret German spy? Trying to sabotage RAF morale?"

"Of course not," Mr Harris spluttered. "I'm a local man just trying to do my job."

"Why do you not sit down and have a cup of tea with us," JJ said, "because we must return to base soon. Briefing at five, you know."

Mr Harris sighed. "I suppose there can't be any harm in it," he said.

Josie grinned to herself as she went into the kitchen. As it happened, she had made Chelsea buns, and they had turned out rather well. She brought through a tray and set up china and cutlery at two tables. She saw Mr Harris looking impressed at the quality of the china.

"It belongs to the lady who owns this house," she said. "She graciously allows us to use it, and the men are very respectful." She looked around. "Where is Dickie today?"

Charlie's face changed. "He's taking a few days' home leave," he said. "His plane didn't make it back, and he took it rather hard."

"His plane?" Josie asked. "But he's ground staff like you, isn't he?"

Charlie nodded. "We're all assigned to a particular plane, you know. Give it our special nickname, know the air crew. And Dickie's was one of the ones that didn't return. He's blaming himself, but of course there was nothing he could have done. Too many German fighters, and we were flying into Happy Valley again."

"What's that?" Josie asked.

"You know. Over the Ruhr. Industrial area. It's our name for it."

"I say, old fellow, you shouldn't be discussing things here," Patrick said. "You don't know who might be listening."

Charlie glanced at Mr Harris. "Oh, right," he said. "But I can't do much harm by discussing a mission that already took place, can I? Now if I were to say where we're off to tonight . . ." He grinned. "But of course we don't even know that yet until the air crew gets their briefing. Unless we're in on the morning's planning with the big brass. So all is well."

Josie poured tea and put out the cakes. Mr Harris bit into his and nodded. "This is quite tasty," he said. "Where do you get the butter from?"

"I don't," Josie replied. "It's marge and lard. We make do with what we can get."

"She does a smashing job," Charlie said, gesturing across from his table. "You should try her scones, and when the local dairyman can spare some cream—perfection!"

Josie gave him a grateful smile.

Mr Harris put down his cup. "So how much do I owe you?"

"This one is on the house," Josie said. "I can't very well charge you when I'd be collecting money illegally, can I?"

He got up. "You'll be hearing from us, then. I'll put in a good word, Mrs Banks. I can see that you are performing a service here. We might even be able to class it as that—services to the military get special priority." He held out his hand, and Josie shook it.

"Thank you," she said.

"Damned cheek," Charlie commented as Mr Harris left the house. "These little jumped-up bureaucrats flaunting their self-importance! I bet he was a greengrocer before the war."

The others laughed. They put down coins on the table and got up, ready to leave.

"I hope they do not make you shut this place," JJ said. "I much appreciate my time here, and your good food."

"I'd be livid if they closed it down," Patrick said. "By the way, where is our dear Kathleen? I should say a word to her before I go."

"She's in the kitchen or her private quarters. I'll get her," Josie said, thinking that Kathleen didn't seem as keen on this relationship as Patrick was, something she found odd.

"Don't bother yourself. I'll go through and find her," he said. "We had a nice long talk about home when you were away in London."

"Give my best regards to Dickie when he returns," Josie said to the other two as they reached the front door.

Charlie nodded. "We're hoping he comes through this all right," he said. "Some of the chaps do crack, you know. It's the constant strain. Worse for the air crew, of course, but not too good for us either. I'm scared they'll give him an LMF label, and he'll be done for."

"What's that?" Josie asked.

"It stands for Lack of Moral Fibre. It means you can't handle the job, and you're demoted and put on to non-essential work. The demotion is done in public, too. Humiliation."

"Then let's hope a few days at home do the trick," Josie said. "I don't know how you boys do it, day after day like this."

"You get used to it, I suppose," Charlie said.

"I confess it gives me much pleasure," JJ added. "Every bomb I drop I think that this is for my country that you invaded and destroyed."

Josie watched them leave. Such young, bright men living with danger and death every day. No wonder some of them, like Dickie, cracked. Her thoughts went immediately to Mike, who had managed to bring a damaged plane home safely. How long before the pressure got to him? She wondered when she would see him again, whether she dared to write to him. She decided she would risk it. She went upstairs and wrote him a letter:

> *Dear Mike:*
> *I've been back from London for a week now. I saw Stan off on his boat train. I'm sorry you had to be part of an awkward situation. I'm afraid he's always been defensive about me. But he's gone now, and I do want to see you again. I heard about your last raid, and I imagine you're quite shaken up. Anytime you want to come and talk, I'm here.*

She paused. How should she sign it? *Yours truly* was too formal. But *Love, Josie* went a step too far. She played it safe and just wrote her name. Then she sealed and stamped the envelope and put it ready for mailing after she had done the washing-up. Kathleen was in the kitchen, sitting at the table with a cup of tea.

"Did you have a nice chat with Patrick?" Josie asked.

Kathleen frowned. "I don't know why he wants to keep on bothering me," she said. "I've nothing to talk about with him, have I? I've lived in England most of my life. I've no ties to home now."

"Maybe your voice just sounds reassuring to him," Josie said. "These poor blokes are living close to the breaking point all the time. That one who plays the piano had to go on leave because the plane he takes care of didn't return from a bombing run. It was too much for him, knowing all those men didn't return."

Kathleen nodded. "They know the risk when they volunteer, don't they? They could just as easily have signed up for the army. The catering corps."

"And have a bomb dropped on them instead?" Josie had to grin. "There's no place that's safe now, is there?" She was about to leave, wanting to go down to the post office before the last collection, when she remembered. "By the way, we had a man from the county council here, claiming we were running an illegal business."

"That you are, right enough," Kathleen said quickly. "I've nothing to do with it."

337

"Right," Josie agreed. "But he's going to try and get us the permit we need, and that will mean a kitchen inspection. Now I know you keep the kitchen spotless, so we've nothing to worry about, but I just wanted to warn you."

"So they'll be poking their noses in my kitchen now, will they? Jesus, Mary and Joseph, there's not been a moment's peace since you came here."

"But you are getting fresh eggs and veggies, aren't you?" Josie said sweetly. "And soon there will be beans and peas and maybe some cane fruit? And I have taken over a lot of the cooking . . ."

"Oh, I suppose you do help out a bit," Kathleen agreed grudgingly, "but it's the constant coming and going that I don't like. I like my privacy. I like to feel safe in my own little home." And she stalked past Josie to her own part of the house.

Josie took the letter and walked into the village. As she returned from the postbox, she saw Lottie coming towards her.

"Hello, love," she said. "How are you getting along? I don't see much of you."

"I'm doing better, thank you," Lottie replied. "The girls at school aren't quite as horrible— at least most of them. And the teachers like me because I'm a good student. But there is a lot of homework, and it's hard to concentrate in such a small house. The other girls are noisy, and Nan always has the wireless on."

"Yes, that must be hard for you," Josie said. It crossed her mind to suggest that Lottie come to the house in the afternoons to do her schoolwork, but Lottie went on.

"So I go to Dr Goldsmith sometimes," Lottie said. "He lets me do my homework in his study and use his books."

"How kind of him."

Lottie continued, "He has wonderful books." Her face became transformed. "Just like my father's study at home. Not just medicine either, but literature and art and geography. And some are in German, which is good for me to read so I don't forget it. I want to be able to speak to my parents when I go home again." Josie saw her expression falter and knew she was wondering if she would ever go home again and if her parents would be there.

CHAPTER 30

Josie did not hear from Mike for two more days and began to worry about him. Was he, too, in a state of shock after that disastrous raid? Or had the incident with Stan made him decide to stay away from her? She felt powerless to do anything but wait. As it happened, the first caller that Tuesday was not Mike but a woman from the council Health and Safety department. She was another of the officious, efficient women who had taken over positions during the war—the "stand no nonsense and get it done right the first time" sort who were making the country run smoothly.

"Mrs Banks?" she asked. "I am Miss Dawson. Health and Safety. Come to inspect the kitchen."

"Righto. Come on in," Josie said.

The woman heard Josie's London accent and frowned. "You are not the owner, I take it?"

"A Miss Harcourt owns the house, but I'm running the tea shop. I'm the one who does the food preparation."

"Very well. Lead on."

Josie led her through. There was no sign of Kathleen. The kitchen was, as always, clean and inviting looking. Miss Dawson looked around. "This is the restaurant kitchen?"

"It's not a restaurant," Josie said. "We just serve tea to some airmen from the local aerodrome in the afternoons."

"On good china?"

"Yes, on good china," Josie said. "They are very careful."

Miss Dawson stalked around the kitchen, peering into every corner. "The stove does not meet standard requirements," she said. "Not enough burners and only one oven."

"It's plenty for what we do," Josie said. "Tea and maybe a dozen scones. We're not cooking roast and two veg, you know."

"And where is the sink?"

"Out in the scullery." Josie pointed.

"Hmm." Miss Dawson made a noise that might have been one of disapproval. "And the food storage?"

"We have a pantry, back here."

Again she looked. "I don't see the right size bins for staples. Your surplus flour is where?"

"Well, since I only get a one-pound ration every four weeks, it's not anywhere at the moment," Josie said. "Surplus is something that doesn't happen here."

"But you are not using your own ration for the food service, are you?"

"What else? Sometimes people share some of their rations, and we keep going as best we can."

"My dear girl," Miss Dawson said, "if you are

running a business, you are entitled to access wholesale supplies, especially if the RAF is involved. I'll give you the address, and you just need to show them your permit."

"I don't have a permit yet," Josie said.

"You should receive it after I make my report," Miss Dawson said.

"So you're going to approve us?"

"I see no reason why not." Miss Dawson nodded with the hint of a smile. "Clean kitchen. No sign of vermin." She looked around. "You do this alone? You do not employ kitchen help?"

"We have a woman who sometimes helps with the washing-up," Josie said. "I do all the baking and serving."

Josie led her back through the front hall. At that moment, Miss Harcourt opened the door from the sitting room. "I thought I heard a strange voice," she said. She gave the newcomer a questioning stare.

"This is Miss Dawson from Health and Safety, come to inspect our kitchen so that I can get a permit for the tearoom," Josie said.

"Inspect my kitchen?" Miss Harcourt drew herself up and stuck out her chin. "This house has entertained the cream of the county for fifty years. You will find nothing wrong with my kitchen. You should consider yourselves lucky that I have agreed to provide this small service to the community here during wartime."

Miss Dawson saw that she was outmatched. "Oh yes, absolutely," she stammered. "And the kitchen was indeed spotless. We are very grateful. Most grateful." She hurried to the front door. "You will be hearing from us, Mrs Banks. The permit should arrive shortly."

"That put her in her place," Miss Harcourt said as Josie closed the front door. "Too many bossy types around these days. I hope she didn't give you any trouble?"

"She came around quite nicely in the end," Josie agreed with a smile.

That afternoon a letter came from Mike. Josie opened it with a sick feeling in her stomach. He was telling her he did not want to see her again.

Dear Josie, it read.

> *I'm sorry to have stayed away, but our little motor car had a disagreement with a tractor earlier this week and is alas in the repair shop. I hasten to add that I wasn't driving her. Since parts are hard to find, it may take a while before she is on the road again, and without a motor car, it's a long walk from my quarters, and I don't have the time to be absent that long right now. I'll try to borrow a bicycle!*
> *Love,*
> *Mike*

Josie stared at the message, feeling the glow of happiness again. *Love, Mike.* She knew that plenty of people ended letters that way, almost without thinking, but those two words made the whole world feel right.

That week, Josie had managed to use two weeks' meat ration on a tiny piece of topside of beef. On Sunday, she roasted it along with potatoes and parsnips and even managed a small Yorkshire pudding to go with it. They were just sitting down to lunch when there was a knock at the front door. Kathleen went and came back with a disapproving look on her face.

"It's your sweetheart come to call," she said.

Josie rushed to the front door. Mike stood there.

"Hello," he said. "I finally managed to have a day off and beg, borrow or steal a bicycle. Is this a bad time?"

"We're just about to sit down to Sunday lunch," Josie said.

"Oh." He looked disappointed. "Then I'd better let you get on with it."

Josie made a quick decision. "Come on in. I'm sure we can stretch it to one more person, if Miss Harcourt doesn't mind." She led him in. Miss Harcourt was already sitting at the dining table. Josie introduced him.

"Squadron Leader Johnson," she said. "He has taken me shopping a couple of times. He's from Canada. Far from home. I don't mind letting him have my share of the meat, if you say he can join us."

Miss Harcourt examined him. "By all means join us, Squadron Leader," she said. "It will make a change to have male company at the table. We may even find that we have a decent bottle of wine left in the cellar. Josie, will you ask Kathleen for the key? A hock or a claret."

Josie went into the kitchen, where Kathleen was now pouring the gravy into a jug.

"Miss Harcourt wants you to give me the key to the cellar," she said.

"What for?" Kathleen glared.

"The gentleman is joining us for lunch, and the mistress wants a bottle of wine."

"Then I'll get it myself," Kathleen said. "I'm the one in charge of the keys here. We don't want you poking about in our cellar."

"Suit yourself," Josie said. "She said a hock or a claret."

"I know what wines she likes," Kathleen said. "I've been in this house since the old master, remember? In those days, it was dinner parties for twelve all the time."

And she swept past Josie.

Lunch went smoothly, with Miss Harcourt chatting easily with Mike, discussing the state of the war and showing considerable knowledge, then Mike answering in a way that included Josie and Kathleen. The unaccustomed wine made Josie feel relaxed and happy. She brought in the treacle pudding and custard for dessert and then excused herself. "You don't mind if we go out for a while now, do you?" she said when Kathleen joined her in the kitchen.

"And the washing-up?" Kathleen asked. "Is that going to sit around for all hours, cluttering up my kitchen?"

"Since I did all the cooking, perhaps you could do the washing-up," Josie said, trying to keep her tone polite and friendly.

"I'm not your skivvy," Kathleen snapped. "You come here, pushing me out of my place, getting all chummy with the mistress, then expect me to wait on you hand and foot."

"You know that's not true," Josie replied, still fighting to stay calm. "I've taken more than half the workload off your shoulders, supplied you with fresh vegetables and even brought in some money that we sorely need. And you've done nothing but make me feel unwelcome since the day I arrived. Fine. Leave the washing-up. I'll do it in a little while."

"It's sinful what you're doing." Kathleen spat out the words. "On the Lord's Day, too. Adultery is a mortal sin."

Josie took a deep breath, her fingers jammed into her palms. "Since I've done nothing I'm ashamed of, I'd watch my words if I were you. The squadron leader is a good man, and a kind man, and sometimes we all need a bit of kindness."

She stalked out of the kitchen. Mike was waiting in the front hall and noticed her red face.

"Is everything all right?" he asked.

"I'm afraid Kathleen was being a bit dramatic again," Josie said. "She has never forgiven me for coming here, even though I have taken over most of the workload. She lets me do the cooking and grow the vegetables but then complains about me nonstop." She opened the front door, and he followed her out. "The trouble is that she's jealous of me. Because the mistress has taken to me, I suppose."

"Some people are just unhappy by nature," he said. "You can't do anything about that."

"Are you happy by nature?" she asked, looking up at him.

"I used to be," he said. "Long ago I was very happy. Definitely a happy child without a care in the world—fishing with my father, helping my mother to bake. But until I met you, I'd forgotten what happiness was like."

"I suppose the war has robbed so many of us of the chance to be happy," Josie said. "But then, for people like me, it's the opposite. I feel like I've been given a second chance."

"Me too," he said. His gaze held hers for a long while. He paused at the front gate. "I'm afraid I can't take you anywhere today. I've only the bike, and I don't think you'd want to ride on the crossbar."

"That's all right. Let's just go for a walk," she said. "There's nowhere really to walk to, but it's a nice day and the air smells good."

"I agree."

"I was worried about you," Josie said. "I heard that so many planes were shot down while I was away. And JJ said yours came back full of holes."

"A slight exaggeration," he said, "but it was definitely a close call. And I'm afraid quite a few fellows weren't as lucky. You remember those two snooty types who gave you a bad time? Rogers and Watson? Both lost in one night. It seems as if our losses get worse all the time. Almost as if the Germans are waiting for us."

Josie shuddered. "Don't go any more," she wanted to say. They walked together in silence until they came to a raised dyke between fields. New crops had now turned the fields bright green. There was wild garlic and Queen Anne's lace growing along the sides of the track.

"I wasn't sure you'd come back," he said at last.

"Why?"

"I thought you might cave in to that husband of yours. He clearly didn't want you out here, did he?"

"No, he didn't. He came around when he saw I was coming back whatever he said."

"I hope I didn't cause trouble for you."

Josie shrugged. "I can't say he was thrilled about my knowing you," she said.

"He's a bully, isn't he?" He touched her arm lightly.

Josie didn't want to admit the truth. It seemed disloyal. "He was scared about going off to fight. So most of it was bluster. He was quite nice on our last day together, as if he wanted me to have good memories of him."

"Well, I'm glad of that." They walked on, then he said, "He's not good enough for you, Josie."

She looked away, staring across the fields to where a windmill turned on the horizon. "I married him, didn't I?"

There was a long pause until he said, "Do you love him?"

"I must have done once. I can't say I feel much for him any more—other than pity, that is."

"But you'll go back to him after the war?"

Now she turned to him, trying to hide the anguish on her face. "How can we say what might happen after the war? Maybe he won't come home, maybe a bomb will drop on me, maybe you won't come back, maybe the Germans will invade and make us all slaves." Her voice dropped. "It's no good making any plans beyond tomorrow, is it?"

"I suppose you're right," he said. "It just angered me so much to see you unhappy. I have to tell you I had this absurd desire to punch him."

She looked up then and smiled. "I like it that you were prepared to fight for me. It makes me feel sort of special."

"You are special."

He reached out and took her hand. They walked on until they came to a narrow stand of trees. Bluebells were growing in the shade, creating a carpet of mauvy blue. Mike sat on an old log, helping Josie down beside him. The only sounds were the stirring of leaves in the breeze and the squawk of a pheasant from a nearby field. Josie felt tension melting away with the serenity of the scene and the wine working through her body. Mike put an arm around her, and she rested her head on his shoulder. Then a gust of wind rustled the woodland, and her normally cautious nature returned.

"We probably shouldn't stay here too long, Mike," she said. "People will talk. 'They were seen going into the woods together, and you know what that means.'"

He laughed, pulling her up to her feet. "Would that be so terrible?" he said.

She hesitated. "No, but . . . we can't always have what we want, can we? I've got to live here right now, and I don't want the reputation of a fallen woman. And you've got to have the respect of your men."

This made him chuckle harder. "I have to tell

you, in the RAF, scoring with the ladies is looked upon as a sporting achievement. But I value your reputation, and besides, the ground is still wet. If I'd had evil desires, I would have brought a blanket with me."

This made Josie smile, too. He put his arm around her shoulder, and they walked on, out of the wood and along the dyke. The breeze had a slight tang of the sea, and a water-filled ditch now ran beside them. He asked her about London and how it looked now.

"I don't know where everybody's going to live after the war," Josie said. "Half the city is lying in ruins."

"Maybe people will come out to Canada," he said. "We have great empty spaces looking for more inhabitants."

"So you'll go back to Canada when this is over?" She tried to keep this a polite question.

"I'm not sure. We'll have to see how things are," he said. "There is something rather special about Nova Scotia. The fishing villages, the hill-sides covered in evergreen trees. Everything is so fresh and clean. But it's very insular, very cut off from the rest of the world. Too insular. Too lonely, probably." He helped her over the steps of a stile. "Now Montreal is a good city, but it's French speaking. You don't get by well there unless you have both languages."

"Do you speak French?"

"Not too well. We all had to learn it in school. So other than that, there is Ottawa—boring place—and Toronto, too big. That leaves the west coast. Beautiful, rugged, but awfully far away." He gave a short, despairing laugh. "No point in any of this discussion. Look, there's another village ahead."

They came into a small village, about the same size as Sutton St Giles—a couple of shops next to a pub, a church with a tall spire and a few houses around a village green with a pond in the middle.

"Shall we see if there's an ice cream or cup of tea to be had?" Mike asked.

"Ice cream?" Josie laughed. "Haven't you noticed there's a war on? And I'm sure everything's closed on Sundays."

The shops and pub were indeed closed, but from beyond the church came the sound of clapping. They followed it and came to a field with a cricket match going on.

"I know nothing about cricket," Mike said. "You'll have to explain it to me. It looks horribly complicated."

"Don't ask me," Josie said. "The only cricket I've seen is what the boys in the park play. I've never been to a real cricket match like this where they wear whites and there's the pavilion and scoreboard and everything. It's so nice and clean and just right. Like this is the way England's supposed to be."

Her lack of knowledge made her feel uncomfortable. "You have to understand, Mike. I don't have much schooling. I'm not educated, like you and like Miss Harcourt. I heard you two chatting away at lunch, talking about things and places I know nothing about. I've grown up in the East End of London. That's the slums. I've never had much of a life. People like me, we grow up, we get a job, we marry, we work, and then we die."

"No," he said. "Maybe that's how it used to be for you. This is your chance, Josie. The world has opened up for you. Already you're reading books and meeting different people and . . . and watching cricket matches." He pulled her on to a bench beside him, and they watched, both trying to make sense of the rules of the game.

"The boys play at the airfield, in their free time," he said. "I must get myself a rule book and then have a go myself. I was good at baseball when I was a kid. This can't be so different. Then you can come and watch me and clap when I hit a four or a six or whatever it's called."

As he was speaking, a big black dog bounded up to them. Josie shrank back, unsure around dogs, but Mike immediately started petting it. "Hey there, old fella," he said. "What are you doing running around by yourself? Are you lost?" The dog put its paws on his knee, trying to lick Mike's face as he laughed and continued rubbing its chest and sides.

At that moment, a small boy came running up. "There you are, Sooty," he called. "Sorry about that, mister. He got away from me."

"It's all right, kiddo. I enjoyed meeting him," Mike said. "I miss my own dog."

"So you used to have a dog?" Josie asked.

"Always. Grew up with them and had a dog around the place until—" He broke off. "Mostly Newfies. Newfoundlands, you know? Great big soppy brutes. There was one called Josh that was extra special when I was going through a difficult time. I actually cried when he had to be put down." He paused, giving her an embarrassed smile. His eyes followed the dog as it was led away. "You didn't have dogs?"

Josie shook her head. "When I was growing up, there was no food to spare for an extra mouth, and after that—well, Stan didn't like anything that took my attention away from him."

Mike looked at her, went to say something then obviously thought better of it. "What's happening now?" he asked as the players were leaving the field to the sound of clapping.

"They are breaking for tea," Josie said, glad she knew that much. Stan had listened to cricket on the wireless.

"Breaking for tea?" Mike burst out laughing. "You English play the most silly games."

"It's a very civilized game," Josie said in mock reproof. "Anything that stops for tea is civilized!"

She got up. "We should probably start walking back."

As they walked in silence, Josie found herself thinking about what Mike had said earlier. She had been given a chance for a new life. She'd already learned that she could run a business, bake buns, make friends and fall in love. That was not bad for half a year.

When they returned home Josie asked Mike if he'd like to come in for tea.

"I think I should be getting back," he said, "and we don't want to antagonize Kathleen again, do we?" He stood looking at her. "This was a great afternoon, Josie. I like being with you."

"I like being with you, too," she said. "It makes me feel that something in the stupid world is worthwhile."

"I'll see you soon," he said. "Let's hope the motor car is repairable."

He blew her a kiss, climbed on to the bicycle and rode away.

CHAPTER 31

When Josie came into the house, she found the washing-up done and the kitchen spotless. There was no sign of Kathleen, but she saw Miss Harcourt sitting in a deck chair under one of the apple trees. Josie went out to her.

"Ah, so you've returned, have you?" Miss Harcourt said.

"Just in time to make you some tea," Josie said. "You're in a good spot there."

"I'd forgotten how pleasant the garden could be," the older woman replied. "I must get busy with the flowers. I'm sure some of these old rose bushes could be brought back to former glory."

"I'll ask Alf Badger to come and take a look."

She was about to walk away when Miss Harcourt said, "This one is better than the other one, isn't he?"

Josie wondered for a second what she was saying, then realized. "But I'm married to the other one," she said.

"So you are. So maybe my advice to you should be to be careful. One false move and a life can be ruined. And you are a decent woman."

"Don't worry about me," Josie said. "No false moves." And she retreated back into the house.

• • •

The promised permit arrived. Josie took the bus into Spalding and stocked up on supplies. She had perhaps overestimated how much she could carry when she realized she'd have to hitch a lift home. She managed to get as far as the road leading to Sutton St Giles and then stood, waiting for a passing lorry. Nothing came past. The sky, which had been bright early in the day, was rapidly clouding up with the promise of approaching rain. Josie worried about the precious flour and sugar getting wet and was about to return to the town to wait in a café for the afternoon bus when a motor car came towards her. It slowed and stopped.

The driver wound down a window. "Hello, Mrs Banks! Can I give you a lift?"

It was Dr Goldsmith.

Josie gave him a grateful smile as she climbed in beside him. "I thought I was about to get soaked," she said. "I didn't realize how little traffic there is these days."

"Nobody can get petrol," he said. "I'm lucky because I have to be at the hospital."

They drove off. Almost on cue, the rain began to spatter on the windscreen.

"I haven't seen anything of you lately," she said. "Have you been very busy?"

"To be honest, I did not feel comfortable coming back to your tearoom," he said. "Those airmen—to them I am a German. An enemy. What do they know about how the Jews are treated over there?"

"You should come back and let them get to know you," she said.

"Maybe."

He slowed the motor car as a tractor turned out from a field in front of them and they had to crawl forward. "As it happens, I have not had time for polite visits," he said. "We have had problems at the hospital. We were bombed, and the surgical unit was damaged quite badly. So we have been operating in makeshift quarters, and we have had to take our turn at fire watching for incendiary bombs at night on the roof."

"That sounds awful."

"It is not pleasant, I can tell you, especially when it is cold and wet and windy. But it has to be done. We cannot risk the whole hospital going up in flames."

The tractor turned off into another field, and the car speeded up again.

"I saw Lottie the other day," Josie said. "She says you let her come to your house to do her homework sometimes."

He nodded. "She is a very bright young girl. So much has been taken away from her. I want to encourage her all I can. And it is important that she does not forget her own language. I think this is a good place for her. A kind woman to look after her and a place to help her forget that she has lost her family. Already I see that worried look is no longer on her face." He turned to Josie for affirmation. "And you. I think this is a good place for you as well. You, too, look as if you belong here now. Is that not true?"

"Perhaps you're right," she said. "But what about you? You don't feel that you belong?"

He shrugged. "People are polite enough. Maybe I shall never feel that I belong, however many years I live here. It is the price I pay. But if I had stayed in Germany, I should probably have been hauled off to a camp by now. Or dead."

They came to a halt beside Miss Harcourt's house.

"Thank you for saving me," she said. "Everything I have bought would have been ruined." She gave him an encouraging smile. "Come back to the tea shop sometime. I'm making really good buns and cakes now."

"Perhaps one day. I must remember to bring you my ration coupons," he said.

"That's kind of you but not even necessary now," she said. "We got an official permit to operate, so I can now get supplies from the government distribution centre. That's where I've been today."

"Splendid," he said. "I shall come and try your new good buns."

Josie tried not to smile at the choice of words.

He was so earnest, so serious. She gave him a cheery wave and hurried into the house.

With the new supplies Josie set to work, studying the cookery book and experimenting with more baking. This coincided with the burst of glorious summer weather. In a flash of inspiration, Josie carried the smallest tables and chairs out on to the front lawn, then approached Rose Finch to buy some of their cream so she could offer cream teas. Local people came, airmen and WAAFs, but not Charlie and his friends. Josie worried about this.

"Excuse me," she said as a group of WAAFs got up to leave one day. "But I haven't seen Charlie Wentworth lately. Do you know him? Is he all right?"

"Charlie?" one of the WAAFs said, glancing at her friends. "Oh dear. We haven't seen much of him either. He's really upset, of course. You heard that Dickie Dennison died, did you?"

"Dickie died?"

The girl nodded. "He killed himself rather than come back after his home leave. He wrote a note to say he couldn't handle it anymore."

"Oh, how terrible." Josie put her hand up to her mouth. "Poor Charlie and JJ. They were good friends. And Dickie—the life and soul of the party. I'll really miss him."

"We all will," the woman said.

"Could you hang on a minute?" Josie said. "I'd like to write a note to Charlie. Just to say I'm sorry."

"Of course," the young woman said.

Josie dashed upstairs, sat on her bed and stared at the writing paper. What did one say?

Dear Charlie, I am sorry to learn of the loss of your friend. It must have been a terrible shock. She paused. What else could she say? Words of comfort? But she couldn't think of any. That things would get better, easier? But they wouldn't. That it was a stupid waste of a life? In the end she added, *He was a good bloke. I enjoyed meeting him.*

That was about it. She signed it Josie Banks, put it in an envelope, addressed it and handed it to the WAAFs.

After they left, Josie went out into the garden and walked around, trying to digest this latest news. She hardly knew Dickie Dennison. He had come into the café, made jokes, played the piano. A nice chap. And now he was gone. And she realized the war was producing more casualties than just those that happened during bombing raids.

Josie tried to put her grief aside. She threw herself into the expanded enterprise. The cream teas were a big success as local inhabitants joined the airmen, and even travellers out for a spin in their motor cars stopped. Josie realized she could bake a double batch of buns in the mornings and offered the excess to the village shop, where they were snapped up every time. She felt the flush of success that her little business had really taken on wings.

One day she noticed a man sitting in the tearoom. It was a blustery day, and the tables were inside. He was observing the other customers with interest, especially the group of airmen. He was ordinary looking—young, dark hair, clean-shaven, not terribly well dressed. A well-worn tweed jacket and an open-necked shirt. A schoolmaster maybe? When he got up to pay his bill, he drew Josie aside.

"Do you have a moment, madam?" he asked.

"Is something wrong?"

"No. The tea was most agreeable."

"Then was there something you wanted?"

"I'd like to have a few words with you, if you don't mind. Is there somewhere more private we could go?"

"What's this about? I have a proper permit for the tearoom."

"No, it's nothing like that. But I do need to talk to you."

Josie looked around the room. There was only the group of airmen sitting beside the piano, none of whom she really knew. She went over to them. "Just leave the money on the table when you're finished, will you? I have to talk to this gentleman."

And she led him out into the foyer. She could hardly take him to Miss Harcourt's sitting room. "It had better be the library," she said, and went ahead into that room. Even in the height of summer, the library felt dark and cold, as if it remained cut off from the real life outside. There were two chairs over by the window, and she motioned for him to sit on one of them.

"Okay, so what is this about?" she asked.

"I'd like a few particulars on you first, if you don't mind."

"I do mind," Josie said. "Who are you? Are you from the county? The police?"

He smiled. "All will be made clear soon, I promise. Now if you could just give me your full name and a little bit about what you are doing here?"

"Are you from a newspaper?" Josie was not going to budge. He saw that.

"I'm afraid I'm from the government, Mrs Banks, and I do need you to cooperate."

"You already know my name?"

"Yes. We do our research ahead of time. You previously lived in London, and you came out here several months ago."

"After my house was bombed and I was hurt."

"Quite." He paused. "Exactly why did you choose this part of the country? What brought you out here?"

"The answer to that is a train, then a bus."

"That wasn't exactly what I was getting at," he said, showing no sign of impatience.

She shrugged. "It's the truth. Someone put me on a train in London. Someone else met me in Peterborough, put me on a bus and dropped me off in this village. I had no say in it. Believe me, if I'd had any say, I wouldn't have come here, out in the middle of nowhere. This house was the only place left to take in an evacuee. The owner wasn't at all happy about it, but she had no choice. So I've stayed, and I'm getting along quite well now."

"In London, what did you do?"

"I was a housewife until my husband was called up. Then I worked in a tea shop. I really liked it. Quiet and genteel. Then that was bombed, and the owner was killed, and next thing you know, I was bombed, too. That's the way it went in London. I was glad to be out of the city."

"Were you ever a member of the Communist Party?"

"What?" She looked up at him and gave an incredulous laugh. "What a bloody stupid thing to ask. Of course I wasn't."

"But your husband was."

"What?" This, too, took her by surprise. "Stan? Stanley Banks? No, you've got the wrong bloke."

"I have it on the best authority that his name shows up on a Communist Party list of members."

Josie hesitated. "Maybe before he met me,

then. He was a bit hot-headed in his young days, but since I've known him, he was only interested in a good meal and a pint at the pub."

"I see." The man paused, looking at her until she began to feel uncomfortable.

"Why are you so interested in the Communist Party?" she demanded. "It seems to me we're fighting Hitler, not Stalin. Isn't he supposed to be our ally now?"

"It's a complicated business," the man said. "There are other factions who would rejoice in the downfall of Britain. The Communists are one of them."

"Well, if you think I'm a ruddy Communist, you really are barking up the wrong tree, mate." She paused. "Besides," she went on, "if I was a Communist, wouldn't I be staying in London and agitating the people?"

He actually smiled then. "Maybe." He scribbled down some notes in a small book. Then he looked up again. "So what about the other occupants of this house?"

"Certainly neither of them is a Communist either, I can promise you that."

"Let's forget about Communists, then. Who lives here?"

"It's owned by a Miss Harcourt. She's proper old-school gentry. And she has one servant left. A woman called Kathleen. Been with Miss Harcourt for donkey's years."

"I see." He nodded. "And you operate a small café here now?"

"You saw it." Josie was still uneasy, not sure why he was questioning her.

"That was your idea, or the homeowner's?"

"It was mine. I saw the local airmen needed a place to come and forget about things for a while. Feel like home, you know. So I started it, and now it's going really well." She paused. "Are there taxes I should be paying that I don't know about? We did get the permit."

"No, nothing like that," he said. "Would you say you are an observant person?"

"Yeah. I think so."

"Then I'd like to enlist your help."

"Not until you tell me who you are and what you want from me."

"Mrs Banks, this conversation is strictly confidential and must be repeated to no one. Do I have your word on that?"

"I suppose so. All right. You still haven't explained—"

"A matter of national security. Do I have your word?"

"That I won't repeat the conversation? All right."

"It concerns the bomber command station nearby. Until recently their losses were average for bombing missions. For the past couple of months, they have become above average. Excessive, one might say."

"Yes, I know they've been hard hit. I feel so bad for those poor boys."

"It almost seems that when they go on a bombing raid, the enemy knows where they are heading and is waiting for them. Almost as if they have been tipped off in advance."

Now she stared at him, her mouth open. She remembered that Mike had used those very words: "Almost as if they were waiting for us."

"You think someone is tipping off Jerry about our bombers?"

"It appears that way, yes."

"Someone on the RAF station?"

"Possibly, although security is tight enough that a radio transmission would be discovered instantly. That person would need to leave the RAF station to transmit the news to Germany."

She saw what he was getting at. "And you think someone might come here to pass along the news?"

He nodded. "That's exactly what we were thinking. You immediately came to mind—you come here, and almost immediately the RAF starts experiencing higher than usual losses."

"Bloody cheek." Josie could hear herself slipping back into cockney speech.

"We had to consider all angles, Mrs Banks. So assuming you are in the clear, I want to enlist your help. Would you be willing to help your country?"

"If I can," she said. "You don't want me to be a spy, do you? I don't fancy myself as no Mata Hari."

He laughed. "In a way, but not Mata Hari, I promise you. I want you to keep your eyes open. If there are any strangers, see if they interact with an airman. Make a note of who comes to your café every day. See if you can actually get their names. Maybe have a guestbook you ask them to sign? Perhaps a pattern will emerge."

"Look," she said, "I still don't know you from Adam. You might be an enemy spy yourself, for all I know."

"Actually I work for MI5. Domestic security. As for my name, you can call me Mr Thomas."

"That's not your real name?"

"No, it's not."

"And how do I get in touch with you?"

"I'll be coming to tea from time to time. I'm a feed salesman calling on local farms, as far as anyone knows around here." He smiled. "But I'll give you a telephone number only to be used in a great emergency. There is a telephone in the house?"

"There is."

"That's good, then. We won't have to come up with a reason to install one. A time you might need to use it is if you actually see a suspicious transaction taking place—a slip of paper passed from one person to another?"

"Hang on a minute," Josie said. "Why would one of the airmen at the airfield want to tip off the enemy? He could be flying himself that night. They don't always get their orders until the evening."

"We have to assume this person is privy to a briefing amongst higher-ups, earlier in the day, and of course he may not be a pilot. He may be ground crew."

"And happily sends off his fellow RAF to their death? Who would do that?"

"One also assumes the Germans are able to infiltrate our armed forces. We've had an influx of central Europeans: Poles and Czechs and Hungarians escaping from the Nazis. Some of them arrived having flown their own aircraft. They often come without papers, unable to prove who they are but keen to join our armed forces. We've only their word that they are not Nazis."

"Blimey." She immediately thought of JJ. Sweet, funny JJ with his strong accent.

He stood up. "I should let you get back to your duties. I will be in touch, and I can't stress enough that we are relying on you. This has to be stopped. And not a word to anybody, you understand?"

CHAPTER 32

After she had seen him out, Josie stood for a while in the foyer, staring at nothing, collecting her thoughts. It seemed impossible that this tranquil place was being used by an enemy spy to pass along information—information that would kill their fellow airmen who flew the bombers, might kill Mike. And if it was one of their own airmen, who could he pass the information along to? She had met all the local people—solid Lincolnshire farmers who showed no interest in the world beyond their village, other than to worry about their sons and husbands who were fighting in faraway places. It was true that outsiders occasionally did stop for tea when she had the tables outside, but that had only been a recent occurrence.

And now she was being asked to spy on her customers. The sick, sinking feeling in her stomach returned. Why was it that every time she felt she was safe and happy at last, something came up to remind her that she wasn't? But she did as Mr Thomas had asked and noted who came to the tea shop and where they sat. She noted no interactions between guests beyond a friendly remark about the weather.

When she went into Spalding next, she found

a guestbook at the stationery shop and put it on prominent display by the door at Miss Harcourt's. "Please sign our guestbook," she said. "I have to prove to the ministry that I'm serving airmen here."

Nobody seemed to object. Life went on its usual slow pace. Josie baked, poured tea, counted the profits, attended WI meetings where not much sewing got done. She remembered that Johnny Hodgkins was known for his black-market activities. A man like him could possibly be persuaded to sell secrets to the enemy. But then, he had never been to the tearoom, and Lil, his wife, had only been in a couple of times. It did occur to Josie that Dr Goldsmith was a German who claimed to have renounced his country because he was Jewish. But was he really Jewish? She had never heard him talk of a temple or a rabbi, even when he was with Lottie, who was also Jewish.

Josie mentioned this to the girl once when they met as Lottie was getting off the bus in the afternoon.

"So, are there any other Jewish girls at your school?" she asked.

Lottie shook her head. "Not one. I don't think that Jewish people choose to live in the English countryside. There is too much prejudice against them."

"Dr Goldsmith does."

"Yes." She nodded, sadly. "He chooses to live in the country because the prejudices are even worse in the big towns. If he had not been Jewish and German, he could have made a lot of money in private practice. But as it is, he prefers the anonymous feeling of a big hospital."

"Aren't Jews supposed to go to their temple? That must be hard for you."

Lottie smiled. "My family was not at all religious. My parents never went to the synagogue. In fact, they sent me to a Catholic girls' school because the education was good. I quite enjoyed being part of that religion. It seems rather comforting, with saints and candles and Mary, mother of God. I think it's lovely that there is a lady one can pray to. The Jewish religion is all about men. I might have converted if I hadn't been banished when the Nazis said no education for Jews."

"And Dr Goldsmith? Does he miss his synagogue?"

"He is more religious than me," Lottie said. "He has a lovely menorah at his house. I don't know. Perhaps he has found a synagogue in Peterborough. It is a big town."

They parted company, and Josie walked back home. Lottie thought that Dr Goldsmith was quite religious. So that should rule him out as a suspect.

July became August, and Mr Thomas did not

reappear. It seemed as if the bombing raids had slowed for the summer, and Josie didn't hear about more disasters with many planes lost. She hoped that MI5 had got it wrong and it was only a coincidence that several flights had suffered disastrous consequences. The days were hot and sticky. Miss Harcourt sat in her deck chair in the shade and read. Josie picked fruit and vegetables, and she and Kathleen bottled them for the winter.

Then one day a contingent of land girls arrived, brought in to harvest the sugar beets and potatoes growing in surrounding fields. Some of them were billeted at the pub, and in the evenings they sat on the green in front of the church, talking and laughing. Josie encountered them when she went to visit the Badgers. She heard accents similar to her own and stopped to speak to them.

"You're the lady who runs the café where the RAF blokes come in the afternoons, right?" one asked her. The girl was wearing overalls and had her hair tied back in a kerchief. Her face was freckled from the sun. Josie said she was.

"We're coming when we get an afternoon off," she said. "We're fed up with no men in our lives." There were more risqué comments, and Josie laughed with them. *That could have been me,* she thought as she walked back. But she was glad that her fortunes had taken a turn.

The land girls were also the talk of the WI

meeting. Harry at the pub was glad of the extra business; so was the shop lady.

"They're hard workers, so I've heard," someone commented.

"My Frankie says they don't complain about the long hours or anything. Just get on with it," Mrs Wilks said. "We should do something for them. Make them feel appreciated here."

It was suggested that the WI set up a dance at the village hall as a gesture of goodwill to the land girls and the airmen. Josie baked extra cakes to serve with the lemonade. No alcohol was to be served. They decorated the hall with banners and paper streamers until it looked quite festive. Josie decided to attend, just to help out, she told herself. She put on the silk tea dress and curled her hair in curl papers. She was helping to pour lemonade when she looked up to see Mike coming in with a couple of other officers.

"I wasn't expecting to see you," she said. "You were going to check out the land girls, eh?"

"Keep an eye on our men, more like it." He smiled. "They won't misbehave if we're watching them. But since I'm here, do you fancy a dance? It's nice and slow."

He took her hand and led her on to the dance floor. He held her close, her cheek against his uniform. "You've saved me a bicycle ride," he said. "I was planning to come out to see you, but it's not my turn for the motor car. The blighter's gone off to visit his family for a week—in Yorkshire."

"Oh dear." She smiled up at him. "That's annoying of him. Wanting to visit his family."

"That was actually what I wanted to see you about," he said.

"Visiting your family?"

He shook his head. "We've been told we have to take regular leave away from base. They are worried about battle fatigue. It's my turn next. So I thought I'd take a little trip to the seaside."

"That's nice for you," she said.

He looked at her before he spoke, his eyes holding hers. "I was wondering if you'd like to come with me."

"Me? To the seaside?"

"That's right."

"That sounds smashing. Which day are you planning to go?"

"I thought we'd leave next Monday. I'll see what hotels are open for business."

"Oh, you mean you're staying there for a few days?"

He nodded. "Yes. That's what I meant."

"Oh. I see." The full implication of this was just becoming apparent. He steered her around a wildly gyrating couple who were attempting a jitterbug and off to one side of the dance floor.

He was still holding her, his hand on the small

of her back. "You deserve a break, too, Josie. Will you come?"

The music changed to a slow waltz. Josie broke away from him and went to sit on one of the empty chairs. Mike pulled up another beside her. She took a deep breath. "You want me to come away with you for a few days? Share a hotel room with you?"

"I just thought . . . you and I." He stumbled over the words.

Josie reached out and touched his arm. "Believe me, Mike, I'd really like to. I'll probably kick myself after you've gone, but it just doesn't seem right. I know, I'm old-fashioned, I suppose, but I'm still a married woman, whether I like it or not, and my husband's off somewhere fighting the enemy. I wouldn't want to betray him."

"That's all right," he said, speaking too quickly. "I'm sorry. I shouldn't even have suggested it. Forget I even said it. I just thought we both needed a little chance of happiness today because there might not be a tomorrow."

This struck Josie right in the heart. She realized what he was saying was true. He never knew which flight would be his last. She looked at him in an agony of indecision. "Look, I love spending time with you. And I've hardly been to the seaside in my whole life, so it would be a real treat, but . . ."

"Would you come if I booked separate rooms for us?"

"Just as friends, you mean?"

"Just as friends."

"I think I'd like that a lot."

"Terrific. Or as the boys here say, 'smashing. Wizard.'" He looked as if she had given him a present.

Later, at home in her room, she stood staring at herself in the speckled mirror on the chest of drawers. "What are you doing?" she asked herself. "You've agreed to go away with a man." A man she really cared about. Were they really going to be able to stay casual and distant when they were far from home and when nobody else was around? She had admitted to herself long ago that she didn't love Stan and was finding it hard to picture herself with Stan when the war was over. And if Stan ever found out she had gone with Mike, there would be hell to pay. On the other hand, didn't Mike deserve a little happiness, too, when each day could be his last? She couldn't deny her feelings for him and suspected he felt the same way about her, but she couldn't be sure.

"Anyway, I've already said yes, so there's no going back now," she told the worried image in the mirror. "What Stan doesn't know can't hurt him."

That weekend she told Kathleen that she'd be

going away. "I think we'll just close up the tea shop for a couple of days, rather than give you extra work. We'll put out a sign and say closed for summer holidays, all right?"

"It seems a shame to close now, when we're making the money," Kathleen said. "I expect I can manage on my own, but I'm not doing any baking in this kind of weather. It will be tea and biscuits and strawberries if we've still got some coming up." She eyed Josie with interest. "So where are you going? Back to London to the relatives there?"

"No, only to the seaside for a couple of days."

Kathleen's eyes narrowed. "You're going with him, aren't you? With that man."

"It's none of your business, Kathleen," Josie replied, a little too sharply. "And I told you before, we are just friends. There is no hanky-panky."

"Men don't invite women away with them just to be friends," Kathleen said.

"I'll make another lot of buns before I go, then you'll have something to serve," Josie said and walked out of the room, feeling her cheeks glowing hot. The problem was that she knew Kathleen was right. Men didn't invite women to go to hotels with them just to be friends. Was she mad to say she would go? And yet she knew she wanted to. She had the feeling that this was her one chance to be happy, and if she turned it down, she'd always regret it.

Telling Miss Harcourt was even harder than breaking the news to Kathleen.

"I have a chance to meet a friend at the seaside for a couple of days," she said. "I'll make sure Kathleen has everything she needs to take care of you properly."

Miss Harcourt eyed her with that birdlike stare, her head cocked to one side. "I hope you and your friend have an agreeable time," she said. "The sea air certainly is most restorative."

"Yes," Josie said. She knew what Miss Harcourt was thinking and could find nothing to reply. She suspected that Miss Harcourt would be looking out of the window when Mike arrived in the little motor car on Monday morning. *It's none of her business either,* Josie told herself, but it did matter. She had come to value Miss Harcourt's opinion of her.

CHAPTER 33

Josie tried to push her concerns aside as she sat next to Mike in the little car and they headed off. It was a glorious summer morning with the countryside shimmering in the heat haze. As they left the village behind, Mike glanced at her and gave her a conspiratorial smile. "We're off on our adventure, Josie. I can't tell you how much this means to me."

"Don't you go getting any ideas, Mike Johnson," she said, although she was smiling, too. "Just friends, remember."

"That's right. Just friends."

They drove on for a while in silence.

"Where are we going, then?" she asked.

"Hunstanton. It's a seaside town on the Norfolk coast. Not too far from here. Nice beaches. Good bathing, apparently."

"You'll be doing the bathing. I'll cheer you on. I don't own a bathing suit," she said.

"Then we'll have to find one for you when we get there," he said. "I'm not going in the sea by myself."

They drove mostly in silence. Josie suspected Mike was as uneasy as she was. Occasionally, she sensed him looking in her direction. She met his gaze, and they exchanged a smile.

"Is there too much breeze with the window open?" he asked.

"No, it's lovely. I like the smell of the fresh air, don't you?"

"I do. And I expect the sea air will smell even better."

They passed low-lying fields, waterways and windmills, through the historic town of King's Lynn, with its impressive twin-towered church, and then through leafy countryside until they came to Hunstanton. It was one of those resorts the Victorians created when sea air became popular. Rows of tall, solid brick houses, green lawns and gardens above the cliffs and a beach to one side. The gardens would have been dotted with flower beds before the war but now were mostly dug up and growing vegetables.

"The hotel is called the Seaview," Mike said, peering through the windscreen. "It should be around here somewhere."

They drove slowly along the esplanade, studying the row of hotels and boarding houses, but none of them was the Seaview. Then they turned into a narrow side street, and there it was.

"False advertising, wouldn't you say?" Mike commented. "I doubt there's a sea view from any of the rooms. It should be called Fish and Chip Shop View."

Josie chuckled.

The narrow front hall wasn't too promising. It

had a lingering smell of yesterday's food. The woman who greeted them looked quickly at Josie's left hand to see if she was wearing a ring.

"Squadron Leader Johnson? Three nights?"

"That's right."

"And Mrs Johnson, I presume?"

"No, this is Mrs Banks. A friend."

"So you'll be needing separate rooms, then." It wasn't a question.

"That's right."

"And your ration books, please?"

"You can have mine," Mike said. "This lady operates a café for the airmen and donates her own coupons, so I'm afraid one will have to do. We'll be taking our evening meal out."

"Suit yourself," the woman said. She went over to a board of keys. "One of you can have room number three, at the back. Quieter there. And the other one's number seven, up another flight." She handed them keys. "Door's locked at ten. Absolute silence after that. Bathroom at the end of the hall. There's a line on the bathtub. Only three inches of water, mind."

Mike carried their bags upstairs and unlocked the door to number three as Josie followed. "Why don't you have this one?" he said. "Fewer stairs.

"This wasn't exactly what I pictured," he said as they stepped inside. It was a narrow room and looked out on to a small back garden and the houses behind. Not a trace of a sea view. It contained a narrow bed, a rack to hang clothes and a small chest of drawers. No chair and no mirror. "Shall we take a look at the other room?"

Josie left her bag and followed him up the stairs. Mike looked back and laughed. "Listen to how the stairs creak. I bet she did this deliberately so she could make sure there was no creeping around after dark."

The other room was equally gloomy, but Josie went over to the window. "It does have a sea view if you lean right over like this," she said. She looked back and grinned. Mike sat down on the bed, and the bedsprings gave an ominous twang.

"It is pretty awful, isn't it?" Mike said. "Should we try somewhere else?"

"I don't suppose many hotels are operating," Josie said. "There is a war on."

"We'll be out most of the time," Mike said, now trying to look cheerful. "Come on. Let's go and buy you a bathing suit!"

They left the motor car parked outside and walked into a high street. They found a ladies' dress shop, although the window display looked as if it had not been changed for many years. The assistant agreed that they might have ladies' swimwear for madam, pulled out a drawer and displayed a navy-blue wool swimsuit.

"Well, it's not exactly Hollywood," Mike said as Josie eyed it suspiciously.

"We don't have much call at the moment," the woman said. "Not getting the usual holiday-makers, are we? The railway station was actually bombed earlier this year. And they tried for the pier, but they missed."

Mike paid for the swimsuit, and they came out into the sunshine. He suggested they explore the front and see which part of the beach was safe for swimming. The first beach they reached was mainly stones, not sand. They continued until they came to impressive cliffs made up of layers of dark-red-and-white rock. Below them were boulders where the face had tumbled. Not too inviting to walk on, so they followed the path over the cliff tops to the lighthouse and stood looking out to sea. They ate a sausage roll from a seaside kiosk for lunch, then went back to the hotel to change into their costumes.

"I'm not at all sure about this," Josie said. "You won't let me drown, promise?"

"I won't let you drown. Promise." He took her hand. It was the first physical contact they had had that day, and it shot a little bell of alarm through Josie, although she didn't draw her hand away. The tide had gone out, revealing sand beyond the stony part of the beach.

"Do you think it's safe?" Josie asked as they undressed. "It's not mined or anything?"

"There would be warning signs if it were," he said. "I see some tank traps further down, but the tide goes out so far here that it would be impractical as a landing area. Come on." Mike took her hand and propelled her forward over the sand. The water that now lapped at her toes was icy. Josie stopped.

"I'm not going in there. It's bloody freezing."

"Coward." He ran ahead and dived into the waves. Then he came up again, a look of horror on his face. "You're right. It is a little cold."

Two little girls ran through the waves, laughing. "If they can take it, we can," Mike said. "And we have to christen that suit." He took her hands and dragged her, protesting, into the waves. A wave swept up to her chest, and she gasped. "You need to get all the way in, then it's better."

She dunked herself. "No, it's not," she called to him. "It's still freezing."

He laughed, dived through a wave and swam away with easy strokes. Josie wished she could swim and that she wasn't afraid of the waves.

"Come on," he called. "It's calm beyond the waves."

She shook her head. "I can't swim."

"Oh no." He came back to her. "This is not a good place to teach you. Maybe there's a swimming pool where we can go tomorrow."

She shivered. "I'm cold, Mike. I'm going back. You keep swimming, and I'll watch."

As she walked out, she started to laugh. "Look at this swimming costume. It's stretching down to my knees, and it's heavy enough to drown me."

"It does look a bit strange," he agreed, laughing, too. "You look like you're being devoured by a sea monster."

They went back to the hotel to change. Josie came out of her room to find Mike coming out of the bathroom, now dressed in slacks and an open-necked shirt. "I don't know about you," he said, "but that swim has given me an appetite. Should we go out and find a cup of tea and something to eat?"

Josie agreed. She felt tension between them now, in a strange hotel together. They walked along the seafront until they found a café that served tea and toast.

"Not as good as yours," he whispered.

The day seemed to stretch on. For supper they bought fish and chips and carried it up on to the green above the cliffs, where they sat watching the sun set.

"Do you notice that?" Mike asked.

"What?"

"The sun is setting over the sea, but we're on the east coast. It must be the only place on this coast that faces west. The bay must curve around."

The sunset was spectacular. Mike put his arm around her, and Josie rested her head on his shoulder. *It's going to be all right,* she thought. *No need to worry.* They stopped at the Queen's

Head pub for a pint. It was almost dark by the time they returned to the hotel. The landlady appeared in the front hall as they came in. They felt her watching them as they went up the stairs. They stood outside Josie's door, looking at each other.

"Well, goodnight, then," Mike said.

"Goodnight, Mike." She could tell he wanted to kiss her, but they were both conscious of the landlady, probably still watching. Mike gave an embarrassed chuckle and headed up the stairs to his room. As Josie lay on the narrow, uncomfortable bed, she asked herself whether it would be so wrong to give in to what they both wanted. Weren't they both entitled to a tiny sliver of happiness?

"Did you sleep well?" Mike greeted her in the morning. He looked hollow-eyed, as if he hadn't had a good night either.

"Ruddy awful, if you want to know," she said. "The bedsprings stuck into my back, and every time I turned over, they gave this loud twang."

"Same with mine." Mike chuckled. "I expect it's deliberate so the landlady can keep tabs on what is going on."

Breakfast was a bowl of unappetizing, lumpy porridge with a slice of bread and margarine.

"I think this is the straw that broke the camel's back, don't you?" Mike whispered.

"Let's find somewhere else."

The landlady was not pleased they were leaving. "I could charge you for the other two nights," she said.

"We'll split the difference, and I'll pay you for one extra night," Mike replied. "But I need my ration book back."

"Talk about the Wicked Witch," he muttered to Josie as they put their bags in the car. "I felt she was watching us every second, didn't you?"

Josie nodded. "No hanky-panky allowed at that hotel, clearly."

"Let's drive along the coast and see if we find somewhere we like better," he suggested. They left the town, and at the far end of the cliffs, where the landscape opened into a sandy bay, they came to a pretty village. Mike checked his map. "This seems to be Old Hunstanton. This looks better, doesn't it?"

"I don't see any hotels," Josie said.

Then they spotted a sign saying "Room to Let" in a window.

"It says *room* and not *rooms*," Josie pointed out.

"We can give it a try," Mike said. "Come on. Where's that sense of adventure?"

The door was opened by an elderly woman. Mike introduced himself, and then added, "And this is Mrs Banks."

"You'll be wanting the one room, will you? I've a big double bed."

"Do you have two rooms?" Mike asked.

"I do. So this lady is your sister, is she?" She was eyeing them almost with amusement now.

"I'm not his sister," Josie said. "But just a friend."

"Just a friend. Ah." The woman nodded. "Well, then. Let me show you the rooms."

They were side by side, facing the sea, both decorated with flowery wallpaper and with a white wicker chair in the window. The landlady offered dinner and breakfast at a reasonable rate.

"A bit better than the last one, eh?" Josie said.

They explored the village, then walked on the sandy beach. After lunch of a cheese sandwich containing very little cheese at a pub, Mike swam again while Josie collected shells. A scream made her look up. A small child had been playing in the shallow water when an unexpectedly big wave knocked him over. Josie saw arms and legs as he was bowled over and started towards him. But Mike got there first, scooping up the child.

"It's okay. You're safe, buddy," he said in his deep, comforting voice. The child's mother was now running towards them, her mouth open in fear. Mike set the boy down.

"No harm done," he said. "He just got knocked over by a big wave. But keep an eye on him, okay? The sea is unpredictable."

The child was howling now, and the mother carried him off. Mike turned to Josie and shook his head. "She needs to keep a better eye on that child. If this beach had a rip current, he would have been gone."

"You would have made a great dad," Josie wanted to say but didn't. It seemed one step too intimate.

"I think that's enough cold water for one day," she said.

"Okay, I agree. The water is damned cold. Come on, let's get a cup of tea." He put a wet arm around her.

"You're making me cold and wet!" she exclaimed, shaking off his arm.

"You don't want me to hug you, then?" he teased, coming towards her. Josie shrieked and ran off as he chased her. Mike caught her. "I'm not going to let you go that easily," he said, grabbing her shoulders and smiling down at her. Josie saw the desire in his eyes.

"Go and get changed, you silly ha'p'orth, or you'll catch your death of cold," Josie said, laughing uneasily because she, too, felt the excitement in the pit of her stomach.

After he had changed on the beach, they went for a walk further along the shore. After the last houses of the village, the beach was bordered by sand dunes, and the scene felt wild and remote. Sandy beach became a narrow strip of pebbles interspersed with seaweed-covered rocks.

"The tide's coming in," Mike said, and just as

he finished the words, a wave, bigger than the rest, rushed up to them. Josie squealed and ran back, but not quickly enough as the cold water splashed over her bare feet and soaked the bottom of Mike's trousers.

"I don't think we can go any further this way," Mike said. "Come on, let's cut back to the road." He took her hand again and led her up into the dunes. Climbing the hill of soft sand was hard going, and Josie was out of breath by the time they had crested the first dune.

"Hold on a minute," she said. "It's like going through the bloody Sahara Desert. I'll expect to see a string of camels any minute."

"That's right. We are in the middle of the Sahara, and I am a wicked sheik," he said, laughing as he grabbed her. "And now I have you at my mercy." Then the laughter faded, and suddenly he was kissing her. And Josie felt herself responding. He eased her down to the soft, warm sand.

"God, Josie. I want you so bad," he murmured. His hands ran over her body as he kissed her again. Josie was conscious of the weight of his body on hers, the warm sand pressing into her back and his mouth, tasting of salt, crushing against her lips. At that moment it felt as if they were alone in the universe and nothing else mattered. Then suddenly a cloud rushed across to hide the sun, and a gust of cold wind peppered them with fine sand. Josie broke away from him.

"I'm getting sand in my eyes," she said, "and in my mouth, too." She brushed at her face.

Mike sat up. "And in your hair, too." He reached out and brushed the sand gently from her hair. "Okay, I give in. The fates are against us. Come on. Let's walk back."

He pulled her to her feet. The wind from the sea was now fierce, the sand stinging at their bare legs.

"It looks like a storm's coming in," he said. "Look at those clouds gathering." He slipped an arm around her shoulders. "I don't remember feeling as happy as this for many years now," he said.

"Since your wife died?" she asked cautiously.

He nodded. Then he cleared his throat and said, "About my wife . . ."

"Yes?"

There was a long pause. Then he said, "Never mind. I didn't think I could be happy again, but then I met you. I think you feel the same way about me. When I was kissing you back there, you didn't want me to stop, did you?"

"But that didn't mean that it was right, Mike. I have to think of Stan—"

"Damn Stan," he said angrily. Then he gave an embarrassed shrug. "I'm sorry, but when did he ever consider you and your happiness?"

"Not often," she agreed. "Maybe never."

"Well, then. Don't we deserve a chance, Josie? I want to make love to you. I know we can't think about the future. This moment—this is all we've got. Can't we make the most of it?"

"I suppose you're right," she said at last. "We might not be here tomorrow. Stan might be dead for all I know, and I do deserve some happiness." It came as a startling revelation. Her whole life so far had been about someone else's happiness, never her own. Leaving school to look after her brothers and sisters, working in the factory she hated, then trying to please Stan. And not once had anyone asked her what it was that she wanted. *Except Madame Olga,* Josie reminded herself. Madame had cared about her, and now she was dead.

As they left the beach, Mike's arm around her, Josie found herself picturing life with him, always happy and free like this, maybe even in far-off Canada. Then a rumbling noise interrupted her thoughts as a flight of planes came overhead, followed by a second wave, heading towards the Continent. This brought her back to reality. There could be no future until the war was over.

CHAPTER 34

That evening they dined in the old-fashioned front room of the cottage. The meal was fish pie with runner beans fresh from the garden, followed by gooseberry fool. "From my garden," the landlady said, beaming with pleasure when they complimented her on the food. "I keep chickens, and the fruit has been wonderful this year. I'd be making jam if only I could get the sugar."

They had just finished dinner when the storm came in. Rain beat against the window and rattled the frame. "I'm glad we're not going anywhere on a night like this," Josie said.

"So am I." His look said it all.

There was no sign of the landlady when they went to their rooms. Josie opened her door, and Mike followed her in, closing the door carefully behind them.

"I want you to know that I have fallen in love with you," he said softly. He reached out and carefully undid the buttons down the front of her dress, letting it fall to the floor. Josie stood like a statue, letting him. Then he took her into his arms and kissed her. What happened after that was a blur to Josie. She didn't remember Mike unhooking her bra, taking off her slip and panties, but then they were lying naked together on her bed while outside the storm raged. Josie had no idea that lovemaking could be like this. It was overwhelming, intoxicating. Afterward, she lay in his arms, tasting the salt still on his skin.

"I can't let you go, Josie," he whispered to her. "I can't let you go back to him."

"Let's not think about it now, Mike. I don't want to think what might happen." She turned to look into his face. "I can't let myself fall in love with you, Mike."

He frowned. "What have I done?"

"Nothing. Everything about you is perfect. Too perfect. It's just that I don't want to lose you either. I don't want to look up at the sky every night, wondering if you're going to come home safely."

Mike stroked her hair. "But don't you see, having you to come home to makes everything worthwhile. I think about you all the time, Josie."

Josie closed her eyes, fighting the turmoil inside her. Of course she wanted to be with him. Of course she was already in love with him.

That night she had a dream. She was back on the sand dunes, and ahead of her she saw a lone figure. She thought it was Mike and started towards him, but then she realized it was Stan, alone in a desert of sand. He was looking around, desperate. "Where are you, Josie?" he called. "I need you here, with me." And he sank to his knees.

She woke up, her heart racing. Mike slept beside her, a look of serenity on his face. In the morning, she told him about the dream. "I don't think we can do this again, Mike. What if Stan really is in danger?"

Mike frowned. "Do you still love him, in spite of the way he treats you?"

"No. I don't think I've loved him for years now. Perhaps I never loved him. He was a way of escape for me. But I married him. I made a promise."

"Do you think he's kept to his promise? Has he been faithful to you?"

"I don't know. But that doesn't make it right."

"Do you want to go back? Forget about our last day?"

"I don't know." She turned away, staring at the blank wall. "I've never felt so happy as here with you."

"It's the same for me, Josie. This is the first time in years that I've remembered what it's like to be happy. To be hopeful. To think there might be a future, after all." He stroked her bare shoulder. "If I asked you to marry me after the war, what would you say?"

"I'd like to say yes. I think I could have a lovely life with you. But how would I feel about deserting Stan when he came back from the fighting, after he's been through so much?"

"Let's not talk about it now, then. Let's just

enjoy the rest of the time we have together, okay?"

"All right," she agreed.

They sat together in silence as they drove back. Already it felt like a dream that was fading. After the dream about Stan, Josie had wrestled with conflicting emotions. She knew how happy she felt with Mike, but the guilt threatened to overwhelm her. Would she have the strength to walk away from a loveless marriage when Stan came home?

Back at the tea shop, Josie now found her mission more challenging. The land girls had agreed to start work earlier in the mornings so they were free by four o'clock. Then they'd come to the tearoom and meet the airmen. Which also meant that RAF men came to meet the land girls. It was a fun, lively afternoon but impossible for Josie to observe if information was handed over. She could rule out the land girls as they were not present when MI5 became suspicious. But the land girls also brought in local farmworkers. Josie looked at the burly local boys, too young to join up, or the older men, too old to serve, and couldn't think that any of them might be involved in helping the enemy.

Dr Goldsmith came in but looked askance at the crowded tables and noisy laughter.

"You have created a monster, Mrs Banks,"

he said. "Now there will be no stopping you. I foresee a chain of tea shops! The Lyons of the future."

Josie laughed. She set him up at a table in the shade, away from the others.

Miss Harcourt was also not happy about the numbers and the noise.

"I thought you mentioned a couple of tables in the sitting room. A quiet little operation, Mrs Banks. Now there is hubbub every afternoon."

"There is also a good amount of cash coming in," Josie said. "I don't take much for myself, you know. Just the tips they leave. The rest goes to you. And besides, the land girls will be gone soon, as soon as the harvest is over. Then it will be back to quiet and boring."

Josie had been so busy that she saw little of Mike. She was glad for this, as she still hadn't come to terms with what she felt for him and what the future might hold. In September a harvest festival was held in the church, which was decorated with woven straw dollies, sheaves of wheat, fruit and vegetables. The children came up, bringing offerings from their gardens, and afterward there was a picnic on the church grounds. It was a happy occasion, and Josie enjoyed feeling part of it. Again the thought struck her that she wouldn't mind staying on here after the war.

Then the land girls departed, and the tea shop became genteel and quiet again. Josie had seen nothing of Mr Thomas for a while, then one day in October he turned up. Josie offered to take him through to the library again, but instead he suggested they go for a walk. They headed away from the village.

"I've kept the guestbook like you said," she reported, "but I can't say I've seen anything suspicious. Of course it was impossible when the land girls were here. The place was overcrowded every day. But then the land girls weren't even here the last time you came."

"That's true," he said, "but I'll take your list, and we'll run background checks on anyone who shows up on a regular basis. Keep up the good work." And off he went again.

Two weeks later he returned, again suggesting that they go out for a walk. This time it was a blustery autumn day with the promise of rain. Josie tied a scarf around her head. "Well?" she said. "Have you found anything?" The wind snatched at her words.

"We've done intensive background work," he said, "not just on people who come to the café but on any of the airmen who might have reasons for sabotage. There were a couple who joined the Communist Party at university. But neither has been to your café, nor do they seem to have left the aerodrome on days when the Germans attacked. We have several foreign pilots whose identities cannot be verified. The Polish pilot whose name I can't pronounce. We can no longer access Polish records. He has been a frequent visitor to your tea shop."

"JJ?" She shook her head. "I can't believe it about him. He's always so friendly and polite, and besides, I've never seen him . . ."

She broke off. She had seen him talking to Dr Goldsmith more than once. They had even exchanged a few words in German. She mentioned this. "There is a local doctor. He's a German refugee here. Jewish. He's been here a long while."

"Yes, we have taken a look at him. He seems to be quite blameless. No recent ties to the fatherland. Parents detained in a camp." He hesitated, then said, "I believe you also know a Squadron Leader Johnson?"

She reacted, unable to hide her surprise. "Mike? Yes, I know him. He's Canadian."

He nodded. "I don't know how much he's told you . . ."

"He was a chemist. He joined up at the beginning of the war. He comes from Nova Scotia."

"He's not exactly who he claims to be," Mr Thomas said.

"What?" Josie stared at him.

"We took a good look at his background. I presume he hasn't told you."

"He's surely not helping the enemy. That's ridiculous. He has to fly the bloomin' planes into Germany every night." The wind buffeted her as she said the words, blowing her hair across her face.

"No, as far as we can tell, he is not aiding the enemy," Mr Thomas said softly, "but he's using an alias. An assumed name. His real name is Mark Jensen. Grandfather was an immigrant from the Danish-German border."

"That hardly makes him a suspect," Josie said angrily. "A lot of people have grandparents from somewhere else, don't they? And he probably changed his name for that very reason, because *Jensen* sounded German."

"I presume he changed his name and took on a new identity because he had been in prison."

"Prison?" Josie could hardly say the word. "What for?"

"He was arrested for murdering his wife."

"No!" Josie stood like a statue, staring at him, unable to breathe. "That's not true. That's not possible. It's bloody stupid. You've made a mistake. You've got the wrong person."

"I wish I were not the bearer of painful news," Mr Thomas said. "I understand you have developed an attachment for this man. But I'm afraid it is quite true. We have the court documents from Halifax, Nova Scotia, and it is definitely the same man."

"He was arrested?"

Mr Thomas nodded. "He was tried for her murder."

"And acquitted?" she asked sharply.

He shook his head. "It was what they call a hung jury. A retrial was scheduled. Because of local sentiment, the charges were reduced to manslaughter. He pleaded guilty."

Josie screwed her eyes shut, as if this might blot out her racing thoughts. "So it was an accident, then?"

Mr Thomas shook his head. "No accident. He drugged her and then put a pillow over her face. They changed it to manslaughter because they didn't think the jury would go with the murder conviction. He did three years in prison."

"Does the RAF know about this?"

"I gather the top brass does. Their feeling is that they'd rather have an outstanding pilot and turn a blind eye to his past." He moved closer to her as the first raindrops were falling on them. "I'm sorry, Mrs Banks. I know this is hard for you, but I wanted you to know the truth, before it's too late."

"Yes." She turned away so that he would not see her anguish. "I would want to know the truth. Thank you."

"But we can count on you to keep on with

what you are doing here? You may be doing your country a service."

"Yes, you can count on me," she said and started to walk back towards the house.

CHAPTER 35

This latest news turned her already conflicted emotions into an agony of turmoil. She couldn't think straight as she went about daily tasks.

"You're burning the milk," Kathleen called as Josie was warming it for the yeast mixture. "What's the matter with you? You haven't had bad news, have you? No letter's come from your husband in a while."

"I'm all right," Josie said.

"Then you're mooning about that pilot. Wanting what you can't ever have. Likely as not, he's got a wife at home in America."

"Canada," Josie replied mechanically. "And there is no wife."

"You're not in the family way, are you? Carrying on with him in that sinful fashion."

"Of course not," Josie snapped, then realized how glad she was that the one encounter had not resulted in a baby. Neither had that time spent with Stan when he was home on leave.

She had no idea what she would say when she saw Mike again. Confront him with the truth? End their relationship on the spot? *Was he going to keep it from me forever?* she wondered. And looming over all were questions: Why had he killed his wife? Had she been unfaithful? But then he had no problem with Josie being unfaithful to Stan. Did he have bouts of rage? A drinking problem? As a chemist, he'd have had access to drugs. And yet he always seemed like such a calm, easy-going sort of person. She realized how very little she knew about him. Anyone could be nice and pleasant for a few hours at a time. Perhaps she'd had a lucky escape . . . and yet the thought of life without him seemed horribly bleak.

The numbers at the tea shop had dwindled after the land girls left, but the cold autumn weather had brought back the regulars—Charlie and his pals, the group of WAAFs, and several women from the village.

"Where's Mrs Adams?" Josie asked. "I haven't seen her recently. She wasn't in church on Sunday."

Rose Finch shook her head. "You haven't heard? She got the telegram. Her husband's ship was torpedoed. So she's gone to stay with her sister over in Sutterton. She doesn't know what will happen to her because they've had the labourer's cottage from the farm, on account of he was assistant manager before the war. She's just hoping the farmer won't make her move out too soon—where would she go?"

"I'm so sorry," Josie said. "You tend to forget about the war out here, don't you? But it's going on all the time."

"We don't have much chance to forget," one of the airmen said, having overheard their conversation. "Three more planes lost last night. JJ here was scheduled to fly out on one of them."

"Yes, I was," JJ said. "But this poor man asks me to swap shifts with him so that he might attend his son's christening." He paused. "I must believe the devil doesn't want me yet." He gave an attempt at a carefree laugh.

"Who was on the planes? Anyone I know?" Josie asked. *Not Mike,* she found herself praying. She saw the airmen's gaze go past her, and she turned around and saw Mike standing in the doorway. She resisted the impulse to run to his arms.

"Do you have a minute?" he asked. He looked as he always did, friendly, relaxed, giving her that hint of a smile in his eyes.

She was conscious of all those faces looking at her and had no idea what to do and what to say. "I need to bring out more tea for these people," she said, flustered. "I don't have time to talk at the moment." She picked up an empty teapot and pushed past him into the front hall.

"What's wrong?" he asked.

"Nothing. I'm just extra busy today." She couldn't look at him.

"You should slow down a bit," he said. "You're working too hard."

"I need to keep working," she said. "I need to be busy, don't you understand?"

He grabbed her arm, looking at her with concern. "Josie, slow down. It's all right. They can wait for their tea. It's not important."

"I really don't have time to talk right now, Mike," she said, trying to calm her racing heart. "What was it you wanted?"

"I just came to tell you—" He paused. "I'm being sent on a training course, over in Manchester. We're getting new heavy bombers—the Lancaster. It's not in service yet, but it should prove really useful. Great big thing, four engines, crew of seven. I have to learn to fly them, then come back here to instruct the rest of the flight crews when they come into operation. That's good, really, isn't it? I won't be flying bombing raids for a while. Just testing aircraft that haven't been approved for service yet." He grinned. "So I thought I'd just stop by to say goodbye. I didn't want you to think something bad had happened to me, or I'd gone off without telling you."

"Right. Thank you." She nodded. "So you'll be gone for a while, then?"

"Six weeks, I think it takes. So I'll be back before Christmas. Take care of yourself, okay?"

"Yes, okay." She paused. "You too. Take care of yourself."

He frowned. "Is everything all right? You look really upset."

She wanted to ask him, to confront him, but she couldn't. "I just had some bad news. I've just heard that one of the village ladies has lost her husband," she said quickly. "His ship was torpedoed."

"That's too bad. I'm sorry." He reached out and touched her shoulder gently. "I have to go. I'll write when I have an address."

Josie nodded. She knew she should have accompanied him to the front door. Wished him well. Hugged him. He would be flying a prototype aircraft, perhaps one that wasn't even fully tested yet. A dangerous mission. And yet, with the unasked questions still screaming in her head, she couldn't move.

"Bye, Mike," she said softly. "I'd better get that fresh tea." And she fled into the kitchen. Inside the kitchen door, she leaned against the cold stone of the wall, fighting back tears. How could he seem so nice, so gentle, so kind and yet have done that awful thing? If she had never found out and had married him one day, would she also have wound up with a pillow over her face?

At least she was glad that she was being given a respite during which she could think how to confront him with the truth. She threw herself into her chores, both inside and out. Alf Badger had told her what needed to be done in the garden in preparation for the winter. What had to be dug out, what needed to be cut back and what could be planted. As she worked, she glanced up at the back of the house. The Virginia creeper that covered the back wall had now turned a brilliant dark red. She admired it for a moment before deciding that it had become too overgrown and really needed to be thinned. She got the shears and started to attack it, realizing she'd need a ladder to do most of the work. It was a tougher job than she had anticipated—it seemed as if the original vine had been strung up with wires. A strand of creeper had wrapped itself around a wire and was threatening to cover a downstairs window. She muttered a few choice words to herself.

At that moment, the window opened, and Kathleen's head poked out.

"Holy Mother of God, what are you doing, woman?" she demanded. "Trying to dismantle the house, are you now?"

"I'm just cutting back the creeper," Josie said. "It's far too overgrown. It will damage the brickwork, and it's shutting off the light to your room."

"Leave well alone. It's not yours to decide. The mistress likes that creeper, especially in the autumn when it's this lovely colour."

"I'm not cutting it down, just thinning it out," Josie said. "It will be coming in your window next, and mine, too, if I don't cut it back now."

"Well, I like it just the way it is, and so does the mistress," Kathleen said. Her face was now red and angry. "I don't appreciate the way you've come here and changed everything. We were getting along quite nicely until you showed up, and now there's not a minute's peace to be had. I'm going to ask the mistress to write to those evacuation people. It's about time you went back where you came from."

Josie sighed, left the creeper and went back to work digging up a vegetable bed. Whatever she did, it couldn't please Kathleen. "Let them have their stupid creeper," she muttered. They'd be sorry when it cracked the wall and let in the rain.

When Josie came in and began preparing the dinner, Kathleen was quite pleasant to her again. "One thing I like about England is Bonfire Night," she said. "It's coming up next week, isn't it? Or would be if there was no war on. When the old man was alive, we used to have a great bonfire in the back garden and fireworks and invite all the village children. Cook used to make toffee apples and sausages on sticks. It was grand. I loved the fireworks, didn't you?"

"It was different in the city," Josie said. "We had a bonfire in the middle of the street, but the nasty little boys used to let off squibs and bangers all around us. They thought it was a big joke to throw a squib under a girl's skirt. I didn't like that at all."

"It was the rockets I liked," Kathleen said. "So pretty when they burst into little stars."

"Rockets were not much use where I lived,"

Josie said. "By the time they exploded, they were lost in the fog usually or blown over to another street."

"I'm glad I don't live in a place like that," Kathleen said. "Do you really want to go back there when your husband comes home?"

"Not really," Josie said.

"You're still thinking of that man." Kathleen wagged an accusing finger at her. "No good can come of it, you know."

"I know," Josie said. "Believe me, I know."

On November 5, when in other times the talk would have been of bonfires and "penny for the guy, gov," Mr Thomas came to visit Josie.

"I think we'd better talk outside," he said, "where we can't be overheard."

Josie looked out of the front door. It was spitting with rain. She sighed and grabbed her coat from the hall cupboard, then tied a scarf around her head.

"You've found out something?" she asked. "More about Mike Johnson?"

"No. Not about him. We've been using a device that tracks radio frequencies," he said. "We've picked up something that may be important. A quick burst of transmission from around here."

"Coming from the RAF station, perhaps?"

He shook his head. "It seems to be coming from around here, meaning around this house. But the transmissions are always so short—literally one or two seconds—that we can never home in on the source."

Josie held on to her scarf as the wind threatened to snatch it away. "You can't think someone in this house is doing the transmitting?"

"It's possible."

"But there is only me and Miss Harcourt and Kathleen."

"Exactly."

"But they wouldn't . . ." She shook her head. "Miss Harcourt is true blue English, and Kathleen—well, she's not very bright, and she likes a quiet life and has no connection with Germany." She paused, thinking. "I'm trying to wonder if it's possible for one of the visitors at the tea shop to slip away long enough to do a short radio transmission."

"Could be possible," he said. "They'd have to have the transmitter hidden in the house. It's too big to carry around easily."

"Miss Harcourt has a radio in the sitting room. She listens to the news all the time."

"That's different," he said. "That's a receiver. We are looking for something that sends the signals. A transmitter."

"What would this transmitter look like?"

"They are usually a wooden box, about the size of a small suitcase. Fairly easy to hide. Might almost be in plain sight somewhere. And there would have to be some sort of aerial. So someone would have had to be in the house long enough at some stage to have set things up."

Josie frowned. "I don't recall anyone being in the house, except the doctor when Miss Harcourt had her heart attack. The visitors in the tea shop don't go wandering over the house."

"Nobody ever asks to use the cloakroom?"

Josie hesitated, trying to recall. "I don't think so."

"And you are with them all the time?"

"No, I'm in the kitchen preparing the tea for them."

"So there is in fact plenty of time when one of them could snoop around a bit?"

"Except they'd be taking a big risk. They could bump into Miss Harcourt or Kathleen—"

"And excuse themselves by saying they were looking for a lavatory?"

"Yes, I suppose so."

"It wouldn't take long. As I said, the transmissions are only a second or two. I presume they have a code for which city was to be bombed. One for Berlin, two for Hamburg, etc. So all they'd have to do is type the Morse code for their call sign and then the number." Mr Thomas held on to his own hat as a great gust of wind snatched away the words he was going to say. "The sort of person who would willingly spy for the Germans doesn't mind taking risks. He enjoys them, in fact. It could well be the same sort of person who enjoys flying bombing missions—flirting with danger."

"Blimey," she muttered.

"So I'm going to ask you to take a bit of a risk yourself. Could I ask you to do some snooping? See if you can find a hidden radio transmitter? If you come across it, don't say anything, but go into the village and call me from the telephone box."

Josie shook her head, giving an uneasy laugh. "It doesn't seem real, does it? Surely nobody would use this house . . ."

Mr Thomas smiled. "I can't tell you how many times since the war started someone has said to me that people they know and trust could not possibly be involved in spying. People never suspect those near them." He glanced up. "It's about to pour. We should get inside." He put a hand on her shoulder and steered her back towards the house. "But just a word of warning. Don't take too many risks, and don't tell anyone what you are doing. I wouldn't want you to put yourself in danger."

Josie had an absurd desire to laugh again. It all seemed so improbable, someone at the house sending a communication to Germany. One of the nice RAF boys slinking out to find a radio and send a signal to the Nazis?

"What did that man want?" Kathleen demanded,

poking her head out of the kitchen as Josie came back in and shook the drops of rain off her coat. "He's been around here several times, hasn't he? Another of your sweethearts?"

"Don't be daft," Josie said. "Why do you think I have sweethearts? I don't exactly look like a film star, you know. He's from the government." Her brain was racing. "Those forms we had to fill out for the tearoom. It seems someone gave us the wrong form, and it's caused all sorts of complications. He's trying to sort it all out."

"Trust the government to make a mess of everything," Kathleen said and went back into the kitchen.

CHAPTER 36

Josie wondered exactly how she'd be able to snoop around the house and not raise the suspicions of Miss Harcourt or Kathleen. She didn't think Kathleen would be hard to fool, but she seemed suspicious by nature and took offence if Josie tried to do any chore she thought was her own.

"I was wondering if we should do anything before winter sets in?" Josie said. "Give all the rooms we don't use a good clean and shake out the dust sheets?"

"What for?" Kathleen said. "Like you said, nobody uses them."

"We don't want mice to set up home in a mattress, do we?"

Kathleen shrugged. "Suit yourself. For my part, I've quite enough to do, thank you kindly. You seem like a glutton for hard work."

"Yes, I don't like sitting still much," Josie said. "And I don't suppose we'll get many people coming to the tea shop now it's so cold and rainy. I wouldn't want to walk all the way from the aerodrome myself."

"I'm not sure how you're going to keep heating it all winter, anyway. We've gone through most of the wood from the vicarage, and our own coal ration won't stretch to keeping another room warm."

"We'll manage," Josie said. "I'll ask the RAF boys. They might be willing to cut up another fallen tree and cart it here."

Josie went up to her bedroom and sat on the bed. The room was now cold and draughty. She went across to the window, trying to locate where the cold blast of air was coming in. The frame had warped, and it didn't close all the way. Then she saw something she hadn't noticed before. That wire that was wrapped around with creeper ran all the way up to the roof. What for? Was it the aerial that Mr Thomas had mentioned? So what was below her room? She came down again and stood in the hall, trying to calculate. Miss Harcourt's study was at the back of the house. She heard the radio coming from the sitting room, which meant Miss Harcourt was busy listening to the news. Kathleen was in the kitchen. So she darted down the narrow corridor and into the study. As well as the central table that held the telephone, there was a big mahogany bureau against one wall, a filing cabinet and bookshelves stocked with all kinds of boxes as well as piles of books. It was the sort of clutter that would take ages to sort through but also a good place to hide a radio. In plain sight, Mr Thomas had said. She started to check the boxes on the shelves. They contained papers or old account books. There were more boxes under the central table. She knelt to examine them. Before she could pull one out, she heard the sound of footsteps. She scrambled under the table and crouched amongst the boxes, wondering how on earth she could explain her presence if she was caught.

The door opened, and she saw Miss Harcourt's prim laced-up shoes come in. She crossed the room, went behind the table to the bureau, opened a drawer and put something inside. From her position of hiding, Josie couldn't see what it was. Then Miss Harcourt crossed the room again, went out and shut the door. Josie let out a sigh of relief and crawled out of her hiding place. It was dusty under there, and she brushed herself off as she stood up. Clearly nobody cleaned that study often. Was that because Miss Harcourt didn't want anyone in there? It seemed impossible to think that Miss Harcourt could in any way be involved with helping the enemy. She hadn't mentioned any German ancestry or any anti-British sentiments. Josie tiptoed over to the bureau to see what she had put in the drawer. It was the photo album Josie had seen her looking at before. Reliving old times, happier days. That made sense. She opened it cautiously. Faded snapshots of long ago—women in long skirts and big hats, men with impressive moustaches and side whiskers. The earliest pictures were posed studio shots of somewhere exotic with palm trees and dark-skinned servants. Presumably Miss Harcourt's childhood in India. Yes, there she was holding hands with a woman in a sari. Her nurse, maybe?

And then there she was as a young woman in England. London. In a ball dress, looking grave and important as she held a fan. And then several photographs of the same young man. *James at Kew Gardens* written in faded script under it. *James rows on the Thames.* One picture of them together. She smiling up at him. And then *James in uniform. About to sail.* The young man dressed in an old-fashioned army uniform, holding a helmet under his arm. To sail where? Around the turn of the century, by the clothing in the other snapshots. The Boer War, perhaps? Josie turned more pages. No more photographs of James. In fact, no photographs for several years.

It was dark in the room, and Josie carried the book over to the window. This was definitely not the same young man as the photograph on Miss Harcourt's desk. Two sweethearts? She picked up the framed photograph and examined it. This was a different army uniform. More modern— the uniform she recognized from her earliest memories of men coming home from war. But Miss Harcourt would have been too old for this sweetheart during the Great War. She would have been at least forty. So a nephew, a godchild? But why keep only one photograph on display in the whole house? She went back to the photograph album. Towards the end, there were pictures of a strange woman pushing a baby carriage, a little boy with a dog—all of them blurred and taken from far away. And on the back page of the album a newspaper cutting: *Local Boy Latest Casualty on the Somme. Freddie Brooks of Grange Farm, Sutton St Mary, aged eighteen.*

Why would Miss Harcourt devote a whole page to a farmer's son? Then a chill crept over Josie. What if it was her own son? A son born out of wedlock whom she had to give up, and the only memories she had of him were those blurred, distant pictures of a happy little boy? That would explain her remoteness and bitterness now. Josie remembered how unfeeling she had seemed about the young men who risked their lives. If her own son had been taken, why should she care about other mothers' sons? And Josie took this thought a step further—if she blamed England for sending her son off to war when he was just eighteen, why not destroy more lives? Why not help Germany? It might have been possible to recruit a bitter, remote woman with nothing to lose. It seemed outlandish but at the same time credible. Someone from the RAF station would somehow pass along the information to her every day, and she would send it from a transmitter hidden perhaps somewhere in this room.

Josie came out of the room just as Miss Harcourt was heading up the stairs. The woman paused, frowned, staring at Josie. "What were you doing in my study?"

Josie tried to come up with a plausible answer. This was no time to confront her. "I was checking for our coal supply," she said. "I seemed to remember that your study didn't even have a fireplace so wouldn't need any coal."

"That's right," Miss Harcourt said. "The room is miserably cold unless one puts in an oil stove. I think it was originally intended as a servant's room." She gave a brief nod and continued up the stairs. Josie watched until the older woman disappeared in the direction of her bedroom, then she darted back into the study. Several minutes of searching did not turn up anything like the radio Mr Thomas had described. Josie decided she was letting her imagination run away with her. But after dinner that night, Kathleen went off to her own quarters, early as usual, and Josie joined Miss Harcourt in the sitting room, where the fire gave off enough warmth. She sat quietly reading until Miss Harcourt said, "So what are you reading now? More books about Canada?"

"No. No more books about Canada," Josie replied. "I've learned everything I needed to know."

"Perhaps a wise choice," Miss Harcourt said. "Too much heartbreak in the world already."

"Yes," Josie agreed. "I don't know how they handle it working at the RAF station. Knowing every night that some of the planes won't come back. Losing friends all the time."

"One gets used to it, I suppose."

"Do you think so? Doesn't it go on hurting all your life?" Josie asked. She looked across at the older woman. "That photograph I noticed in your study—was that a relative of yours?"

"Of sorts."

"A young man who died in the last war? You must have been very fond of him, because it's the only photograph on display anywhere in this house."

"Yes," Miss Harcourt said. "I was very fond of him."

Josie took a deep breath. "I know this is damned cheeky of me, and I'm always poking my nose in where it's not wanted, but was it your son?"

Miss Harcourt's face flushed scarlet. "How the devil . . . You had no right . . ." Then she sighed. "Yes, Freddie was my son. His father and I were to be married, you see. But James was in the army. His regiment was sent off to South Africa, to fight the Boers. And he never returned. He fell in battle."

"I'm so sorry," Josie said. "What an awful shock for you."

Miss Harcourt squeezed her eyes shut, as if trying to blot out the memory. "I told my father.

He was horrified. Furious. He sent me away, and when the child was born, he insisted on putting it up for adoption. At least I managed one thing—I had Freddie given to a farmer nearby. That meant I could see him sometimes. Not actually interact with him, you know, but watch him from a distance. He grew up to be such a handsome, sturdy little boy. Just like his father. And then when he turned eighteen, he was called up for military service. I met him. I told him the truth and that when he returned I'd like to help him establish a career. He was not as surprised as I thought he'd be. He'd always known he was adopted, and he seemed happy to know me. He sent me the photograph . . ." She shut her eyes again. "He was killed his first week in France. In the last year of the war. Nineteen eighteen. A few more weeks, and it would have been over. It was all so cruel and meaningless. I vowed I'd never feel anything for anybody again."

"I'm sorry for you," Josie said. "It must have made you hate your country for sending him off to die like that."

"I can't say that I hate my country. I think it was a stupid, meaningless war that claimed millions of lives unnecessarily." Miss Harcourt shrugged. "It was the same for so many mothers and sweethearts. Most of England was mourning somebody. But at least they'd had a chance to hug their sons, tuck them in at night. I had nothing."

Josie was wondering what to ask next when Miss Harcourt said, "This war, of course, is quite different. This time we have no choice. This madman Hitler must be stopped at all costs."

That was clear enough for Josie. She decided to take the risk. "Would it surprise you to know that someone around here has been helping the enemy?"

"We have a spy in our midst? In this little community? How would you know that?" she asked. She looked at Josie long and hard. "There is more to you than meets the eye, isn't there, Mrs Banks? You were not a simple evacuee. You were sent here to root out a fifth columnist."

"I have been helping a bit," Josie said evasively. "And I'm not supposed to mention this to anyone, but I could use your help. I'm afraid it seems that someone at RAF Sutton Deeping is passing along information about where the bombers are headed each night, so that the Germans are waiting for them."

"The traitor is at the RAF base?"

"One of them," Josie replied. "But it also seems that he or she is passing along the information to someone outside the RAF station who then radios it to Germany."

"Someone in this village?"

"It appears it might be someone using this house."

Miss Harcourt gave a short gasp. "So you suspected me."

Josie gave an apologetic shrug. "Your study seems to be close to where a wire goes up to our roof. I thought it might be the aerial I have to look for. And that photograph—I thought perhaps you might . . ."

"Have been angry enough to betray my country?" She shook her head. "My dear, I am made of sterner stuff than that. English through and through. I would be ready to stop the invading tanks with my pitchfork." She paused, frowning. "Do you think it's one of those people who take tea at your café?"

"It has to be, doesn't it? I've supplied their names, and the blokes at MI5 have done background checks, and so far nothing has come up. But someone must have hidden a radio transmitter here, and I can't see how anyone would have done that—in broad daylight, with me coming in and out all the time."

"A true spy would be clever and well trained." She frowned. "So the information is passed across at this house, to one of the local inhabitants, you suggest—but as for actually sending the message from this house . . . who could do that?"

"There's only you and me and Kathleen," Josie said. The two women stared at each other. Miss Harcourt shook her head. "Surely not Kathleen. My dear, the woman has just enough brains not to burn the bacon when she cooks it. And as for being a German spy—why, she couldn't even point out Germany to you on a map."

Josie's brain was racing. "The only thing I can think of is that one of the airmen who comes here quite frequently is Irish. His mates didn't think he was the type to take afternoon tea. They teased him about it. And he was always so keen to chat with Kathleen, although she didn't want to give him the time of day. Why would a young bloke want to chat with a middle-aged woman, apart from homesickness?"

"He's Irish, you say?" Miss Harcourt was still frowning. "The Irish have no great love for us."

"He's Northern Irish—part of Great Britain. His name is Patrick O'Brien."

Miss Harcourt looked up sharply. "She has a nephew called Patrick. She showed me pictures of him when he was a young boy. Handsome little chap. If he was secretly working for the IRA, trying to reclaim Ireland from the English, what better way to help Germany win than to infiltrate the RAF and send planes to their destruction?"

Josie shook her head. "I find it hard to believe. He seems like such a nice, easy-going sort of bloke. And as you say, how would Kathleen know what to do with a message? Can you see her operating a radio?"

"There's only one way to find out," Miss Harcourt said. "We must search her room."

"How are we going to do that? She never leaves the house, and she guards that place fiercely. She gave me a right dressing-down when I tried to wake her up on the night of the bombing."

"I'll think of something," Miss Harcourt said. "We must catch her unawares."

The next day, Josie looked for Kathleen in the kitchen. She was in the back garden, bringing in laundry from the line. Josie went out to join her. "Here, let me help with that," she said.

Kathleen nodded and handed Josie the basket. Josie's eyes were drawn to the shed. She remembered how Kathleen guarded the shed, too. She had always supervised Josie when she went in and out with tools, never let her have the key. Josie had always thought of it as silly possessiveness until now.

"Hey, Kathleen." Josie hoisted the basket on to her hip. "I'd better make sure the tools are all safely inside the shed and nice and dry, or they will rust. I can't see myself doing much gardening for a while. Do you have the key on you?"

"It's in my room."

"I'll go and get it if you like"—Josie gave her a smile—"when I take this lot in. I don't think any more will fit in the basket."

"No, I'll get it." Kathleen forged ahead of her into the kitchen, put the clean washing she had been carrying down on one of the chairs and then found the keys. "Come on, then. I need to finish getting these in before it rains."

"I can let myself into a shed, Kathleen," Josie said. "You don't have to watch me. I'm not about to swipe the tools."

Kathleen walked ahead of her and opened the door. "They all seem to be safe enough in here," she said. "I don't think you've left any outside that I know about."

"I think you're right. Well, better be safe than sorry, eh?"

Reluctantly she came out again, watching Kathleen lock the door and shove the keys into her pocket. In the brief time she had looked around, she had seen nothing like a radio and really no place to hide one. But there had been a scrap of paper lying on the bench. It had the number two written on it. That could be anything, but it was worth noting. All she could do now was wait for Miss Harcourt to make her move.

It happened later that afternoon. There had been no guests at the tea shop, and Josie was putting away the tea things on the dresser when she heard a shout from upstairs.

"Kathleen!" came the call. "Come quickly."

Kathleen glanced at Josie.

"It's the mistress! I hope she hasn't fallen," Josie said. "You better go."

Kathleen went up the stairs, and Josie made as if to follow her. She heard Miss Harcourt say, "Grab the broom. There's a mouse in my bedroom. I saw it run under the bed. You know I can't abide mice."

Josie didn't wait another second. She came up the stairs with the broom and handed it to Kathleen. Then she dashed back into the kitchen and through the door leading to Kathleen's private quarters. The bedroom was painfully simple, with a narrow bed, wardrobe, chest of drawers and a small armchair. Beside the bed was a commode containing a chamber pot. Josie shut the commode again hastily. She looked under the bed. Nothing. The wardrobe contained pitifully few items of clothing. A hatbox, containing two hats— one summer, one winter. A suitcase on top of the wardrobe was empty. The drawers in the dresser were too small to hide a radio. In frustration Josie came out and opened the other doors leading off that narrow hallway. One was the uniform cupboard with black maids' uniforms hanging beside fancy footmen's livery. Nothing there either. Then the former butler's pantry with the household silver in a glass case, a table with the accounts book, a wine decanter—all relics of a bygone age. Josie glanced at the accounts book and saw a sheet of paper sticking out between pages. It read *1 B, 2 H, 3 F 4 R 5 S 6 Bo 7 K 8 D . . .*

Was this what Mr Thomas had suggested? One would be Berlin, two Hamburg, three Frankfurt, maybe? Josie didn't know enough about German cities to identify the rest, but she took the sheet of paper. A rapid search of the tiny room did not turn up a radio. But this gave her hope. It had to be somewhere. She went back to the bedroom, and on impulse opened the commode, took out the chamber pot, and there beneath it was a brown wooden box. She didn't have time to open it before she heard footsteps. Kathleen burst into the room.

"What in the name of God do you think you are doing?" she shouted. "Trying to steal from me now, are you? Get out of my private quarters."

"Not trying to steal, Kathleen," Josie said. "Just trying to find proof that you are an enemy spy."

The colour drained from Kathleen's face. "What are you talking about? What nonsense would you be spouting now?"

"They know about you, Kathleen," Josie said. "The radio. And the codes. One for Berlin, two for Hamburg. You sent all those poor boys off to their deaths."

"You'll pay for this." Kathleen took a step towards Josie. She was a big-boned woman and Josie involuntarily retreated.

"No, you will, Kathleen," Josie said. "They shoot traitors, don't they? Firing squad? At least it's quick."

Kathleen opened her mouth but said nothing. There was panic in her eyes. "You should never have come here, poking your nose in." She darted out of the room. Josie assumed she was making a break for it and went to follow, but Kathleen returned brandishing the big kitchen knife. "I'll tell Miss Harcourt you've run off to be with that man," she said. "They'll never find your body."

"Don't be so bloody stupid," Josie said, sounding braver than she felt. "They're on to you. They know this signal comes from this house. They've already tracked you down."

She saw Kathleen's expression falter. "He made me do it," she said. "Patrick made me do it. He told me I had to do it for Ireland. To make us free. He came to me late last year when he was posted here. I didn't want to do it. It didn't seem right . . ." She broke off. "But then you arrived, and I saw she liked you better than me. I was afraid she was going to throw me out, and I'd have nowhere to go, and I thought I'd pay her back, pay you back . . . you and your fancy man."

"So Patrick left the number each day in the shed, did he? No wonder you were so protective of it."

Josie tried to remain calm, but she could see how agitated the woman was, her hand shaking as she held the knife. Now she lunged at Josie. "You've caused nothing but trouble since you've been here. It will give me great pleasure to stick this into you . . ."

Josie looked around to defend herself, reached

back and grabbed a pillow from the bed, holding it in front of her.

"You can't get away, you know," Kathleen said. "You're trapped. I'll tell Miss Harcourt you were the one who was sending the messages, and I bravely killed you."

"You'll do no such thing," Miss Harcourt said, looming up behind Kathleen in the narrow hallway. "Put down that knife immediately, Kathleen."

Kathleen gave a little cry, spun around, slashed at Miss Harcourt and fought her way past. Josie went to chase after her, but then she looked at Miss Harcourt, who was leaning against the wall, clutching at her arm. "Did she hurt you?"

"Only a scratch, I think," Miss Harcourt said, then stared at blood running down her arm.

CHAPTER 37

Josie called the police as well as Mr Thomas.

"She won't have got far," the policeman said, and this proved to be true. Kathleen was found hiding out in the nearby woods. Miss Harcourt was taken to the local hospital, where her arm was stitched up, luckily not a dangerous wound. Mr Thomas arrived. A trap was set for Patrick O'Brien. They were waiting for him when he came to leave the number for the day in the shed, and he, too, was caught. Josie would have liked to have been part of the excitement, but she felt she should stay with Miss Harcourt at the hospital until a police car drove them home.

"It's been a terrible shock," Miss Harcourt said as Josie put her to bed. "Kathleen has been part of my life for over twenty years. She never was the friendliest of mortals, but at least I felt she was loyal and devoted to me. And now to find out this about her."

"It was her nephew who made her do it. I think he had a cruel streak, actually. He'd make sure he spoke to her when he came to tea and watch her squirm with embarrassment. She was probably terrified of him." Even as she said this, she realized that she, too, bore some responsibility. It was her coming that had made Kathleen feel

433

angry and insecure enough to strike back at the world.

"All the same, she could have told one of us," Miss Harcourt said. "We would have put a stop to it."

"Yes, we would have." Josie looked at the old lady's face. The haughty, scornful look was gone, and she looked tired. "Don't worry. I'll stay with you. We'll manage, the two of us. You might have to learn to do a bit of dusting and polishing, but that won't hurt you."

Miss Harcourt smiled then. "I don't suppose it will. You're a good girl, Josie. I may call you Josie, may I not? A kind heart and a good worker."

When Josie was on her own that evening, she had a chance to examine what this decision might mean. She would still be here in six weeks when Mike came back from his training. She had received a letter from him almost immediately. It had somehow evaded the censor, since it had been sent from a hotel through the normal post.

> *Dear Josie,*
>
> *Well, here I am, safely installed in a local pub when several of us guinea pigs are learning to fly these great lumbering kites. We all feel they've been rushed into production, probably without the normal amount of testing, but we can see*

they'll make a difference if they actually fly! They'll carry enough bombs to do serious damage—take out a whole factory complex or rail yard.

I miss you already. I think about you all the time and can't wait for my six weeks here to be up.

Love,
Mike

His address was on the envelope. Josie stared at it, feeling her eyes stinging with tears. Should she write back, *Dear Mike, or whatever your real name is—why have you lied to me? Why did you kill your wife?*

But she couldn't. It was the sort of thing she had to ask face to face, watching his expression. It was impossible to guess how he'd answer. At the very least, he had kept the truth from her. At the most, he was a cold-blooded murderer, a man with two sides, and she was well rid of him.

Mr Thomas came to deliver the news that Patrick O'Brien was in custody and linked to an IRA cell that was actively trying to disrupt the war effort.

"Well done," he said to her. "You have quick wits."

"It was more luck than anything." Josie gave an embarrassed grin. "I'd never have suspected

435

Kathleen in a million years. It was only seeing that wire that I thought might be an aerial."

"If you'd like to work for your country, we could use women like you," Mr Thomas said.

Josie laughed. "Oh, I'm not the sort to go around catching spies."

Mr Thomas smiled, too. "I didn't mean that. We need people for operation support—filing, reading through material to find clues. You'd enjoy it. You'd be good at it."

Josie shook her head. "I'm not going back to London for love or money. I've been bombed once, and once was enough, thank you."

"But we have facilities outside of London. Nice country houses. Good food. Think about it."

"I've got Miss Harcourt to look after now," Josie said. "I can't leave her in the lurch after she's had a nasty shock. Kathleen was with her for years, you know."

He nodded with understanding. "Well, if you change your mind, you have my card and my telephone number."

The news about Kathleen spread rapidly around the village, and Josie was besieged by the local women when she went in to do the shopping next.

"She attacked you with a knife? Fancy that," Rose Finch said. "Who would have thought it of Kathleen, being a spy for the enemy?"

"Anyway, we're glad that you and Miss Harcourt are safe," Annie Adams said.

"How is she going to manage without Kathleen?" Lil Hodgkins asked. "When you go back to London, I mean? She'll never cope with that big house alone, and I don't know where she'll find another servant these days."

"I could come and help out," Annie said, as if the idea had just occurred to her. "Looks like I'll have to leave my cottage anyway, and I don't mind a bit of hard work."

Everyone agreed this was a good plan all around, and Josie put it to Miss Harcourt, who thought it was a splendid solution. Annie moved in, and it was clear the place was going to run smoothly.

"I have an idea," Josie said as November came to an end. "Why don't we have a Christmas party? Everyone needs cheering up, and we've made a bit of money from the tea shop."

"I suppose we could . . . ," Miss Harcourt said hesitantly. "Nothing too elaborate. My father had these huge parties, you know. Sit-down dinner for twenty."

"I was thinking more of a tea party, Father Christmas, little presents for the kiddies."

"Yes, that might be fun," she agreed. "I've got plenty of knick-knacks around the house to give as little presents."

"I know where we can find a tree," Annie said.

"And I've got my decorations stored away as well."

It was good to have something to plan for.

"I wish I could make a pudding," Josie said, "but you can't find dried fruit anywhere."

She was in the kitchen, going through recipe books to see what she could possibly bake with their limited ingredients, when there was a knock at the front door.

"I'll go," Annie said. She came back with a white face. "It's a telegram. For you, Josie."

Josie went to the door and saw the telegraph boy standing there, holding out the small envelope. "For Mrs Banks," he said.

Josie knew what that meant. How many other women had received similar news? It meant Stan had been killed. Her hand trembled as she opened it.

Private Stanley Banks severely wounded in action. Now transferred to Royal Herbert Military Hospital, Woolwich.

Miss Harcourt was just coming down the stairs.

"What is it, Josie? Bad news?"

"It's my husband. He's badly wounded and has been brought back to hospital in London. I have to go to him."

"Oh dear. I am so sorry." Miss Harcourt reached out and gave Josie's shoulder a tentative touch. "Yes, of course you have to go straight away. And I presume you'll be looking after him for some time."

"Yes, I suppose so," Josie said flatly. Mechanically she went upstairs and packed her things. At least that would solve the problem with Mike. She sat down and wrote to him:

> *Dear Mike,*
> *I'm afraid Stan has been sent back to England severely wounded. I have to go to him right away. This means I won't be seeing you again. I'm sorry. I really hoped things could be different.*
> *Love,*
> *Josie*

At least that was ending things on a good note, so they both could have good memories. Whatever Mike had done, she loved him. She had known true love for the first time.

She noticed how her scant possessions seemed to have multiplied during the year she had been here. Clothing from Miss Harcourt, the summer things she had bought with Stan and various gifts from Mike, including the ridiculous swimsuit. No point in taking that. She'd not be near the sea again. The Wellington boots Mike had bought her were in the scullery. She probably wouldn't need them either, but she couldn't bear to be parted from them, so she went down and crammed them into the suitcase Miss Harcourt had lent her. From the top dresser drawer, she took her little jewellery case, opened it briefly and pulled out the bag containing Madame Olga's rings. It seemed impossible that just one year ago she had been working in the tea shop, chatting with Madame Olga. She looked at the big flashy rings with their fake stones and thought of them on Madame Olga's pudgy hands, along with her red nail polish. On impulse she put on the fake diamond and tried to smile. So much loss in one year. So much gain, too, and now that was to be taken away.

Josie said goodbye to Annie, then went in to Miss Harcourt.

"I'll be off, then," she said. "I want to thank you for taking me in. I've had the best time here. I won't ever forget it."

"No, thank you, my dear," Miss Harcourt said. "You brought me back to life. I wish you all the very best. Do come back to visit if you can. And if . . . if your husband does not recover from his wounds, you know you always have a home here."

Josie nodded, blinking back tears. Then she picked up her suitcase and didn't look back as she walked down the front path. The bus having gone early that morning, she waited to hitch a lift into Spalding. It was a cold, bleak day, with a bitter east wind that cut through her flimsy over-coat and pushed her along. It matched her mood. She'd walked for about a mile when a motor car came to a halt beside her.

"Mrs Banks. Where are you going?"

It was Dr Goldsmith. He leaned across to open the door for her. "Jump in. I'm on a late shift at the hospital today, so I'm just driving in."

"Then you could take me all the way in to Peterborough, couldn't you?" Josie asked.

"Of course. Do you need the station?"

"Yes. I'm going back to London," Josie said.

"For a visit?"

"For good." Josie stared out of the window as the stark, empty fields flashed past.

"Oh dear. Miss Harcourt will miss you. The tea shop will miss you." He paused. "I'll miss you."

"I'll miss all of you, too," Josie said. "Please give my love to Lottie and tell her that I sent my best to the Badgers and the girls."

"May I ask why you are leaving?" he asked. "You are not happy here?"

"Oh, I was very happy. Happier than I have ever been," she said. "I just got a telegram that my husband has been shipped home, badly wounded. I don't know if he'll make it or not."

"I'm so very sorry," he said. "But he's able to get good medical care now. Let's hope for the best, shall we?"

For the second time, he reached across and

covered her hand with his own. *He's a nice man,* she thought. *A lonely man. A man who also deserves something better than the life he has.*

The journey to London passed in a blur. It had started to rain, and through the rain-streaked window, the rows of sooty tenements and factories looked more depressing than ever. Almost every street had a bomb site on it. What had once been a church now just had a tower standing beside a burned-out shell. This was London. London where she'd now be trapped forever. She wondered where she would stay while Stan was in hospital, where they would live when he came out. There was an old poster on the carriage wall, above the seats. *A day at the seaside* was the caption. Immediately Josie was back with Mike, laughing in the cold water and then lying in his arms, his warm breath on her cheek. She blinked hard to shut out the image.

It took a long time to work her way across London from King's Cross. The Northern line tube took her down to London Bridge, and then it was two buses to Woolwich and then to Shooter's Hill. The Royal Herbert was an enormous complex of buildings with an impressive facade at the front. Josie hesitated before walking up those front steps. Once inside she was directed to the correct block. It was now raining hard, and she was soaked through by the time she had lugged her suitcase into a building that smelled of disinfectant and death. But a nurse received her kindly and led her up the stairs. "I'm afraid you're in for a bit of a shock, Mrs Banks," she said. "We've done what we can for him, but he needs a lot of loving care now if he has a chance of making it."

They entered a long ward of maybe twenty beds where tall windows looked out on to a wooded area. On a sunny day it might have been a pleasant view, but at this moment the rain peppering the windows enhanced the cold and dreary feeling. There were curtains around some of the beds, and from behind these came moans of pain. The nurse whispered to the sister on duty, who took Josie aside. "Your husband came to us in a very bad way, Mrs Banks. His vehicle hit a landmine. I'm afraid they had to remove his left leg. We hope we have saved the other. He's still very weak, but he has a good chance of recovering now you are here to encourage him."

"Before we go to him, I was wondering about where I can stay," Josie said. "I just came in from the country and . . ."

"We have a dormitory for loved ones of critical care patients," the sister said. "You can stay there until he is released."

She walked ahead of Josie down the ward and pulled aside a curtain around a bed at the end. Stan was lying there, apparently asleep.

"He's on a lot of morphine at the moment," the sister said. "The pain of the amputation, you know. So he may not be exactly himself."

Josie stepped up to the bed. Stan had a dressing over one eye. His face looked grey, and part of his hair had been cut away.

"Mr Banks. Look who I've brought for you," the sister said.

Stan opened his one eye, frowned and then said, "It's my Josie. What are you doing out in Africa, Josie?"

"You're in London now, you silly sod," Josie said. She bent to give him a kiss on his cheek. "And you don't have to worry. I'm here to take care of you now."

CHAPTER 38

The next week passed with one day after another spent on the hard chair beside Stan's bed and nights spent in the narrow bed in a dormitory for women—porridge for breakfast, some kind of unidentifiable stew for lunch, bread and jam for tea. Some of the time Stan was conscious, sometimes rambling, sometimes coherent.

"You should have seen it, Josie. All that sand. It gets in everything. All the food tastes like sand. It's good to be home again, eh?"

As he recovered and was weaned off the morphine, he started coming to terms with reality. "I won't be good for much ever again, Josie. You're stuck with a cripple. A useless, bloody cripple. It would have been better if that bloody explosion had killed me like it did my mates."

"Don't say that, Stan." Josie managed to sound positive. "You'll learn to get around. There will still be things you can do and things you enjoy. You've got two good arms. You can make things. And you can still have your pint, can't you? Listen to the radio. And get out on fine days . . ."

"You'll have to be the breadwinner, old girl," he said on another occasion. "Find a job that can keep the two of us. Maybe that factory will take you back. At least we won't have to worry about where to live for now. We've got Shirley and Fred."

Josie tried not to think about her life in the country. She went with Stan to his rehabilitation appointments, where they taught him to use crutches. And then, right before Christmas, he was discharged.

"Normally we'd keep you longer," the sister said, "but the Royal Arsenal Hospital has been bombed, so we're having to take in civilians as well as you army blokes, and we're full up to the gills. You'll need to keep changing that dressing on the wound and doing your exercises, and then in the spring you can come back, and we'll talk about getting you fitted with a prosthetic leg."

They were driven across the Thames through the Blackwall Tunnel and then to Shirley's house in Whitechapel.

"We've turned the front parlour into a bedroom for you until you're up to stairs again," Shirley said as she ushered them inside. "And we've got a commode for you, so you don't have to go out back to the lav."

"Good of you, Shirl," Stan said. "You're a godsend. I don't know what we would have done without you."

Josie was glad that she didn't have time to think. She had to change the dressing on the stump of Stan's leg, empty his commode, wash him and bring him his meals. She slept on a camp bed beside him, as he was still in a lot of pain. He cried out often in his sleep. Josie felt intensely sorry for him—a man still in his prime reduced to being useless—but she also couldn't help feeling sorry for herself. *This will be my life,* she thought. *Taking care of him, going out to work as soon as he can be left, sitting with him in the evenings.* It was clear now that he was going to recover. He was getting stronger every day. She tried to be cheerful and optimistic for his sake. But every time she went out shopping, she saw the Christmas decorations in the shops and thought about Christmas at Miss Harcourt's. The RAF boys, the village women and children, the party she had been planning. And she felt as if her heart was breaking. It all seemed so unfair.

"I don't know what bloody kind of Christmas it will be," Shirley complained. "We can't even get a ruddy chicken, let alone a turkey. You'd think with four ration books we'd have enough, but no, it seems you need six or eight to get a chicken. So what are we stuck with? A can of corned beef with a bit of holly in it for our Christmas dinner?"

"I can make us a nice meat pie if we can get stewing beef," Josie said.

"Good luck with that," Shirley replied. "And you can't find an onion for love or money, so I don't know how you're going to flavour it."

Josie went out hunting amongst the various

butcher shops of her old neighbourhood and eventually came back with a rabbit.

"A bloody rabbit? Who wants to eat that?" Stan demanded.

"You'd be surprised. It tastes like chicken," Josie said. "We got them quite often out in Lincolnshire when a farmer shot one. You'll see. It will be good."

"I must say you've turned into a good cook, Josie," Shirley said. "I reckon you could get a job in a café. Do quite well for yourself."

"Let's just get Stan back on his feet first," she said, then winced at her choice of words. "I didn't mean that—you know what I meant."

Two days before Christmas, Stan declared that he was tired of staying cooped up and he wanted to go to the pub.

"You're not up to that yet, Stan," Josie said. "Where would you sit? Someone would bump into you, and you'd fall over."

"We can take him to the lounge, not the public bar," Fred said. "I say let him come if he wants to. God knows he's got little enough to cheer him up these days." He put a hand on Stan's arm. "We'll take care of you, mate, won't we?"

"I still don't think he should go," Josie said. "I know it's only on the corner, but if it's slippery or icy, he's going to fall, and we'll be back to square one."

"You always were a killjoy, Josie. Always did

know how to make a bloke feel miserable," Stan said, already trying to stand up.

"I'm trying to take care of you." Josie's patience snapped. "I've given up a lot for you, Stan. A life I liked, a job I liked, people I liked."

"Yeah. People you liked a bit too much, from what I saw," he said. "What's the matter? Miss getting your jollies from the air force?"

It took every ounce of Josie's strength not to hit him, not to scream. Instead she said, "Go to the bloody pub if you want to, but they'll have to look after you because I'm not coming!" She stomped upstairs to the spare room where they kept their things and stood staring out into the darkness. Downstairs she could hear Shirley and Fred laughing as they tried to get Stan into his overcoat, give him his crutches and then help him out of the front door. When they had gone, Josie let herself finally cry. She was just wiping her eyes when she heard the air raid warning siren echoing out. How were they going to get Stan into a shelter? she wondered. He'd never make it down steps into the Underground. *Bloody fools. They should have thought of that first.*

Her thoughts turned to her own safety. Shirley and Fred had a backyard shelter, but she remembered her panic last time they tried to get her into it. The air raid warning grew louder. So did the drone of approaching planes. Immediately memories swirled around her brain: the deafening roar; waking up buried in the rubble not able to move. The panic rose in her throat. Was it going to be like this every time the bombers came over?

"Enough is enough!" she said out loud. She made up her mind. She opened the front door and walked out into the street. People were streaming past her, clutching valuables, carrying babies, dragging along crying children. The street emptied out, and she stood alone as the drone of planes became louder, now punctuated by the anti-aircraft fire. A distant thud, then another as bombs were dropped. The first planes were caught in searchlights—big black crosses in the dark sky. So many of them.

"Here I am!" Josie yelled. "Come and get me! Take me now! I've nothing to live for. I don't want to live another moment."

The first wave of planes passed over.

Josie stretched up her arms to the sky as the second wave approached. A loud boom sounded at the docks, followed by the red glow of fire.

"Look at me, you silly sods," Josie screamed. "Look at me. Don't you think a bomb is worth wasting on me? Finish me off now." She danced around in frustration. Then there was a whooshing sound, a deafening explosion, a sheet of flame. Josie felt the intensity of the blast. The air was sucked from her lungs, and she was blown backwards. As she tried to stagger to her feet, the air filled with dust and swirling debris.

She put her hand up to her mouth, gasping, trying to find where her house was. She waited for the dust to settle, and there it was, still standing. So close. It had been so close. Half a street away, and she would have been out of her misery.

Then, in horror, she remembered Stan, Shirley and Fred at the pub. How close had they been? At that moment the all-clear wailed out. Other people had emerged from their shelters and were standing out in the street, staring, or even making their way towards the glow of the fire. She could already hear the clanging of a fire engine bell. She hadn't gone far before she realized: the pub on the corner was no more.

CHAPTER 39

"I'm sorry, Mrs Banks," the policeman said. It was past midnight when he paid a visit. Josie was still awake, still in shock, sitting at the kitchen table with a cold cup of tea in front of her. He looked elderly, with his uniform stretched tight across a paunch—almost too old to still be in the police force, but perhaps he had volunteered to return when the younger men went into the army. "Mr Banks and Mr and Mrs Ward were identified amongst the dead. Their identity cards were found on them."

Josie nodded.

"A sad business," he went on. "All those people packed in there, and a direct hit. None of them had a chance."

As she still said nothing, he asked, "Is there a family member or a neighbour you could go to for the night so you don't have to be alone?"

Josie shook her head. "I just came up from the country. There is nobody here."

"What about next of kin? They'll have to be notified. You'll be in touch with your husband's family, will you?"

"Shirley was his only sister. Their parents and three brothers died during the flu epidemic, so they were raised by an aunt, who has also since died," Josie said. "I know he has cousins, but he wasn't in touch with them."

"And Mr Ward?"

Josie shrugged. "Fred was my husband's brother-in-law. No relation to me, so I don't know much about him. I heard talk of a brother who was in the forces. Apart from that, I couldn't tell you."

"Then don't worry about it right now," he said. "The Red Cross will be coming round in the morning, and you'll be contacted about the release of the bodies and funeral arrangements."

"Oh. Right." Josie hadn't got as far as thinking about funerals. What she had been experiencing was an overwhelming feeling of guilt that she had wished Stan dead and now it had happened. It was almost as if she had caused his death, and Shirley's and Fred's, too. She tried to quieten the whisper that she was now free, forever free of them.

"At least they died instantly," the old copper said, giving her an encouraging smile. "That's one comfort, isn't it?"

But Josie was picturing Stan trying to use his crutches to get to safety as patrons stampeded, as the building burned and collapsed around him. She felt a wave of pity for him, but behind it was the guilty realization, a little louder now, that she was free. The policeman left her then. She made herself another cup of tea, then went to bed in Stan's bed in the front room, curling up with a hot water bottle to try and get warm. She sensed the smell of him on the sheets. She tried not to think, not about Stan and not about the future.

The next day a Red Cross volunteer came to the house.

"I gather you were only visiting here. The house belonged to your husband's sister and brother-in-law?" she asked.

"They were only renting it. They didn't own it," Josie said.

"Will you want to take over the rent, then?"

Josie almost said "Not bloody likely" but restrained herself and shook her head. "No, I'll be heading back out to the country as soon as I've arranged for the funeral."

"There is the question of furniture and personal effects," the woman went on. "Is there a relative of the Wards who would be entitled to them?"

"Fred had a brother. In the army, I think. I never met him."

"We'll try to contact him, but I think the best course at the moment would be for us to remove the furniture so that the landlord can relet the house. There are so many people who are home-less at the moment. And the furniture donation will be most welcome, too. You'll let us know when you leave, then?"

Josie nodded. "I should be arranging for the

burial, shouldn't I? I don't know much about funerals. Then there's my sister- and brother-in-law. Stan would want me to take care of them."

"If you don't, they will be buried in one of the mass graves," the woman said.

Josie knew there was money in Stan's post office savings book and decided she had to do the right thing. She had no idea when the bodies would be released from the mortuary and remembered, with a flash of irony, that tomorrow was Christmas Day. She awoke to a holiday with no church bells. There were already paper chains up in the living room and a bottle of port as a treat. It seemed so incongruous now. She needed to keep herself busy, so she cooked the rabbit she had bought and took most of it round to the neighbour next door, who had several children. The woman then invited Josie to Christmas dinner. It was strange to see other people being festive, children being excited about presents, although most of them were handmade. She pictured Miss Harcourt's house. Would Annie have found the perfect tree? Would it be decorated nicely? She couldn't wait to go back and be with them.

Nothing was open on Boxing Day, but the morning after, she went to a mortuary and arranged for a plot in the big cemetery by the Hackney Marshes.

"Will you want a plot big enough so that you can be buried beside your husband later?" the mortician asked.

It didn't take more than an instant for Josie to decide this wasn't what she wanted. "I don't think so, thanks."

"Then if you wanted to save money, we could bury him beside his sister and brother-in-law."

Josie nodded. "All right. Let's do that. Stan would want to be with his sister."

She paid for the arrangements, which took a big chunk out of Stan's savings account, and waited for the bodies to be released. This didn't happen until after the new year. The funeral was held on a bitterly cold, wet January 3. She stood on the flat, exposed ground beside the Thames while the wind snatched at the black hat she had found in Shirley's wardrobe. She had invited Shirley's neighbours, but the lady next door couldn't leave her young children, and the woman on the other side had gone back to work in the munitions factory. So Josie stood alone as the bodies were lowered into the ground. The minister seemed as anxious to get through the service as she was, and after a sprinkling of earth, they headed, with the pall-bearers, for the nearest pub, where Josie treated them all to a whisky.

She was still feeling numb, and not just from the cold, when she came back to Shirley's house and started to pack up her things. Her own case remained largely unpacked, but Josie reasoned that she had paid for the funeral and therefore should not feel guilty about helping herself to a few of Shirley's possessions. The rest would go to charity anyway. She wasn't going to be greedy, and there wasn't much she wanted. Shirley's style of clothing was more flashy and bright than Josie's, but she did find two pairs of good shoes, a new petticoat and stockings, a new woollen vest (much appreciated in the bitter cold) and various items of clothing that could be altered, since Shirley was bigger boned and taller. Shirley also owned a beaver lamb coat that Josie tried on with delight. She had always dreamed of owning a fur coat.

And so, on January 4, 1942, Josie took a taxi to King's Cross Station carrying two suitcases. She had written to Miss Harcourt that she was coming back but hadn't yet received a reply. It was only now, on the train, that she allowed herself to think about Mike. He was going to be there. She would have to see him. And she admitted that she wanted to see him. She could not break off her relationship with him without knowing the truth, or at least hearing his side of the story. During those long, cold nights when she slept in the empty house, he crept often into her dreams. Once she even dreamed he was holding her in his arms, and she awoke smiling. But she wasn't born stupid, as her father used to say. She knew how many women had gone with dubious men because they "would change for me." If he had a temper or a jealous streak she hadn't seen yet, she wanted to know about it. She was determined to be straight and outspoken with him.

She changed trains in Peterborough, then took the small branch line to Spalding, arriving in time to catch the afternoon bus out to Sutton St Giles. It had been snowing, and the sky was heavy with the promise of more snow. But the snow could not dampen her mood. Josie found herself smiling with anticipation. She'd be hugging Lottie and the girls, sitting in Nan's warm kitchen, seeing Charlie's and JJ's smiling faces when she opened the tea shop again . . .

The bus stopped not far from Miss Harcourt's house. Josie hefted the two big cases and set off through the snow, wishing she had worn her gumboots. She was about to open the gate when a man standing beside the front door stepped out to stop her.

"Here, where do you think you're going?" He was in RAF uniform and looked about twelve.

"I live here," Josie said angrily. "At least I used to live here, and now I'm coming back."

"Not any more, you don't," he said. "This place has been requisitioned since the new year. Taken over by the RAF. We've had to bring in more pilots for the big new planes we're getting . . ."

"The Lancasters?"

"How did you know about them?" He looked amazed.

"I've heard," Josie said defiantly.

"Well, they need more crew members, so we've had pilots transferred here. They all need somewhere to stay, so we've taken over this house."

"What has happened to the ladies who lived here?" Josie asked, her voice trembling.

He shrugged. "I don't know anything, ma'am. I was assigned to this duty yesterday, and here I am. You could ask at the RAF station, at the office that handles billeting. Someone might know there."

Josie's temper snapped. "I can hardly walk with two suitcases half a mile to the main gate, can I? In the bloody snow?"

"You could leave the cases here on the porch," he said.

"No, that's all right," she said with a resigned sigh. "I'll go into the village. I'll have to spend the night at the pub, if they've a room, and then decide what to do next."

She was about to leave when the thought struck her. "Squadron Leader Johnson—he's not staying at this house, is he?"

The young man's face became guarded. "Squadron Leader Johnson? You mean Mike Johnson?"

"That's the one. He must be back from his training in Manchester by now."

"I'm afraid the squadron leader was flying one of the planes that didn't come back from a sortie a couple of weeks ago."

"Didn't come back?" Josie tried to process this.

The airman repeated: "His plane was one of the ones that didn't return. Four planes lost that night."

"Oh. Oh, I see." Josie turned away and staggered blindly up the path.

The familiar route into the village seemed to have turned into a mile-long trek. She stumbled blindly along, trying to come to terms with her latest reality. No Miss Harcourt. Nowhere to live. And no Mike. At least her last letter to him had been kind. He had died with a good memory of her. But she—she would never know what had happened long ago in Nova Scotia.

The cluster of houses ahead never seemed to get any closer. She was out of breath, her hands burning from carrying the two heavy cases, and before she arrived, the first flutter of snowflakes landed on her new fur coat. The shop was already closed, the houses already shuttered and dark. She stood looking around her at the familiar sights, fighting back tears. She had looked forward to this so much, and now it had been taken from her. She turned towards the church, which looked like a Christmas card scene with its churchyard heaped with snow.

"Come on, God," she said out loud. "Enough is

enough. Are you going to take everything away from me any time I'm happy?"

At that moment, she heard someone coming towards her, whistling "We're Going to Hang Out Our Washing on the Siegfried Line." A man came into view, and it was Alf Badger. He paused, frowning when he saw her standing there.

"Why, it's never Mrs Banks, is it? What a lovely surprise. Have you come to visit?"

Josie fought to keep her voice steady. "My husband died, Mr Badger. He was killed in a bomb. So I came back to be with Miss Harcourt again, only . . ."

"Only the poor old thing's been turned out into the snow, eh? Nasty shock for you, I'd imagine."

"What's happened to her, do you know?"

He came up to her and picked up the suitcases as if it were the most natural thing in the world. "Let's not stand here, freezing. Come on. Come inside and have supper with us, and then I'll tell you all about it. Nan will be so pleased. So will the girls."

He stomped ahead, and it was all she could do to hurry after him. He put down the suitcases, opened the door and called out, "Nan, girls, come and see who I've just found."

Nan appeared from a back room and clapped her hands in delight. "Mrs Banks! Well, I never. What a lovely surprise. So you've come to visit us?"

"She's come back, Mother," Alf said. "Her husband didn't make it, and she thought she was returning to live with the old lady again."

"Oh dear. What a nasty shock for you," Nan said. "Well, take off your coat and sit down. I'll get you a cup of tea."

Before she could sit down, Sheila and Dorothy came bursting through the doorway.

"Lottie, come down and see," Sheila called. "It's your lady. She's back."

There was a clattering of feet on bare boards, and then Lottie appeared, beaming at Josie. "You've come back? For good?"

"I'm not sure now, love," Josie said. "I was planning to stay with Miss Harcourt again. Get my tea shop up and running. But now . . ." She turned to the Badgers. "Where did you say she'd gone?"

"Well, you'll never believe this, but she's moved in with that doctor," Nan said. "You know, the German man. It seems he heard about her being turfed out, and he said he'd had all that room to himself, and he'd welcome the company. So she's gone there, and Annie Adams is taking care of them both. So it suits all around, it seems. We all felt sorry for her, the way it was handled, so we ladies from the WI all went over to help her pack up her personal stuff. It's locked away in an attic, but I don't reckon those RAF types will take good care of her furniture, do you?"

"I'm glad she's got a place to stay," Josie said. "She'll be good company for Dr Goldsmith."

"Our Lottie goes over there quite often, don't you, love?"

Lottie nodded. "He helps me with my homework when he's not on a late shift. He's very clever, you know. I'm taking chemistry now, and he can explain so well." She gave a little smile. "And Miss Harcourt—well, she's read a lot of books, and she's travelled, too, so she tells me things."

"That's good." Josie tried to sound positive. It seemed everyone now had a place where they fit in nicely. She was the only one who didn't.

She accepted the cup of tea. "I really shouldn't stay long," she said. "I should find out if the pub has a room for me."

"Oh no, dear," Nan said. "They've billeted more officers at the pub. The whole place is full of them now."

"Then I've no idea where I can stay the night," Josie said. "Perhaps the vicarage?"

"You'll stay right here with us," Nan said, glancing at Alf.

"But you don't have any room."

"Well, we've a spare bed in the girls' room because Dorothy likes to share with Sheila, don't you, my love? And Lottie prefers her space in the attic. So if you don't mind bunking in with the girls . . ."

Josie wiped back a tear. "That's so good of you. Of course I'd love to stay the night. And tomorrow I'll have to decide what I'm going to do next."

"They are using civilians at the RAF station now, so I've heard," Alf said. "But I don't know that they'd have a place for you to stay."

Josie shook her head. "I don't think I could take that, waiting for the bad news every morning about which planes didn't come back."

Alf nodded. "No, it's hard for all of them. So many losses. But let's not think about it tonight. In the morning, things will seem brighter, won't they?"

They ate a hearty stew followed by a jam roly-poly and accompanied by Alf's homemade parsnip wine, which packed quite a punch. Josie went to bed, hearing the gentle breathing of the little girls beside her, and drifted off to a peaceful sleep. In the morning she prepared to walk to the doctor's house. More snow had fallen during the night, so she rescued the Wellingtons from her case, remembering as she put them on the day Mike had bought them for her. It was a long walk through the snow, and she was red-faced and panting by the time the house came into view. Annie Adams opened the door, a look of amazement on her face.

"Miss Harcourt, it's our Josie come back."

Josie was ushered in to where Miss Harcourt

was sitting by the fire. Josie sat opposite her, and they exchanged news. Miss Harcourt examined Josie with her steady gaze. "It must have been a hard time for you, my dear. In some ways I expect you are relieved it's over, aren't you? I never thought there was much love lost between you and that husband of yours."

"I suppose I did love him at first," Josie said. "But he wasn't easy to live with. And it was a merciful release for him, as he'd have been an invalid for the rest of his life, but I can't help feeling guilty about it."

"Of course you can't. But the truth is that you really are free now. Free to marry again, if you want to."

"I don't want to," Josie said, almost snapping the words out. Then she sighed. "I'm sorry. There is nobody I want to marry. I'll have to find a job and somewhere to live and just get on with things."

"I'm sure the doctor wouldn't mind you joining us here," Miss Harcourt said. "He's been most kind, and I think he really enjoys our company, doesn't he, Annie?"

"I'd say he does. And my cooking," she added with a grin.

That evening Dr Goldsmith affirmed what the women had said. "My dear Mrs Banks. You would be most welcome to join the ladies here. I have enough bedrooms, you know. The word will get around the hospital that I now have a harem." And he gave a self-deprecating smile. Josie agreed to stay, at least for a few days. Dr Goldsmith drove her over to the Badgers' to pick up her suitcases.

It was indeed pleasant at the doctor's house. He had an extensive library. Annie was a good cook, and Miss Harcourt was good company. But Josie couldn't settle. She wrote to Mr Thomas: *My husband was recently killed, and I am now free to offer my services wherever you can use them. Only I prefer not to be in the middle of London if that's possible.*

A letter came back a few days later: *As it happens, they are looking for recruits at a country house in Buckinghamshire. I can't tell you what they do there because it's all very hush-hush. But I do know it's valuable work and you'd be needed. What's more, it's a lovely setting with good food and good company. I'll give you the address. It's a place called Bletchley Park . . .*

Josie announced to the others at dinner that she'd be leaving the next day. They all seemed disappointed she was going.

"I do like it here," she said, "but it's not right that I should be enjoying myself and doing nothing when every able-bodied adult is needed. So I'm going to work for the government—doing filing and office stuff, I expect, but I've got a place to stay, and that's the main thing."

Dr Goldsmith drove her to the station the next morning. "I'm sorry to see you go," he said.

"And I'm sorry to be going, but it's the right thing to do. I've had too many shocks and disappointments, and the last thing I want is time to think and brood."

"I can understand that, but I'm going to make a proposition to you. I wondered if you'd stay on . . . if I asked you to marry me."

"Marry you?" Josie gave a nervous laugh. "But you hardly know me."

"I've seen enough to know you are a kind and generous woman, and I think you'd make a good doctor's wife."

"I'm really touched, Dr Goldsmith, but I wouldn't want anyone to marry me out of pity."

"Oh, it's not pity," he said quickly. "I have come to have the highest regard for you. You would want for nothing."

"Oh dear." Josie gave a little gasp. "What you are offering is really tempting. I know you're a good man. A kind man. But I wouldn't be the wife for you. You're a foreigner, and however long you've lived here, you'd never understand the English. If I was your wife, any time I opened my mouth, they'd know I was a cockney, and they'd look down on me—and you."

"Every time I open my mouth, they know I'm a German. Do you not think they thus look down on me even more?" he asked. "Look, I know that I am Jewish, and that may be a problem."

"Of course it's not that," Josie said. "I wouldn't care what religion you are."

"And I am considerably older than you . . ."

"Not that much, surely," Josie said. "I'm nearly thirty. You can't be more than forty."

"Forty-two," he said. "It is an age difference to be sure, but I would try to make you happy and hope that one day you would come to love me."

Josie put her hands up to her face. "Don't ask me this now. I've lost everything, Doctor. I might say yes because I'm clutching at straws."

"My name is Jakob. Then I will leave the offer open, Josie," he said. "I will not ask you to give me my answer right away. Think about it. Get back on your feet. Try out this new job, and one day you may say, 'Yes, I believe I could be happy with him.' "

Josie looked at him tenderly. "You really are a nice man," she said. "I hope you do find a woman and fall madly in love with her. And she with you."

"I think I already have fallen for one woman," he said.

CHAPTER 40

As the train carried her towards Bedford and the house called Bletchley Park, Josie had time to think and reconsider her actions. She told herself she was a bloody fool for turning down Dr Goldsmith's proposal. He wasn't bad looking. He was quiet and kind, and she'd have a lovely house. What more did she want? Love, she told herself. She wanted to marry a man she loved. Her first marriage had been one of convenience, a chance to escape. She was not going to make that mistake again. It was time for her to make her own life.

Her first impression of Bletchley was not a good one. The small station stood beside grimy, terraced houses and a brickworks. The smell of brick dust burned in her nostrils. She enquired about a taxi but was told it wouldn't do her much good.

"He can only go as far as the main gate, love," the porter told her. "They don't let anyone past without clearance. And it's a good long walk up to the house."

Luckily the snow in this part of the world was only a dusting, but the suitcases were heavy, and she was gasping for breath as she approached the perimeter fence. The high barbed wire and the armed guards at the gate were off-putting. What was she getting into? she asked herself. She showed one of the guards the letter she had been sent. They checked her off on a list and then directed her to go straight to the main house.

"You can leave the bags here for now in the gatehouse," the guard said, looking at her more kindly now. "No sense in taking them all the way up there when you'll be billeted some-where else."

Josie gave him a grateful smile as he took the cases from her and put them inside the small gatehouse. Then she set off up the drive, came around a corner, and there was the mansion, a sprawling red-brick building, situated on the far side of a lake where swans were swimming. A group of young men were throwing a rugby ball around on the lawns. It looked remarkably peaceful and elegant, and Josie's spirits rose. Inside the entrance hall, she stood, admiring the sweep of the curved, polished-wood staircase, the stained-glass windows throwing patterns of colour on to the floor and the panelled ceilings. It was elegant beyond anything she had experi-enced, and old doubts crept in. "This is no place for you, my girl." She heard her mother's voice. "Getting above ourselves, aren't we?"

The woman who ushered her into a small office seemed to agree. "I'm not sure why you are here or whether we have a suitable assignment for you, Mrs Banks," she said. "Other than catering, that is. We can always use extra kitchen staff."

Josie wouldn't actually have minded working in a kitchen, but her pride kicked in. "Mr Thomas seemed to think I might be useful," she said and handed over the letter. The woman scanned it.

"Mr Thomas? Oh, I see. Tom Worthington. We are familiar with him. Well, if he thinks you can be useful, I'm sure you can." The woman's tone changed. "But before we go any further, you are required to sign the Official Secrets Act."

"What exactly do you do here?" Josie asked.

"That will be made clear to you only when you have signed."

"I have to sign before I know what I'm letting myself in for?" Josie asked.

The woman gave an apologetic smile. "I'm afraid that's the way it works. What we do here is top secret. If you wish to work here, you will swear that you will never divulge anything that happens at Bletchley to another soul. Is that clear?"

Josie had to grin. "I don't actually have another soul to divulge it to," she said. "Everyone I loved is dead. So yes, I'll sign your paper for you."

Again the woman eyed her, and Josie could see the questioning in her gaze. Did they want an uneducated cockney at this place? But she took back the papers after Josie had signed them.

"Right," she said. "I'll hand you over to our Miss Godfrey, who will show you the ropes."

Miss Godfrey turned out to be another of those efficient and terrifying women, but she told Josie to follow her. "We did receive a communication from a certain member of MI5," she said. "He thought you had quick wits and good powers of observation, so I'm taking you over to the index."

They left the warmth of the main building and headed for a row of long huts. In contrast with the elegance of the main building, these were austere and drab in the extreme.

"You'll be working with a lot of young Cambridge men," Miss Godfrey said as the full force of an icy wind met them. "They are all rather full of themselves, but don't take any nonsense. And there are quite a few debs, too. You know—former debutantes. But don't be discouraged. We are all working with one goal, and you will only be judged here on the quality of your work and what you can offer."

"What exactly will I be doing?" Josie asked, now a little nervously.

"Well, what this place does is intercept German messages. We have a machine that has broken their code, you know. Brilliant work. Do you speak fluent German?"

"I don't speak any languages, not even English too well," Josie replied, making the woman smile.

"That's all right. There are plenty of jobs that don't actually involve translation."

Josie was taken into one of the huts—a long, ugly wooden structure. It smelled of oil stoves. The floor creaked. The place was partitioned into small rooms, and a draught blew through the narrow passage that linked them. *Not exactly the luxury of the main house,* Josie thought. From some of the partitions came the clatter of typewriters, and Josie began to feel panic rising that she didn't know how to type, nor could she speak a foreign language. What use could she be?

She was introduced to a middle-aged male supervisor, a big balding man wearing horn-rimmed spectacles, whom Miss Godfrey addressed as Commander, and who gave the impression that he wasn't sure what use she would be either.

"But we're rather short-staffed at the moment," he said, "so I suppose you'll have to do for now. We'll see how you get along, shall we?"

With those encouraging words, he led her to a bigger room at the far end, where the pertinent information from intercepted messages was written on index cards and then filed or sent on to the appropriate armed forces. This seemed like something Josie could do, and she gave a sigh of relief. She took her place at a rickety table and looked around at the other workers. There were four others in the room, much younger women, and they seemed to find it interesting that Josie should be joining them.

"It's bloody awful here," one of them said when they stopped for a tea break. She introduced herself as Cynthia—the others being Diana, Audrey and Beth—all girls who might have been former debs. "Freezing cold in winter, unbearably hot in summer, and if you are billeting with us, which I think you will be, the food will probably poison you, so make sure you take your main meal up at the cafeteria. The old cow takes our ration books and then serves us toast and dripping. But we've all survived so far." She gave Josie an encouraging smile. "What brought you here?"

"I was bombed twice," Josie said, "so I wanted to get out of London. And I did a bit of work helping to catch a German spy."

That got her immediate respect. "Was he disguised as a nun?" one of the young women asked.

Josie laughed. "I don't think I'm allowed to talk about it, but there were two of them. Not nuns. Quite unlikely spies."

"Well, our work here isn't nearly as glamourous," another of the girls said in her smooth, aristocratic voice. "Quite tedious most of the time—you know, copying down figures or names—but every now and then we hit upon something important, and we know we've done a good thing."

"And life is quite fun when we're not working," Cynthia said. "We have dances, and we put on plays and operas, and on fine days we have tennis and rounders and picnics on the lawn."

"The chaps are mostly a hopeless lot," the small dark one called Beth said. "More interested in math than in girls."

"Or in boys than in girls," Diana added, and they all burst out laughing.

At the end of the day, she was driven in an army jeep down to the town, where she found herself rooming with Cynthia and the others. It certainly wasn't luxury, looking out on the railway line, but the younger girls seemed to take it in stride. Josie had never been in a situation like this. At first she worried that they were all young and upper class, but they adopted her instantly as a surrogate mother and dragged her into all their plans and shared worries about boyfriends and generally treated her as a pet from another species. Josie equally felt that they might be creatures from Mars. Much of their conversation was unintelligible to her. Cynthia mentioned a certain "chap" as being NSIT.

"What's that?" Josie asked, and the other three laughed.

"Not safe in taxis," Cynthia explained. "It's part of our code so we can warn other girls."

Josie didn't mention that she had never taken

a taxi with a young man. A different universe, that's what it seemed like. But they were nice enough to her. And she scored a major triumph when she confronted the landlady about their rations.

"I've been here over a week," she said, "and I haven't seen a bit of meat yet, nor an egg. Now I know you have five ration books, so that should let you get a decent bit of meat."

"Meat's not easy to come by," the woman said, folding her arms defiantly.

"Then I'm afraid we might be looking for somewhere else to stay, and we'll let them know up at the big house that this place isn't suitable for nicely brought-up young girls like these. We're doing valuable war work, you know."

"Here, hold on a minute," the woman said, taking a step towards Josie. "I'll see what I can do—all right?"

"You were absolutely brilliant," Cynthia said as she returned to the bedroom. "I'd never have had the nerve."

Josie realized that her class had been an advantage for once. She had faced the landlady as an equal, knowing how to spar with her. And sure enough, a meat pie was on the menu that evening.

The work, as Cynthia had said, was mostly tedious, copying information to index cards and filing them or sending on the information if it was deemed important. But one day Josie, working on U-boats, noticed something as she wrote.

"Here," she said, going over to Diana, who worked beside her. "Look at this. This U-boat has changed captains and has left the fleet it was with. It seems to be heading off alone. I wonder what it's chasing?"

"Show the commander," Diana said.

With trepidation, Josie did so. At first he seemed uninterested, but the next day he came back to her. "Well done. Sharp eyes," he said. "That U-boat was shadowing one of our battle-ships. Thanks to you, we've sunk it before it could sink us."

And he put Josie on to another job, scanning intercepted messages for anomalies. Josie didn't know what an anomaly was and was afraid to ask, but she soon proved to be rather good at it, especially the figures. She worked so hard that she had put aside all thoughts of returning to Lincolnshire and accepting Dr Goldsmith's proposal. She wrote to Miss Harcourt, and that lady wrote back to a government post office box number, as Josie was not allowed to give her address. All was going smoothly in the village, except the extra RAF men were taking over the pub and getting drunk too often. Dr Goldsmith added a few lines to the bottom of the letter— non-committal greetings that did not mention his proposal.

A year passed. Other people went home for Christmas. Josie stayed. They had a fun party with plenty of booze, turkey, goose and an actual Christmas pudding. They put on a silly panto-mime, and Josie helped with the costumes. She had begun to feel that she did actually belong here—that she had a purpose in life.

"You know, after the war, you should go to university," the commander who ran her hut said. His initial scepticism had been replaced with approval. "You've a good mathematical brain. You could teach."

"Me? University?" She laughed.

He nodded. "I've seen your work. You are twice as fast as some of the other women."

"It's hard to think about life after the war," she told him.

"I know. But things are starting to go our way," he said. "Rommel has been defeated. We've landed in Italy. It will only be a matter of time before we win."

"You really think we're going to win?" she asked.

He nodded. "Oh yes. No doubt about it. We've got the upper hand now."

That made her feel hope for the first time. After the war. What would she do? Where would she go? Could she really attend a university at her age? Would she want to? Wouldn't she rather go back to Miss Harcourt and help her reclaim the house? But wouldn't she be bored after the pace of life at Bletchley? And what about marrying Dr Goldsmith? She certainly had more to offer as a potential doctor's wife these days. *Let's just get the war over first,* she told herself.

Then, at the end of 1943, everything changed. She was going through a column of names, part of a report detailing British prisoners of war, and she saw his name. *Johnson, Michael.* It was a list from a Stalag Luft—a camp for RAF officers. It had to be him, although Michael Johnson was a common enough name. She was in an agony of indecision. She had felt a great surge of happiness when she realized he was alive, but wouldn't it be wiser not to communicate with him—to forget about him and get on with life now? But then she thought of him in a prisoner-of-war camp. He'd already been in prison, Mr Thomas had told her. He'd experienced what it was like. This must seem like hell for him—alone with nobody to write to him.

She shared the news with her housemates. "Do you think I could write to him? Am I allowed to use information we've gained here?" she asked.

"Oh, for heaven's sake, Josie," Diana said. "If it's a chap you're keen on, of course you should write to him. Poor man, stuck in one of those hellholes. He'd love to get a letter from anyone."

She didn't share with them what she knew about his past. It was too painful to contemplate. And as she lay in bed that night, the room shaken each time a train passed on the main line, she tried to examine what she knew and what she felt about him. She still could not come to terms with Mike as a murderer. He was a kind man, a gentle man. She remembered him petting that dog, scooping the child out of the waves and the way he looked at her with such tenderness. The court had downgraded his charge to manslaughter, hadn't they? Didn't that mean that they thought his wife's death was probably an accident? *He gave her the wrong drugs by mistake,* she told herself. And she knew she had to write to him.

And so she wrote.

Dear Mike,

I hope I'm writing to the right Mike Johnson, but it seemed too much of a coincidence that there are two squadron leaders called Michael Johnson in RAF prison camps. So I hope it's you. I thought you were dead. They told me your plane had not returned, so I assumed you hadn't made it. And I just found out you were alive. I don't know if they'll deliver this letter or let you write to someone at home, but I want you to know that I'm thinking of you. I'll find out if I'm allowed to send

you any supplies. Is there anything you desperately want?
  Love,
  Josie

There. She had done it. She found the Red Cross delivered letters and parcels to prisoners and handed over her message. She didn't receive a reply for a couple of months and had almost given up hope when one came.

Dear Josie,
  What a wonderful surprise, getting your letter. I can't tell you how much I've been thinking of you, stuck here in this hell of a place. We are lucky, I suppose. It's not as bad as some camps because we are officers and pilots, and thus they respect us. No terrible punishments unless someone tries to break out—which happens quite regularly. I'm not stupid enough to try it. They only get shot, and I'd prefer to stay alive, in spite of everything. I probably can't tell you much about the conditions because it would be censored. The food is awful, of course. Barely enough to keep us alive. Thin vegetable soup and a slice of black bread a day. But the Germans themselves aren't eating much better, so we are told.

How is your husband progressing? Has he recovered from his wounds and gone back into the army? Are you staying in London? I think about you all the time. Those days with you were the happiest I have known in years. Just knowing you still think of me gives me a warm glow.

I wish you the happiest of lives, and I hope that your husband realizes what a treasure he has and treats you accordingly.

With affection,
Mike

PS. If you are allowed to send anything, I would really appreciate a bar of soap and some warm socks.

Josie went out and bought soap and socks, then added a jar of Bovril, a tin of corned beef and a packet of biscuits. She would have loved to send chocolate, but there was none to be had. She added a small packet of writing paper, in case he had none. She packed them up and realized she should write a note with them. Should she tell him about Stan? Would that give him a false hope? Then she decided that hope was what he needed to keep him alive. And so she wrote the note, telling him that Stan had died, Miss

482

Harcourt's house had been taken over by the RAF and she was now working in a government office, enjoying her role.

In May she got a letter back on her writing paper.

I can't tell you how much your gifts have meant to us. We heat water over the stove in our hut in a former paraffin can, and I give each man a mug with a little Bovril in it. So nourishing. And the corned beef! You'd have thought it was filet mignon the way we all smacked our lips and moaned in ecstasy.

The weather is finally improving. We can see distant mountains from our grounds. They let us out to play football, or at least they did until two stupid blokes tried to dig under the wire fence. They were shot in front of us, and they made us stand to attention outside all day. Now we're not allowed out again.

Josie, I am sorry about your husband. I'm not sure if you are or not. I think you might feel free. But maybe I'm wrong. I guess we all must love the person we marry at the beginning. Anyway, your news gave me hope like I haven't had in ages. Please stay alive until after the war. I know I will try extra hard now.

Josie stared at the letter. *I guess we all must love the person we marry at the beginning.* Did that tell her that he stopped loving his wife because . . . ? Stopped loving her enough to kill her? Because she betrayed him? Tried to leave him? Josie tried to understand, but it didn't make sense. He had never shown any signs of uncontrolled anger or jealousy. She wanted to write and ask him for the truth, but she couldn't.

CHAPTER 41

Spring became summer. The Allies landed in Normandy. The end was in sight. At Bletchley Park, they were working harder than ever, intercepting communications that revealed how desperate the enemy was becoming. But Josie received no more letters from Mike. She wrote to the Red Cross about him, but they couldn't help. Nobody had any information since the situation had deteriorated inside Germany. Had the Germans shot their prisoners? Had he tried to escape and come to a bad end? She couldn't stop thinking about him and worrying. She continued to send letters, just in case he still received them, but no replies came. In the end she had to accept the inevitable.

Church bells rang out across Britain in 1945 when the war ended. There were street parties and parades, welcoming the heroes home. At Bletchley they had a crazy party with dancing on the lawns, fireworks and lots of booze. Everyone was hugging and promising to write, looking forward to going home. Only Josie had no home to go to.

Cynthia sent out invitations to her wedding and made Josie promise to come. Josie saw the address: *The Earl and Countess of Buckley,*

Forthington House, Derbyshire. And she had to smile that they had shared a room, terrible food and long shifts in a hut. Now the world would go back to normal, and there was no way she'd attend a wedding at Forthington House.

With no real plans, and certainly no desire to return to London, she headed back to Lincolnshire. If the RAF had vacated Miss Harcourt's house, she'd need help getting it up and running again. Josie felt a twinge of excitement as she got off the bus, and there was the village of Sutton St Giles, now with Union Jacks flying, bunting strung across the street and draped around the pub. Miss Harcourt's house stood empty, vacated by the RAF. This made Josie feel alarmed that Miss Harcourt might have died since Josie had last received a letter from her. She was reassured in the village shop that Miss Harcourt was still staying at the doctor's house, so Josie left her bags behind the counter and walked the half mile to the big square Georgian in the middle of the fields. There she found Miss Harcourt and Annie. Josie was given a warm welcome. She felt strange and awkward, sitting in a proper sitting room and being served tea by Annie.

"I want to know all the news," she said. "How is Lottie?"

Miss Harcourt beamed. "Dr Goldsmith has helped Lottie get into Cambridge. She starts in September. Reading chemistry."

"How lovely for her. But what about her parents, now that the war's over?"

Miss Harcourt shook her head sadly. "We have been trying to find out, but from what Dr Goldsmith tells me, I think there is little hope they will be found alive. Millions of Jews were exterminated, so we understand. All the Jews in Germany are gone. Such a terrible thing."

"And the other two girls? What will become of them? Has Sheila gone home?"

Miss Harcourt sighed. "Sheila's mother made it quite clear that she is not keen to have her back. Another new man in her life, so we gather."

"Poor little thing," Josie exclaimed. "So what will she do?"

"Nan and Alf are going to keep her, of course. And Dorothy's father—well, he's just come back from the Far East. He's not sure what to do with a daughter, and Dorothy doesn't want to leave the Badgers, so they are keeping her, too, for now."

"I'm glad," Josie said. "It's a good thing to grow up in a home with love."

"Yes," Miss Harcourt said. "Love might have been a good thing in my early years. And yours, I'd imagine."

Josie nodded. Miss Harcourt stared at her.

"There was an airman, I remember. A handsome pilot? What became of him?"

"He was in a prisoner-of-war camp. But I

haven't heard from him in over a year. So I have to assume . . ."

Miss Harcourt nodded with understanding. "So, what are your plans now? Will you go back to London, do you think?"

"Oh goodness me, no," Josie said. "I could never live in that dirty old city after being in the country so long. I'm used to fresh air! My supervisor where I was working told me I had a good brain and should go to university. That seems rather far-fetched, but I might think of a teacher's training college maybe, if they'll have me. I get along well with kids, even if I don't have any of my own. But first I thought you might want some help getting your house back in order. I don't suppose they've left it in the best condition."

"I haven't seen it yet," Miss Harcourt said. "Frankly I'm afraid to. But it doesn't really matter because I have decided to sell it."

"Sell it?"

"It's too selfish for one person to have such a big property. And I'd never be able to get the staff to keep it running properly these days."

"Will you go on living with the doctor?"

Miss Harcourt shook her head. "I understand he's decided to go out to Australia. Lots of refugees are going there, so we're told. He can be of great service. Such a good man. Annie is also going to Australia, to her daughter. She's applied for a passage."

"But what will you do? Where will you go?" Josie asked.

"I shall move into one of those homes for distressed gentlefolk. I always despised them, but now I realize I welcome the company. There is one in Shoeburyness—on the coast, you know. That would be pleasant. Walks along the promenade. I have written to them."

"That will be nice for you," Josie said. She tried to give a bright smile, but all she could think was that everybody had somewhere to go, and she had nowhere.

That evening when Dr Goldsmith came home, his face lit up when he saw Josie.

"I can't believe that you have returned to us," he said. "What a lovely treat. How long are you going to stay?"

"Not long," Josie said. "I just wanted to make sure everyone was all right."

After dinner he took Josie out on to the back lawn. A fountain was playing. Rooks were cawing in a big old yew tree. It was all so peaceful and serene, as if a war had never happened.

"I don't know if they told you," he said, "but I have applied to go to Australia. It is a new country, plenty of opportunity, lots of room, and they need doctors. They are inviting refugees from all over Europe, and they won't care that I have a funny accent." He paused. "I think it would be a good place for you, too. Nobody will care if you were born in London or Timbuktu. I know you turned me down before, but my offer still stands, Josie. Will you come with me?"

"Australia?" Josie hesitated. "Let me have time to take it in."

"Of course. Take all the time you need. I don't suppose I'll be able to leave for several months. So many people have applied for a chance to emigrate."

That night she lay in bed, mulling this over. Australia was such a long way away. She didn't know much about it, but she had seen pictures of long, sandy beaches and koalas and kangaroos. Strange and exotic and foreign. But a doctor's wife would be a good life. Respected, able to do some good. And he was a kind, decent man. He'd take care of her. Maybe in time she'd come to love him, if she could ever love again.

In the morning she offered to take Miss Harcourt to her house. The doctor dropped them off on his way to work, and they went up the path together. Josie could feel the old woman's hand trembling as she held Josie's arm. Inside it was as bad as Josie had dreaded—peeling wallpaper, scuffed and damaged furniture. There were rings on the black lacquer of the piano where mugs and glasses had been placed. The piano seat had a slit in it. They had even used a painting as a dartboard. Josie saw the pain on Miss Harcourt's face. In the three years they had been apart, she had aged considerably and now looked like a frail old lady.

"I'm sorry," Josie said. "Perhaps we shouldn't have come."

"Oh no, dear. I had to see it. Just another casualty of war, but it doesn't even seem to matter now. The whole world has changed. Big houses and servants are things of the past. They'll probably tear it down and build a housing estate."

"Come on," Josie said. "Let's go into the kitchen, and I'll make you a cup of tea, if the RAF haven't pinched all your supplies."

"I'm sorry you won't have your tea shop any more," the old lady said. "You brought a lot of happiness, I think."

"Yes. It was nice of you to let me use the room." Josie sat Miss Harcourt down at the kitchen table and looked around for supplies. "No milk, of course. Why don't I run into the village and get some?"

"Oh, it's not worth the effort," Miss Harcourt said. "Let's just call a taxi to take us back to the doctor's house for now. I think I've seen enough for one day."

They came out of the front door, and Josie took the old lady's arm to escort her up the front path. As they reached the gate, she glanced up and saw a man walking towards them. He limped and walked with a stick, but he was wearing an RAF uniform that didn't fit well. Josie stopped. Stared.

Blinked. Then she started to run towards him.

"It is you," she shouted. "It really is you."

Mike dropped the stick and opened his arms. They wrapped around her as he hugged her so tightly that she could hardly breathe. Then the tears came, and she cried on his shoulder. "I thought you were dead," she sobbed. "I didn't hear from you, and I thought that . . ."

"They kept moving us as the Allies came closer. They took us to the east. The Polish border. I think they planned to kill us all, but then the Russians arrived in the nick of time, and we were freed. It's taken me a while to get home, and I had no idea where I'd find you. I just hoped you might be here . . ."

He took her face in his hands, gazing at her as if he were seeing a miracle. He was so thin, his face like a skeleton, his eyes hollow. His head had been shorn.

"Come inside," she said, glancing back at the house. "I was about to make tea, but there's no milk. Where are you staying?"

"I was going to spend the night at the RAF station. I've already been officially demobbed, but I figured they'd put me up there if necessary."

"You can stay here," she said. "I'm sure Miss Harcourt won't mind. I'll stay with you. It's in a bit of a mess, but we'll muddle through."

She sent him inside with Miss Harcourt, then ran all the way to the village and came back with milk, eggs and bread. Later, when Miss Harcourt had been taken back to the doctor's house and they were alone, they took chairs out into the back garden. It was a mild summer evening, and swallows flitted through a pink twilight.

"You've hurt your leg?" Josie asked.

He nodded. "Broke it badly when I parachuted out and they shot at me on the way down. And they never set it properly, so I'm not likely to play football again. At least not for a pro team." He gave a sad chuckle. "But you—you look marvellous. So fit and healthy. You're like a miracle, Josie. It seems too good to be true."

Josie swallowed hard. "Mike. We have to talk . . ."

"There's another man in your life now?" She saw the alarm on his face.

She shook her head. "About your wife. I need to know before anything more happens. I need the whole truth."

He nodded. "Of course. So you heard. I thought the news would cross the Atlantic in the end. I was a coward not telling you before. Stupid to think I could keep it from you. I did try to tell you once, when we were at the seaside together, but I chickened out halfway. I thought you'd want nothing more to do with me." He sighed. "I'm not sure how much you've been told."

"Did you really murder your wife? I didn't want to believe it was true."

"But I did," he said. "I did kill her." She gave a little gasp and moved her hand away from his. He turned away, staring out across the overgrown garden, then went on. "She developed an aggressive brain cancer. She only had months to live, and it would have robbed her of her sight, her memory—everything. She asked me to let her go peacefully while she still knew who she was and who I was. 'You have access to the right drugs. You know what to do,' she said. So I gave her drugs to put her to sleep. I held her hand all the while and told her I loved her." Tears started running down his cheeks. "And when she was fully asleep, I put a pillow over her face."

Josie took his hand. "Oh, Mike, I'm so sorry."

He nodded. "It was the hardest thing I've ever done."

"But surely nobody could think that was a crime? It was an act of love."

He shook his head. "The law doesn't see it like that. It didn't matter to them that she had months to live and I put her out of her suffering. She was alive and I killed her. That's murder. I was arrested and tried." He paused, fighting to regain his composure. "The prosecution tried to make all kinds of claims—I wanted her insurance money, or just wanted to be free of a basket case. There was a hung jury. There was going to be a retrial. They came to me and told me that if I pleaded guilty to manslaughter, I'd get off lightly.

A couple of years in jail. I didn't want to do that, but I saw there was a real chance they'd stick the murder conviction during the retrial, and it would be life behind bars. So I agreed. I got five years, and I served three." He paused again, staring out past her. "When I came out, it was terrible. A small community, you know. Everywhere I went, people whispered: 'That's the man who killed his wife.' The hospital didn't want me back. So I changed my name—you knew that? They told you that?"

"They said you were Mark Jensen?"

"That's right. I became Mike Johnson. The war was about to start. I took flying lessons. I moved to England and joined the RAF. I told my superior officer the truth, and he agreed to let me keep the new identity. I'm so sorry, Josie. Sorry that I didn't tell you before. I just didn't want to lose you."

Josie laughed. "You silly old thing. I spent all this time worrying that you were a psychopath, a man who went around killing women. If only you'd told me the truth right away, of course I would have understood."

"Well, you know it now," he said.

"I do. I always thought you were a kind man, and that was the ultimate act of kindness. And bravery, too. I'll go anywhere you want to, Mike. I'll do anything I can to make you happy."

"You can make me happy by saying yes."

"You don't even have to ask. I've loved you since the day you picked me up off the ice and fell down yourself in the process."

He was beaming now. "We'll get married right away. So where do you want to go? What do you want to do?"

"Me?" Josie paused. "I've had all sorts of thoughts about what I'd want to do, but right now I only have one thought, and that's to be with you. But what about you? Do you want to go back to being a chemist? Working in a hospital again?"

"I think not. Once you get a taste for flying, it's hard to let it go. I'd rather start a flying school somewhere. Or run a small airline back in Canada or Australia, maybe New Zealand."

"A small airline? And where's the money coming from, eh? Don't tell me you got rich in a prison camp."

He smiled. "They did pay me my normal RAF stipend for the time I was in the camp, as a lump sum. Not much, but it's ready cash right now. I still own some property in Canada. We could sell that and use the money to set up somewhere else. And I'd only start with one plane—there will be planes going cheap after a war. Easy to convert to civilian use."

"Am I going to have to worry about you every time you fly off?"

He shook his head. "Nah. Flying's pretty safe

now—unless someone shoots at you. So where do you want to go?"

"Wherever you like. Not somewhere too cold, though. I've been cold enough during this war."

"I agree. Let's look into New Zealand, shall we? It's supposed to be a beautiful country, and not enough people yet."

"All right. But first we need to get married."

"Right here?"

She nodded. "Right here."

They smiled at each other, and he reached out to take her hand.

CHAPTER 42

Josie and Mike visited the vicar to have the banns published for the wedding. Josie asked Lottie, Sheila and Dorothy to be bridesmaids, and Mrs Badger set to work making them dresses. Josie wondered what to do about a dress of her own. Everything was still on coupons, and it seemed frivolous to spend money on a proper wedding dress that would be worn only once.

"I think I'll just wear a summer dress," she said. "No sense in being too fancy, is there?"

"We could go into town and see if we can find you a new one," he said. "And we should get you an engagement ring, too. Make it formal."

"Don't be daft," she said, giving him a playful slap. "I'm only going to be engaged for a couple of weeks. That's a waste of money we don't have."

"But it doesn't seem right . . ."

"Stay there." She ran upstairs, then returned, showing him her left hand, a large, sparkling stone on her finger.

"Who gave you that?" Mike demanded. "Your last husband? I didn't realize he was a big spender."

Josie laughed. "Stan? His idea of treating me was a packet of crisps at the pub." She held up the ring for him to see. "This is one of the rings that belonged to my old employer at the tea shop," she said. "She wore them all the time. They're all paste, unfortunately. Not real. But quite pretty, eh? It will do the job."

"I'd still like to get you a real one," he said, "but I accept that we need to save money at the moment. But let's go into town to get your wedding ring, anyway."

They took the bus into Spalding and asked to look at wedding bands. The elderly jeweller beamed at them. "Let me show you what I have. I see madam already has a lovely engagement ring . . ."

"Oh, it's not a real stone," Josie said hastily.

The jeweller frowned. "You surprise me. I could have sworn . . . May I perhaps take a look?" He took the ring from her, retreated into a back room then returned. "You are mistaken, madam. This is a fine diamond. An unusual cut— antique, foreign, obviously, but five carats. A lovely stone."

Josie looked at Mike, then burst out laughing. "That crafty old thing," she said. "She told me her rings weren't real, but they were. We can buy your plane!"

"It would have to be a very small plane," Mike said, also chuckling.

"But I've got more of them. All the stones are big."

They were married on a warm summer day. Josie wore a wreath of orange blossom and jasmine in her hair and a flowery silk dress. Mike was in his uniform. The three girls wore dresses of white muslin that looked quite fancy, with big pink sashes around the waist. Mrs Badger confided that the sashes had come from an old bedspread and the underskirts from an old sheet. The ladies of the WI provided the cake and the wedding breakfast, and the whole village danced until late at night.

"I shall be sorry to move away," Josie told Mike. "They've been good to me here. They made me feel like I belonged, that I mattered."

"Well, you do," he said. "Don't ever put yourself down again, Josie. You do matter. You brought them hope. Your tearoom—it was a good thing."

Josie nodded, her eyes brimming with tears.

Mike took her into his arms. "You could open another tea shop in New Zealand if you wanted to. Or you could do your teacher training, if that's what you want. Or . . ." He paused, smiling down at her. "You could be my partner in the airline."

Josie laughed. "Me? You're not going to get me up in a plane."

Mike smiled, too. "I meant handle the business side. Make sure I don't cook the books."

"Let's just see where life takes us first, shall

we?" Josie said. "Right now I just want to be with you."

"Sounds good to me," he whispered. "Do you think we can just slip out now?"

He gave her a challenging smile. Josie's eyes moved to the exit door, and together they crept away.

ACKNOWLEDGMENTS

A big thank-you to everyone involved in this book: Danielle and my team at Lake Union, Meg and Christina and the whole team at Jane Rotrosen. I couldn't work with better people. Penny and Roger Fountain helped with the RAF Lincolnshire research, and my dear husband, John, is always my first reader—and biggest critic!

ABOUT THE AUTHOR

Rhys Bowen is the *New York Times* bestselling author of more than forty novels, including *The Venice Sketchbook*, *Above the Bay of Angels*, *The Victory Garden*, *The Tuscan Child*, and her World War II novel *In Farleigh Field*, the winner of the Left Coast Crime "Lefty" Award for Best Historical Mystery Novel and the Agatha Award for Best Historical Novel. Bowen's work has won twenty honors to date, including multiple Agatha, Anthony, and Macavity Awards. Her books have been translated into many languages, and she has fans around the world, including an online following of over two hundred thousand fans worldwide. A transplanted Brit, Bowen divides her time between California and Arizona. To learn more about the author, visit www.rhysbowen.com.

Center Point Large Print
600 Brooks Road / PO Box 1
Thorndike, ME 04986-0001 USA

(207) 568-3717

US & Canada:
1 800 929-9108
www.centerpointlargeprint.com